Rafael Sabatini, creator of some of the
was born in Italy in 1875 and educa
Switzerland. He eventually settled in England in 1892, by which
time he was fluent in a total of five languages. He chose to write in
English, claiming that 'all the best stories are written in English'.

His writing career was launched in the 1890s with a collection of
short stories, and it was not until 1902 that his first novel was
published. His fame, however, came with *Scaramouche*, the much-
loved story of the French Revolution, which became an international
bestseller. *Captain Blood* followed soon after, which resulted in a
renewed enthusiasm for his earlier work.

For many years a prolific writer, he was forced to abandon writing
in the 1940s through illness and he eventually died in 1950.

Sabatini is best-remembered for his heroic characters and high-
spirited novels, many of which have been adapted into classic films,
including *Scaramouche, Captain Blood* and *The Sea Hawk* starring
Errol Flynn.

Chivalry

Rafael Sabatini

HOUSE OF
STRATUS

This edition published in 2001 by House of Stratus, an imprint of
Stratus Books Ltd., 21 Beeching Park, Kelly Bray,
Cornwall, PL17 8QS, UK.
www.houseofstratus.com

Typeset, printed and bound by House of Stratus.

A catalogue record for this book is available from the British Library
and the Library of Congress.

ISBN 07551-153-0-9

Contents

Chapter 1

THE LADY OF ROVIETO

i

When his father was hanged, his mother died of a broken heart.

For the same reason he is known to history merely as Colombo da Siena. His arms – azure, a dove statant argent – are of his own adoption and, in rebus, merely expressive of his patronymic, for all that he came of an armigerous house and possessed the right to a patrician name and to some famous quarterings. Behind his disdain of one and the other lies the tragedy that was not without influence on his life. He was, in fact, the only son of that Lord of Terrarossa, Sigismondo Barberi, whom the Florentines dispossessed and deservedly put to death for treachery. He was ten or eleven years of age when he was left orphaned and destitute to face the world; and that he did not perish is due to a saintly brother of his mother's, a Franciscan of the Large Observance, who sheltered him in his early years from evil.

Later, as the lad grew, deepening in resemblance to his mother and displaying other qualities which endeared him to Fra Franco, his uncle, the question arose of finding a place for him in life. The friar would have made a determined attempt to obtain his reinstatement in the lordship which his father's villainy had forfeited; and that humble little brother of Saint Francis was not without influence. But in this he met the sternest opposition from Colombo.

'Since the forfeiture was deserved and just, it stands as an expiation. In some sort it serves to cancel the offence. If we retract a payment, we revive a debt. So, let it be.'

After vain arguments, the friar yielded to the clarity and honesty of the boy's logic, abandoned the attempts he was setting on foot, and addressed himself to other prospects for his nephew.

In later years Colombo would frequently insist that his natural inclinations were entirely pacific. He loved Nature and would have found his proper vocation in her service and in agrarian pursuits. But it also happened that he was equipped with rather more than the perception which, as his namesake the Genoese navigator was to demonstrate, is necessary so as to apprehend the obvious. It is, I fancy, the whole secret of his success in life, as it is of many another's. It showed him in his nonage that a man born into the turbulence that constantly distracted the Italian Peninsula in the second half of the Quattrocento, should make haste to determine whether he would range himself with the sheep or with the wolves, since mankind in that time, and particularly in that land of unrest, offered no further choice.

The sheep were the toilers: the merchants, the peasants, the craftsmen, the artificers, even the clergy. The wolves were the princes and those who served them in their quarrels over the soil upon which those toilers had their being. To be industrious, productive, law-abiding, was to be in danger of unending harassment, to be constantly in peril of being plundered, fined, ruined, or even slaughtered.

Considering all this, Colombo reached the conclusion that if his natural inclinations did not urge him to become a wolf, even less did they urge him to remain a sheep.

Thus he states his case. But whilst scarcely conscious of it himself, his history states it otherwise. Accounting extinguished the house from which he sprang, there were in him from an early age the vague stirrings of an ambition to found another, infinitely more splendid, that should be entirely the work of his own hands and brain. Since he could not be a descendant without shame, he would render himself an ancestor of whom his posterity should be proud.

It is not to be asserted that he had deliberately set out with this intention when at the age of sixteen we find him trailing a pike in the service of his native Siena. Rather did the notion grow in him with his own vigorous and rapid growth until it took definite shape during that Sicilian campaign when first his name was blared from Fame's trumpet across the length and breadth of Italy. He was in his twenty-eighth year by then and he had learnt the trade of arms under that great soldier Bartolomeo Colleoni. From modest beginnings in Colleoni's company, with the command of ten helmets, he had risen rapidly to the position of one of that famous captain's most trusted lieutenants.

Then, soon after Colleoni entered Venetian service, Colombino – by which affectionate diminutive he had come to be known in the company – had separated from him, and forming a small condotta of his own, of a hundred lances, he had taken his sword, as it were, to Bellona's market-place.

In the Sicilian campaign of which before all was over he was constrained by the favour of fortune to take complete command on behalf of Aragon, he won not only fame but enough wealth to acquire the homestead and vineyard on Montasco, in Sienese territory, which he was gradually and nobly to extend.

He was resting there after his labours in the summer of 1455, and with him were two other condottieri who had linked their fortunes with his own and had come to range themselves under his banner: the tough, elderly, worldly-wise Florentine soldier of fortune Giorgio di Sangiorgio, and the portly, jovial Aragonese Don Pablo Caliente.

I suspect that it would be at about this time that he began to dream of scaling the summits. He did not lack for models. There was Colleoni himself, now grown old, but still nominally Captain-General of the Venetian forces, covered with honour and lord of great possessions. There was Francesco Sforza, now Duke of Milan and disputing with Venice the prepotency in the north, whose beginnings had been as humble as Colombino's. There was Carmagnola, who had won to sovereignty before he had lost his head. And there were a dozen others whom Colombino could call to mind who by the trade of arms had raised themselves to princely estate. Like them so might he come by the sword to found a dynasty. Already the Sicilian war had set his feet upon the road to those heights.

Nor were his ambitions a mere greed of power and possessions. He was imbued with the conviction that where he governed he would govern wisely and well, so that the governed should bless his name and find in him, not a ravager, but a protector. He was guided by ideals belonging to the age of chivalry rather than to his own age, which was already accounting chivalry a chimera. He entertained knight-errantly notions of succouring the helpless, of upholding the weak against the insolent strong; notions to be expressed in a benign rule, different, indeed, from the ruthless despotism practised by the Princes of the states that made up Italy.

You realize that much though Colombino had learned in eight-and-twenty years of a life that had been rich and varied in its experiences, he had still to learn that in the world of his day ambition and chivalrous ideals could not journey far as yoke-fellows. It was about to be demonstrated to him at the date at which, after this brief prelude, I am about to take up his history, or, at least, so much of it as it has seemed to me worth while to assemble from the various sources in which it may be sought.

Scarcely had he come to rest at Montasco, scarcely had he, as it were, doffed his harness and turned his mind from thoughts of war to matters concerned with the noble mansion he was building and to considerations of the husbandry he found so attractive, when the call reached him to a task that was not merely to weave a dominant pattern into the tapestry of his destiny, but was to bring a change into his outlook, and so into his very nature. It was just such a call as his chivalry must leap to answer. It came from the Sovereign Countess of Rovieto, that Eufemia de' Santi, who, with nothing in her life to place her in the memory of posterity, has yet been given by the brush of Antonello da Messina a fame as enduring as his canvas.

It was the end of a hot day of August, and Colombino sat at supper with his two captains in a room of the princely house, a part of which was still in the making. They were sitting with windows wide to the welcome breeze of sunset, when from the distance they heard the hoof-beats that announced a messenger breasting the hillside.

Someone from Siena, they supposed, until a servant entered with the letter whose source he announced. When Colombino had read it, he tossed it to his captains and by a gesture invited their attention to it.

Sangiorgio took it up, scanned it, frowning, and was thoughtful at the end. But when Caliente had read it, he, on the contrary, was moved to jovial satisfaction.

'Praised be Our Lady for this mark of favour. I never hoped we should find work again before going into winter quarters. It serves to show that your fame will now give you little rest, Don Colombo.'

There was a flash of white teeth in the Spaniard's broad, good-humoured face, with the vivid red lips that told of the rich abundant blood in his veins, and the heavy jowl that was blue from the razor. The contrast between him and the tall, angular, and saturnine Sangiorgio, was stressed now by the fact that the older man looked as sour as Don Pablo was gay. Tugging at his dagger of grizzled beard, Sangiorgio took the letter again, and read it a second time.

It was from the Countess of Rovieto, and she wrote at length. Filippo della Scala, Lord of Verona, was arming to invade her territory, to enforce a claim to it based on his kinship with her late husband. The resources of Della Scala, strained by his share in the long-drawn struggle between Venice and Milan, did not permit him to engage for his purposes one of the free companies that stood for hire in Italy. Therefore, he had sent his agents into the Swiss cantons to recruit among the mountaineers who were to be had upon reasonable terms. This made Time her ally, thanks to the warning she had received. Forestalling him, it was her aim and hope to strike the first blow, to invade his territory whilst he was still unprepared; and when he sued for peace, she would impose such terms that there would be a definite end to his pretensions. To carry out this design, she invited into her service Messer Colombo da Siena and his Company of the Dove.

When at last Sangiorgio looked up, Colombino nodded to him across the board.

'A woman of spirit, that. A woman who understands the cardinal principle of war: that attack is the best defence and that victory often goes to the first blow. A rare woman, on my soul.'

Sangiorgio wrinkled his long beak of a nose, dropped the sheet with a suggestion of scorn and made a gesture as of dusting his fingers. 'Rare, yes. I thank God for it. If there were more such women there would be fewer men.'

Colombino raised his brows; Caliente swung his bulk round as on a pivot, so as to face his brother captain. Sangiorgio explained himself.

'Her history is more interesting than savoury. You need to learn something of it. She was born in the year that Lucca broke from Florence. So that she cannot yet be more than three and twenty; and already she has disposed of two husbands. The first was a patrician of the Milanese House of Visconti, an injudicious fool who went about Rovieto roaring his jealousy of a Roman visitor, Gerolimini, until he suddenly dropped dead, stricken, most oddly, in midwinter, by a malarial fever. Faith in that fever is not increased when we discover that she married Gerolimini three months after Visconti's death. And then Gerolimini, who suffered from the common ambition to govern, refused to understand that the consort of a sovereign is not necessarily a sovereign himself.

'It was a presumption for which a judgment overtook him. He broke his neck in a fall from his horse, one day whilst hunting. At least, that is how the records run. He was hunting alone at the time. When they found him, he was in a supine condition as if he had been laid out, and no sign of damage or disorder to his garments.

'As you say, Colombino, a rare woman, and a fortunate. Perhaps even a dangerous.'

Colombino's answer was cold with reproof. 'At present she is, on the contrary, a woman in danger.'

'Which is just when such a woman will be most dangerous.'

'Shall we leave old wives' ill-natured gossip, and come to business?' Colombino pointed to the letter. 'What concerns me is her desire to hire us.'

But Sangiorgio was not to be reproved out of his sardonic pessimism.

'It may well concern you. I ask myself how does she propose to pay. Her father, Todescano, all but ruined Rovieto before he died. She, following with filial piety in the footsteps of her spendthrift sire, has completed Rovieto's bankruptcy. Della Scala, she says here' – and contemptuously he flicked the document – 'is without resources to hire one of the mercenary companies in Italy. She, with still fewer ducats, invites the Company of the Dove into her service. How will she pay for it? I ask again.'

'That is what I had better go and ascertain,' said Colombino.

'I could make a guess that would save you the trouble.'

'Ribaldry is natural to an old soldier.'

'And credulity to a young one. I began that way myself. I've learnt wisdom since, which you call ribaldry. And that letter wouldn't take me to Rovieto.'

'I shall set out tomorrow,' said Colombino quietly.

'Is she beautiful at least?' Don Pablo asked his brother captain.

'They say so.'

'Then why scowl? Or are you so old that you've forgotten everything? A beautiful woman, Giorgio, is worth any journey.'

Sangiorgio looked from the smiling Don Pablo to the thoughtful Colombino.

'God help you both,' he said, and gave his attention to the wine.

ii

As prompt in action as he was swift in decision – and it has been said that this was the whole secret of his successes – he was in the saddle before sunrise on the morrow, riding down the slopes of Montasco to take the road north, with ten lances to escort him and lend him consequence.

His dispositions had all been made last night before seeking his bed; and since speed was of the first importance, they were made on the assumption, ignoring Sangiorgio's pessimism, that the business side of the matter would be agreeably settled.

To his captains his orders were to marshal, equip, and follow with the Company of the Dove. In those days its strength was of three hundred lances of three men to the lance, and at the moment these were at rest in quarters provided for them up and down the Sienese contado. Further, his captains were provisionally to enlist Falcone's condotta of three hundred men which was known to be idle at Imola and any other small free companies that should suffice to make up a total strength of two thousand men, which Colombino accounted sufficient for the business.

Nor did he neglect other matters. He held, before sleeping, a long consultation with his steward Palombari on matters concerned with his building plans and also with the planting of some vines that were being brought from the district of Orvieto, which Colombino believed should do well in the soil of Montasco.

Three days later he was at Rovieto, and his meeting with the Countess Eufemia was one of mutual surprises.

Lightly though he might have held Sangiorgio's account of her, yet enough of it had remained in his mind to lead him to expect to look upon a Maenad. Instead he found a child, as it seemed to him; and this not merely in years, but in spirit; for Colombino still nourished the belief that a countenance is the mirror of the soul, and here he beheld a countenance that was all candour, gentleness, and golden loveliness. So slight and virginal and innocent of aspect was she as to defy belief that she was in her second widowhood, and to put to shame the vile slanders of which Sangiorgio, by more than innuendo, had made himself the mouthpiece.

On her side she had expected, from Colombino's name, to behold a diminutive man. She had drawn a mental picture of him short and sturdy and most likely bow-legged from the saddle, one who as a result of his trade would be rude and uncouth. Instead she beheld a tawny-headed youngster, some six feet tall, broad at the shoulders, tapering thence to the waist and over lean, athletic flanks to the ground. His shaven face, with its starkly defined bone structures, its lofty brow and powerful jaw, its dark solemn eyes and stern mouth, was remarkable, if not for beauty, at least for strength. Borrowing assurance from success, he bore himself with the airs of a great prince, and he came dressed like one, in a fur-trimmed houppelande of dove-grey velvet, with a girdle of hammered gold and a heavy gold-hilted dagger on his hip.

Her eyes on their first sight of him, when he stepped into her council chamber, fell away as if before an effulgence. Then they returned, not only to observe but to admire; and this with a boldness which the mere softness of her eyes translated into candour.

His reception was formal, which did not at all surprise him, for he had already learned that states are very much like individuals, and that the smaller their consequence the greater is the ceremony with which they seek to inflate it.

The officer of the guard who received him in the courtyard of the citadel passed him on to a chamberlain, who in turn delivered him over to a gentleman-usher, by whom he was conducted to the council chamber where her highness waited.

On a shallow dais at the head of the council table she was enthroned in a great gilded chair of state, which should have lent importance to her, but merely served to stress her small daintiness and childlike airs. At the table, three on her right, and two on her left, sat the five members of the Council of Rovieto, all of them elderly, sober-looking men. These five rose as Colombino entered and inclined their heads in greeting. The Countess, retaining her exalted seat, graciously waved him to the foot of the table, where a stool had been set, and invited him to sit.

Then, when the others had rustled down again into their places, drawing their robes about their knees, it was the Countess herself who addressed him. She uttered a few words of welcome and of thanks for his prompt response to her appeal, stilted words which had been obviously prepared for the occasion, and then, more fluently, she came at once to an exposition of her needs and her intentions.

Whilst these elaborated the matter of her letter, they added so little to the information which it had contained that he was almost impatient for the end of her address. And scarcely had she ceased when he was speaking.

'Yes, yes,' he approved her closing words. 'It is ever the first blow that counts the most. Often, when it strikes one who is unprepared for it, it proves the last.' Whilst his eyes were fully and squarely upon her, he was conscious that the five councillors had turned their heads in his direction and were owlishly regarding him. He went smoothly on. 'Already I have so disposed that my lances should be here by Sunday. By Tuesday of next week I should cross the frontiers of Verona. I'll be upon Della Scala before he is even aware that I am marching.'

Eyes as blue as the Adriatic shone upon him with intoxicating wonder. Sensuous lips, alluringly red in the winsome pallor of the little face, were parted in a sudden smile. 'The eagle or the hawk were a more proper device for you, Ser Colombino, than the dove.'

'Della Scala shall say that presently.' He rose, swaggering a little and displaying himself, his glance enveloping her like a flame; and so they remained, absurdly, staring at each other, until one of the councillors cleared his throat with a rasping sound, which in itself was a herald of hostility.

It was old Della Porta, the dean of the Council, who thus harshly broke the spell that was settling upon those children. Lean and vulturine with his bald head and long beak of a nose, he sat forward, tapping the table with his knuckly fingers. He was a practical man who took his office seriously and whose humour consequently had been soured by endless endeavours to check the wayward wastefulness of his mistress. He had been dismayed by her high-handed resolve to call in a mercenary company which they had not the means to pay, and he was rendered now the more impatient of these assumptions that already all was settled where yet there had been no mention of a contract or its essentials.

'And the terms, Messer Colombo?'

Colombino, still with his eyes upon the Countess, scarcely seemed to awaken. He sighed audibly. 'Ah! The terms?'

His vagueness went to swell Della Porta's irritation.

'The terms, indeed. We must know to what we engage ourselves.'

The other four grumbled their concurrence.

By his peremptory tone Della Porta had drawn at last the Captain's eyes upon himself.

Considering that gaunt unloveliness, the young man descended from his ecstasy. He remembered that he had to find wages for his troops.

He sat down again, and leaned his elbow on the table. It was not clear to any why, indeed, he had risen. He became coldly practical.

'The monthly pay of a lance in the Company of the Dove is twenty ducats, with fifty ducats each for my two captains, and say thirty ducats each for some three other captains of fortune who will be enrolled with their companies, so as to make up a strength of two thousand men, which I judge necessary for the enterprise. Then there will be ten ducats apiece for the sutlers of the Company, of whom there will be fifty. And, of course, the rationing of my troops and the fodder for their horses will be your affair during the term of our engagement.'

One of the councillors groaned, another swore softly. Della Porta, in tight-lipped silence, was setting down figures on a sheet. Colombino watched the quill as it scratched and spluttered, yet conscious that Madonna's eyes were upon him the while. At last the

11

bald old councillor flung down the pen in an obvious heat. His face was white.

'In round figures that will be not less than twenty thousand ducats a month.'

Colombino spread his elegant hands. 'War is not cheap. You'll observe, sirs, that no provision has yet been made for wastage in the course of the campaign, loss of horses, tents, munitions, and the like, which it is impossible to estimate in advance. Nor do your figures include any provision for myself. Normally I require a thousand ducats on the contract, a thousand ducats monthly as my pay, and three thousand ducats upon the successful close of a campaign.'

The Council became visibly agitated. 'God save us!' exclaimed one of its members, whilst another in sour sarcasm offered the comment: 'You grow rich at that trade, sir.'

Colombino smiled into his eyes. Upon occasion he could employ, said Caliente, a smile that would have melted the heart of a Gorgon.

'If I do, it is an assurance that I close my campaigns successfully.' He had hardly at this date undertaken as many as the answer would imply. But it sufficed to silence his critic.

Della Porta was stroking his bald head in agitation. At last he exploded into speech.

'We have not the means, sir. I must be frank. We have not the means to pay you.' And with a reproachful eye on the Countess, he added: 'We had not the right to bring you here.'

Ignoring him, her silvery voice followed swiftly upon his raucousness.

'You said, I think, "normally," Ser Colombino.' She was leaning forward and there was entreaty in every delicate line of her. 'Can that mean that it is in your generous mind to make an exception from your norm?'

'Unless it is, sir,' interposed a councillor named Pagolo, 'your journey to Rovieto has been vain.' He was almost rude. 'I'll be even more frank than Messer Della Porta. Our treasury is empty, and taxation has so drained our people that little more is to be extracted, however much we squeeze them.'

'Messer Pagolo,' the lady's voice reproved him, and there was a touch of acid in its sweetness, 'we did not bring Messer Colombo here to weary him with Rovietan politics...'

'What I ask myself, madonna, is why we brought him here at all.'

Colombino's sudden rising silenced the general ill-humoured rumblings that applauded Messer Pagolo. He stood squarely confronting the Countess and his question was a challenge.

'Is this, indeed, the case?'

She winced under his peremptoriness. She seemed to shrink in her vast chair of state, and to grow yet smaller and more childlike, so that his heart reproached him for the brutality he used. There was a breathless fluttering of her bosom, and very wistfully she fell to studying her fine white hands where they lay in the lap of her gown of royal blue. She fetched a sigh for only eloquent answer.

'Alas!'

A moment he stood in silence, straight and tense, his solemn eyes inscrutably considering her. In that moment he took one of his swift decisions.

'I am dismissed then? You are not to engage me?'

But it was Della Porta who made bold to answer him. 'Not unless you can materially abate your terms.'

The Captain, however, did not seem to hear him; for with his eyes upon the Countess he continued to wait for her reply. None came. She sat with those demurely folded hands, her abashed gaze lowered to them, a stricken little figure, calculated to awaken all a man's chivalry by its lovely wistfulness. Sangiorgio had he been present would have accused her of depending upon the eloquence of her silence. But in the absence of that curmudgeon, Colombino heard only the voice of his ideals, of his knightly aspirations to succour the afflicted, and of something more. Here in this lovely lady, beset by a greedy enemy who proposed to dispossess her, with none to lean

13

upon in her hour of need save these unfeeling cross-grained dotards, was a subject for chivalrous endeavour.

He turned at last to the council table. 'Messer Della Porta, will you give me leave alone with her highness for a little while?' The question was a dismissal that included his brethren with Della Porta.

But the councillor scowled. 'To what end, sir? We here compose the Council of Rovieto, and it is our sacred duty...'

He got no further. Madonna Eufemia cut into the pompous sentence with a voice suddenly sharp. 'You have leave to go. All of you.'

Della Porta made as if to speak, then checked, and expressed by the compression of his lips his awareness of the futility of resistance. He rose, bowed, not without a suspicion of irony, and waved his fellow councillors before him from the chamber.

There was a spell of silence between the soldier and the lady after the door had closed. She sat very stiffly in her tall chair, grasping the arms of it, whilst he paced the length of the room, on the grey walls of which frescoed vermilion demi-lions climbed to the groined ceiling. When he came to a halt before her, it was to perch himself unceremoniously on the edge of the massive board. His houppelande fell open, and he swung a long, shapely, vigorous leg that was clad in creaseless grey like all the rest of him.

Still at a loss for words to express the thing in his mind, he continued to consider with reverent eyes this woman who seemed made for love, whilst she, fluttering a little under his odd regard, waited for him to break the silence.

At last he approached the position by one of those skirmishes on the flank which he had found so profitable in the field.

'It is being said of me, madonna, that I am as hard in a bargain as in action. And God knows it's true enough. I have been inclined to adapt my prices to the needs of those who hire me, rather than to the work that is to do. Considering your desperate need, I came intending to ask twice what I have asked for my condotta and twice the sum I have named as my own price. Upon perceiving your necessitous condition, I halved my pretensions. Considering further, madonna, it comes now to this: that my price to serve you shall be what you choose to make it.'

'What... What I choose to make it?' Ingenuous eyes of heavenly blue opened wider in candid wonder. 'What I choose to make it?'

'It is no riddle, lady.' There was a kindling in his voice. 'It is not for a slave to talk of wages.'

'A slave?'

He stood up again.

'It is what the lovely sight of you has made me.'

There was a startled, questioning wonder in her glance. Then a smile that was no more than a deprecatory shadow flitted across that little face, pale as a lenten rose.

'You have known me less than an hour.'

'That is just the time that I have loved you.'

Thus, judging the moment come, he staked all upon that bombardment. Either the citadel would lower the bridge to him, or he would be beaten back in rout, a presumptuous assailant who challenged more than he could sustain.

It brought her to her feet abruptly, her countenance now aflame, and her voice held the warmth of injured pride.

'You go very fast, sir.'

'Always, madonna. Speed makes for victory.'

'I am a woman, not a fortress.'

'I thank God for it.'

At this she began a laugh that changed into a sob, and left him puzzled. She stepped down from the dais, as if to approach him; then she checked and set a hand to her broad, low brow. It was a gesture of bewilderment, almost of helplessness.

'Let me understand. Do you say that because of...because of this, you will serve me without guerdon?'

'Without guerdon, madonna, beyond such guerdon as love claims.'

'Oh! Oh!' She was white again and breathless. Her lips twisted scornfully. 'Not so nobly selfish, after all. You are to be paid, then, when all is said.'

'What I am paid in love I can pay back. In love there are no debts.'

'I am at school, I think.'

'Have done!' he cried. 'I'll not be mocked.'

'I see. I am to take your insolence seriously.'

But the masterful young captain accounted that skirmishing had gone far enough. He put forth a hand, and pulled her to him. Thus, abruptly, she found herself in his arms, her breast against his breast, his eyes probing her own, as if to scan the soul within their limpid depths.

Startled, ruffled, by his hands, affronted by his assumptions, she struggled with the fierceness of a kitten, but struggled with an increasing feebleness, until at last, as if her strength were spent, she lay resigned, her head against his shoulder. And then, accounting this a surrender, without more ado he bowed his tawny head and kissed her on the lips.

She grew heavier against him, as if faint, her round eyes narrow now and a queer smile at the corners of her mouth. She sighed.

'By your coils I judge you more colubrine than columbine.'

'So that my coils hold you, their nature is no matter. I may be a dove in name, but I am a hawk by nature. Where I stoop, I bind.' His ardent young lips played over her face and neck, and set her quivering. 'When will you marry me?'

At that question she grew suddenly not merely still, but stiff.

'Marry you?' quoth she, aghast.

'What else were you supposing?'

'Mother in Heaven! Not content, my dove, to be a hawk, you aspire to become an eagle.'

'Would you mate with less?'

'It is the mating that would make you so,' she proudly reminded him.

He smiled. 'Yet without that mating you are unmade. Della Scala will drive you from your eyrie. I ask no more than I can earn: to share the nest I shall have preserved.'

She delivered herself from his arms and stood confronting him. If still by her slightness suggesting the child, yet there was a dignity about her that was of the woman accustomed to command.

'Is that your price?'

'When you shall have confessed that you love me. Not before.'

'You need that, too?' She laughed as she looked up at him. 'You would fit the place, for you were surely born to rule. You command all things. Even love. Oh, yes. You command that, my lord.' And then sharply, she concluded: 'I'll marry you when you have broken Della Scala.'

Some little colour kindled in his cheeks. His eyes sparkled. 'I am content,' he said, and there he checked his exultation so as to deal once more with matters practical. 'I will ask, then, only that you provide the ducats for my lances.'

The intrusion of business at such a moment shocked her, as her countenance announced. 'Lord! Will you palter? With a princedom in your grasp?' Then she showed him that she, too, could be practical even amid transports. 'Levy the means to pay your men from the Veronese when you invade them.'

'It is contrary to usage,' he objected. 'And it is imprudent until the end is assured.'

She flung back her head the better to laugh at him. But all that he noticed was the lovely line of her neck that was thus displayed more fully.

'Usage? By my faith, we conform with usage, you and I, as we do with prudence. You've yet to face the Council with this bond of ours.'

'With you beside me I'd face Hell unshaken.'

Upon that assurance he gathered her to him and kissed her again, then let her go recall her councillors, who waited glooming in the outer gallery.

When she had told them of the bond, but not how it was forged, Della Porta, perceiving a harlotry in this, was once again confirmed in his conviction that he served a woman whose wickedness was unfathomable.

Similar was Sangiorgio's view when, a week later, he marched the glittering Company of the Dove and the enrolled auxiliaries up to the walls of Rovieto and encamped it in the meadows by the river.

'So that's the price she pays you for your service! Body of God! I might have guessed that it would be just so that she would mend her bankruptcy, abusing your youth and your…'

'No more of your infamies!' roared Colombino in a sudden white-heat of passion. 'It is of the family of all the other lies that are published against her. And you are no better than a bawdy fishwife that you must be retailing them. It was not she, let me tell you, who offered the price. It was I who demanded it.'

'You would suppose so,' growled Sangiorgio, unabashed, his leathern, weather-beaten cheeks aglow with anger.

'Suppose it? Do I not know what passed?'

'To be sure, you'll believe you do. There's nothing clumsy in that woman's arts. She looks like a saint in a cathedral window. Are you married yet?'

Colombino controlled his wrath. He answered loftily. 'That is for when Della Scala is broken.'

'I could find it in my heart to pray he breaks you instead. It might prove the lesser evil. Her husbands are not lucky, Colombino.'

But at this Colombino loosed his passion again, and it was such as Sangiorgio had never yet seen in one who normally was of a calm rarely found in men of twice his years. He came striding across the tent towards his captain, his hand reaching for the dagger on his hip.

'The Devil burn your filthy tongue, Giorgio! Will you make it the agent of scandal about that sweet saint? Go look in her face, you fool, and behold in it the evidence of your baseness.'

Sangiorgio was a brave man; but he was also prudent. He deemed it best to drop a subject so inflammatory. But as he went thereafter about the business of his command, he seemed to his men and to his fellow officers to be suffering from loss of spirit.

Three days later the Company of the Dove departed on its warlike errand. With blare of trumpets, with azure and silver bannerols fluttering above a forest of spears, trailing in its wake a great siege train of arbalests and rams and leathern cannon hooped with steel, it paraded under the walls of Rovieto thronged with townsfolk, and past the Tower of Luna, from the battlements of which the Countess viewed it, her Council in attendance.

Colombino rode last of all, with two esquires to bear his lance and shield and helm. Save for his tawny head, encased in a skull-cap of crimson velvet, he was in armour, a glittering silver figure on a white charger, whose housings of blue and silver trailed almost to the ground. He raised his mace aloft to salute the Countess as he passed, and the slight, fair, childlike figure waved a blue scarf to him in answer.

iii

Colombino came down upon the Veronese with the swift, sudden fury of a summer hurricane. It is a method of campaigning that has distinguished other great soldiers before and since his day, and one that presently came to be regarded as his normal practice.

Della Scala, whose agents were still levying troops in the cantons, was taken completely by surprise. It passed his understanding. Building confidently upon the state of exhaustion of the Rovietan treasury, and the Countess Eufemia's consequent inability to raise an army against him, he had been going leisurely about his preparations and was still entirely unready. That of all mercenary companies the Company of the Dove should have been hired to invade him increased his wonder and his rage. He had heard of the exorbitancy of Colombo da Siena. Where had the Countess found the gold Messer Colombo would demand before he would put an army in the field? He set his spies to discover the answer to this question, and he raged the more when eventually they brought it to him. If Colombino should, indeed, come to reign in Rovieto, as the consort of the Countess, the Lord of Verona would never again find it possible to sleep in peace. Such a neighbour, he supposed, would keep him constantly alert.

From what had happened by the time Della Scala had news of the compact made, it looked as if that unpleasant future were neither improbable nor distant. The fortresses of the Veronese had been going down before the forward sweep of the invader, like so many Jerichos, at the mere sound of his trumpets. An inadequate army hastily assembled to hold him in check until reinforcements could be obtained, and until Verona could be victualled for the siege that was clearly imminent, was smashed to atoms in a single engagement with the Company of the Dove.

Within a fortnight of crossing the frontiers of the Veronese, Colombino had swept up to the walls of Verona. Since the place was too strong to be carried by assault, at least until hunger should have emaciated its defenders, he drew up his lines of circumvallation, linking them across the river, above and below the city, by chains of barges, and he sat down to besiege it.

Della Scala was reduced to despair. Ruin complete and utter stared him in the face. Odd countrymen who found their way into the city brought him news of dreadful ravages in the countryside. Not only was the Company of the Dove victualling itself by ruthless raids, but Colombino was paying his lances with gold extorted by way of indemnities from the fiefs he had reduced. Della Scala swore in terms picturesquely blasphemous that the man was behaving like a brigand. He swore, too, a frightful reckoning. This when his rage was hottest. In cooler moments, realizing his impotency, he doubted if he would survive to present it. Next, as men do when they see little prospect of help from man, Filippo della Scala turned his thoughts to Heaven. He ordered public prayers and processions and made extravagant votive offerings. Then, coming to doubt the efficacy of even these spiritual measures, he taxed his wits to discover physical means of meeting his difficulties.

Here again, both he and his brother Giacomo discovered in themselves a sterility of invention that was reducing them to hopelessness until Giacomo, remembering something, conceived the notion of buying Colombino. Before attempting, however, to act upon it, the brothers took counsel with their illustrious kinsman, Agostino della Francesca, whom they held in high esteem for his learning, his address, and his worldly wisdom.

It was after supper one October evening, by when the siege had endured a fortnight, that whilst they still sat at table, Filippo with gloomy candour exposed his anxieties. One slender hope he still possessed. A captain of his, one Pantaleone, a bold, resourceful, and devoted fellow was abroad awaiting an opportunity to bring a convoy through the lines on some dark night. If he succeeded, then Verona revictualled might be in case to hold out until the besiegers should be compelled to go into winter quarters. If that happened, then, by the following spring, Della Scala reinforced should be able to give a very different account of himself.

Agostino shook his auburn head. Like his cousins, he was a tall, big-boned man, yet of a peculiar grace which they entirely lacked. Virile, there was yet something oddly effeminate about him, something curiously androgynous in the beauty of his face, and particularly about the mouth which, wide and full-lipped, was at once sensual and cruel.

'Colombo will be as aware of this as you are. From what I know of him, he is capable in such conditions of protracting the siege into winter.'

'That,' cried Filippo, 'is impossible! Such a thing has never happened.'

'But it may with this fellow. He has a gift for innovations. Nor in your place should I count for a moment upon Pantaleone's deceiving the vigilance of his lines.'

This put Filippo out of temper. Whilst he sought advice, he desired none that should destroy his already too slender hopes. The younger Della Scala intervened.

'Impatience will not serve, Filippo, nor is our weakness repaired by being ignored. Let us rather recognize it, and seek how it may be countered.' After which exordium, Giacomo introduced the only notion in which he found grounds for real hope.

But again Agostino shook his head. 'To offer a bribe is merely to encourage him by advertising your own weakness.'

'Does that matter if he accepts?'

'Why should you suppose he will?'

'His father was Barberi of Terrarossa. These things run in the blood, and like his father, Messer Colombo will have his price.'

'Maybe. But have you gold enough to pay it? This dove flies high. You tell me, yourselves, that he plays for the sovereignty of Rovieto as the consort of the Countess. What can you set in the scales against that?'

'What then?' roared Filippo, like a goaded bull. 'In Hell's name, what then? Must we sit here inert until we starve?'

'You'll not avoid it by listening to counsels of despair,' said Agostino.

'There are no other counsels left,' Giacomo flung in. He was irritated almost as deeply as his brother by this logical opposition. 'You smile at me, Agostino! My God, you can smile! Yet if we go down in ruin, you will share our fate. You have forgotten that?'

'I have not. I study to be calm, so that I may keep my wits about me.'

'And very fruitful they are proving,' sneered Filippo.

But he did not sneer next morning when Agostino brought him the fruits his wits had borne in the night. They left him aghast. They were of a perfume that slightly nauseated him at first, and awakened that scorn of his kinsman which slumbered in the depths of him, begotten of the difference in their natures.

Agostino propounded his rascally notion without hesitancy or any tinge of shame. Whilst few men really liked or trusted him, he was, and knew himself to be, possessed of that indefinable quality which when exerted women find irresistible. The *histoire galante* of this handsome, swaggering Veronese, a tale of easy and successive triumphs, might well be worth the labour of writing. Something of a fifteenth-century Casanova, his story would delight those who have been enthralled by the memoirs of the later Venetian amorist.

His present scheme was built upon his faith in these powers of his and upon the widely reputed frailty of the Countess Eufemia. The task ahead looked easy to him, and this confidence pervaded his exposition of it to the brothers in that same room where last night they had dined and where they came now to break their fast.

He would slip out of Verona alone, make his way to Rovieto, and seek sanctuary at the hands of Madonna Eufemia, representing himself as a fugitive from the ruthlessness of the Scaligeri. This alone should lend him interest in the eyes of the Countess. Having thus won, as it were, across the threshold, it should not take him long to make himself master of the house. That was his own phrase. They found it obscure, so he enlightened them with a laughing frankness scarcely decent.

'I have attractions. At least, so it has been found. And I have some little experience in these affairs. So, I believe, has Madonna Eufemia. We should do very well together.'

The brothers stared at him. Then Filippo swore in his black beard, and asked to know in the name of all the saints how this lewdness should help Verona.

Agostino, looking from one to other of their puzzled faces, laughed outright. 'Dullards! Isn't the sequel plain? When I shall have gathered this fragrant little fruit, when it lies here in the hollow of my hand, let word of it go to Colombino. That will be the moment to approach him with your offer of a bribe. Don't you see? Not only should it tempt him then, when the situation will show him his risk of losing the greater prize for which he plays, but he will perceive in the acceptance of it the means to square accounts with a faithless jade.'

He threw back his head to challenge their applause, a handsome, glittering figure, as he stood, hand on hip, in a patch of sunlight from one of the arched windows.

The applause, however, was slow to come. Giacomo's approval was as gloomy as his countenance.

'Ingenious,' he admitted, and added: 'Infernally ingenious.'

'Infernally, as you say,' grunted Filippo. 'I like things reasonably decent.'

Agostino opened wide his eyes. His cruel mouth grew scornful.

'Is this your thanks? I show you a way to save yourselves, I offer to do the work myself, and incur the risks, and you, Filippo, can tell me only that you like things decent.' He moved in agitation about the chamber. 'You'll never have heard, I suppose, that necessity knows no laws.'

'Why all this heat?' wondered Filippo, already seeking to retreat from those grounds of decency on which he had thought to stand. It was true enough, as Agostino reminded him, that necessity knows no laws; and the choice of decent weapons was a luxury no longer within his means. So he swallowed his reluctance at a gulp. 'Why all this heat?'

'At your ingratitude.'

'You take us by surprise,' said Giacomo, coming to his brother's aid. 'You rob us of breath. That is all. We are not ungrateful. We are amazed, and if we are reluctant it is because we are considering that you may leave your head in the business.'

'Ay,' growled Filippo. 'Have you thought of that?'

Mollified, Agostino laughed once more. 'Not whilst it has any brains in it,' said he. His faith in himself was as massive as the Mole of Hadrian.

iv

Agostino della Francesca, whose energy matched his guile, lost no time in acting upon the plan conceived and at last agreed by his kinsmen. Soon after dark that night, and before the moon had risen, he put off alone in a boat from the castle, and slipped down the river towards Colombino's barges. He did not wait to be discovered by the guards, but himself proclaimed his approach.

When they hailed him, as he trusted that they would, into Colombino's pavilion and the presence of that captain, he told a harrowing tale of being in flight from the vindictive wrath of the Scaligeri, who suspected him of sedition. He ended on an appeal to the condottiero for sanctuary.

His person had been carefully arranged so as to lend colour to his tale. His fine clothes were rent and disordered. He was without weapons. A bloody bandage swathed his brow, and blood, from a scalp-wound which it covered, smeared his handsome face.

Consistently, since he fled from vindictiveness, he displayed vindictiveness in his turn. He was very free with information as to the desperate conditions in Verona, and he displayed such an eagerness in this betrayal that the truth of the rest of his story was not to be doubted.

He aroused, however, little interest in Colombino, who heard him indifferently, asked few questions, and carelessly dismissed him. But since there was always a possibility that the fellow might be a spy, Colombino would not have him about the camp.

'If you seek sanctuary, you may find it in Rovieto. Your quarrel with Della Scala will make you perhaps welcome there.'

So far all was precisely as Messer Agostino had calculated. He thanked the condottiero effusively, and took his leave. He went to purchase a mule in the camp – he was well supplied with gold – and cheerfully suffered himself to be conducted beyond the lines.

In Rovieto it was Della Porta he sought in the first instance, and was by Della Porta invited to come and repeat his tale of the conditions in Verona that day to the Council. When he presented himself in the council chamber, he came washed and combed and dressed with more than ordinary care and all the richness of his rank, a resplendent figure calculated to awaken interest in a lady who had never been known to regard male beauty with restraint. The bandage of fresh linen swathing his brow announcing a wound, taken if not in her cause at least at the hands of a common enemy, was an added commendation. Then his contemptuous words on the subject of his cousin Filippo della Scala and his assurances that the tyrant was as good as beaten already uplifted them all into giving him a warm welcome to their midst.

To convince him of the readiness of her hospitality, Monna Eufemia, languishing a little under his ardent eyes, gave orders that quarters should be accorded him in the citadel, and invited him to sup with her that night. Della Porta, knowing her ways and considering in what relationship she now stood to Colombino, was filled with a vague alarm which increased steadily and became less vague as the days flowed on.

And they flowed into weeks without any confirmation of Agostino's jubilant assurances that the end of Verona was already in sight.

October was nearing its end, a month had sped since Agostino's appearance in Rovieto, and still Della Scala held out. But he held out at terrible cost. Gaunt famine stalked the city of Verona, and men were dying in the streets. Such few victuals as still existed within those grey walls were jealously husbanded for the garrison, inadequate to nourish even these.

It is to be doubted if Della Scala would have held out so long but for his obstinate hope that Pantaleone, who was still at large, might yet succeed in bringing his victualling convoy into the city. As for the hopes he had founded upon Agostino's unsavoury stratagem, these had perished by now. The conviction had been borne in upon the brothers that Agostino must have failed. Possibly detected, or at least suspected, if he had not been slain he must certainly lie by now a prisoner in Rovietan hands; otherwise he would have found some way to make a sign. For single messengers still contrived to slip through the besieging lines and bring word of events in the countryside. It was one of these who came to hearten Filippo della Scala with word that on the night of the Feast of Saint Raphael, the twenty-second of October, after the moon had set, Pantaleone would attempt to bring his convoy by barges from the north, and he warned the Lord of Verona to open the water gate at midnight, so as to admit him.

This was Della Scala's last hope. If he were revictualled, he could hold out until the besiegers should be compelled to go into winter quarters. And as the weather was now turning colder, this could not, he thought, be very much longer delayed. Nor was he without justification. It was a subject that was already troubling Colombino. Of his auxiliaries, Falcone and his three hundred men and Lanciotto da Narni who had brought a hundred had already marched away on the ground that it was becoming too cold under canvas for their troops. Other desertions threatened, and even Sangiorgio was complaining of the difficulty of subduing the murmurs of those who remained.

Aware of the point to which the garrison of Verona was reduced, Colombino refused to contemplate the waste of all that had been done by raising the siege at such a moment. Another week, if they were steadfast, might see the end of the resistance; but another week might also see the end of his company's patience.

It became necessary to enliven matters. If he could discover a weakness anywhere, he would attempt an assault. He entrusted the task of a close survey of the defences to Caliente, who as well as being a superb cavalry leader was expert in all that concerned fortifications.

Don Pablo made his inspection carefully, and came to report that in his view a bastion on the western side of Verona was easily vulnerable. Colombino went out with him to survey the spot, and having assured himself that the Spaniard's report was just, he went back to mature a plan of assault.

On that same night Pantaleone made his attempt to succour the city. His barges came gliding on the bosom of the stream, with scarcely an oar dipped and never a gleam of light to break the moonless gloom about them. Nevertheless they were detected. The vessels with the food that was to renew Verona's fainting life were rounded up, captured, and towed down to Colombino's camp below the city.

The din of that brief battle fought afloat bore news of the failure to Della Scala, and set the seal upon his despair. Gaunt and haggard, the Lord of Verona faced his brother.

'It is the end. Nothing remains but to ask for terms.'

Giacomo was moved to the profanity of the impotent. He raged against surrender.

'But for that swaggering coxcomb Agostino, I might have ended matters a month ago by buying this son of a Judas. It's not yet too late. Let me make the attempt even now. I'd give all that I have sooner than that we should become the mock of that Rovietan harlot.'

'As God's my witness, so would I,' concurred the Lord Filippo. 'So be it, then, Giacomo. Try this before we throw down our arms.'

And so it came to pass that at an early hour, before the late sunrise of that chill morning of the last day of October, the younger Della Scala went forth from a postern, and came, under a flag of truce, into the bustling camp of the besiegers, to be at once conducted to Colombino's pavilion.

They were rude folk, these Scaligeri, untouched as yet by that spirit of art and letters that was already so vigorously permeating the life of Italy or by the sybaritism that was the natural offspring of this love of beauty. Therefore Messer Giacomo opened wide his dark eyes at the luxury he found here, the rich Eastern hangings, the bearskins that covered the ground, and the tinted and gilded leather of the abundant furniture. In his Spartan eyes there was an effeminacy here that must have moved his scorn but for the commanding presence of the man for whom it made a setting.

Colombino in a rust-red surcoat that descended to his knees and was open like a tabard at the sides, revealing the lynx fur that lined it against the cold, stood to receive his visitor.

'I give you welcome, Messer della Scala.' Stately and gracious the young man bowed his red-gold head which was bare. 'If you will sit, I will have my captains summoned.'

But Giacomo ignored the hand that courteously waved him to a couch. He came a step nearer, loosening his cloak. He glanced over his shoulder at the guards who had conducted him, and who waited, like statues, under the brown canvas awning borne on poles that made a porch for the pavilion. He lowered his voice.

'My errand were best delivered, sir, to you alone.'

Colombino stared. 'Your errand? But, then, is it not concerned with terms?'

'With terms. Oh, yes. And yet it is important that we be private.'

'As you please.' The condottiero shrugged, and waved away the guards. 'Accommodate yourself. Be seated.'

Colombino himself went back to the chair from which he had risen, set at a gilded table on which there were writing materials, maps, and papers.

There, after a brief and more or less unintelligible prelude, Messer Giacomo disclosed the purpose of his corruptive visit. No sooner had Colombino perceived whither the Veronese was going than he set hands to the arms of his chair, to heave himself up, so that he might hurl from his tent this smug patrician who insulted him by these assumptions of his venality. But even as his fingers closed upon the lions' heads that decorated the chair's arms, he checked the impulse, and let Messer Giacomo continue to the end.

With lowered eyes, and a mask of blankness upon his face, Colombino heard him out. Then he looked up, and laughed.

'It may be, sir, that your brother takes the costliest way to end this siege.'

Giacomo's heart leapt within him at the words. He glowed with satisfaction in his own acumen which had so rightly judged the son of Barberi of Terrarossa.

'Let my brother be the judge of that. Will you name the sum, Messer Colombo?'

The condottiero, with a huckster's smile, shook his head slowly. 'I would rather hear your brother first.'

'It is scarcely for the buyer to name the price,' said Giacomo, in his secret contempt not even troubling to be tender of the soldier's feelings. 'Still... Since you prefer it so... What should you say to fifty thousand ducats?'

'Say to it? By the Host! I should say that you hold me cheap, my lord.'

'That, be assured, is not the case. Name your own price, sir.'

Colombino considered him with a glance of mockery. 'I'll tell you this: less than two hundred thousand ducats would not even tempt me.'

Giacomo's broad face lengthened at the mention of so vast a sum. 'By the Blood! An emperor's ransom!' But Verona's need was desperate. 'If I were to offer that?' he asked breathlessly.

'I might accept, with certain conditions.'

'Conditions? You would saddle with conditions such a sum?'

'I must protect my patron, after all. You are not to suppose me just a common scoundrel who sells his master. If your brother will agree to a year's truce with Rovieto, I will consider.'

Giacomo's smile was not pleasant. 'I see. You must protect not only your patron, but your face as well. Of course. A year is no great matter. I am empowered to answer for my brother. He will accept the condition.'

Colombino swallowed the insult of Giacomo's present manner as calmly as he had swallowed the insult of his opening words. He inclined his head a little.

'Very well,' he said quietly. 'I will consult with my marshals. Return for the answer in three days' time.'

That knocked the insolence out of the Veronese. The swift change to dismay that overspread his countenance was ludicrous. To Verona in her present extremity three days were an eternity. In three days most of them would be dead of hunger. So much Giacomo could not admit, or this scoundrel would, he was sure, increase the price.

'What have your marshals to do with this?' he blurted out.

'Do you imagine such a thing can be done without their participation? They'll want their share of the plunder. How else do you suppose that they will acquiesce? And even then, however plausibly I may put the matter to them, it is always possible that I may not bring them to my views.' Abruptly he ended. 'Impossible to pronounce until I have conferred with them.'

Giacomo had come to his feet. He stood now with clenched hands and set jaw. 'Could you not determine by tomorrow?'

Colombino raised his brows. He smiled his understanding. 'In such sore straits, are you?' Then his smile broadened with his thought. 'Perhaps I can help you, there. I might, in earnest of my friendly intent, permit the victualling barges we captured yesterday to pass into the city at once.'

His eyes watching the other's face saw the sudden incredulous relief that overspread it. Without giving him time to speak, Colombino picked up a quill from the table.

'First, however, set me your offer down in writing: the price you pay and what you pay it for. Here is a pen, and there the ink. Set it down.'

Giacomo came slowly forward. 'Why this?'

Colombino was impatient. 'So that the barges may go, of course. This will explain it to my captains: show them that you are already conditionally bound.'

The Veronese took up the pen, and stooped to the table. He wrote laboriously, uttering the words as he scrawled them:

'In the name of my brother, Filippo della Scala, Lord of Verona, I offer the sum of two hundred thousand ducats for the raising of the siege of Verona and the withdrawal of all hostile troops from Veronese territory, and further I undertake in my brother's name that he shall not bear arms against Rovieto for a year from this date...'

There Giacomo paused, and straightened himself again under the impulse of a sudden thought.

'There is one thing I might require where so much is being paid.'

'Ah?'

'Does it happen that you have in your hands a kinsman of ours, Agostino della Francesca?'

Colombino remembered the fugitive patrician who had come to him bleeding and in rags more than a month ago for sanctuary against his Scaligeri cousins. Wondering a little, he yet answered frankly:

'Why, yes. He is at Rovieto, I believe. What of him?'

'I will add the condition that he be given a safe-conduct to return to Verona. You will hardly deny us that.'

'A safe-conduct?' Colombino questioned, and not even the surprise in his tone showed Messer Giacomo the blunder of asking for a safe-conduct for a man who had represented himself to Colombino as escaping from Scaligeri wrath. To have asked Colombino to deliver up in bonds this fugitive would have been reasonable, and could have excited no suspicion. But a safe-conduct was a thing of no effect unless there were on the part of Messer Agostino a willingness to avail himself of it. And this, if Messer Agostino were what he had represented himself, there could not be. It seemed to follow that the man's flight had been a pretence, his tale a lie.

With the scent of treachery strong in his nostrils, Colombino slyly asked: 'You insist upon that condition?'

'I beg for it.'

'Very well. Set it down.'

Whilst Giacomo wrote on, and finally signed the document, Colombino was considering. When the Veronese flung down the pen, its task accomplished, the condottiero drew a bow at a venture.

'After all, perhaps I owe no less to Ser Agostino. It was he who named to me the sum I have now asked. But for his obstinacy in the matter of the year's truce, this siege might have been ended a month ago.'

He read the stupefaction in Giacomo's dark face. 'Agostino discussed this with you?'

'Does it surprise you?'

Giacomo reflected, his lip between finger and thumb. Then he shrugged, and betrayed all. 'Why, no. Not when I come to think of it. It may well have seemed to him the easier course. But the fool should have informed us of your insistence on the truce.'

For the moment this was more than enough for Colombino. What the alternative purpose Agostino della Francesca had come to serve, what purpose he might be endeavouring to serve even now in

Rovieto, Colombino could not guess and could not ask. Nor did it signify.

He took up once more the pen that Giacomo had laid aside. 'It is a whim of mine that you should add to the condition of a safe-conduct for Messer Agostino della Francesca, the following words: "who is the friend and kinsman of Filippo della Scala, and was empowered by him to negotiate on his behalf for the raising of the siege of Verona, or to take such other steps as might deliver the Lord of Verona from his present difficulties." '

Giacomo frowned his bewilderment. 'Why that? What reason for it?'

Colombino was easy and affable. 'So that it may go upon my records. I like things done in orderly fashion.'

But this was Greek to Messer Giacomo. He could perceive no sense in it, and he knew that deliberate nonsense is a common mask for evil purposes. His tone became hard. 'I'll need a better reason.'

This was check to Colombino. But he maintained his easy, affable smile. Then he walked past Giacomo, to the entrance of the pavilion. He drew aside the canvas curtains. 'Come here,' he said, and when Giacomo stood beside him, he pointed to the string of laden barges moored among the rotting sedges by the river's brim. 'As soon as you shall have signed and sealed the document in the terms I've uttered, those barges shall start for the city, and your starving men shall eat their fill.' He paused, and whilst Della Scala still continued to scowl at him, still tormented by doubts, Colombino mockingly put the question: 'Is that reason enough? Will you write now?'

Rendered reckless by despair, Giacomo went back to the table and bent again to the task.

'Seal it,' Colombino commanded. 'You wear a ring with the Scaligeri arms. It is fortunate. So.' He took the document. 'For the rest, come for my answer in three days' time. Your urgency will now be less, since I send you the means to feed your people. Return on Sunday.'

Giacomo had not left the camp before Colombino's orders had gone forth for the release of Pantaleone and his men, to the end that they might take their barges into Verona by the Water Gate. At the same time he sent for Sangiorgio and Caliente. They came at speed, making no attempt to dissemble their surprise at the orders he had issued, indeed, demanding to know the meaning of them.

For answer Colombino told them that hostilities were suspended until Sunday.

'An armistice?' said Sangiorgio, incredulously.

'An armistice.' Colombino was grim.

Caliente exploded. 'Por Dios y la Virgen!' he swore. 'An armistice at such a moment, with the city about to fall into our hands, with the weakness discovered in the Madonna Bastion, and the attack upon it settled?'

'It is an armistice to render the attack more certain. Lulled into a sense of security, the Veronese will relax their vigilance. Thus the assault to be delivered on Saturday night should carry the place before they are even aware of it.'

Neither of the captains could believe his ears. It was incredible that this leader, so fastidiously chivalrous in all his measures, should seriously intend so dastardly a violation of an engagement.

'But the treachery of it?' Sangiorgio reminded him, his tone almost one of awe.

'These gentlemen of Verona shall find in me, so far as they are concerned, the character with which their foul assumptions have had the temerity to endow me. Read that.' He set Giacomo's document before them, and waited until they had read.

'Filippo della Scala dares to send his brother here to me, to propose a bribe. They suppose me so corrupt that they offer me gold to betray my employer. In the hour of their defeat, they suppose me so false to my undertakings that I am to be seduced into selling them the victory.' His countenance inflamed, he was giving now a free rein to the passion he had curbed whilst Giacomo had been with him. 'And so persuaded are they of my vileness that they approach me almost without circumlocutions. "What is your price to sell the Countess of Rovieto?" Those are almost Messer Giacomo's very words. Flattering, is it not? The fellow never suspected how near he was to a broken neck when he put that question. He escaped it only because I had this sudden inspiration of how their vile assumptions should be met. I would behave to them exactly as the faithless traitor they suppose me should behave. Now, sirs, do you understand? Do you still think that I am to consider knightliness when I deal with huckstering seducers such as these?'

Don Pablo, who was seated on the fur-spread couch, smacked his massive thigh with his plump hairy hand. 'You have reason, God help me!'

But Sangiorgio, standing tall and gaunt with bowed head, his fingers tugging at his dagger of a beard, was thoughtful.

'Even so, it will make an ugly tale. Men may see only your treachery, and never learn of the treachery it was employed to meet. The Scaligeri will not proclaim it, and we may not be believed.'

'But I hold the proof. Why else, do you suppose, did I have Messer Giacomo set it down in writing?'

'Writing can be denied. Colombino, my friend, this will not serve. You are in the trade of arms. Loyalty is as much a commander's stock-in-trade as skill.' He became emphatic. 'You have a name for chivalry which you cannot ruin just to be even with these dogs.'

'Chivalry! I'll be chivalrous with foes who are chivalrous themselves. But with tricksters I'll be a trickster. To be aught else is to be a fool.'

'It is no shame to be a fool in the service of honour,' said Sangiorgio.

'Wait,' said Colombino. 'There is something in that paper you have both missed. The allusion to Messer Agostino della Francesca. There, too, we have treachery, and of a sort that is yet to be discovered.' He made clear his inferences from that request for a safe-conduct. 'I am starting now for Rovieto to discover it. The armistice gives me leisure to do so.'

And then he showed that Sangiorgio's opposition had shaken him a little. No decision about Saturday night's assault on the Madonna Bastion need be taken until he should return. Meanwhile, however, let Caliente carry forward his preparations for it.

V

Colombino set out that afternoon, escorted by only ten lances, travelling lightly that he might travel the more swiftly. The little company rested awhile towards sunset, then rode all night, although after midnight it turned bitterly cold, and before daybreak as they came into the Rovietan uplands it was snowing heavily.

There was something urging him besides the matter of dealing with Ser Agostino. It was not so much alarm of what that agent of the Scaligeri might attempt against Madonna Eufemia, for she would be well guarded, and Della Porta would see that no harm came near his mistress. It was a hunger of his eyes to behold again in the flesh that gentle loveliness of which in all this month he had carried the vision ever before him. He had been starved the more, because whilst in the last fortnight he had sent impassioned letter after impassioned letter to Madonna Eufemia, each a lyrical pulsation of a devotion that grew deeper, it seemed to him, with every hour, yet he had in all that time received but one brief cold and formal letter from her in return. It was not in his heart to blame her. It is not for the saint in Paradise to be making passionate answers to her votaries. Nor was he a coxcomb to suppose that he could yet have moved in her the deep tenderness by which he was exalted. This was something that would follow when by loving service he should have proved his worth, as, God helping him, he would. But he had the hope to do something meanwhile towards lessening her aloofness, and in this hope he rode, warmed by it against the chill of that grey morning.

It was the first of November, the Feast of All Saints, and High Mass was being sung in the Cathedral as Colombino and his lances rode across the square, their hoofbeats softened by the snow, and up the steep, narrow street that led to the citadel.

Dismounting in the courtyard, he learnt from an officer whom he questioned that Messer Agostino della Francesca was, indeed, still in Rovieto, and at that moment at Mass with her highness.

'At his prayers, eh?' Colombino's lips made a straight grim line. 'That is very well. Send a messenger to tell him that he is required at once by Messer della Porta; that the matter is urgent.'

Then, having ascertained that Della Porta was above, in his apartments, Colombino went up the stone staircase in quest of him.

He found him in that long bleak room where first the captain had beheld the Countess, and the announcement of Colombino's presence disturbed the old councillor in labours that were engaging him with his secretary. To judge by his appearance when presently the secretary had been dismissed and the condottiero was admitted, he was in prey to a disturbance deeper than could have resulted from the interruption of his work. He stood in his long, fur-trimmed surcoat, leaning against the table from which he had risen, a gaunt figure of consternation.

'Why are you here, sir?' was his odd greeting, quaveringly delivered. 'Why... Why have you left your post under Verona?'

'Verona will not dissolve between this and my return. My marshals have their orders. The assault that will certainly carry the place is to be delivered on Saturday. Meanwhile, I make holiday; and something else.'

He strode past the aged councillor, towards the fire, loosening his cloak as he went. Beneath it he was all leather, with steel at his heels and waist and throat, and he creaked and jingled martially as he moved.

The councillor's scared eyes followed him. 'What... What else?' he asked.

'You shall learn in a moment.' Colombino answered him over his shoulder. His first concern seemed to be to warm himself. The logs hissed and spluttered under his wet heel, and for a moment the soldier spread himself to the almost instantly ensuing blaze. Then, turning again to the anxiously waiting councillor, he asked on a softened note for news of the Countess.

Della Porta answered vaguely, a man whose thoughts were obviously wandering. He shambled up and down the long grey room, his hands clasped behind him, and his bald head craned forward on his long, stringy neck. In his grey furred gown he had, thought Colombino, the air of a gigantic and uneasy vulture. Presently his aimless pacings took him to the window. He stood there, his knuckly hand upon the stone sill, and peered out.

'What are they doing down there, those men?'

'They will be men of mine. They fulfil my orders.'

'Your orders?' Della Porta turned. His face was grey, and he was shaking. For what he had just seen below was a headsman's block being set up on the snow in the middle of the courtyard. 'Your orders?' he repeated.

Colombino was spared the trouble of explaining himself by the opening of the door. The officer who had carried Colombino's message came in quickly, followed by scuffling, clanking sounds from the stairs behind him.

'Sir Captain!' he cried out as he entered. 'Your men are doing violence to Messer Agostino.'

'To be sure,' was all that Colombino indifferently answered him, without moving from the hearth.

Della Porta sat down heavily at the long table in the room's middle, and a groan escaped him, to increase the mystery which Colombino sensed here rather than perceived. He was frowning down upon the councillor when Agostino della Francesca, a magnificent glittering figure, in white and gold, came writhing and struggling in the grip of two men-at-arms.

At sight of the martial figure, standing straight and tall and stern against a flaming background, Ser Agostino fell suddenly still. But that was only for a moment. In the next he had broken into violent imprecations and more violent threats. Messer Colombo da Siena he announced with many unnecessary and furious words would be required to answer to the Countess of Rovieto for this violence.

'Oh, yes. No doubt. But that need not concern or excite you, for you'll not be here to witness it.'

'What's that?' From pale that they had been the cheeks of the Veronese went now grey-green.

'Have you a soul to make, Ser Agostino? If so, you have ten minutes in which to make it. Your treacherous sands are run.'

With dilating eyes Messer Agostino stared at him for a long moment. Then, rousing himself, he swung to the old man who was rocking in distress.

'Della Porta!' he cried. It was an appeal for help.

Della Porta groaned again. He flung out trembling hands towards Colombino. 'Sir! Sir! What is your intent?'

Colombino paid no heed to him. His eyes, at once stern and sad, were fixed upon Agostino. He spoke very quietly. Inwardly this killing in cold blood revolted him. But his duty and the nature of Agostino's offence imposed upon him the necessity.

'We need waste no words, Messer della Francesca. You know what you came here to do, and if I do not yet perceive your ultimate design, that is no matter. I have it on your cousin Giacomo della Scala's word that you are here to take such steps as may deliver Filippo della Scala from his present difficulties. That is enough. What wages you were to have earned I do not know. But the price you are called upon to pay is neither more nor less than the price demanded of every man who is caught in treachery as you are caught.' Abruptly he added, with a wave of the hand, 'Take him away. Let justice be done.'

They dragged him writhing, screaming, and protesting from the chamber. As the door closed, Colombino shuddered, whilst Della Porta started up in panic, knocking over his chair.

'Sir! I beg that you will wait at least. At least. The Countess should be summoned, sir. If...if...what you have said is true...'

'True? My God, what do you suppose me? I hold the proof. Should I act summarily otherwise?'

'But... But...' Della Porta shuffled forward, quaking, blinking, stammering. 'Her highness should be summoned, none the less. It may go very ill with us all...'

Colombino shrugged and interrupted him. 'It is not worthwhile to disturb her highness at her devotions. This is no great matter.'

'No great matter? Oh, my God!'

How great a matter it was the old man dared not tell him. He turned away in despair to find himself another chair into which he might collapse. And thus with no further word between them they awaited the coming of Madonna Eufemia, Della Porta in terror, Colombino with his lover's impatience a little overcast by the shadow of the justice he had done.

She came at last.

Alighting in the courtyard from the litter in which she was borne, she checked there in horror and amazement.

A block, smeared with fresh blood, stood in the snow in the middle of the little square. At the foot of it lay a mass over which a crimson cloak had been thrown. Beside it a lance was planted in the ground, and on this lance was impaled a head, from the waxen face of which a pair of glazed eyes stared foolishly.

With fixed gaze Madonna Eufemia advanced a pace or two. Then she smothered a scream, and staggered as if about to fall. But mastering the faintness that assailed her, she asked a question, hoarsely, of a man-at-arms.

'Who has done this?'

His answer, brief but complete, sent her speeding to the stairs.

Colombino above heard her quick approaching steps, and as the door opened he was leaping eagerly to meet her, when her aspect checked him. So disordered was her countenance that he scarcely recognized it for her own. Its gentle, innocent loveliness, its very youth was blotted out by rage.

'You dog! You beast! You murderer!' Thus foaming at the lips she greeted him. 'As God's my witness, your head shall go the way of his.'

The colour receded from his face until his very lips were bloodless. He seemed to crumple a little, to lose some of his splendid height and dignity of poise. Thus for a long moment they stood regarding each other, and each was breathing labouredly.

For spectators they had Della Porta, too palsied to rise from his chair, and behind her a little group of men and women, two of the councillors, two or three of her lackeys and as many of her men-at-arms, and behind these again a half-dozen of Colombino's men brought up at speed by their sergeant who had scented trouble from the manner of Madonna Eufemia's departure from the courtyard.

At last it was Colombino who broke that heavy, anxious silence.

'So!' he said. 'So! I seem to have found here more than I was seeking.' There was such reproach and agony in his voice as only heartbreak lends. 'What was he to you, this man?'

She recoiled a step or two, and crouched like an animal about to spring, her litheness stressed by her close-fitting gown of black velvet with a fiery glow of cabochon rubies at her girdle.

In her rage, in her vindictive desire to wound, to punish, to lacerate his soul before she had the head hacked from his body, she cast all dissimulation to the winds. Sobbing and snarling through her shuddering lips she answered him.

'It is fitting you should learn it before you die. Agostino della Francesca was my love, and would have been my husband. He was my peer, a natural mate for me, not the son of a degraded traitor, a braggart upstart, who traded on my need to make of my own self the price of his hireling service.'

'Ah!' he said slowly. 'That is your justification, is it?'

'I need none, sir. I but tell you this, so that you may know what mercy to expect.'

But Colombino's bloodless lips were curling in a terrible smile.

'Yes. He was your peer, as you say. Your peer in all things. And that is why I took off his head, although at the time I knew only the half of his offence.'

'As I shall take off yours!' she shrilled. 'Or,' she mocked him wildly, 'do you look for mercy?'

Anger restored his strength. He straightened himself again, and threw back his head. His voice boomed now through the vaulted chamber.

'Mercy? Mercy, do you say? Mercy is for such treacherous things as you and he.'

'You dog! Have you not yet vented enough of your jealous spite?'

41

'Jealous...?' He checked on the amazed word. Then he laughed dreadfully and without mirth. 'So that is what you supposed. Why, yes. It would be. But I did not even dream I had a rival in that poor Judas, who like yourself – your peer, as you have said – could keep faith with none.' He pulled Giacomo's parchment from the breast of his tunic, and stepped close up to her. 'Look, woman. Read. Learn why I took off his head, as you must have taken it off once you saw this. Because to serve his kinsman of Verona he came here to betray you.'

To guide her staring eyes, his finger traced the accusing lines above the Scaligeri signature and seal.

She shuddered as she read. When it was done, she put a hand to her brows in a gesture of helplessness and pain, and the lithe, delicate little figure swayed like a lily-stem in a breeze. One of her women ran to her, and supported her to a chair. She sank into it, and sat there stricken, her white hands interlocked and wedged between her knees.

Colombino turned aside, and went to hand the parchment to Della Porta.

'There is the evidence that will justify the judgment I have executed.' He paused there, and then added: 'Since the price I was to have received for my service has meanwhile been treacherously squandered, it follows that my engagement to Rovieto is at an end. I take my dismissal.'

'Sir! Sir!' cried Della Porta, starting up.

Colombino, standing stiffly, looked at him, and the old councillor fell back from the glance as from a blow.

Then erect and leisurely he walked out of the room beckoning his men to follow him and without so much as a glance at the lovely, golden-haired little Countess, who, whimpering now, was huddled in the chair to which she had been helped.

Mechanically, insensible to the fatigue upon him from his night-ride, he gave the order to saddle, and with an escort as weary as himself, but without the burden that he carried in his heart, he set out once more for his camp under Verona.

He reached it on the following evening, having rested the night at an inn upon the way, and in his countenance the shrewd-eyed Sangiorgio read that this stony-faced man who returned was no longer the Colombino who had ridden forth. He was a man who, meeting betrayal where he had placed his greatest faith, conceived himself deluded by all the ideals he had cherished, a man who found himself under the necessity of readjusting his views and discovering for his life a more practical but less noble orientation.

Listlessly he sent a messenger to summon the Scaligeri for his answer. To Messer Giacomo, when he came, he delivered himself with the same listlessness.

'I am prepared,' he announced, 'to raise the siege on the payment of the two hundred thousand ducats. The condition concerning your kinsman Della Francesca I am no longer able to fulfil, because Messer della Francesca has lost his head. As a set-off, however, I waive the condition exacted from you of a year's truce with Rovieto. Once I have raised this siege your hands are free.'

Messer Giacomo would have protracted the interview. But Colombino curtly dismissed him.

'That is all, sir. I have no more to say. You have three days in which to find the money. When it is paid, we depart into winter quarters.'

And so Messer Giacomo went back to tell his brother: 'I knew that Barberi's son would succumb to the lure of gold. If that poor fool Agostino had heeded me, he would be with us now.'

In Colombino's tent Sangiorgio shook his head over the business and gloomily told him that men would say exactly what Giacomo was at that moment saying. He spoke of honour.

Colombino sneered. 'Honour! Will honour pay my troops? It is necessary in this world to be practical before being honourable, and I must have money for my men. Besides, it is no longer my concern to force a capitulation. I have left the service of Rovieto.'

And because unable to bear the sorrow and reproach in his captain's eyes, Colombino blurted out the whole shameful story. He found relief. Some of the poison went out of him on that relation of the events.

'I have done nothing that I am not justified in doing. The Lady of Rovieto made an end of the engagement when she dishonoured the terms of it. There is nothing in my actions that hurts my honour.'

There was a wistful smile on the old soldier's deeply lined face. He sighed as if in relief.

'So that honour still counts with you, child.' He came to stand over the young condottiero, and set a hand upon his shoulder. 'Nor have you real reason to repine. Presently, when this wound heals, you'll give thanks. A dangerous woman, as I warned you. There is death in her kiss. Agostino della Francesca is the third who has found it there. Praise God that you could kiss her and still live.'

Chapter 2

THE LADY LACKLAND

i

As long as life pulsates in him man moves as if persuaded that it will never cease to do so. For which reason age seldom sets a term to schemes and plans and measures that concern the future.

At sixty-nine that shrewd little man Onorato da Polenta might more properly have been employed in making his soul than in addressing himself to the reconquest of the dominion of Ravenna, from which Venice had twenty years ago expunged him. After all, there was no man of his house to succeed him. His only son Azzo had been put to death by Venetian justice for violating the decree of banishment under which he lay jointly with his father. His only nephew Cosimo da Polenta was in holy orders. There remained his daughter Samaritana, but since in the circumstances the legacy of Ravenna would be a legacy of strife, it would be a folly to suppose that it was on her account that the Lord Onorato determined to come out of his exile in Crete and put his case to the arbitrament of arms.

For twenty years he had watched and waited for the opportunity he now perceived. He had been prophetically confident that in the end Venice must pay dearly for the greed of which his own dispossession had been an instance, and at last it seemed to him that his prophecy was fulfilled. Not content with being mistress of the sea and of vast colonies beyond it, the Most Serene Republic had raised great armies so as to extend over a vast sub-Alpine territory her dominion on the mainland. She had reduced into vassalage the states of Treviso, Vicenza, Padua, Brescia, Bergamo, and a half-dozen lesser tyrannies, including that of Ravenna. The great wealth amassed in trade and by the arts of peace had been squandered in war for the gratification of imperial aims; and whilst superficially Venice now appeared stronger than ever before in her history, in reality she had been bled white by the great mercenary companies under Carmagnola, Colleoni, and other captains hired to fight her battles. Although the long war dictated by the forward policy of Doge Foscari against the Duke of Milan had brought her all that she coveted, yet it had left her without the necessary strength to hold her conquests.

In the words of Onorato da Polenta the present Venetian State was a wall built without mortar; let one stone be removed, and the entire structure would crumble. It was to preach this gospel that, greatly daring, he came out of his Cretan exile, and with his daughter Samaritana crossed to Italy in his sixty-ninth year.

He found it easy by his fiery arguments to persuade his fellow sufferers in the North of the correctness of his views. Men are ready enough to credit what they hope. But it was not so easy to persuade any of them to set about pulling his own stone from the mortarless wall of Onorato's picturesque image. Everywhere the answer was the same.

'Dear Onorato, what you say leaps to the eye. Do you, then, make the first attempt. Wrest your own Ravenna from the talons of the winged lion, and we will complete the prostration of the beast by following your example, blessing your name.'

It was in vain that Onorato protested that he did not command the means for such an undertaking, and that what he was proposing was a league that should band them all together against the common foe; in vain that be talked eloquently of the strength that lies in union.

Disgusted with them, he went off at last to Milan and Francesco Sforza. But Francesco shook his crafty red-gold head. Venice was not the only one to be exhausted by the long-drawn war. What but exhaustion, did Onorato suppose, had reconciled him to leaving Bergamo and Brescia in Venetian hands?

Still the Lord Onorato would not be denied, and by his persistence he wrung at last a conditional promise from the Duke of Milan.

'I could perhaps muster strength to support – that is, to follow up – a well-delivered blow. But I am certainly in no case to initiate a fresh campaign.'

A temperament still sanguine even at sixty-nine led Onorato to construe this into an undertaking. And meanwhile in Milan he had heard much talk of Colombo da Siena, and in particular that from his abundant confidence in himself he had been known to consent to serve for payment upon results and out of resources to be supplied by the conquest in view. If Onorato could persuade him to enter his service on such terms, he would avert the failure with which he was threatened by the lukewarmness of those upon whose enthusiasm he had counted.

So the Lord Onorato set off again on his travels with his daughter, and came to Siena on a day of early April, when the land was turning green.

He sought there the good offices of that cultured young patrician Camillo Petrucci, whose house was coming to be regarded as foremost among those – the Salimbeni, the Piccolomini, the Malavolti, and the Spallanti – who disputed for prepotency in the Sienese Republic. Camillo's generous heart was moved to sympathy with these wanderers, this Lord Lackland and his daughter, as he called them, half in jest, half in compassion. He gave them noble entertainment, hope, and encouragement; highly commended the Lord Onorato's wisdom in seeking the services of Messer Colombo, in admiration of whom the young Sienese was almost lyrical; and himself undertook to conduct him to Montasco and lend his support to the Lord Onorato's proposals.

Father and daughter in mule litters, Petrucci riding, with a half-dozen men of his own for escort, they travelled some fourteen miles down the narrow valley of the Arbia, through Monteroni, turning westward just short of Buonconvento, and then breasted the gentle slope upon which Colombino was spreading his vineyards, dominated by the stately, four-square red house, half-villa, half-fortress, the building of which he had only just completed since his return four or five months ago from his ill-starred Rovietan adventure.

In this business of building, embellishing, and equipping his stately home, the condottiero had sought to smother the ache which the treachery of Eufemia de Santi had left in his young heart. For this treachery she had paid bitterly by now. At the first touch of spring, a month ago, the Scaligeri with their Swiss levies had marched into Rovieto and annexed it to Verona with scarcely a blow struck. For the Countess, perceiving the utter hopelessness of resistance in her defenceless condition, had fled at the enemy's approach, and was now a landless wanderer somewhere in Italy.

Colombino, however, was not of those who can find vindictive solace. It comforted him not at all that the Countess should have fared so ill. A measure of gloom remained in him, despite the resilience of youth and of a spirit naturally joyous. A measure of hardness was also now discernible which had certainly not been his before, but for which Sangiorgio opined that presently he would be the better in the career that he had chosen.

Out of his fatherly concern for his young captain, Sangiorgio had lately been praying that work might come to engage them before long, so that absorbing himself in it Colombino might completely escape the thoughts that so often set that upright line of pain between his level brows.

Meanwhile, now that the house was finished, Colombino was finding no little measure of distraction in the planning and setting of his vineyards. He was breaking the hillside into terraces, for the better sunning of the choice vines he had brought from Orvieto, from Naples, and from Sicily, and here as the Lord Onorato was borne up the gentle, winding ascent, he found the activity of an ant-heap, an army of labourers swarming with spade and mattock over the slopes between the terraces that made of the hill a Titanic staircase.

To Onorato da Polenta, whose life had been spent in court and camp, it seemed an odd thing that a captain of fortune should engage his mind upon such peasant concerns as these. But as he advanced, he found the concerns to be more than merely those of husbandry, and he was impressed by the boldness of the conception which he found in execution: the vast deep terraces, each edged by a colonnade of square rough-hewn granite pillars, roofed by beams over which orange and lemon trees were being trained to form long shaded galleries. Even more was he impressed by the provision he beheld for irrigation. Into each of the terraces, somewhere about the middle of its length, a great estang of granite had been partially sunk, to receive and store the waters of a mountain torrent, thus harnessed to his needs by Colombino's engineers, and conveyed by stone channels in sparkling cascades from the estang of each terrace to that of the terrace next below, until, from the widest and deepest of them all, a miniature lake at the foot of the hill, the overflow, controlled by sluices, escaped into the river Ombrone. Nor was the work merely utilitarian. About some of these vast square basins there were colonnades, bearing trellis-work to shade the water and its neighbourhood in which tables and seats of stone had been set. Others were hemmed about and partially enclosed by dense hedges of yew, in which niches had been carved where marble figures gleamed white against the dusky green.

The house itself stood some little way below the summit of the hill, screened thus from the north. Its façade was pierced by Gothic windows of delicate tracery, with slender mullions carved in close spirals. Each corner was flanked by a square tower and the whole was crowned by battlements that were roofed and tiled. A miniature moat, for ornament rather than defence, made an island of it.

With jingle of mule bells and hollow beat of hooves upon the timbers of the drawbridge, the two litters were borne under the tall arch of the gatehouse, followed by Petrucci and his little troop. They entered an unpaved courtyard, now half in shadow, where grooms at once came forward, whilst a young chamberlain in black with a gold chain on his breast issued presently onto the broad steps to receive the visitors.

They were ushered into a wide hall that was paved in black and white marble chequers, the ceiling in blue and gold mosaics displayed in its middle a silver dove, the walls were hung in tapestries of rusty red and blue, with glittering trophies of arms displayed at intervals.

Here an officer in gorget and cap of polished steel, armed with a short blue tasselled partisan, was on guard, and it was into his care that the chamberlain delivered the little Lord Onorato, his tall, handsome daughter and the splendid Petrucci, whilst he himself went forward to announce them.

If the strangers had been impressed by the nobility of the setting in which they discovered this soldier of fortune and the evidences of the princely state he kept, they were impressed more deeply still by his commanding presence and the urbanity of the reception he accorded them, following upon their presentation by Petrucci.

The young Sienese he embraced with a warmth which proclaimed the depth of the friendship that bound them. Then having set them at their ease, he mantled himself in a coolness which, whilst nowise impairing his perfect courtesy, yet seemed to increase his dignity. This coolness he retained whilst listening to Petrucci's statement of the mission which had brought the dispossessed Lord of Ravenna out of his banishment and to the Lord Ravenna's own more elaborate exposition of his hopes. And this notwithstanding that the presence of the Lady Samaritana was calculated to inspire warmth in a man of any sensibility.

A tall, slender girl, not yet twenty, of dark tresses and a warm pallor of countenance, she possessed something of the elusive beauty, the stateliness and the grace of that other famous woman of her house, the ill-fated Francesca da Polenta, who some two centuries before had gone to be the Lady of Rimini, and there had died, of one death, as Dante has it, with Paolo Malatesta.

A year ago it might have been impossible for Colombino to have regarded her with the cold, almost hostile indifference which now invested his eyes when they transiently rested upon her. It would have been impossible for him to have viewed the wistfulness by which her gentle face seemed clouded without stirrings of that chivalry to which on the threshold of his career he had vowed himself, or to have listened to her father's tale without an immediate desire to arm in his service, for this sweet lady's sake. But sore and sick at heart still from the treachery of which he had so lately been the victim, his vision was so warped that in womanly grace and beauty he beheld only hollow lures of evil.

The Lady Samaritana, sitting erect, with folded hands, demure and still as an image in an altar niche, with her downcast eyes and wistful mouth, he set down for a proud, cold, calculating piece, and so dismissed her from his thoughts, giving his cool attention first to Petrucci and then to the Lord Onorato.

When their tale was told, Colombino sat back, chin in hand, and slowly asked a question.

'To seize Ravenna would not be difficult, even if Venice should put an army into the field. But when it has been seized, how do you propose to hold it against Venetian resources?'

To Camillo Petrucci it seemed that Colombino was delivering checkmate. But not so to the lean, grizzled little Lord of Ravenna. His dark, kindly eyes under their tufted brows glowed with a mild excitement of debate, his wide, humourous mouth was smiling as he delivered with vehemence his answer.

First he had Francesco Sforza's promise to support the undertaking. Second, the example of Ravenna must be followed by the other vassal states which Venice had seized, and the Venetian Empire on the mainland must inevitably crumble beyond repair.

Colombino was not impressed.

'These are but possible contingencies. They are not certain. Duke Francesco, for instance, does not move without prospect of profit. What shall he stand to gain?'

'The weakening of Venice!' cried Onorato. 'Is not that gain enough for a prince who aims at undisputed prepotency in the North?' And then, since the subject of gain had been introduced, he used the prospect of a rich reward as a means of stirring the Captain from the discouraging apathy he discovered in him. He talked of ducats, recklessly. A hundred thousand was the sum he offered, to be levied upon the city of Ravenna so soon as it should be in his hands.

But the offer, fantastic for an undertaking that might be accomplished in a month, did not dazzle the condottiero.

'It needs thought. For you, sir, it is none too wise to begin your restored rule by such a levy. For me, there is the risk that Venice may be in sufficient strength to frustrate me. It is not a heavy risk, or one that ordinarily would daunt me. But it exists.' He rose, as if to mark the conclusion of the matter. 'I will consider, my Lord. Give me until tomorrow to resolve. Meanwhile, I am sensible of the honour your proposal does me. You will stay to dine.'

When, after dinner, the Lord Onorato, a little crestfallen but still hopeful, took his leave and departed with his daughter, Petrucci remained behind, and soon showed that his intent in doing so was to plead the cause of the Lord of Ravenna.

'My dear Camillo,' he was answered, 'that cause is all but hopeless, but for the liking Onorato da Polenta aroused in me, I would not even have consented to give the matter further thought.'

'Though you say Onorato, I've a notion you might mean Samaritana.'

'His daughter?' Colombino looked at him, almost sullen-eyed, and shrugged. 'I scarcely saw the girl.'

'Yet she's a girl to fill a man's eyes.'

'Some other man's, perhaps. And anyway, my mind was busy with the problem of the Lord Onorato's case: the problem of how he is to hold Ravenna when it is taken. Until there's a solution to that, this campaign is a mere waste.'

'In your place,' said Petrucci slowly, with the suspicion of a smile, 'I could find, I think, a solution that would profit me.' And he went on to answer the question of Colombino's glance. 'The House of Polenta is at the point of extinction. Onorato's only son is dead; his only nephew is in holy orders. The Lady Samaritana succeeds to his dominions.'

'Which at present do not exist.'

'That is your opportunity. Convert this Lady Lackland into the Lady of Ravenna, then let them see that, if she is to maintain her hold upon that lordship, she'll need a soldier at her side to share it with her. It's a pity you did not look at her more closely. As I've said, she's a woman worth looking at, especially by a young ambitious captain who is invited to restore her house.'

Colombino's face had darkened. 'I want no woman for a ladder by which to climb.'

'Scruples are very well, but here...' Petrucci was saying, when he was interrupted.

'It is not only a matter of scruples, but of experience.' Colombino opened his heart. 'Once, not long ago, I dreamt just such an unworthy dream. Nor was ambition then the only, or even the real spur. I was no mere fortune-hunter taking advantage of a woman's needs. I was a lover first, desiring only to serve. But since I sought also to profit, I found in betrayal perhaps no more than I deserved. I have learnt my lesson, Camillo. I've no mind it shall be read to me again by your Lady Lackland.'

But Petrucci shook his head. 'The lesson you should have learnt is that a man may not serve at once two masters: love and ambition; tyrants both. Here, since your heart is not engaged, you will be on sounder ground. Think of it, Colombino. Here is offered you such a crown to your career as rarely comes to a captain until he has grown old, and not often then: sovereignty and the founding of a dynasty. Shall I say a word to Onorato da Polenta that will set the door ajar for you?'

'I beg that you will not.' The soldier was emphatic, almost indignant, and Camillo, with a sigh, let the matter drop.

But he had sown in Colombino's mind a seed which presently began to put forth roots, and this with such tenacity that they would not be torn up. There ensued for him a season of conflict. When ambition urged him to take the road that Petrucci had shown him, his chivalrous ideals revolted against the cynicism of a loveless marriage for worldly ends. Then, remembering what through love he had suffered and how his simple faith had been abused, he mocked himself for still permitting chivalry to fetter him. Here, as Petrucci had pointed out, was a chance of greatness such as might never come again. Let him take it, marching alert and wary to his ends, without any fond emotion to obscure his sight.

Thus for two days his thoughts continued tossed about without coming anywhere to rest, and when at last he rode into Siena, to seek the Lackland Onorato in Petrucci's palace on the Campo, it was to announce a decision which still left the deeper purpose undecided.

'Look you, my Lord, that I can bring you to Ravenna I do not doubt. The rest can wait. The means by which you are to maintain yourself in your dominion can be determined when once more you are in possession of it.'

Petrucci who was present looked at his friend, and wondered. When he observed the searching glance which the young condottiero bent upon the Lady Samaritana, who was also present, he suspected that Colombino might have been moved to the wisdom of at least considering what he had proposed. The rest, thought Petrucci, Samaritana, at once so stately and so demure, should herself accomplish. She was dressed that day in silk and velvet of the brown of leaves in autumn, voluminous of skirt, but fitting so closely from neck to waist as to reveal the lovely lines of her maiden breast. Heavy outer sleeves of velvet hung like a mantle from her shoulders down to the level of her knees, whilst inner tight-fitting sleeves of silk encased her arms and half-concealed her long, slim hands. A broad, flat velvet cap partly covered her intensely black and lustrous hair, and a narrow frontlet of black velvet crossed her brow to stress its white purity.

Furtively considering her, Petrucci told himself that Colombino was a fool if he refused this gift of Fortune which with a little trouble and address he might make his own.

The Lord Onorato was a man exalted. His humorous mouth twitched in excitement as he asked questions and received answers concerned with the means that Colombino would adopt, and Samaritana's eyes lost some of their wistfulness, a little colour crept into her pale cheeks to see at last this promised fruition of her father's hopes.

Colombino's last words to Onorato were: 'Depend upon it, within a month I shall have taken the field.' Then, whilst the little man laughed and rubbed his hands, the captain turned to take his leave of Samaritana, and employed in doing so more words than he had yet addressed to her in their total.

'If I take now a reluctant leave, madonna, it is in the confident hope that I shall have the happiness of setting you in Ravenna before many weeks are past.'

With that he took her hand and bowed his tawny head to set a kiss upon it. He had a feeling then that only the firmness of his grip had prevented that little hand from eluding his lips.

Remembering this, her silence and the trouble in her glance, he sighed more than once as he rode back to Montasco; and if some of his sighs were for her, some were for himself.

ii

True to his pledge, Colombino within the month opened the campaign for the reconquest of Ravenna, and the battle of Civitella, which added fresh laurels to his brow, was fought in the early days of May. For Venice despatched an army in haste with orders to push forward, meet, and destroy him as he came down the foothills of the Appenines, long before he so much as set foot upon Venetian territory.

Venice little suspected that in these anticipatory measures she was doing neither more nor less than Colombino had desired and reckoned. His dispositions, indeed, had begun by startling Onorato da Polenta. Within a week of their agreement little else was being talked of in Siena but the fact that Colombino was marshalling an army to invade the Veneto, and it followed that from Siena the news would go out over Italy like a ripple over water.

Onorato was not merely startled, he was angry. The wide, humorous mouth was grimly scornful as he inveighed to Petrucci and others against the insanity of a captain who made boastful proclamation of his intentions. In the end he went off with his fury to Montasco, which he found in a hum of preparation, the courtyard and the military quarters in the eastern wing swarming with men-at-arms.

When the old man furiously remonstrated with Colombino, reminding him of the old military axiom that surprise is at any time worth a thousand lances, the young captain smiled upon his ingenuousness.

'I desire to be honest,' said he.

'Honest!' Onorato's consternation ascended yet steeper heights. 'This is not a joust, sir. It is war!'

Colombino explained himself. 'If Venice had disbanded her armies, there would be grounds for your misgivings. But she has not. Colleoni is now too old to take the field; but not too old to advise; and knowing his methods, I have a notion what his advice will be. At present Belluomo is in the pay of Venice with an army twice as strong in numbers as any that I can muster. For Belluomo I have no great respect. But numbers are numbers; and it would nothing profit you to have me seize Ravenna merely to be pinned there by Belluomo's vastly superior force. That is what surprise would accomplish.'

He paused, so as to allow the Lord of Ravenna to grasp and appreciate that cardinal fact; and already Onorato was staring at him with round eyes and open mouth, whilst in the background

Sangiorgio was quietly smiling and Caliente broadly grinning. Colombino resumed.

'It follows, then, that my aim must be first to meet Belluomo in the open, and there either destroy him, or at least so weaken him that I shall afterwards be in sufficient strength to deal with the forces remaining to him for a siege. Thus we shall temporarily disable Venice, and you will be given the opportunity to consolidate yourself before she can arm again to come against you. It is to ensure this that I am widely publishing my preparations. If I know Colleoni's mind at all, he will send Belluomo's army to bar my passage into the territory of Ravenna, and that will be my opportunity. There is no other course that will serve our ends, my lord.'

The Lord Onorato, who had come to storm, remained to worship, in awe of a soldier who pushed strategy to such lengths as these. And whilst he commended and apologized in one, Colombino was admonishing him.

'Trouble no more about me, my lord. What I have undertaken I will accomplish if it be humanly possible. Your own work should now lie in Milan with Duke Francesco. Let him know what is preparing, so that he may be ready to follow it up when the moment comes. Once I am in Ravenna, I may have to look to you to relieve me with troops from Milan. We must prepare for every contingency.'

Obediently the Lord Onorato had set off for Milan, and there he learnt of the battle of Civitella and how completely it fulfilled Colombino's calculations.

Belluomo had reached the plains of the Forlivese when his scouts brought him word that Colombino's army was at the head of the Valley of the Ronco. There, Colombino had deliberately paused, so as to rest his men for the engagement upon which he counted hereabouts.

Belluomo pushed on, and on the morrow beheld Colombino's army coming to meet him down the hills through the grey olive trees that straggled over their flanks. The Venetian took up at once a position that should serve as a starting-point for one of those games of living chess which still made up a campaign between mercenary forces, who desired neither to suffer nor to cause unnecessary casualties. Usually these manoeuvres for position were pursued until one side obtained a strategic advantage so obvious that it only remained for the other to admit defeat and lay down its arms. Colombino, however, had so far prevailed by departure from, rather than observance of, these antiquated methods, and it was soon plain to Belluomo that it was the enemy's intention at once to deliver battle. He could scarcely believe in his own good fortune, for with twice Colombino's numbers there could be only one issue for the young captain from this rashness.

Swiftly and exultantly he took his measures to ensure that foolhardy young man's destruction. And even with his superior numbers there was nothing foolhardy about Belluomo's dispositions. He was a captain who took no chances, and he followed very definite and settled principles of war. He adopted now the time-honoured practice of dividing his forces into two battles, each of some two thousand five hundred men, and each therefore equal to the whole of the opposing army.

Retaining one of these under his own command in the position already taken up, so as to check Colombino's advance, he sent the other, under the best of his lieutenants, Gravedonna, round the hill to the north, so as to menace Colombino's left flank. And he allowed the manoeuvre to be plainly seen, calculating that, so as to elude the threat of these pincers, Colombino must drag his army up the southern ascent. It would then be for Belluomo to deal with him by a converging movement of all his forces.

It was all so clear and plain in Belluomo's mind that already he counted the victory won. But, to his profound amazement, as if the young man intended to promote his own destruction, instead of the southern retreat upon which Belluomo reckoned, he beheld him come steadily on down that narrow valley, following the course of the stream. Already he was not more than a half-mile away. Let him but continue this advance a little, and his danger then would be not merely of being outflanked, but of being taken in the rear by

Gravedonna's division and so of being inevitably crushed between the two Venetian battles.

Belluomo was stirred to compassion. The poor lad made it evident that he had still a deal to learn of the difficult art of war. He was not to be taken seriously, and because of this pitying contempt, Belluomo did not even trouble to stand to receive the threatened attack, but moved forward so as to expedite matters and be the sooner done.

And now, at last, the poor lad called a halt, and had summoned Caliente to his side. Sangiorgio spurred up, with an urgent prayer that his captain should give attention to the danger of Gravedonna's flanking movement.

'There is no danger,' he was quietly answered, and Colombino expounded: 'It will take that division the best part of an hour to reach the summit, and some little time longer to marshal its ranks before the attack is launched. By that time there will be no flank to attack, and the battle should be over.' He turned in his saddle. 'Don Pablo, are you ready?'

Caliente, a colossal figure in his armour, astride of a charger that was like an elephant, grinned through the open visor of his helmet.

With his mace he pointed to the orderly mass of horsemen behind him, numbering close upon a thousand.

'You will charge at once, then. And you will charge through. Understand that clearly. Let nothing tempt you to do more or less. No matter in what disarray you fling them, no matter what advantages you may see in a protracted engagement, you will go right through their ranks. Like a spear. Let that be your only aim. And when you are through, ride gently on until you hear my trumpets. You understand.'

'As if I were a spit and that battle a capon.'

Colombino nodded, his face stern, his lips tightly compressed. 'Forward, then, and Saint Michael ride with you!'

Don Pablo rose in his stirrups, he swung his ponderous mace above his head, a trumpet sounded, and with a gathering roll as of thunder a thousand horsemen, their armour flashing in the sunlight, were launched upon Belluomo's force. The gentle slope of the ground increased their impetus, the check which their charge imposed upon the advancing host by its suddenness had a demoralizing effect. Before Belluomo could station his pikemen to meet this act of madness, Caliente's men were upon them. The front rank crumpled back upon those behind. For a moment the sheer mass of the Venetians in that narrow place resisted the Spaniard's onslaught, then the ranks opened, as instinctively the disordered men flung themselves to the right or the left out of that murderous line of charge.

From his station above, with Sangiorgio at his side, Colombino beheld Don Pablo's squadron cleave its way into the middle of that heaving mass, and check there a moment whilst the valley rang as with the din of some Titanic smithy. Then Don Pablo ripped onwards until he was clear of the press through which he had cut that murderous furrow, his men riding more gently now, but with all the air of being intent upon escape.

Behind them, under the furious command of Belluomo and his officers, the Venetians, disordered and confused were rallying and attempting to re-form their ranks.

Colombino looked to the left. Gravedonna's columns had not yet reached the brow of the hill. He made a sign and his trumpets blared out. Then he charged with the remains of his cavalry, some four hundred horse, whilst Sangiorgio followed with the foot, a thousand strong between pikemen and crossbowmen, the sutlers' wagons coming last.

Don Pablo acting faithfully upon his orders, wheeled his horsemen at that trumpet blast, and came thundering back again, timing his charge so nicely that Belluomo's force was caught simultaneously between Colombino's two divisions, and cracked there like a nut between two stones. The Venetians, demoralized as any force must be that has lost perception of which is its front and which its rear, scarcely resisted.

By the time Gravedonna brought his columns to the heights over which they were to have made their flanking movement, he perceived, to his dismay, that nothing remained but to ride hard to the assistance of the main battle, which already had all but ceased to exist.

Belluomo himself was in flight up the hillside to the north with a little troop to form a bodyguard, whilst in the plain his men were throwing down their arms and calling for quarter.

Before Gravedonna came up, to be received with a hail of crossbow quarrels and to be arrested by Sangiorgio's pikes and compelled to retire before the menace of Colombino's horsemen skirmishing on his flank, the battle of Civitella was at an end. Of Belluomo's division, not more than three hundred escaped to rejoin their captain, who now with Gravedonna on the ground from which Colombino had launched his attack was marshalling the Venetian forces afresh and disposing to recommence the battle in an endeavour to retrieve the fortunes of the day.

But Colombino did not wait for this. With calm speed he gave his orders.

If the dead among Belluomo's following were comparatively few, there were upwards of five hundred wounded and disabled, and some twelve hundred prisoners ringed about by a division of Don Pablo's horse. In no case to encumber himself with these, Colombino was content to render them impotent by depriving them of horses, arms, boots, and most of their clothing. Having possessed himself of Belluomo's vast baggage, which included a magnificent siege-train, stores, arms, tents, and general supplies, he entrusted all this to Caliente, who, driving the horses before him in a herd, was ordered to march northward at once upon Ravenna.

Behind him came Colombino and Sangiorgio, and fighting rear-guard actions all the way, they fell steadily back before Belluomo's depleted army, and came three days later safely to Ravenna, where Caliente, well received by the inhabitants, had already installed himself in the vast new fortress twenty-four hours earlier.

Thence, having despatched a messenger to Onorato da Polenta in Milan with an account of the events, Colombino put off at last his harness, and took his ease, whilst in the marshy plain to the south of the stronghold, the dejected and disgruntled Belluomo sat down to besiege him.

By this Colombino was no longer exercised. A siege by Belluomo, shorn of half his forces and bereft of siege artillery, was no longer a formidable affair. Besides, the victory of Civitella had introduced new factors. Onorato da Polenta should have no difficulty in prevailing upon Francesco Sforza to lend his support, now that so little remained to be done. Once the Duke of Milan's troops appeared before Ravenna, Belluomo would once more find himself between two fires, and the rout of the Venetian army should then be complete.

iii

Annibale Belluomo, foiled and smarting, laid siege to a city which he knew himself unable to carry by assault. But because he did not intend to remain in this situation, because he must redeem his reputation in the eyes of his harsh Venetian taskmasters, and because he burned to be avenged upon the insolent Colombo da Siena, whom he regarded as having been singularly and unfairly favoured by fortune, he sent to Venice for reinforcements and another siege-train.

The siege-train came at the end of a week, a siege-train vastly inferior to the one Belluomo had lost. But the only reinforcement Venice sent him was a commissioner, a lean, white-faced, tight-lipped member of the Council of Ten, the Procurator Francesco Gritti. His mere appearance in the camp before Ravenna, arguing Venetian loss of faith in her condottiero, filled Belluomo with uneasiness.

Seated in Belluomo's pavilion, his black robe drawn about his lean shanks, as if his bloodlessness felt cold, although it was a sunny day of May, Messer Gritti was harsh, sneering, and uncompromising in the terms of censure which he did not hesitate to employ.

Annibale Belluomo, a large, florid, paunchy man, of a gaudy taste in dress, with the strength and the courage of a bull, stood abashed to listen.

'You ask for reinforcements at a time when you should know that the Most Serene Republic has disbanded all troops in her pay saving only those of your condotta. That in retaining you, from among the captains who served her, the Republic made a wise decision is something which the facts now appear to contradict.

'For what was to do here, the troops at your command, in competent hands, and even in incompetent ones, should abundantly have sufficed. Your force numbered fully twice that of the young captain who opposed you, and it was vastly superior in equipment. Yet in a single ill-judged and ill-fought engagement, you have suffered these advantages to be lost. Half your force has melted away, broken and destroyed, and your equipment – including the most complete and powerful siege-train ever put into the field – is now in the possession of the enemy. It will not surprise you that the Most Serene has little confidence left in you, or that unless with what force remains you can retrieve the confidence you have lost, the consequences may be very grave.'

The condottiero, sweating at once with fear and rage, muttered abject platitudes about the fortunes of war.

'It is easy for you men of the robe to sit snugly in the council chamber and criticize the operations in the field, for never having seen an engagement, you know nothing of the incalculable chances that are involved. Fortune was unjustly favourable to this fellow from Siena. He prevailed by a rash audacity which no soldier of experience could have dreamed of committing, and one which by all the laws of war should have resulted in his destruction.'

'The more shame to you, then, that it resulted in his victory.'

'But – God give me patience with you! – that is what I mean by the fortune of war.'

Messer Gritti shifted in his chair. He tapped the table before him with a long, bony forefinger. 'The Most Serene demands in her captains the ability to control fortune. Have you forgotten Busoni who was Count of Carmagnola?'

Belluomo turned purple at that allusion to the great captain whom the Republic had beheaded for the ill-conduct of a campaign.

'In the name of God! You'll not compare me with Carmagnola! That was a traitor.'

Eyes that were cold and grey as steel regarded him steadily from under level black brows. Lips that were thin, crafty, and cruel smiled almost imperceptibly in scorn.

'The results were the same; and it is by results that we judge a man. What shall assure us that you are honest?'

'This,' said Belluomo, 'is too much.' He mopped the sweat from his brow and from his short, thick neck.

Messer Gritti went coldly on. 'I bring you a siege-train to replace the one you have lost. It is inferior, far inferior; but the best we can supply. And, anyway, with the remaining men at your command it should be sufficient for your purpose, provided that you display more zeal than hitherto.'

'I vow to God I have never lacked for zeal!' roared Belluomo.

'For skill, then.'

'Nor yet for skill!' He banged the table with his massive fist.

'Then it seems to me that you condemn yourself. For only honesty remains.'

'For a man determined to think ill, perhaps. But there is still fortune, as I have told you; and that is all that has been lacking.'

Messer Gritti, that cold fish of a man, was not moved by this vehemence.

'See that your fortune changes before it completely submerges you. You have no time to lose. Is it necessary that I should tell you that Ravenna must be reduced before its treacherous example can infect other states now in Venetian vassalage? That is a calamity we need not perhaps at present contemplate, nor its consequences, to you, who will be held responsible.'

From that awe-inspiring interview, Belluomo went to work with the zeal of a man who was fighting not for his employers but for his own life.

Within the ensuing week he had conceived and executed three several plans for carrying the city by assault, each of which had been repulsed with heavy loss. The vigilance and skill of Colombino made easy work of it.

Reeling back to his pavilion, sick at heart, through the grey mists of a summer dawn, after the defeat of his third attempt, Belluomo found Messer Gritti there, awaiting him.

The pale-faced procurator was like ice in his anger.

'I will do you the justice to admit that at least you are honest. For it begins to become plain that you are opposed to a soldier far greater than yourself.'

Than this he could have administered no more cutting whiplash. Belluomo strode to his couch, and clanked down, his bespattered armour still upon him. 'If you have so high an opinion of the fellow the more fools you and your Council of Ten for not hiring him to your service when you might have done so.'

'It's an omission that may yet be repaired.' The procurator, who had been pacing the pavilion, halted before the soldier, and held out a strip of parchment. 'Read that.'

Belluomo slewed round, so that the increasing daylight might fall upon the writing. But he need scarcely have troubled, for the Venetian gave him full information.

'Whatever else you may lack, you possess at least vigilant outposts. A man was caught an hour ago attempting to cross the lines. In your absence they brought him to me. That letter was in the lining of his shoe. An elementary method of concealment. It is from Onorato da Polenta, enjoining Colombo to stand firm, since Francesco Sforza, enheartened by your defeat at Civitella, is raising an army to come to his relief. Three weeks, you'll observe, is the utmost time required. Three weeks.'

Belluomo took the bitterness in the man's voice to be a reflection of the bitterness in his soul. And he was dangerously near to being maliciously glad of the mental torment of this fellow who had so tormented him with his cold, sarcastic hectorings. He actually laughed, although without mirth, as he returned the scrap of parchment. Then, whilst unbuckling the straps of his harness, he delivered himself.

'I told you a week ago that reinforcements would be needed. Now perhaps you believe me.'

The answer was barbed with contempt. 'You had no thought for this, but only for your own incompetence when you clamoured for more troops.'

'Do you read thoughts now? How do you know what is in my mind?'

'What is in your mind I can tell with tolerable certainty. And that is nothing.'

Belluomo, suddenly white, ventured for once to give as much as he took.

'If you had been less of a fool, with your airs and your sneers, if you had possessed some scraps of this competence of which you make so much pestilent chatter, you would have perceived that this thing was inevitable.'

The procurator quivered as if he had been struck. But he refused to display heat. He remained coldly superior. 'And why, pray, is it inevitable? Because your blundering has made it so. In the face of that you should study humility.'

Belluomo was tugging at a strap. He paused. 'Look you, Messer Gritti, you may put the blame where you please. I care not a rat's tail for your opinion. I won my spurs at my trade long ago, and my military reputation is not at the mercy of your judgment, I thank God.'

'You have occasion to thank God for that. Do you read Plautus?'

'Plautus?' Belluomo stared. 'Who's he?'

Messer Gritti sighed. 'A pity you have no learning! It might help you to understand me when I say that you remind me of his Miles Gloriosus, a braggart, rhodomonting captain, full of sound because otherwise empty and hollow.'

'And I remind you of him!' Belluomo heaved himself up. 'By God, sir! I find you intolerable.'

'Ah! Then, if in nothing else, we are in harmony at least in our opinions of each other. But we are not here to quarrel upon them. We have a situation to face and a duty to perform.'

'Then face it by doing what I advised a week ago. Send to Venice for more troops. Let the Most Serene hire Gattamelata to support me.'

'We have three weeks. Gattamelata could not take the field in six.' Messer Gritti gave reasons, coldly, passionlessly technical. They convinced Belluomo and humbled him.

'What then?' he asked helplessly.

'Is it possible that, in spite of all your thrasonical ranting, you ask me that?' The procurator paused, his lips tight. Then from the table he took up another strip of parchment exactly like the first. 'Look at this.'

Belluomo took it, and read with deepening wonder. Again it was a letter from Onorato da Polenta. But its contents were the very opposite of the first one.

These in doleance to warn you not to lean upon false hopes. My endeavours here have failed. Milan either cannot or will not lend assistance. Therefore, you must depend as I do entirely upon yourself and the resources at your command. The courage and address you displayed at Civitella permit me to wait with confidence.

ONORATO DA POLENTA

Bewildered, Belluomo took up again the first letter. He compared the two, and could not doubt that they were in the same hand, even to the flourish adorning the signature. He raised his puzzled eyes. 'What does it mean?'

'In the first place, that I am a skilful penman.'

'You mean that you… Oh! But to what purpose?'

'Let me help your perplexities. First, you must find me an intelligent man, if such a one exists among your following, to take the place of the captured messenger. Second, this message should sensibly lessen Colombino's confidence. Third, whilst it is so lessened, we deliver an attack upon his loyalty. It means, my captain, that dull arms must yield to the toga. My wits must supply the lack left by your military blundering. I must step in and take charge so that we may not perish by your ineptitude.'

'Ah!' Belluomo became sarcastic in his turn. 'It follows that we shall see fine things.'

But Messer Gritti paid no heed. Pacing calmly to and fro in the pavilion, he expounded further.

'This Colombino is a greedily acquisitive rogue. It has just come to my knowledge that in the campaign between Rovieto and the Scaligeri his faith was bought by Della Scala for two hundred thousand ducats.'

'Lord! Does your wisdom put faith in scandalmongers?'

'No. Not in scandalmongers. I had a visitor two days ago; a lady, as you may have heard. The sometime Countess of Rovieto, who is now landless and dispossessed because of this rascal's treachery. Some lingering hopes that she bases upon Venetian assistance prompted her to seek me, to tell me that if we are in difficulties here, we can always purchase our way out of them.'

'And you believe it? Bah!'

'We need not dispute a matter which we are about to test. This letter is to pave the way. If you will find me the messenger I need, the rest can wait until tomorrow.'

That messenger, a cross-gartered peasant, approached Ravenna in the dusk of that May evening, and, having softly drawn the attention of a sentinel on the ramparts, swam the moat and gained admission by a postern.

Colombino was at supper with his captains when the letter was brought. He read it twice, first in bewilderment, then in suspicion, and tossed it to his two captains, who, having read, looked at him in dismay.

'Malediction!' said Caliente. 'It's unfortunate.'

'It's curious,' said Sangiorgio, and pulled his beard. 'Curious, yes. More curious than unfortunate,' Colombino opined. 'If the Lord of Ravenna had desired to discourage us he could hardly have done better. Shall we take a look at this messenger of his? It might be prudent.'

The clown was fetched, a stolid, dull fellow by his air, showing a natural awe of these soldiers.

But Colombino, very affable, put him entirely at his ease.

'Don Pablo, give this worthy lad a cup of wine. He's wet, and shivering with cold.'

The wine was poured and gratefully drunk. Colombino lounging in his tall chair considered him with friendly eyes.

'You deserve a hatful of ducats for the service you've performed and the risks you took. Tell me, from whom did you have this letter?'

'From the Lord Onorato himself, may it please your potency.'

'You are sure of that? Sure that it was the Lord Onorato himself.'

'I've been too long in his service to be mistaken, my lord.'

'Ah! You were in Candia with him when he was exiled there.'

'In Candia. Yes, my lord.'

Don Pablo jerked up his head, and looked more fully at the messenger.

'Then you would be with him last year, when he was in England.'

'To be sure I was, magnificent.'

Colombino's affability increased. 'And how did you like England?'

The fellow grinned. 'I like Ravenna better.'

'I've been disputing with my captains here a matter that you can settle, having been so long in the Lord Onorato's service.' Colombino stood up, displaying his imposing height. 'Don Pablo Caliente here has wagered me that the Lord Onorato is fully as tall as myself, and I have laid him ten ducats that I am the taller by an inch. What should you say, my friend?'

The clown considered him for a moment, blinking. 'Faith, it'll be a near thing between you, my lord. I'll not dare to say.'

'You are wise,' said Colombino. He sat down again. 'Wise, but not wise enough. You were insufficiently schooled by those that sent you.' His manner had lost none of its amiability. 'They should have told you that the Lord Onorato is a little man, at least five inches shorter than myself; that his place of exile was Crete and not Candia; and they should have told you enough to prevent you from being gulled by a tale that he was ever in England. Now, my friend, your bubble's pricked. Will you tell us the rest, of your own free will, or shall the engines squeeze it out of you?'

The clown was on his knees clamouring for mercy, Don Pablo was expressing a joyous amazement in morphological Spanish oaths, and Sangiorgio was grim.

'You shall come by no harm here, my lad,' Colombino assured the terror-stricken peasant. 'And you'll find my service better than that of the knave who hired you to this treachery. Be wise, then; by which I mean, be truthful.'

iv

Messer Gritti did not keep them waiting for the second act of the little comedy he had prepared.

Towards noon of the morrow there came to Colombino in the quarters he had established in the Casa Polentana, the home of the Lords of Ravenna, an officer bringing word that a little troop under a white flag had ridden up to the South Gate. Ser Annibale Belluomo came to request a parley and desired safe-conduct.

When eventually he was ushered into the state chamber of the palace, where Colombino waited to receive him, he did not come alone. With him, preceding him into the room as if by right of rank, came the tall, gaunt, funereal Messer Gritti. Save for his white, crafty face and the linen bands at throat and wrists, the statesman was all black, from his lank hair to his square shoes, and he walked delicately, as if he stepped on eggs. After him, in vivid contrast, rolled Belluomo, portly, blond, and florid, all in flaming scarlet, with a clank and jingle to his swagger.

From the table at which he had been writing, Colombino rose to receive them. In the long surcoat of grey velvet, with a gold chain at his neck and a caul of gold thread confining his thick tawny hair, he looked the courtier rather than the soldier, and in his reception of them he displayed the urbane dignity of a prince.

'This honour is unexpected; but you are none the less welcome, sirs.' His fine hand, innocent of any jewel, waved each in turn to a seat, then he resumed his own chair, so placed that his back was to the tall windows and the sunlit garden beyond.

'Command me,' Colombino invited.

Messer Gritti cleared his throat and loosed his harsh voice.

They came, he announced, in terms that had obviously been rehearsed, to avoid that precious time should be wasted, valuable property destroyed, and good blood shed in vain. Next he proceeded to demonstrate that Ravenna's resistance was futile. Venice commanded almost inexhaustible resources, which she would not hesitate to employ. Conceivably Messer Colombo was counting upon assistance from the Duke of Milan. If so, he built upon sand. Messer Gritti had sure information from dependable agents of the Serene in Milan that Francesco Sforza would not, and could not if he would, lend any assistance. Did, then, Messer Colombo, consider it worth his while to persist until starvation must compel him to admit defeat? Would he not be better advised to surrender whilst he might do so with the honours of war, rather than forfeit by the protraction of this siege every right to merciful consideration?

Belluomo, listening to those measured periods, delivered in that harsh, monotonous voice, expected at the end defiance and derision from the young soldier to whom they were addressed. Instead, however, to his amazement, Colombino remained thoughtful, chin in hand, and the eyes he raised at last were mild and dreamy. It looked, indeed, as if the spirit had been slain in him by that forged letter. When presently he spoke it was in the subdued voice of a man who is beggared of confidence.

'All this may be as you say, sir. But it remains that I have pledged my service. I am paid to hold Ravenna for my Lord Onorato da Polenta.'

It was a statement that opened wide the door for Messer Gritti, and eagerly, confidently, he entered.

'You are paid? What are you paid, if I may presume to ask?'

Colombino answered frankly, a further evidence of despondency. There was a glitter now in the steely eyes of the Venetian.

'And is it only in the hope of this hundred thousand ducats that you hold the city?'

'What else? With me war is a trade like any other. I do not pursue it for my distraction, or for barren glory.'

The procurator leaned forward, his elbow on his knee, and significantly lowered his voice. 'Has it occurred to you that you might possibly find the Most Serene Republic a more generous pay-master?'

Colombino sighed. 'Unfortunately I am not in the pay of Venice.'

'What hinders you from entering it?'

The abruptness of that question clearly startled the young condottiero. His suddenly quickened glance faltered before the Venetian's glittering eyes. He covered his mouth with his hand. Then at last he spoke, with the hesitation of a tempted man.

'There is my obligation to the Lord Onorato.'

'That obligation is ended by the situation, which properly considered is a situation of defeat – ultimately assured, if not immediate. You merely go to meet the inevitable in accepting it at once. And I am prepared to assure you that the Most Serene and ever-generous Republic will signify her satisfaction for the pains you will have spared her and for avoiding the ruin of her property here in Ravenna, by a payment of two hundred thousand ducats.'

Thus he came straight to the heart of the matter, wrapping the proposed betrayal in neat speciousness, supplying Colombino with all the justifications that a traitor ever needs. Having spoken thus boldly, he sat back, his waxen hands on his black-clad bony knees, and waited. His patience was not tried. Almost instantly Colombino cast off languor and hesitations.

'Do you pay in advance?'

Messer Gritti caught his breath. From Belluomo there was an inarticulate grunt that was prompted by disgust. The things they said of this fellow were true, then. Treachery was in his blood. He was a disgrace to the trade of arms.

The procurator stroked his shaven chin. 'You shall be paid in advance what moneys I have at hand – some fifty thousand ducats – as an earnest of our compact. We pay the balance when Ravenna is surrendered.'

Colombino regarded him steadily for a moment. Then, abruptly, he rose.

'Fetch the gold, and we'll talk of this again. In the meantime, I will consider.'

They took that dismissal, but as they rode back to the Venetian camp in the marshy lands south of the city, Belluomo shook his great head over Messer Gritti's self-laudatory hymn of victory.

'I can't bring myself to believe in it. It is too easy. It'll not surprise me if you end by being hoist with your own petard.'

The procurator vouchsafed him a glance of contempt. 'You understand men as little as you understand your trade. Fortunately the conduct of this business is in my hands.'

Belluomo kept his temper as best he could. 'We shall see what we shall see.'

What he saw that evening when they went again into Ravenna accompanied by two men bearing the sacks of ducats was evidence that he was wrong and Messer Gritti right.

Again Colombino was alone when they were admitted to his presence. A map of the city and its surroundings was spread upon his table.

'If I sell you the place without more ado, I ruin my career as a captain of fortune.' His uplifted hand restrained Messer Gritti's interruption. 'This thing must be so contrived as to make it clear that

I yield to military necessity. For this I shall lose some credit. That will be your gain, Messer Belluomo.'

The big soldier looked at him now with undisguised dislike. He threw out his broad chest. 'That consummation is in any case inevitable.'

Colombino bowed his head. 'If I had not recognized that probability, I should never have listened to your proposals. Here now are mine.' He turned to the map, and beckoned them forward. He was very brisk.

'On a night to be determined you shall carry the city by assault. Thus: You will march a force of not less than a thousand men round to the north, going wide of the city, so that the movement may not be suspected. You will have to do so in any case, so as to cross the canal, which you can do only here, two miles to eastward, by the Bridge of San Sisto.' He indicated on the map the bridge over the canal which connected the city with the sea, built since the days when the Adriatic had flowed through Ravenna as it now flowed through Venice and before it had receded.

'With this force, you will open an attack on the Venezia Gate. You will make it violent, with a full display of strength, so as to justify me in bringing my entire garrison to the threatened point. Once this is accomplished, which will be exactly a half-hour after the attack has opened, a second force of yours – five or six hundred men will suffice for this – will launch a genuine attack against the South Gate which by then will be utterly undefended. You will throw an improvised bridge across the moat there, and with rams or gunpowder you can break down the postern in a few minutes. As there will be no defenders, there will be no resistance. The noise will be drowned by the greater uproar across the city here on the north. Once a dozen men are in, they possess themselves of the machinery of the drawbridge, and in as many minutes they will have lowered it to admit the whole body of assailants. This force will charge straight across the city, to take me in the rear. Perceiving the peril and not knowing its extent or the numbers with which I shall have to deal, it will be natural for me to withdraw my men into the citadel in the best order possible, leaving the invaders free access to the Venezia Gate, which they will open to your main division.

'Thus you make yourselves masters of the city. The obvious sequel is that from your position of advantage you summon me to surrender, offering me the honours of war. In all the circumstances it will be seen that I shall have no alternative but to accept.'

There he paused, and looking shamelessly from one to the other of them, inquired did the plan receive Messer Belluomo's approval.

It was Messer Gritti who answered. Even in that moment he could not repress his sour, sneering humour.

'The military credit that will accrue to Messer Belluomo assures you of that.'

The sarcasm quenched the gleam in the eye of the Venetian captain. He shrugged and grunted, whilst Colombino resumed.

'We are agreed, then. This is Friday. If Sunday night will suit you for the attack, that will suit me. Let the action in the north commence a half-hour before midnight, and that on the South Gate at midnight precisely.'

The procurator's glance consulted Belluomo. The captain nodded. 'Sunday night,' he agreed curtly.

Colombino swept aside the map. 'Then it but remains that you jointly sign this bond for a hundred and fifty thousand ducats due to me, and payable on demand.'

Messer Gritti frowned. 'Why this? Is not my word enough?'

'In a transaction so delicate it is imprudent to forgo full payment in advance. If I consent to that, at least I must have the nearest possible equivalent to the gold.'

Messer Gritti considered yet a moment. Then he shrugged. 'Ever the man of business, Ser Colombo. I marvel you should have been content to devote yourself to the trade of arms.'

'I find it sufficiently remunerative.'

Belluomo could not contain himself before so much cynicism. 'Conducted as you conduct it, sir, it must be.'

But Colombino laughed without shame. 'Do you sneer at me? You should be grateful. I make things easy for you.'

'The devil burn your impudence!'

Colombino laughed again, and proffered the pen to Messer Gritti. The procurator had been studying the document.

'It says nothing here of the consideration for which the gold is due.'

'God give me patience, sir! Should I suffer that to be set down? You must suppose me simple. Come, sir, do you sign or not?'

Messer Gritti plucked at his nether lip. 'After all...' He checked, shrugged, and took the proffered pen. He signed, and then Belluomo laboriously scrawled his signature below the procurator's.

Messer Gritti departed chuckling at the thought that if the corruption of Colombino had been expensive, it was cheap compared with the alternative.

'Provided,' said the ever-uneasy Belluomo, 'that the rascal keeps faith with us.'

'You may depend upon that,' sneered Gritti. 'For enough ducats the dog would sell his own mother. That little Countess of Rovieto knows her man.'

He had proof of his acumen that very night. Another messenger was captured at the outposts; a departing one this time. Upon him they found the following letter addressed to Onorato da Polenta:

My lord – Your letters quench my last hope, which lay in speedy relief by the Duke of Milan. Ravenna has already suffered three severe assaults. These we have repulsed. But a fourth, I fear, must carry the place, as we are in great distress and running short of victuals, of which I account it my duty to send you word.

Messer Gritti leered as he rubbed his knuckly hands. 'Thus that plausible double-dealer prepares the ground for his treachery.'

His last doubt dispelled by this, Messer Belluomo made his dispositions for Sunday with the greater confidence.

Soon after the May night had closed in, he marched his thousand men away to the east through the marshes, then crossing the canal by the distant Bridge of San Sisto, he followed the road round to the northern side of Ravenna.

Gravedonna was left to command the body of five hundred foot that was to charge into the city from the south.

Gritti remained in the camp with what was left of the army: a thousand men who would march at dawn into captured Ravenna, but who might meanwhile rest.

Punctually at a half-hour before midnight Belluomo opened his demonstration at the Venezia Gate, and skilfully maintained it until an explosion beyond the city informed him that Gravedonna had blown in the postern. Very soon from the din and uproar within Ravenna he gathered that Gravedonna was in the city and about the work assigned to him. He stood ready now to enter as soon as the gate should be opened from within. Time passed, and the gate remained closed. The sounds of battle within the city, instead of sweeping onwards towards the north, were actually receding. He began to fear that something had miscarried. There was for a little while almost a lull, followed at last by a terrific distant uproar, not merely from the south of the city, but from a point somewhere beyond it.

At the sudden conclusion forced upon him, a dreadful fear surged up in Belluomo to receive almost instant confirmation. Those sounds of battle must be coming from his own camp. What dreadful treachery was here?

In frenzy he wheeled his men, and led them at breakneck speed through the night, back by the way they had come, heading for that distant scene of action. Whilst overhead the sky was clear and starry, a shallow mist rising from the marshes made perilous that reckless night ride over this treacherous ground. But of this Belluomo recked nothing. He reached the bridge, and led the way over at a gallop. His silvery armour revealed him for a moment in the gloom to those immediately following. Then he vanished, abruptly as if the earth had swallowed him. And, indeed, something akin to it had happened. A resounding splash in the waters below announced the way he had taken.

Where the bridge had been when they had crossed earlier that night, there was now an open chasm, and through this a dozen of his riders followed him into the canal before in roaring confusion the remainder of his company came to a halt upon the brink.

The condottiero was saved by a miracle from drowning. His armour must have sunk him had he parted company with his charger as they hurtled down together. He was unsaddled, it is true; but his hands had wound themselves into the horse's mane, and to this he clung with desperate strength. Shallows fortunately were not more than a dozen yards away, and to these by luck or instinct the plunging half-foundered beast brought its gasping rider.

Alternately panting and trumpeting with rage, the waterlogged Belluomo clawed his slippery way up the slime of the bank, to slide down again and yet again under the weight of his armour, until his men came to his assistance. At last, hoisted to dry land, he sat down, helpless, shivering, and exhausted, with his head in his hands, to endeavour to conjecture what had happened.

It really set little strain upon conjecture.

Gravedonna, having blown up the postern, had entered the city unopposed, and had gone boldly forward until he came to the open space below the great fortress and within a half-bowshot of the Venezia Gate. Here suddenly he found himself surrounded by a force of more than twice his numbers and challenged to surrender if he would save the lives of his men. He realized that he was in a trap, and, casting the blame and responsibility upon those who had so readily believed that Ravenna would be delivered to them, he made no more ado. His five hundred, deprived of their arms, were marched into the citadel.

Thereafter, whilst Belluomo was riding wildly for the Bridge of San Sisto, where he would find himself cut off, Colombino led out the whole of his forces and like a thunderbolt fell upon the unsuspecting Venetian camp. Taking it thus completely by surprise, he made short work of it. In the first pale glimmerings of dawn the inhabitants of Ravenna beheld a mob of over a thousand prisoners on foot, herded ignominiously into the city by Colombino's horsemen to go and join the other prisoners in the fortress. After them came Belluomo's supply wagons, laden with victuals, a drove of bullocks, a herd of sheep, carts piled with tents, ammunition, arms, and accoutrements, the spoils of that ridiculously easy victory.

And among the prisoners, but apart, and treated with great deference by his captors, came Messer Francesco Gritti, whose cunning had been so sedulously employed to this end, and whose soul was now in bitterest ferment.

It remained only to deal with Belluomo.

Daybreak found him there on the canal's brink, chilled to the marrow and to the soul. He was utterly without orientation. To cross this pestilent canal he would have to go west beyond Ravenna. And to what purpose should he now cross it? He was soldier enough to understand exactly what had occurred. Colombino's craft, taking advantage of Gritti's attempt to corrupt him, had divided the Venetian army into three parts, and he had dealt separately with two of them as easily as when he pleased he could now deal with the third.

Belluomo's only course in this pass was to ride north, for Venice, and so save what was left of his condotta. But either this did not occur to him, or else in defeat his fear of the lords of Venice was greater than his fear of Colombino. Be this as it may, there by the canal, Colombino still found him, when he rode forth in strength at sunrise.

What little heart remained in Belluomo went completely out of him when he held that orderly force, two thousand strong, glittering in the morning sunshine as it advanced upon his inferior and dispirited following where it stood with its back to the water and its retreat cut off.

He staggered up in miserable plight, an appalling figure, plastered with mud and still oozing slime from between the joints of his harness.

Accepting the inevitable, he sent an officer forward with a trumpeter to ask for terms.

V

It was a bitter day for Annibale Belluomo. The splendid army which Venice had entrusted to him had melted away under the arts and wiles of the infernal Colombino, in whose hands he was now a prisoner. Nor was he treated even as an honourable prisoner should be treated. Terms had been refused him. Unconditional surrender had been demanded and in this he had been constrained by his circumstances to acquiesce. He had, it was true, been permitted to wash and reclothe himself; but for the rest he had been locked in an underground cell like a criminal, and when towards evening he was haled away to the Casa Polentana, he went with a halter round his neck. The only grain of comfort afforded him was to find Messer Francesco Gritti walking beside him with a similar decoration, silent, livid, his eyes smouldering.

No sooner was Belluomo in his captor's presence, in that same pleasant room where they had been earlier received, than he loosed the fury begotten in him by this treatment and fiercely reproached Colombino for this outrage upon all the usages of war between captains.

'As a captain,' Colombino answered him, 'I dealt with you in the field. Here I am to deal with you and your associate as seducers who sought to corrupt the commander of a stronghold. You must have forgotten that, since you dare to complain of your treatment.'

His words, delivered in calm, deliberate tones, sent a shiver down Belluomo's spine. He hung his head as he stood beside the proudly fierce, almost disdainful Messer Gritti.

Colombino was seated, as before, at the stout oaken table, his back to the windows which had been flung wide to the fragrance of the garden. Behind him stood his two marshals, Sangiorgio and Caliente, and on his left, away at the long table's end, sat the Lord Onorato's nephew, Cosimo da Polenta, a tall, handsome, dark-complexioned man of thirty, who was tonsured and wore the black garb of an ecclesiastic.

Guards with ordered halberts stood immediately behind the prisoners.

Having silenced Belluomo by his answer, it was to Messer Gritti that Colombino chiefly addressed himself, and as he proceeded Belluomo's own humiliation was softened in the contemplation of that of his illustrious fellow prisoner. He tasted in that hour some of the sweets of vengeance upon this man under whose constant sneers he had so keenly smarted.

'Messer Gritti, you esteem yourself, I think, a very subtle man; and no doubt you are encouraged so to esteem yourself, for you deal in arts which are accounted subtle in Venice, as I have had occasion to observe. But the most subtle of minds may be reduced to naught by presumption; and I judge you, Messer Gritti, to be a very presumptuous man. This I shall hope for your own future benefit – assuming that you are permitted to live to profit by the lesson – to demonstrate to you.'

He paused there a moment, and then, in his calm, dispassionate tone, slowly, like a man who chooses words with care, he continued to pour the corrosive acid of his judgment upon the Venetian's soul.

'Your first presumption is of knowledge of the military art. Great soldiers, sir, are not created in the council chamber. They are either born, like poets, or else made laboriously by experience in the field. Since this presumption of yours led you to override the captain appointed by the Most Serene Republic, the responsibility for the failure here of the Venetian operations must also be borne by you. This I am fully representing in letters to the Council of Ten, which I have prepared.' He touched a sheaf of parchments that lay before him.

'Your next and far grosser presumptions were that I am a knave and a traitor. Heaven alone knows why you should have had so poor an opinion of me. But I am concerned with what you thought, and not with why you thought it.

'Presuming me a fool, you forge a letter to deceive me. And such a letter!

'Ask yourself, Messer Gritti, if your wits are not entirely addled, had the case been as that letter pretended would Onorato da Polenta have troubled to write it? That question, and the answer to it, would have occurred to any intelligent schoolboy; and yet one and the other appear to have escaped the acumen of a subtle statesman of Venice.

'You perceive now, no doubt, how my suspicions were aroused. But you should have foreseen it; then it must also have occurred to you that your messenger would be in my hands to be questioned. Such a simple, obvious matter! You will imagine what I asked him. A really subtle man would have imagined sooner and schooled his messenger more fully. Then he would not have betrayed himself by agreeing with me that the Lord Onorato is as tall as I am, that he had been banished to Candia instead of Crete, and the like. It became necessary, when we found him lying, that we should extract all the truth from him. There are artless persuasions, well within the scope of such subtlety as yours: filthy, abhorrent ways of which you will have experience; the rack, the boot, and a simple, nauseous business with knotted whipcord, known as woolding. I take pride in the thought that I had recourse to none of these, and that by gentler measures I obtained all that it mattered for me to know before you sought me on the morrow upon the presumption that I am for sale.

'Do you realize now into what jeopardy you walked? With the evidence in my hands of what you had done, I should have been justified in hanging you at once; and I should certainly have hanged you without compunction if I had not perceived a better use for you, perceived how I might take advantage of your shallow-pated presumption so as to lead to destruction the army whose commander you were overruling.'

The procurator of the Republic could stand no more. Reckless of all peril, he spewed up the venom that was choking him.

'It was no presumption to assume you a traitor to be bought. For that you are. You were bought by della Scala to betray the Countess of Rovieto, as your father Terrarossa was bought to betray Florence and was hanged for it, as you will hang at the end.'

Caliente took a step forward, breathing hard. Colombino's calm hand restrained him. There was no change in the inflexion of his voice.

'You are a brave man, Messer Gritti, or else a very rash and foolish one, to use those words when the halter is round your neck.'

'If I am to hang...' the Venetian was beginning.

'I understand,' Colombino interrupted him. 'You are presuming now upon that. But again you are mistaken. Possibly, at least. Whether you hang or not depends at the moment upon whether the Council of Ten, with all the facts before it, as I have scrupulously set them down, shall consider it worth while to preserve your life. If the Most Serene Republic should not have had enough of your subtleties and should consent to honour the bond by which you engaged her to pay me one hundred and fifty thousand ducats, I will undertake on my side to procure from the Lord Onorato when he arrives your pardon for the attempt to corrupt the commander of his forces.'

'Honour the bond?' Fury made the Venetian foolish. 'Have you honoured your engagement under that bond, you double traitor?'

'Have the rods to the impudent dog,' growled Caliente. 'I'd have cracked his scraggy neck between my fingers for the half of what he has said to you.'

'Sh! We must be patient with him. He is very dull of understanding, poor man. He does not even perceive that the gold he was to have paid me for betraying Ravenna is now to be paid to me as his own ransom. It would be a poor compliment to him to set his value at less. Indeed, when he comes to think of it calmly, his vanity may be wounded by my moderation.' Then he turned again directly to address the procurator. 'Understand me clearly, Messer Gritti. You are not to suppose that you can escape punishment for your offence against me. Either I hang you in the Lord of Ravenna's name, or I fine you in my own. Regard it that way. You may ransom yourself, or the Most Serene may ransom you, by the payment of this bond. It goes to Venice now together with these letters setting forth in detail the events, and making quite clear your own responsibility for them.

'My messenger for this occasion shall be Messer Annibale Belluomo, whom I set at liberty to that end. Thus I discharge at the same time a duty by a brother soldier. For these letters should serve to ransom Messer Belluomo's reputation, justly at the expense of your own.'

Abruptly he waved a hand to the guards. 'Remove your prisoner, and take the halter from the neck of Messer Belluomo.'

One of the soldiers touched Messer Gritti's arm. But he did not immediately turn. He stood shaking from head to foot, his eyes blood-injected and baleful as they glared at Colombino. He mouthed a moment before he could find words.

'You brigand! You vile, treacherous brigand! Don't think that you'll sit long in the saddle, you upstart son of a felon! I shall yet live to see you in the dust where you belong.'

Caliente bawled an order. 'Take that chattering crow away quickly, or – God forgive me – I may forget that he's a prisoner.' And he stalked after them, hastening them with his fury as they hustled the Venetian out.

Belluomo watched the procurator's departure with the suspicion of a smile. Unenviable as was his own position, yet his uppermost feeling at that moment was that Colombino had effectively avenged him upon a man at the hands of whose self-sufficiency he had suffered so much.

Next morning with the letters and an escort of a score of his own men, generously set at liberty for the purpose by Colombino, he set out for Venice.

Chapter 3

THE LADY OF RAVENNA

i

There exists a letter from Colombino da Siena to the Lord Onorato da Polenta, beginning 'Veni, vidi, vici.'

It was penned on the day after the rout of Ravenna's besiegers, and was borne to Milan by Messer Cosimo da Polenta, the Lord Onorato's cousin, the tall ecclesiastic who had been present when Colombino dealt with Messer Gritti.

If Colombino chose his model for that sentence too recklessly for exactitude, yet the overstatement is pardonable in view of the elation in which he wrote. And for the moment it was at least more or less applicable to the army that Venice had put into the field. Between Civitella and Ravenna that had most certainly and completely been destroyed, and destroyed almost at sight by a commander disposing of less than half the original Venetian force.

Colombino's repute, which already had stood high, soared now to altitudes that not even the great Colleoni had reached. The valour he had displayed and still more the craft, so dear to the Italian mind, brought him such fame that his name was being mentioned with awe in the courts of Italy as that of a military wonder-worker. Of this he beheld the reflection in the Lord Onorato's manner towards him and in the deference paid him by the ambassadors of the powers, who hastened presently to Ravenna to felicitate Onorato upon his restoration.

These things, however, did not befall until a fortnight after the victory.

In the meantime the gold for Francesco Gritti's ransom had arrived from Venice, sent, not, indeed, by the State, but by the family of Gritti, which was amongst the wealthiest of the Republic and had taken the view that duty demanded no less. Messer Gritti had departed humiliated and fuming, swearing that he would yet have real value for the gold and that Colombo da Siena should rue the day when he had mocked him and so unconscionably mulcted him.

The increase of wealth which this gold represented permitted him to enrol in the Company of the Dove five hundred of the mercenaries captured from Venice.

It was not for Venice to make a grievance of this. It is true that it was the Italian custom to release all mercenaries at the end of an engagement. But it was a custom that, like a good many others, Colombino disregarded, to the disgust of contemporary captains of fortune. And it was a custom of which Venice herself had never approved when to ignore it had been to the disadvantage of her enemies. The Most Serene Republic, therefore, could hardly now complain if Colombino ignored it to her own.

By this further strengthening of his forces, Colombino lessened the chances that Venice would make any attempt at present to reconquer Ravenna. The Turks at the time were giving her a good deal of trouble in her overseas dominions, and claiming all the resources she could spare, weakened as she was by the long-drawn war with Milan.

Ultimately, however, there would probably come a day of reckoning unless by the display of force the Lord Onorato could avert it. For it was true then, as it always has been and always will be true, that to ensure peace you must be prepared for war. Of this the Lord Onorato was well aware. He remembered Colombino's admonition at the outset that to seize Ravenna would not be difficult, but to hold it would be quite another matter, and he still trusted to the faith he had expressed when he had answered that the example of Ravenna would be followed by other states under the Venetian yoke, amongst which a league could be formed against the predatory Republic.

When, however, the festivities, the banquetings, the joustings, and the stage-plays with which his restoration was celebrated had come to an end, and the Lord Onorato had leisure to scan the horizon, he beheld there no sign of the clouds upon which he had so confidently counted.

The people of Ravenna were loyal to him; they had not been comfortable under Venetian rule. Venetians had filled all the public offices, and Venice had controlled to her own advantage Ravenna's industries and trade. Therefore Ravenna had welcomed the restoration of the Polentas, and it could be depended upon to form a militia to maintain it. But the past had shown how inadequate that would be against the might of Venice, with her professional soldiers.

Although six weeks were sped since the home-coming of Onorato and his handsome daughter, Colombino had as yet shown no sign of determining his engagement. He still occupied himself with matters of fortification and military administration, as if he were to remain indefinitely in command. His captains had withdrawn to quarters in the citadel; but Colombino himself continued at the Casa Polentana, and was daily at the Lord Onorato's table, as much one of the family as Samaritana or Messer Cosimo, and very friendly with them both.

In Samaritana, whose voice he heard for the first time when she came to Ravenna, he found no affectations of reticence. She was as frank and at ease in her speech with him as became a maid of her station, and if the wistfulness he had first observed still hung like a veil about her, yet at times she displayed a gracious liveliness and could spice her utterances with wit.

Watching her as she moved with her slim, leisurely grace, Colombino found himself admiring her, found himself taking pleasure in the contemplation of her, and giving thanks that since she was the ladder by which he was to climb she should be as good to look upon as he now found her.

Love, he assured himself, had no part in this. Love, he would have told you in those days, was a paltry mirage on which men wrecked themselves. His aims being what they were, he thanked God that she was not humpbacked. That was all. She counted in his schemes for no more than she mattered to them.

If at moments his conscience pricked him, if an inner voice assured him that this was unworthy, a calculating outrage upon knightliness, he would harden himself again in the recollection of the treatment he had received at the hands of Madonna Eufemia, and in the persuasion that all women being alike the only wisdom for a man lay in using them for his ends, leaving sentiment to poets and other idle dreamers.

Colombino, who could conduct negotiations with a strategy scarcely inferior to that which he displayed in the field, made no move until he perceived signs of the Lord Onorato's apprehensions that he would be left by the other small states of the Venetian Empire to stand alone. Then on a day of early August, when the Lord of Ravenna had ridden over to the great citadel to view the works of fortification by which Colombino claimed to have improved it, the Captain broached the matter.

'My task here is at an end, my lord. Indeed, in the matter of these works, it has been carried further than was in the bond. I have restored you to Ravenna, which was my undertaking, and I recognize that the time has come when you would wish to dismiss me.'

They were walking upon the ramparts, whence the view extended over miles of the flat lands towards Commachio in the north, now lying under a quivering haze drawn from the marshes by the heat. The Lord Onorato abruptly checked in his step, and so brought them to a standstill. Prepared though he had been for this, yet his dismay was plain.

'Wish to dismiss you? That is not a happy word.' He sighed. 'It is the last thing we could wish, Ser Colombino. If you go, you remove the shield that guards us. I have thought of this.'

'That problem was present from the outset, as you'll remember that I told you in Siena. But it is your problem, my lord.'

'Yes, yes. I have considered it. A solution has occurred to me. At present Venice has her hands full, and a moderate display of force should suffice to moderate her predatory temper. If you were to accept from me an annual retainer to serve me in my need and we were to publish this engagement, that should be enough just now to keep Venice quiet.' He paused, and added, in some hesitation, 'I had thought of some ten thousand ducats yearly, the rate of pay for actual service to be determined when the need for it arises, if it should.' Again he paused before asking, 'What should you say to that, Ser Colombino?'

'That as a retainer it is generous.' But his tone was discouragingly formal, and the lip he made was dubious. 'I will put it to my captains.' And he changed the subject instantly, to point out the advantages of a ravelin which he had thrown out beyond the ditch so as to protect the bastion on which they were standing.

If he put the matter to his captains as he promised, he forgot to report their answer, nor mentioned the subject further so that it was left for the Lord Onorato to bring it up again some days later, asking him if he had considered.

Again Colombino made that dubious lip, and again he dismissed the question casually with a promise to think about it, whence the old despot might infer that it was of little interest to him.

Onorato became anxious. He pressed Colombino for an answer on the morrow. Again Colombino demurred. He showed himself troubled.

'I am in a difficulty, my lord. The desire to serve you, the love I bear you, is in conflict with the love I bear myself. This retainer might prove an obstacle to greater enterprises. That, too, is the feeling of my captains. But I'll consider further.' As before, his tone left little hope that he would consider favourably.

And then from the great world outside came rumours that were of assistance to Colombino. Sauntering one morning with Onorato in the gardens of the Casa Polentana, he alluded to them. War clouds were gathering in the south. There should be work there for the Company of the Dove as soon as Colombino let it be known that his sword was in the market. It became necessary, therefore, more precisely to consider his departure.

Thus did he deliver at last his answer to the proposals Onorato had made him; an answer that ignored them and plunged the little despot into consternation. Limp from this the old man sank to a marble seat set in the bay of a yew hedge that was solid as a wall. He nodded gloomily.

'Your sword is in the market, eh? And, of course, I have not the means to bid for it. I am to conclude, then, that you will think no more of the retainer I proposed?' There was a shade of bitterness, as if of reproach, mingling with the regret in his voice.

Colombino, standing so straight and tall above that frail seated figure, fetched a sigh.

'Should you do so in my place, my lord?'

'Perhaps not. Perhaps not. I do not complain, sir. You have served me very well. But if you withdraw yourself thus completely, all that you have done may prove vain in the end, and Venice may soon be free to avenge herself upon me.' His hatred of Venice rang in his voice, was evinced in the hand he clenched upon his cane as he stabbed the ground with it.

Colombino spoke very gently. 'Because I am aware of it, I have postponed decision, reluctant to make the only decision possible to a man of ambitions. And I have ambitions, my lord, as you would have did you stand in my shoes today. The power to lead I have already shown, and of my power to govern I am no less confident. Do you see, my lord, whither my ambitions lead me? Francesco Sforza, who is Duke of Milan, was less than I am in his beginnings. I may not aspire quite so high. But neither am I modest.'

If this should not suffice, Colombino was prepared to be more blunt. Meanwhile, however, it might plant a thought in the mind of the Lord of Ravenna, and the soldier waited with a calm that was entirely simulated.

Onorato was peering up at him, a frown between his grizzled brows. It was a long moment before he spoke, and by then a flush had crept to his cheek-bones and a glitter to his old eyes, betokening the excitement astir in him. And then at last the question came which told Colombino how his suggestion had taken root.

'Would the lordship of Ravenna satisfy your ambition?'

'The lordship of Ravenna?'

The old man poured out his mind. 'When I am gone, if Venice waits so long, she will claim Ravenna on the grounds that I have no male successor. It was with that possibility in view that my son was murdered by her agency. Do you think that I can die in peace whilst there is a chance that Venice may profit by that infamy? There are no means I will not take to frustrate such a consummation. That is why I ask you, who are the man to hold this lordship and perhaps even to increase it, whether to be Lord of Ravenna would satisfy your ambition. Whether you would consider the prospect of succeeding me a sufficient retainer in the meantime.'

Colombino affected not yet to understand. 'But upon what grounds would my right to this succession be established?'

'By marriage with Samaritana. Thus you would secure her future with your own.'

In Colombino's heart there was sudden laughter. The fruit had fallen into his lap before he had troubled seriously to shake the tree. But his rugged countenance was grave to solemnity. He remained so long in thought that the Lord of Ravenna, who was a Lucifer for pride, aroused him testily.

'Well? Does even that need reflection with your potency?'

'Oh, my lord! You'll realize that I am a little overwhelmed.' He laughed shortly. 'I am conscious of no merit in myself to command this honour. If you have well considered, and provided that the Lady Samaritana shares your views, there can be but one answer. I make solemn oath that I shall study to deserve so great a prize.'

The Lord Onorato breathed relief. Leaning heavily on his stick he heaved himself up. 'That is well. We will count it settled, then. I shall inform Samaritana at once.'

This was to move at speed, indeed. Could it possibly be that he had already taken her feeling in the matter? Incredulously Colombino asked the question.

'I have had no thought to take it.' The old despot's tone implied that he admitted no right of hers to any feeling in conflict with his wishes. Then his dark old eyes played over that tall, virile figure, and a little smile tightened his thin lips as he thought in his heart that she would be difficult to please if her feelings were other than of satisfaction. He continued to look at Colombino and his glance deepened in kindliness. He reached up his left hand and set it on the young captain's shoulder. It was a gesture of affection. 'I tell you, child, this solution of my difficulties is one in which I take joy. I could not have found a happier one.'

And Colombino, deeply touched, a little shamed even as he thought of the guile employed to bring Onorato to take him for his son-in-law, bowed his head.

'Sir,' he answered solemnly, 'I vow that it shall be my endeavour to keep you of that opinion.'

The old man patted his shoulder. 'I know you will, and I trust that for you, too, there is happiness in this. Samaritana is a good girl: docile and yet no fool.'

It was an opinion he was to change within the hour. For a shock awaited the Lord Onorato at his daughter's hands.

He sought her at once in the bower she had made her own, a chamber hung in blue and grey, delicate as her own person in its furnishings of ebony with ivory inlay and painted coffers, and fragrant now with the late roses clustered in a silver bowl. He found her there with her woman-in-waiting, Monica, the sister of the castellan of Ravenna, and he did not even trouble to be private with her so as to communicate tidings of which the town would presently be free.

She heard him with a face of panic, from which all the blood receded whilst he talked, and in the background the listening Monica, a matronly woman in her fortieth year, had turned almost as pale.

'Why, what's this? What ails you?' cried Onorato at the end, by when her disorder was no longer to be overlooked.

She sat, stiff and straight, clutching the arms of her tall chair.

'It grieves me that…that I cannot do this, since it is your wish. But I cannot. I cannot even consider such a marriage.'

Onorato looked at her between anger and amusement.

'Not consider it? By the Blessed Mother! You're not asked to consider it. You're asked to perform it. That's all. And count yourself fortunate. Colombino is a man whom most women would be glad to take to husband. Ha!'

'It happens that I am not one of those women.' She gathered strength from the tyranny of his attitude. 'I look for something better in a husband than a swashbuckling adventurer, a man who takes the name of the city of his birth because he cannot name his father.'

'Prattle!' said the Lord of Ravenna, in relief. 'If that's your reason you're in a mistake let me tell you. Colombino doesn't want for a father or a name. For the rest, if you seek something better in a husband, you're likely to waste your life in seeking.'

'I should prefer that.'

'No doubt, being a fool. But I have my preferences, too, and I know what's to your advantage. One of these days you'll realize how fortunate that is. So we'll say no more about it.'

Ruffled, he was already turning away, when she checked him.

'I am, I suppose, one of God's creatures with a soul of my own, even if I am your daughter.'

'Oh, admitted. This marriage will help you to save that same soul.'

'It will not.' She rose, and for all her pallor she stood as straight and firm as a lance. 'No loveless marriage ever accomplished that.'

'Tcha! Loveless marriage! Loveless balderdash! Get you married, girl, and the love will follow. You need a man here; or you will when I am gone. A man, do you understand? So that your heritage may not fall into the hands of Venice. Without Colombino at your side you wouldn't hold Ravenna for a week, ninny. Now perhaps you understand. So no more of this.'

Again he turned to go, accounting the last word spoken. But again she detained him.

'Oh, but there is more.' She was fluttering a little, and as she spoke, Monica from the background made a movement as if to come to her. 'My faith is already pledged, and I will not be false to that. Nothing shall ever make me.'

He came back slowly from the door which he had almost reached, his eyes fixed upon her. Monica moved as if to bar his way. He waved her back. He spoke with ominous quiet. 'What are you telling me?'

With what calm she could command she answered him, confessing that there was one in Crete to whom she had secretly plighted her troth when they were on the point of breaking their exile there.

His eyes grew baleful as he listened. 'High time I had you safely in wedlock, my girl! What are you? Some scullion's daughter to bestow yourself; and secretly? Why secretly? Was there cause for shame? Who is this Cretan lover, in God's name?'

She gulped before she answered him. 'Ottavio Moro,' and added quickly. 'Now you will understand the secrecy.'

He showed her a face of horror. 'Moro! The Doge's nephew? The Republic's Procurator in Crete?' He caught her wrist in a grip of fury, pulled her to him, and thrust her off again. 'By all the fiends of Hell! Have I a daughter so monstrous, so lost to pride that she pledges herself to one who is of the blood of my worst enemy? Is it nothing to you that the Mori dispossessed your father, that they murdered your brother? Do you dare to stand before me with that white insolence and tell me that this Moro dog is your lover? Blood of God!' He stepped back from her, raving. He handled his cane as if he would strike her with it.

Monica was suddenly at his side clutching his arm. 'My lord! My lord!'

He flung her off, his anger lending strength to his shrunken frame. 'Will you cackle at me? Hold your infernal tongue!' He smashed his cane down in fury upon an ebony table. 'Oh, God! The shame of it! I have for daughter a wanton baggage who runs to the arms of the first fortune-hunter who beckons her, and this a man of a house that is smeared with the blood of mine! Don't you see, fool, the ends this rascal served? Your brother, the heir to Ravenna, murdered, the way is clear for him to the lordship of Ravenna by marrying you. Thus, in one way or another, Venice is to prevail here.'

'All that is false, false!' she interrupted, and would have added more but that he afforded her no opportunity.

'Listen to me, unnatural girl! I'll see you wed to a Moor of Africa rather than to a Moor of Venice.* So dismiss the thought for all time, and pray God to forgive you for it. As for me, if you would deserve my forgiveness in time, never let me hear of this again. Never! You have supplied an added reason why your nuptials with Colombino should be hastened.' He swung round, and stamped to the door. On the threshold he turned, still trembling in his passion. 'See to it that we never hear of this again,' he repeated, in menace, and went abruptly out.

With a little moan the slender, supple body sank down into the chair, and she found Monica's arms about her, and Monica's crooning voice in her ear.

'Comfort you, child. Comfort you. Messer Colombino will never constrain you against your will. He is noble and chivalrous. I would that it were he you loved.'

'That can never be,' said the defiant Samaritana. 'Nor will I ever marry him. Never. I may be as unnatural as my father says. What do I know of these feuds? Ottavio's hands are clean of our blood whatever his kinsmen may have done. I will wait for him, or I will die a maid. I care not.'

Presently came her kinsman Cosimo, sent by her father whose horror he shared upon learning of Samaritana's dreadful entanglement. She was fond of this courtly young priest, and because of her affection for him, and also because he was smooth and calm in his remonstrances, she listened to him patiently. But in the end he, too,

---

* Polenta's bitter pun will be clear to readers with a knowledge of Italian; 'Ti vedró sposa d'un moro d' Africa piútosto che d'un Moro di Venezia.'

grew heated by what he called her obstinacy in error. He found himself insisting in vain upon the feud between her house and the Mori who had so terribly wronged it, and the advantages to Ravenna of her union with Colombino, a great soldier who would know how to preserve her domain and hold at bay the might of Venice. Before the unnatural indifference to matters of sacred duty begotten in her by her ill-starred passion for Ottavio Moro, Cosimo departed in despair.

But the Lord Onorato had recovered his calm by the time Cosimo returned to him with his tale of failure. The old man had whittled down to grimness the fury that had earlier possessed him.

'It matters not a finger-snap what her inclinations may be. I was a fool to use so many words with her. She knows what is to do. It will be for Colombino to make her like it.'

ii

From his window on the following morning, Colombino beheld Madonna Samaritana walking alone in the garden. It occurred to him that the setting was a pleasant one for the little comedy he had to play, and upon that he went forth.

Neither Onorato nor Cosimo had given him a hint that the lady was not proving as docile as her father had pronounced her.

He came up with her in a little enclosed garden where a lily-pond was hedged about with yew. In green with trailing draperies, a white veil covering the dark hair above her pallid face, so straight and tall and slender, she looked, herself, something like a lily to him in the morning sunlight.

At the sound of his footstep she looked over her shoulder, and her eyes widened a little when she saw who came. He bowed low.

'I find you happily, my Samaritana,' said he. 'I come to vow that my life shall be spent in deserving the honour and the joy of which I cannot pretend that I am yet worthy.'

Smiling into her startled eyes, he took her hand, and he was bearing it to his lips when it was gently withdrawn. Adopting the advice that Monica had given her, she had been schooling herself in what to do when this moment came. There was a stone seat before the pond set in the shade of a yew. She moved towards it.

'Shall we sit, Ser Colombino? I have something to tell you.' And when, nowise discomposed by her gravity, he had taken beside her the seat to which he was bidden, she looked at him fully with eyes of timid candour. 'May I be frank with you, Ser Colombino?'

'It is what I should most desire. Now and always.'

'And you will be patient with me? Patient and gentle?'

'I hope that I could never be other.'

'You will not account it an offence against you if I say that I do not love you?'

'I should account it a miracle if you did. That is something that I must yet deserve and earn.'

She shook her head. The wistfulness that haunted her eyes was deepened. 'You are foredoomed in your endeavours, sir.'

The smile that lent a beauty to his rugged face was now displayed. 'It has been said of endeavours of mine before, and I have proved the prophecy a false one. Yet to no past endeavour have I brought the fervour I shall bring to this. Therefore, I am confident.'

'Ser Colombino, you must understand me. I can have no love to give you.'

Her cold firmness banished his smile. He became grave. Before the searching gaze of his dark eyes, she lowered her own.

'You are very young, Samaritana. You are aware only of what you are; not of what you may become. Speak to the present, if you will. But do not speak to the future, which I shall hope to have some hand in shaping. I bring you service and devotion: such service and devotion as cannot leave you indefinitely indifferent to me. Do not, then, distress yourself at what you perceive upon the threshold. Beyond it I shall see that happiness is spread for you. It is to tell you this that I have sought you now, to vow that I shall live with no other aim in view.'

For a space of silence her hands worked nervously in her lap. At last very softly and on a note of intercession she answered him.

'If my happiness were sincerely your aim, you would withdraw at once from a suit that is rendering me desperately unhappy.' And now her eyes were raised to his again, as she half-turned towards him. 'I implore it of your chivalry, Ser Colombino. I beg it of your generosity.' To the intercession in her eyes and voice was added the intercession of the long, slender hands she held out to him.

He was troubled, as his countenance showed. It is even possible that he was a little wounded in his vanity. He sighed as he looked at her.

'Give me a little time to win your favour. I am so confident of winning it, meaning you well as I do.' He rose. 'I will leave you now. You are still startled by the suddenness of the matter. It is not a moment in which to be importunate. Indeed, I hope that you may never find me that.'

'Wait!' She, too, had risen. 'You do not yet understand. It is that my love is already given; that I am pledged; and that neither honour nor affection would suffer me to break that pledge.'

'Pledged? But how is that possible when your father...' She broke in, and forth came the whole tale of that lover in Crete. He frowned as he listened.

'A Venetian, and of the House of Moro! Lord, child, had you raked the world through you could hardly have found a lover more likely to be denied you. No wonder that you have kept the matter secret.' He came close to her, and set a hand upon her shoulder. 'Child, most of this world's unhappiness springs from reluctance to accept the inevitable with resignation. Do not you be the victim of that. I counsel it in all affection. Put this impossible lover from your thoughts, before your spirit is broken between your yearnings and your father's bitter opposition. I do not plead for myself when I urge this; but for you.' He went on at some length in that strain, and came even to speak of her duty to Ravenna, and of her assured enjoyment of her heritage with himself at her side to guard it for her.

They were words of mere worldly wisdom and they fell upon the rocky soil of obstinate passion, where they could find no root-hold. Because he showed himself gentle and considerate, she preferred to set her hopes upon the chivalry of which these were evidences. But if she drew at the moment comfort from his consideration, soon this very consideration was to drive her to despair. For as his wooing began, so did it proceed: patient, unobtrusive, gentle, and understanding, but under all this with the insistent assumption that her mood was one that presently must change, that reason must prevail with her.

Maddened by this, and since he merely met gentleness of repulsion with stouter gentleness of insistence, she became more plain-spoken, lost patience, abused him, and roundly declared him odious. He treated her anger as the anger of a child, let her abuse pass him by, and so drove her to the verge of secret frenzy.

But it was not secret enough. If her father was permitted to see no signs of it and allowed to deceive himself with the belief that, however reluctant, at least she had bowed to his will, Monica, who knew all the truth, could not keep a still tongue. The news of Samaritana da Polenta's betrothal to Colombino da Siena, which from palace and citadel had flowed into the city and from the city in ever-widening circles over the countryside, was followed now by a rumour that the lady was being forced into unwilling wedlock and breaking her heart for a lover left in Crete.

Meanwhile, in an air of sullenness and mistrust the preparations for the marriage went steadily forward. August was out and they were within a fortnight of the date appointed for the nuptials, when one noontide Monica brought a sealed note to her young mistress.

'It was slipped into my hand as I was leaving San Vitale after Mass.'

Samaritana turned the oblong letter in her hands, inspecting the plain seal. 'By whom?'

'By a fat clown who bade me give it to you secretly, swearing that it was something for your service.'

Samaritana broke the seal, and read:

If you would be rescued from the damnation that awaits you
in a loveless marriage come to me between the twenty-first and
the twenty-second hour today or tomorrow, in the borgo, at
the third house on the right beyond San Francesco, and ask for
Monna Caterina.

Beyond that it bore no signature.

Samaritana stood considering. It was odd. It might even be
dangerous. But she was by nature as brave as by circumstances she
was desperate.

Opportunity could easily be made, because it was her frequent
custom to visit the sick in the borgo. And so upon a pretended
errand of mercy, cloaked and hooded and with Monica to attend her,
she set out late that afternoon, and on the very stroke of the twenty-
first hour was at that third house beyond San Francesco.

Whilst Monica remained below, Samaritana was led by the man
who opened to them to a gloomy tapestried chamber above-stairs,
where a woman, young, golden-headed, and pallidly lovely, rose to
receive her; a child she seemed, small and slight, all innocence and
candour, disarming apprehension and bringing at once relief to the
agitation in which Samaritana had reached her presence.

She received the daughter of the Lord of Ravenna with easy
assumptions of equality; took her by the hand, and led her to a
chair.

'Dear madonna, assure yourself that in me you have a friend; the
friend in need whom they say is the best of all. More. You have one
who is in your own sad plight, and who by helping you will help
herself.'

Samaritana loosed her cloak, and waited with quiet dignity to
hear more.

What she heard was a moving tale of this slight, lovely child's
hopeless passion for Colombino. She was, she announced, Eufemia
de' Santi, the dispossessed Countess of Rovieto, and once, not so
long ago, she and Colombino, who at the time had been her captain,
were affianced in marriage.

'But there was bitter misunderstanding,' she lamented, 'the work of treacherous men, who sowed mistrust between us. This not only wrecked my happiness, but was the cause of my subsequent ruin. For Colombino, lending an ear to lies and misconstruing what he saw, went off in dudgeon and left me to my fate at the hands of my enemies. You may have heard the tale.'

Samaritana shook her head, her eyes glowing now with interest, and the Countess resumed.

'No matter. The details are of no consequence. What signifies now is that I have come to Ravenna so that I may serve you, and so that in return you may serve me.'

'I see. I see.' Samaritana was eager. 'I am to make your peace with him; bring you together once more.'

'Just that. I offer you the means to deliver you from a bridegroom whom all the world knows to be distasteful to you, so that in return you may restore to me the lover I have lost. I am quite frank with you.' There was a plaintive helplessness in her smile. 'I should not know how to be other. But for my lack of guile I should not be where I now am.'

To Samaritana it did not seem that this lack of guile required to be protested. It was so manifest in the candid eyes raised from that fair little face to the proud, cold countenance of the Lady of Ravenna. And the Lady of Ravenna abated now something of her normal pride in her eagerness to learn precisely how she was to employ the knowledge gained.

The little white-and-gold Countess took from her scrip a tiny phial filled with a liquid as colourless as water.

'Here,' she said, 'is a magical water of very singular power. It will turn the affections of him who drinks in any direction in which they are desired, and away from any who does not desire them.'

Samaritana's dark eyes grew wide in awe as she gazed at the phial and from the phial to the Countess. And it was awe scarcely tinged by incredulity. For, after all, there was nothing here to strain belief. The existence of magical philtres endowed with the oddest powers was a fact notorious in Italy, and from her cradle she had heard common talk of such things, although never until now had she gazed on one.

Yet mechanically she asked: 'How can that be?'

'Ah! That, madonna, I cannot answer. That is among the many secrets of life that we do not understand. All that I know, and this I know positively, is that it will do as I have said. How it does it...' she smiled a little, and shrugged. 'If I knew that I should be more than humanly wise.'

She rose, and crossed to Samaritana, proffering the phial. 'Take it, and so help us both to our desires. If you could pour it, or the half of it – even less would be sufficient – into his wine, I make oath by my soul's salvation that there will be an end to his importunities. He will never speak to you of love again.'

She pressed the phial into Samaritana's still half-reluctant hand.

'It... it will do him no injury?'

Pale innocence opened wide the eyes of the Countess; her red lips parted in a vague smile.

'Unless I were sure, very sure, that it will not, should I ask you to give this philtre to the man I love? Should I wish to injure him since I am pining for love of him?'

Samaritana nodded. 'That is true. Yes.'

'It will turn him from you. It will bring him to me. You should not consider this an injury, being cold to him.'

Samaritana sat thoughtful, frowning at the little vessel in her palm. Of her thought, however, wedded to her hope, faith was now born.

'I shall be very deeply in your debt,' she said, 'if this will accomplish all you promise for it.'

The low lids of Madonna Eufemia veiled her eyes. 'I am confident. But even if you are not, it is surely worth the attempt. Nothing will have been lost by it. Much may have been gained.'

'Yes. That, too, is true.' said the bemused Samaritana.

'But there is a condition necessary to ensure success.'

'Ah!'

'After he has drunk, you must call me to his mind, so that I may fondly abide there. You must say to him: "In that draught you are pledged by Eufemia of Rovieto." You may even say, if you choose, that the draught contains a potion I have sent him with my love. That will suffice. If his thoughts turn to me as the philtre begins to act, we may be doubly certain of the result we both desire.'

This had a specious, reasonable sound. It seemed to Samaritana to supply just what had been lacking to complete her belief in the potion. She nodded again.

'That I can well understand.'

'But,' the Countess warned, 'on no account be premature or you ruin all. Say no word until he shall have drunk. You understand that, too?'

'Oh, yes.' Samaritana rose. 'How to thank you…' she was beginning, bringing at last some warmth into her voice.

Monna Eufemia interrupted her. 'You owe me nothing. Each here is equally in the other's debt; for each of us but serves the other's ends. You'll not forget my words for him: "That draught is a pledge of Eufemia da Rovieto's love." You'll see how his eyes will light when they are spoken.'

iii

It had become Ser Colombino's custom since his betrothal to pay a visit each morning to Monna Samaritana in her bower, with Monica ever in discreet attendance.

There for the better part of an hour, under cover of a cool outward amiability, a battle of wills would be fought, an amatory onset by the condottiero determined to prevail resisted by the lady with all the determination of a garrison prepared to starve before surrendering.

But on the morning after that secret visit of Samaritana's to the borgo, Colombino at once perceived signs that the citadel weary of resistances might at last be considering a capitulation.

On an ebony table that was inlaid with ivory figures stood a dish of peaches, a jar of honey; a golden jug of wine, and some delicate glasses from the Murano workshops. There was nothing unusual here. Samaritana was fond of peaches sliced into a mixture of wine and honey, and would commonly engage herself upon some such collation, as if pointedly to beguile the tedium caused her by Colombino's presence. What was unusual this morning was that she should so far depart from her normal chill aloofness as to offer wine to her suitor. Almost it startled him. But this was merely the first of the surprises awaiting him. There was a marked change in her bearing. If this could not yet be described as warm, at least it was less cold by many degrees than hitherto. Actually, for once, it was she who led the conversation, where, normally, she followed with lagging and reluctant step.

'We saw you riding in the city yesterday, Ser Colombino. How the townsfolk worship you! I did not see one who did not smile as he greeted you. It is not the least of your victory here that you should have known how to endear yourself to the people.'

He displayed none of his astonishment. He fell willingly into her mood. He smiled and sighed in one.

'Just as without effort we may possess that which we do not prize, so sometimes not all the effort of which we are capable will suffice to command that which we desire.'

She stood straight and tall by the table to which she had crossed in offering him the wine. Her glance brightened as she looked at him. She even laughed, as she gently rallied him.

'That would seem to approach an admission I have never heard from you before.'

He gave her a keen glance, and discovered signs of excitement. The flush on her cheek, usually so pale, and the glitter in her dark eyes almost suggested fever.

'It is my prayer that time and fortune may remove the occasion for that admission.'

'Are your prayers heard, Ser Colombino?'

'When what I ask is good for my soul I must suppose they are.'

She laughed for answer, as we laugh at an evasion, and as if growing uncomfortable under his steady eyes, she turned, took up the jug, and with her back to him, screening the action, she poured the wine. As she turned again, he was beside her in a stride, to take the fine glass she would have brought to him, in which the wine glowed clear and golden as a topaz. Its colour drew a comment from him.

'If I know wine at all, this comes from grapes that were sunned on the Orvietan hills.'

'You prove your knowledge, indeed, and your quick judgment. This is from Orvieto.'

He smiled. 'Had I not been a soldier I must have been a husbandman. As it is, I am a little of both, and of the two, I think that my vineyards at Montasco are closer to my heart even than the Company of the Dove. Of late I have brought there some vines from Orvieto, for to my taste there are none in Italy that yield a better wine. And yet it is my ambitious hope that with care I may still improve their yield in Tuscan soil.'

He took the glass from her as he spoke. In surrendering it her hand trembled so that a little of the wine was spilled across their fingers. To repair the damage, he set the glass down again upon the table, and reached for a napkin. He wiped his fingers and then her own. He delayed caressingly over the task, and for once, for the first time since the commencement of his wooing, she did not shrink under his touch. She stood, indeed, in a sort of helpless fascination, suffering him to have his will. Perhaps it was this unusual attitude that brought him to consider her again. Straight, tall, slim, and supple she stood in her sheath of ruby silk, with a linen gorget that sharply defined the long oval of her face. The contemplation of her kindled a sudden warmth in his heart, a pleasant consciousness that here was a prize worth winning for its own sake, apart from the endowment of a lordship which she brought him. So chaste and proud and noble did she seem to him in that moment that she put to shame the callous, coldly calculating nature of his suit. He stooped over the slim fingers that he held, and very reverently pressed his lips upon them. This, too, she tolerated; and not until his own fingers relaxed their grip did she withdraw her hand. Subconsciously he observed that it was her left, and that her right hung clenched and idle at her side.

She moved away from him, returning to her tall-backed chair in the embrasure of the Gothic window, whilst he remained standing by the table observing her slow grace with appraising eyes. Then with a little sigh he slowly turned to take up the wine she had poured for him.

The glass stood in a shaft of sunlight, otherwise he might have been less quick to notice, even as he was about to put forth his hand, that the colour of the wine had subtly changed during the moments since it had been poured. The clear golden topaz upon which he had commented was clouded now with a faint opalescence. It was so slight that it might well have gone unnoticed by any man less studious of wine and any eyes less intimate with its varying hues.

If his consciousness was startled, he gave no sign of it. With a sudden terrible suspicion in his mind, a tightening at his heart, he completed after that moment's imperceptible pause the movement of taking up the glass. He did not, however, yet raise it to his lips. He merely moved it to the table's extreme edge, where he could easily reach it from the chair which presently he resumed. Without appearing to look, he saw that two pairs of eyes – Samaritana's and Monica's – were watching him, and, it seemed to him, with a furtive intentness. Monica, indeed, for the first time since his entrance had raised her glance from the frame of needlework which until this moment had absorbed her attention.

He lounged in his chair, one leg clad in white thrown over the other that was clad in red, apparently as easy in mind as in body, whilst his wits were burrowing keenly.

Her unwonted graciousness this morning was now explained. It had been assumed so as to throw him off his guard. She was, then, as guileful as any other member of her faithless sex, and he a fool to have harboured a momentary illusion that she might restore to him his lost ideals.

That clenched right hand which he had observed to hang idle at her side, until it furtively sought the scrip that hung from her girdle of hammered gold, was now remembered and explained. It had held a phial, whose contents had gone to trouble the wine. What was it that she had poured for him? What should it be but poison? Despairing of being delivered of his urbanely insistent wooing by any other means, she had resolved upon his death. He was curiously conscious of a sudden spasm of pity for her and of shame for an insistence that had driven her to such lengths.

But, after all, he recognized that he was proceeding upon no more than assumptions. They might be justified. Probably they were. But he must have positive knowledge before he could determine upon any action.

For some moments he talked idly of trivial matters, toying with the tassels of the lacing at his breast, the very picture of a care-free man, whilst he considered, and, at last, devised the test that might reveal the truth.

He sat up abruptly, and broke gravely upon the light talk he had provoked in her. 'Samaritana, there is something of great, and to you – alas! – perhaps of welcome importance that I have to say.'

Thus he riveted sharply her attention.

'If in my suit to you I have been persistent to the point of arousing your resentment, it has been because of the strong hope within me that in the end I should win you to a willing agreement. Of late, to my deep sorrow, I have come to persuade myself that this hope is vain. I see how steadfast is the love you have pledged elsewhere. I account it as hopeless as is my own love for you. But that is not my concern. What concerns me is that I should be unworthy of the knighthood to which I aspire if I were to maintain my insistence in the face of that.'

He paused, and his eyes over which he had cast a veil of wistfulness observed her pallor and the tumult at her breast, whilst Monica, scarcely less startled, sat now with needle entirely idle.

'I have sought to order my life by ideals of chivalry that are perhaps out of fashion. And chivalry forbids either that I should continue to importune or that I should suffer you to be importuned by others on my behalf. I owe it to you not only to withdraw, but to do it in such a manner that no blame can attach to you. I do it at great cost, because, Samaritana, you have come to stand so in my life that my dreams have woven all my future about you. Perhaps it is just because of this that I can no longer take from you what is not freely given, nor suffer that you should be distressed.'

He uncrossed his legs, and stood up.

'You may trust me to make all easy for you. That will be an amend for any heartache I may have brought you.'

She stared at him with troubled dilating eyes.

'I…I scarcely understand. My father…'

'Your father will not distress you. My course is very plain. At the risk of giving deep offence, I shall tell the Lord Onorato that I have changed my mind; that upon reflection I have come to see that it is too early yet in my career to assume the burden of a wife. I shall seek to turn aside his resentment. If I should fail in that…' He shrugged resignedly. 'Why, then, I must submit to his anger. That is all.'

Dread was now stamped upon her bloodless face.

'I trust, Samaritana, to earn your approval, and so, at last, a kindly thought from you.' He took up the glass, and with his eyes upon her he very slowly raised it. 'I pledge your happiness with the lover of your choice.'

He stood a moment as if awaiting some acknowledgment from her. But she made no sound. She continued to stare at him with those awed eyes, a faint writhing movement of her slim body and the clutch of her bands upon the arms of her chair being further evidences of her tension.

Very deliberately he bore the glass to his lips. As it reached them, his nostrils keenly sniffing detected a faint bitter-sweet odour reminiscent of crushed peach-kernels. Here was confirmation of his every suspicion. Under the staring eyes of the women he lowered the glass again an inch or two. Over the rim of it almost, he addressed Samaritana, a queer smile twisting his lips as he spoke.

'Must I still drink?'

She continued dumbly to regard him, as if the question froze her. He laughed, and set down the glass once more. His manner now was one entirely of bitter amusement.

'It occurred to me that by removing the necessity for my assassination I might at the same time destroy the will to persist in it. It seems that I was wrong. It seems, too, that you are more foolish than I supposed; for my death would inconvenience you infinitely more than my peaceful departure.'

'Your death?' She came to her feet as she spoke. Stridently she repeated the question. 'Your death?'

'Was not that what you desired?'

'0 God! How can you suppose it?'

'It seems a reasonable supposition when you put poison in my wine.'

'Poison! That is false. I swear it. There is no poison in that wine.'

'You swear it? By what do you swear it?'

'By my soul's salvation.'

'A potent oath. But women have been known to be forsworn. A draught would persuade me better than an oath. There stands the wine.' He waved her to it with the lightness he had assumed. 'Will you drink, madonna?'

'If that will convince you,' she fiercely agreed, and swept to the table, there suddenly to pause in horror as she remembered the powers attributed to the philtre. Monica, too, had risen, and came now waddling forward in alarm. But Colombino never heeded her. He towered dominant before Samaritana, but his tone was still mild and tinged with mockery.

'You hesitate? But why? What is there to affright you in this innocent draught of Orvietan?' Then his tone hardened. 'I had hoped to find you merciful at least. Such a foolish gull was I that when I realized what you were attempting against me, I took the blame upon myself. I had pressed you too hard with my wooing. To you the prospect of marriage with me had become as a sanctioned rape, and in your despair you availed yourself of the only weapon in your reach. Thus in my feeble-mindedness I reasoned. To test it I announced my renunciation of you and my departure. But so deep has your hatred grown, so bitter your vindictiveness, that not even this can appease you, can bring you to stay your murderous hand.'

She looked at him with eyes of pain and anger. Her breath was coming in short gasps, her breasts convulsively rising and falling within their ruby sheath.

'A test? It was a test? I understand. You are very cunning, sir. All the world says so. Yet cunning will often lead a man too far astray. There is no poison in that wine. I swear it yet again.'

'So I hear. But you will not drink it.'

'No. Because… Because…'

And forth now came the astounding truth in words that tumbled over one another: that she had poured into the wine no more than a philtre, whose purpose and properties she avowed, whilst saying, however, no word of whence she had procured it.

'That,' she ended defiantly, 'is why I will not drink.'

He listened with raised brows and a faintly mocking air of belief that of intent betrayed its own pretence.

'But you have supplied an added reason why you should. By what you tell me the draught should bring you to love me, and loving me you would find it easier to marry me.'

Her brow was dark with sullen anger. 'I see that you do not believe.'

'But you can so easily convince me. Come, Samaritana. This draught will transmute your hatred into love, your distaste into desire. Therefore it encloses your life's happiness. Can you hesitate?'

'You mocking devil! If I did not hate you before, I hate you now. I have told you all the truth, only to provoke your derision, only to be held a liar. If you were not a base upstart, if you could understand the minds of such as I, you would know that whilst I might kill you to be quit of your odious pursuit, yet I should never lie to you.'

'I have heard such words before. They are the jewelled robes in which Falsehood hides her festering sores. But they shall be stripped away, and your falsehood laid naked. Wait.' He took up the wine and carried it with him to the door. There he raised his voice to call, and presently came steps in answer to that summons. He was heard issuing muttered orders. Then, as the steps retreated once more, he came leisurely back, holding ever that glass of wine, and crossed to his chair.

'If you will sit, madonna, I shall not keep you long.'

'What are you going to do?'

'I shall not test your patience,' was all he answered her, and perforce content with that she sank wearily to her own chair, whilst Monica went to stand protectingly over her, glaring ever and anon at him.

Thus in silence they waited until presently two of Colombino's own grooms came in, leading an old pale-coloured hound. He rose, ordering one of them to hold the dog firmly and the other to force apart its jaws. Down the struggling beast's throat Colombino poured the half of the wine from the glass. The glass itself with the remainder he flung through the open window, then stood watching the uneasy hound.

Results followed swiftly, and very soon the poor writhing animal lay still, at fullest stretch, with glazed eyes and a froth about its parted jaws. Samaritana, who had risen, looked on in stark horror, Monica's arms about her.

Colombino waved an imperious hand to the grooms. 'Take it away, and bury it. Say no word to anyone of how it died.'

When they had departed, Colombino stood squarely before the stricken Lady of Ravenna.

'Is it enough? You have seen the working of your love-philtre. You have seen in what case I should have been if I had drunk the wine you poured for me. And you pledged your soul's salvation that it was not poisoned. Have you exhausted falsehood? Or can you think of more to explain even this?'

Humbled, bruised by the lash of his scorn, horror-stricken at the proof he had supplied, she answered only with a sob, and there the matter might have ended for her had not Monica been moved to a passionate outburst.

'She has told you no lies, sir, the gentle dove. You are a scoundrel so to taunt her. What she told you, she believed. She was tricked by that evil woman in the borgo, who gave her the philtre. You ~will know, sir, what you have done to the Countess of Rovieto that she should seek your life. But if you behaved to her as you have behaved to my lady here, by my faith, she had good reason to play the lying witch.'

'What's that? The Countess of Rovieto?' Colombino was suddenly a changed man, alert and stern. 'Was it she supplied this poison? And for me?'

'But not as a poison. Not as a poison. As a love-potion.' And now the whole tale was poured forth by Monica, and at last taken up and amplified by Samaritana.

And at the end of it she held out her hands to him in supplication.

'You have all the truth now. Indeed, I have not consciously lied to you by a single word.'

From her scrip she plucked a scrap of paper, and pressed it upon him. It was the note she had yesterday received from the Countess.

'Yes,' he said. 'It is the hand of that Jezebel. But it no longer needed even this.'

'I believed her,' Samaritana was protesting passionately. 'I take the Holy Mother in Heaven to witness that I believed her. Messer Colombino, I will make amends. I will prove my faith.'

'Prove it?' His brows were knit.

Vehement, distraught at the reflection of how near she had been to doing murder, she answered him. 'All my life hereafter shall give proof. I will be your willing and consenting wife. You shall hear no more of resistance to your will. Thus...thus will I make amends to you.'

So beaten down was her proud spirit by sheer horror of the thing that unwittingly she had all but done that she fell on her knees before him to implore forgiveness.

He stooped, set his strong hands at her elbows and drew up. Still holding her he spoke. 'It needs no such proof. I have done you wrong enough, and most wrong perhaps in my thoughts this morning.' His tone became very gentle. 'When I marry I shall hope to be a husband, not a penance; a lover, not a hairshirt to a woman's tender flesh. So quiet you. There is no further question of our marriage. That is a dream dispelled. I take my leave, though in any need, remember, I shall be ready to come to your call.'

His hands slid from her elbows to her wrists. Then he raised them, kissed her fingers, and was gone, leaving her in a frozen bewilderment.

Chapter 4

THE LADY OF OTTAVIO MORO

i

Colombino did not see her again before departing from Ravenna. He bore with him the sorrowfully ironical perception that he had renounced her in the very moment in which his love for her was born, and that it was this love which had dictated the renunciation. He had in fact done the very thing that earlier, and as a means of testing the extent of her intentions, he had pretended to do. It was her offer of surrender as an amend that, persuading him of her shining honesty, had aroused in him something akin to worship and had made an end of that cynical spirit in which for worldly ends he had aimed at marrying her. Thus, he reflected, too, if that evil woman Eufemia de' Santi's crafty plot to murder him had failed, at least it had dealt him a wound that would not soon be healed.

Another in his place might have sought that house in the borgo with intent to square the account. Colombino's mind was not even crossed by the vindictive thought. Perhaps there was too much else to occupy it. His interview with Onorato da Polenta alone was enough to distract a man's wits for days.

He had found Cosimo with the Lord of Ravenna; but he was not concerned to express in secret a matter that presently would be common knowledge.

'My lord,' he had said, his manner very formal, 'there is likely to be war in the Kingdom of Naples over the succession. My company grows restless in this idleness at such a time, and my captains are naturally anxious to be at work. May it not displease you that we shall be marching south at once.'

The Lord Onorato could not believe his ears. They were in his closet, the small room in which he transacted his affairs, and he had been discussing with his nephew the matter of some repairs to San Vitale, of which Cosimo was a canon. It was into this atmosphere of peace that Colombino had cast his bombshell.

'You are marching south? What the devil do you mean, you are marching south? Your wedding is within a fortnight.'

Colombino's countenance was grave to sadness. Slowly he shook his tawny head. 'Alas! My lord, there will be no wedding.'

'No wedding?' Onorato came suddenly to his feet, pushing back his chair, and Cosimo, echoing the question in consternation, rose with him.

'I will enter into an agreement with you to be at your call upon a retainer, which you may fix at what you will. But...'

'The devil take you and your retainers!' The little man was livid. 'Of what do you tell me? We have gone a long way since there was a question of retainers. Has that unnatural girl of mine refused again? Does she set us at defiance? If so, I vow to Heaven...'

'My lord,' cried Colombino, to check this rising fury and turn it into other channels, 'only just now Madonna Samaritana was protesting her willingness to become my wife.'

'But then...I don't understand.'

'It is just that reflection persuades me I should be doing my interests an ill service to bind myself in wedlock at this stage. The trade of arms to be properly pursued demands that a man shall remain free of family cares. That is all, my lord.'

'All!' cried Cosimo.

115

But Onorato was snarling and incoherent for a moment. 'So! So! Body of God! The Polentani are no longer worthy of your ambitious lordship's alliance, eh? You aim higher, do you? And you wait until a fortnight from the nuptials to discover it, then come here to tell me with this cursedly prim indifference; to tell me that you propose to put this shame upon my daughter and make my house a laughing-stock! It is to be said in Italy that an upstart captain of fortune disdained the hand of Onorato da Polenta's child! Are you dead to decency that you dare to stand before me and tell me that? Or have I misunderstood you?'

And when he ceased, Cosimo took up the tale. 'You are, indeed, your father's son, and you'll end on a gallows like that traitor Terrarossa.' He swung to his uncle. 'I warned you, sir, that you were dishonouring our house by this alliance, that you were defiling your daughter by sending her to the arms of this brigand.'

Colombino stood very straight and stiff. His face was grey, and the austere squareness of its lines had become so marked that it almost looked as if hewn of granite.

'Sir,' he cried out, 'you are a priest, and so I may not call you to account and chastise you for your words. Remember it for your honour's sake.'

'Honour!' raged Cosimo, his dark face aflame. 'Do you use that word? If I am a priest I am also a man...'

'And so am I,' Colombino cut in, 'and being a man I am subject to human weaknesses including that of anger. I'll go before it masters me.'

He strode to the door. But on the threshold paused. He looked back at Onorato da Polenta, who had sunk into a chair, and sat crumpled there, his head bowed, his hands between his knees. As Colombino looked, the anger faded from his face, and only sorrow remained. He had almost come to love this frail little Lord of Ravenna whom he had restored to his dominions. And there was something of heartbreak for him in this parting.

'My lord, it grieves me more than I could tell you that we should part thus. Tell the world that it was you dismissed me, on what grounds you will. I'll never contradict you. Thus there will be no slight upon your house, for as God's my witness, it is the last thing I should wish to see. And if you need me ever...'

But there the fierce pride of Onorato exploded. 'Need you, you rascal? I? Go to the Devil.'

'You have a safe-conduct to him, I think,' sneered the bitter Cosimo.

Colombino sighed, turned and went out, and down the stairs of the Casa Polentana in which he had dreamed of sitting one day as master. In the street a groom waited with his horse. For it was his daily custom before dining to ride over to the citadel so as to deal with his company's concerns.

He mounted the big white charger and rode off, affectionately greeted as he rode by every citizen he met, each beholding in him the future Lord of Ravenna.

In the quarters he had made his own in the citadel, he sent for Sangiorgio and Caliente to receive his orders. They were very brief.

'Our work in Ravenna is done. I am starting for Siena at once, to let it be known that our swords are in the market. I leave you to pack and bring the Company after me with all speed. You should be able to set out by the day after tomorrow. That is all.'

The sternness of his face at once suggested a mystery of pain and forbade inquiry into it at the moment.

Sangiorgio was tactfully practical. 'What lances shall I order to escort you?'

'None. I am in haste, and I'll travel light. A couple of grooms will suffice to bring my gear.'

His departure, however, was delayed by matters of detail concerning the Company upon which his captains found it necessary to take his orders, and the afternoon was well advanced before at last, equipped for travel, he set out.

Caliente and Sangiorgio went with him as far as the gateway, and stood for a moment watching him as he rode briskly away. Then the corpulent Spaniard turned bewildered eyes upon his gaunt companion.

'Will you tell me what it means, Giorgio?'

Sangiorgio shrugged. 'It's plain, I think. He's grown weary in time of the simpering disdain of that cold piece he was fool enough to think of marrying. Give thanks.'

'I do. It was in my mind to take my leave of him after the wedding. I have none of the arts of peace, and I should hate to grow fatter than I am.'

They turned and sauntered across the wide courtyard, where the dust was being raised by the hurried marshalling of troops.

'But for the way he looks at women,' said Don Pablo, 'Colombino would be a flawless captain. That's where he's vulnerable. That's the heel of our Achilles, and mark me, one of these days a woman will be the ruin of him.'

Now whilst that might, of course, be possibly true of some woman and of some time, it was very wide of the truth so far as Samaritana da Polenta and the present were concerned.

The Lady of Ravenna was at that very moment confronting the wrath of her father and her cousin on Colombino's behalf.

Onorato da Polenta had come storming into her bower with the news of the unpardonable affront that Colombino had put upon their house.

'You can say that you dismissed him, or that I refused to marry him. He is too generous to deny it.'

This was to nourish his frenzy. He glared at her, and grew suddenly suspicious. 'You're oddly reconciled. What part had you in this?'

'You have seen my part. I was never willing. You employed constraint. And this is the end.'

'The end? You think so. Ha!'

Then Cosimo questioned her more directly. 'Samaritana, do you suppose that your unwillingness is responsible?'

'What else should I suppose?'

'Yet, when we asked him just this, he told us that as lately as today you had announced yourself ready to become his willing wife. Was he lying to shield you?'

'No. That is also true. I did so surrender. But it was too late. In the sight of my reluctance he had taken the chivalrous resolve to leave me free.'

'Chivalrous!' roared Onorato. 'Chivalrous to put this shame upon my house; and he an upstart smirched with the dishonour of a father who was hanged!' He sank into a chair, and took his head in his hands. 'To have come back after twenty years of exile, to have striven and suffered merely to be crowned by this affront!' Then he was on his feet again, striding to and fro like an angry old wolf. 'I am too old to demand a personal satisfaction. I have no son to cleanse our honour of this stain, and you, Cosimo, might as well have been a woman since you chose to take holy orders.' He stopped in front of him and bombarded him with some of his wrath. 'But for that folly of yours, there would never have been any question of bringing in this adventurer to succeed me. Anyway, there it is. You are no more competent than I to send a challenge to him. There's only one thing left.'

'What's that?' Samaritana asked him sharply.

His eyes were malevolent. 'Does nothing occur to you? Do you suppose I can suffer this man to live?'

'He is the man to whom you owe everything that you today possess. He is the man who brought you back to Ravenna.'

'He was paid for it, hired to it in the way of his trade.'

'And,' added Cosimo, 'by withdrawing now and leaving us defenceless, he cheats us in the end.'

'That is not true. You know it is not true, Cosimo. A priest should disdain falsehood and malice. Messer Colombo was paid to bring us to Ravenna, but not to keep us here.'

'What do you know of that?' her father challenged her. 'I was present, in his house at Montasco when he warned you that to restore you to Ravenna would be easy. But that to keep you here would be your own affair.'

'You defend this traitor? God forgive you! Are you so shameless that you do not burn at the affront?'

'I have told you that I do not account it that. But the very contrary.'

He advanced upon her as if he would have struck her, his hand raised. Then he let it fall heavily to his side again, and turned.

'Come, Cosimo,' he said. 'Come away before I do a mischief to this ninny I begot in an evil hour. We waste our time. Come.'

From his own point of view, could he have known it, he had done worse than waste his time. He had betrayed his intentions against Colombino to one who in that hour was moved to deepest kindness for the Captain. She must be watchful. Colombino must be warned to take measures for his safety. That was her first concern, and in this she enlisted the assistance of her woman.

Monica employed herself industriously. Two hours later she brought word to her mistress that a man of the Lord Onorato's confidence, named Masaccio, had just ridden out with six knaves, his business being to track down Messer Colombino, who was known to have left Ravenna an hour ago attended by only two grooms.

Samaritana was in panic. If Colombino had been indeed her lover, she could scarcely have been more distraught. She raved against the folly of his riding off without an escort, raved against her own impotence, her weakness, her lack of men to do her will.

'But there are Messer Colombino's men in the citadel. A word to them, and…'

'And they'll hang my father. Can't you see, Monica? If I warn them of the danger, they'll require to know whence it proceeds. They'll hold my father, and if harm comes to Messer Colombino there can be no doubt of what they will do. Let me think. Oh, God help me!'

She paced the chamber, her hands to her brow, fighting down distraction so that hers might be at least the power of thought. The best she could do, when at last she was able to reflect clearly, was little enough, but she addressed herself to it with courage. She laid with Monica plans that terrified the waiting-woman, then sent her to prepare them. Three lines she wrote to Don Pablo Caliente: 'Danger threatens Messer Colombo da Siena. You are warned to send an escort after him at once. A half-score men will suffice. But let them set out instantly and ride at the gallop. The urgency is great. Waste not a moment.'

A messenger was found to bear that unsigned letter, with orders to deliver it and depart, so as to avoid being questioned as to whence it came.

Then in the riding-dress of one of the Lord Onorato's pages, booted to the thighs and in a cloak grotesquely heavy and ample considering the heat, her face in the shadow of a round hat, Samaritana slipped from the Casa Polentana by the garden gate. The fluttered and anxious Monica was to cover her retreat by announcing that she was not well, that she had sought her bed and was not to be disturbed. All things considered, there was nothing in the tale to strain belief.

At the end of the lane a groom was waiting with a horse, which at a word he surrendered without suspecting this cloaked stripling to be the Lady of Ravenna.

Samaritana went quietly out of the city, and then at a breakneck pace along the road that runs south by the sea with the aim of outriding Masaccio and overtaking Colombino in time to put him on his guard.

ii

Colombino rode with intent to reach Rimini that night, and lie there. But the distance, not far short of fifty miles, is one that would have taxed the endurance of his horse, even had he travelled with discretion, instead of riding, as he did, at a pace in keeping with the tumultuous gallop of his thoughts.

It befell that in the darkness of a starry night he found himself just beyond the ancient Rubicon on a foundered horse, whilst the grooms who had followed, disgruntled but uncomplaining, were in no better case.

They had brought up in the neighbourhood of Bellaria, and within half a bowshot of a lonely tavern, the Neptune Inn, a ramshackle building, standing back a little from the highway, almost on the very edge of the sea.

'That at least is fortunate,' said Colombino, as he led his lame horse towards the rhomb of yellow light that fell from the open door.

Precisely how fortunate it was he did not yet suspect. Before morning he was to realize that if chance had made him call a halt any earlier or any later, the long odds were that this night would have seen the end of him.

At close quarters the dilapidated house, with a bush of withered, dusty rosemary hanging as a sign above the door, looked not merely uninviting, but forbidding. Such as it was, however, it offered a roof.

From the threshold he surveyed the unpaved common-room through a haze of smoke, his throat and nostrils assailed by acrid odours, in which rancid oil and garlic were predominant.

A long, heavy oaken table occupied one side, and a couple of trestle tables against which benches were ranged lined the opposite wall. The place was indifferently lighted by a brass oil lamp overhead. From each of the three beaks of this a long narrow tongue of flame, ending in a pennon of black smoke, waved in the draught from the open door.

By the hearth a man squatted on his heels, turning some spitted pieces of flesh over a fire of logs. He looked over his shoulder at the newcomers, then he rose, holding the flesh-laden spit as if it were a rapier. Out of an evil, unclean countenance red-rimmed eyes pondered the guest with more challenge than invitation.

Conquering his nausea, the young Captain advanced, leaving the door open. He thrust back the wide black hat he wore, and left it to hang from his shoulders by the cords from which it was slung. His thick, tawny hair, bushed out behind, was confined in a golden net upon which there were tiny jewels.

The taverner surveyed his height and breadth of shoulder, his princely air and rich apparel, and made a tardy effort at civility. But, matching his own forbidding house, he was a man in whom civility came neither naturally nor easily.

Colombino peremptorily made known his wants: food and wine and a lodging for the night for himself and his grooms. At once cringing and surly the taverner answered that food and wine he could supply, if my lord were not too exacting; but that accommodation for the night he could not offer. Of this objection the soldier made short work. He could go no farther, and the common-room must serve his needs. His tone precluded argument.

Because of the foulness of the place, and the night being hot, he insisted that the door should remain wide as he had found it. Upon this depends all that follows.

Masaccio and his six cut-throats upon Colombino's spoor, riding in haste, and with fresh horses obtained at Cesenatico an hour ago, were drawn by the glow of that open door and the promise it held for dusty throats. With no suspicion that their quarry was so near, with no thought other than to drink a cup of wine, those rascals pulled up at the Neptune Inn.

Colombino, seated at the oaken table, with his grooms at the end of it, below the salt-cellars, looked up at the sound of halting hoofs.

There was a mutter of talk out there in the gloom, and then a raucous voice broke into a bawdy song. The singer advanced into the light, a burly, bearded ruffian, clad mainly in leather with here and there a hint of steel. At his heels came six others similarly accoutred.

On the threshold the jovial leader stood arrested, goggle-eyed, the snatch of song perishing on his lips. Behind him pressed his companions, as goggle-eyed as himself to behold Messer Colombino seated there as if awaiting them. Then Masaccio expressed his incredulous amazement in an unclean oath and his satisfaction in a laugh.

'Here's luck beyond belief! And we might have ridden by. Devil's body! I sweat at the thought.' He flung forward, leering. 'Well met, your potency. I bring you a message.'

The insolence of the knave's glance, confirming the evil mockery of his tone, brought the Captain instantly to his feet.

The movement appeared to prompt decision in the other. A more subtle rogue would have made pretended innocence of intention until within striking distance. But Masaccio was an animal without subtleties; indeed, of a certain rough honesty. His bellow sounded the charge, and he lugged out his sword as he bellowed, thus giving Messer Colombino at least full warning of what was coming.

Loyally the Captain's grooms put themselves in the way of those rascals, and so delayed them for a moment. In that moment Colombino vaulted over the table. Entrenched behind it, his back protected by the wall, sword in hand and with his cloak swiftly swathed about his left arm, he felt himself in better case to make his stand and perhaps bring these cut-throats to a parley.

Parleying, however, was not in their business. Having knocked over the grooms, the pack leapt at the victim, and for some five strenuous minutes an incredible battle raised the dust from that unclean floor.

The taverner, in the background by the fireplace, remained at gaze, in affright.

The table, meanwhile, was proving a stout rampart. Every attempt to remove that barrier, too ponderous to yield to one man's strength, was frustrated by the Captain's vigorous swordplay. One rascal only was so rash as to attempt conclusions with him. Advancing within striking distance, he had thrust boldly across the board. Colombino used his left arm as a buckler, and before the ruffian could disentangle his blade from the Captain's cloak, a swift estramaçon came to sever the sinews of his sword-arm.

Disabled and drenched in blood, the man reeled back, a howling discouragement to his fellows. Let Masaccio curse them for cowards as he would, there was not another amongst them quite so rash as to take the wounded man's place. Instead, they addressed themselves once more to the removal of the table, so that all might come together upon their prey. They went about the task with system. Two of them stood by to ward the Captain's blows and make a cover under which two others might drag away the board.

Not all Colombino's vigour and address could have averted the inevitable end if there had been no intervention. It happened, however, that just as that glowing open doorway had attracted the notice of these assassins, so did it attract the notice of another party, riding north from Rimini.

Colombino was persuading himself that his sands were run when that salvation came.

A broad-shouldered young man, very richly apparelled, surged suddenly upon the threshold.

'By the Eyes of God, does it take six of you to kill a man?' Thus he announced himself, and at the ring of his voice the assassins fell back and wheeled to face him.

He came briskly forward, with jingling spurs and a swagger that swayed his crimson cloak; and men came crowding after him to the number of ten: rough, seafaring men by their outlandish garments and their swathed heads, armed with short, curved, ugly-looking swords of Turkish pattern.

Masaccio and his fellows backed away in apprehension towards the hearth, where the taverner continued a helpless, uninterfering witness.

The newcomer laughed with a queer gleeful ferocity, and rapped out an order.

'Cut me those brigands down.'

But as the murderous blades flashed forth, Colombino stayed them.

'Hold!'

Their quick, fierce master, swarthy and handsome in a brutal way, raised his black eyebrows until they were merged in the fringe of blue-black hair that hung straight across his shallow brow.

A little out of breath from his exertions, Colombino answered the amazed inquiry of that glance. 'They are not brigands, sir. They are poor hireling cut-throats.'

'Be they one or the other, their deserts are the same. My men will soon...'

'No, no!'

Colombino raised his fine, long hand. Of a ruthlessness in battle transcending perhaps that of any mercenary of his day, yet his horror of slaughter in cold blood was also greater. He would never have recourse to it even in action where surrender was to be obtained. That, indeed, was the mercenary's code, and by that code he chose now, with singular generosity, to be governed towards men whom he regarded, not as personal enemies, but as mercenaries hired for this undertaking.

'They are merely servants. Their master has, perhaps, a just quarrel with me. 1 have none with them. Let them go their ways.'

'When but for me they would have had your blood?'

'In their master's service. They did no more than they were bidden. Let them depart, sir.'

The other swore ill-humouredly, by the oath betraying his Venetian origin and by his humour the blood-lust of his nature. 'By the Body of Saint Mark! You are a singularly foolish man. I'd have the heads off their dirty necks, and send them back in a bale to their murderous master. That is what I should do.' His glance was an invitation. But as Colombino merely smiled and shook his head, he shrugged. 'After all, the affair is yours, not mine. If you are resolved...'

'I am as to my wishes, sir.'

'Why, then...' He swung to the murderous pack. 'You're in luck you kennel-rats. Away with you while it lasts. You'ld have fared differently with me.'

Masaccio slunk forward, hang-dog. He checked a moment, looking at Colombino, and seemed about to speak. Then he passed on, his cut-throats going after him in a huddle that showed their lingering apprehension. But on the threshold Masaccio paused again, letting his men go on and scramble for their horses. He spoke, and his voice trembled with emotion.

'As God's my witness, my lord, you shall never regret this saintly clemency. Masaccio is your man from this hour. For any service. I make oath of that, by the Bones of Saint Peter. Remember it, Ser Colombino.' And with a wave of the hand he plunged out after his men.

Colombino laughed as he called after him: 'I'll remember it when I want a throat-cutting.'

Then he turned to give thanks at last to his preserver, to be met, before he could utter a word, with the fierce harsh question:

'What name did that rascal give you?'

Colombino pondered the dark countenance before him, with its great cliff of a nose and its aggressive, square, cleft chin.

'My own. Colombino.' With a touch of conscious pride he added: 'I am Colombo of Siena.'

As he moved to one of the trestle tables on which stood a beaker and some cups, he was followed by a laugh.

'Colombo da Siena! You are Colombo da Siena, and it's your life I've saved! Now that is droll. Infernally droll.'

Colombino, still breathing hard, laid his bare sword on the table, and poured himself a draught of that vile wine. His throat was full of dust, and his need of drink had momentarily dulled all his faculties. He drained the cup, then let himself sag down wearily to a three-legged stool that was at hand. He was mopping his brow, when his preserver spoke again.

'It's the queerest chance. Had I not passed when I did, those cutthroats would have saved me trouble. Oh, but I don't repine. I'm a man who likes to do his own work with his own hands.'

The sinister mockery was not to be missed. The Captain looked up, frowning. 'I don't think I understand.'

'But you shall. As God's my life, you shall.' He stood, squarely before Colombino, his arms akimbo under his crimson cloak. 'I've just crossed from Crete, so that you should understand me. Did you ever hear of Ottavio Moro?'

Looking at him more closely now, Colombino traced in that coarsely handsome countenance a resemblance to Cristoforo Moro who was Doge of Venice and whom once, when in the service of the Republic, Colombino had known. So this was that lover of Samaritana's, who had been the Republic's procurator in Crete. The menace in the fellow's manner was explained. But Colombino's easy tone did not betray that he perceived it.

'And you are he. Faith! The queerest chance, as I think you said. I was supposing you in Crete.'

'Very comfortable, no doubt, in that supposition. I left my duty there to cross to Italy, so that I might have a word with you. I landed at Rimini this afternoon, and I was riding to Ravenna. It is considerate of you to spare me the trouble. You'll guess my errand.'

Colombino smiled, but with a curling lip. He was moved to scorn by the airs and postures of this Hector. 'You might have spared yourself further. You are behind the fair.'

He saw the other's face turn white and wicked. He saw the hairy jewelled hand settle instinctively on the hilt of his dagger. 'Do you tell me that you are already wed?'

If there was fury in the tone, there was also pain, and it was this that Colombino answered. 'No. There has been no wedding. But do not imagine that this will profit you. I know that Samaritana da Polenta thinks she loves you. But for your betrothal something more is necessary. You do not and never will possess the Lord of Ravenna's consent. He wants no Venetian blood in his grandchildren. Sooner a Turk's.'

Moro flung out a hand in contemptuous anger. 'I can dispense with the consent of Onorato da Polenta. But that's no concern of yours. For you there is all you'll need in my purpose with you. Unless you're a numskull you'll have guessed it.'

'I might be a numskull and still guess it from the fire you breathe. You've crossed from Crete to seek me, you say.'

'And at need to kill you.'

'It's an irony that you should begin by saving my life.'

'I've already remarked it.'

Colombino sat there, a hand on his booted thigh, considering Messer Ottavio Moro. And the more he considered him, the less he liked him, the more insistently he asked himself under what delusion could Samaritana have laboured when she imagined that she loved this gaudy, ruffianly, theatrical Rhodomont. It would, he thought, be a sweet and knightly deed to rid the world in general and Samaritana in particular of such a fellow. In marriage to him only damnation could await that chaste and delicate lady.

It was perhaps an ungrateful view to take, considering that he owed his life to Moro. But, then, this was an accident deplored by the Venetian; and by deploring it he had cancelled the actual debt.

'I understand, of course. It is not for me to deny your pleasure, Ser Ottavio. There is a spread of turf outside, and there, when daylight comes, on horse or foot, naked of body or fully armed, as you please, I shall be at your service.'

With that, accounting the matter ended, Colombino put out his hand to take his sword. But Moro, leaning forward, by a swift, sweeping movement, sent the weapon hurtling across the room, to be recovered by one of his men.

The act brought Colombino to his feet whilst the other was explaining it.

'No need to wait for daylight. Are you a fool, or do you suppose me one, to think that I'll cross swords with you.'

'I see. You mean to murder me. A knightly intention.'

'Knightly? What have I to do with knightliness?'

'Nothing, as I might have guessed.'

The blood mounted to the Venetian's face. 'You cheap adventurer! Are you so besotted with vanity as to suppose that a man of my blood will meet the son of Terrarossa in single combat? I know you, you see.'

'You say that with ten swords at your back, to a man you dare not meet. You do yourself great honour. In the Venetian manner, I suppose.'

As he spoke he was calculating his chances, although weaponless, of a sudden seizure of this assailant. A sudden grip, and he might snatch Moro's own dagger and set the blade at his throat before his knaves could move to hinder. On the very point of launching himself, his keen ears caught from the distance, faintly, a sound of approaching hooves. That gave him pause. No need, perhaps to risk his desperate chance. As the light of that doorway had drawn others, so it might draw these fresh travellers, too. Let him temporize, then, and even as he was deciding, Moro supplied the means.

'I hold you, and you had best realize that your sands are run this night unless you accept my terms.'

'Oh, there are terms?'

'You may have the honours of war if you will own defeat. Capitulate. Confess that you cannot hold what you have had the temerity to seize, and you may have your life.'

Colombino stroked his chin. 'This needs considering,' said he slowly, his ears intent upon that distant clop-clop.

'Consider, then, and resolve. But quickly. I have no time to waste on you.'

The hoof-beats were very rapid, and rapidly grew louder. These travellers were riding at a gallop, and there must be at least six of them, perhaps more. But now they caught Moro's attention, too, and like Colombino he perceived the chances of an interruption. To avert them he issued an order.

'Shut that door.'

A couple of his men sprang to do his bidding. Closing the door, they masked the light and thus extinguished Colombino's new-found hope. He must now depend upon himself alone. Either he must take the desperate chance of a sudden onset or else make a cowardly surrender which this Venetian braggart would no doubt proclaim widely hereafter.

The man's harsh voice came to rouse him. 'Well, sir? Have you resolved?'

Colombino shrugged resignedly. 'You hold me in check. I have no choice, it seems.'

'You are not without prudence, my valiant captain.'

'The odds are a little heavy even for me,' Colombino excused himself. 'You have my word that I will …'

'Your word!' The interruption came on a laugh of scorn. 'The word of Terrarossa! I'll need some better security than that. You shall write a letter to Onorato da Polenta, declining the alliance with his daughter in terms which shall leave you no doorway of retreat.'

'And these terms?'

'The question is: Will you write as I shall dictate? It is that or the end of you.' He waved a hand to that line of men, waiting with drawn swords. 'Come, sir. Decide.'

Colombino perceived here a faint advantage. It must be that the letter he demanded was more valuable to Moro than the mere death of his rival, or else that death would already have been launched.

There was no reason why he should not write in renunciation of something which he had renounced already, saving that this abject surrender to force seemed to him dishonouring.

'How shall this profit you?' he asked. 'How shall my withdrawal, by murder or otherwise, clear the way for you? I tell you again that Onorato da Polenta will never bestow his daughter on your father's son.'

Ottavio Moro scarcely controlled himself. 'Leave that. Come to what concerns you. Will you renounce, or will you be permanently removed?'

The hoof-beats, rattling upon the dry hard road, were now abreast of the place. But he no longer founded hopes upon those travellers.

'Very well,' he said. 'Let me have the wherewithal to write.'

But in the act of calling upon the taverner for pen and ink, Moro checked. The incredible was happening. The riders had left the road. They were pounding across the turf towards the door of the inn.

To Colombino it was a miracle. To Moro little more than an irritation.

'Hell! Who will these be?'

'Friends of mine, I hope,' said Colombino.

'Much that will profit you, or them,' Moro taunted him, for he had gauged their numbers, and knew himself in superior force.

131

Then the door was flung open, and Colombino saw that here was no miracle; no accident even; just the natural sequel to what had gone before.

On the threshold stood the burly form of Masaccio.

iii

'It's you, is it?' growled Moro. 'What the devil have you come back for?'

But Masaccio was not heeding him. After a glance through the room, he spoke over his shoulder to someone behind him.

'He is still here. And safe and sound as I promised you. Come and see for yourself.'

A slim stripling, a lad, as it seemed, booted to the thighs and cloaked thence to the neck, came to stand in the light, at Masaccio's side.

Colombino, whose eyes like those of every man in the room had turned upon these intruders, caught his breath to behold under the round black hat the pale, oval, lovely face of Samaritana da Polenta.

Following Masaccio's pointing hand with almost fearful eagerness, her dark eyes swept to him without so much as a glance for the others, and from her lips he was greeted by an outcry of passionate fervency.

'God be thanked for this mercy!' She stepped down and ran to him, still without eyes for any other, and she caught him by the arms. 'Oh, God be thanked!' she cried again. 'When I met Masaccio, riding back, I thought that I should die in my despair. It seemed that for all the fearful haste I had made, I was too late: I could hardly believe Masaccio when he told me that he had been foiled in his evil work, that you had been preserved by...'

There abruptly she broke off. She had turned, her eyes seeking his preservers, and they had alighted upon Ottavio Moro, straight, grim, and scowling, in his crimson splendour. Speechless for a moment in sheer amazement, going pale at sight of him, she had loosed her hold of Colombino's arms, and had swung more squarely to confront her lover.

'Samaritana!'

The sound of his voice restored her to speech and movement. She stepped towards him, her head forward.

'Ottavio! It is you, indeed? And here?' She uttered an odd, excited laugh. 'A miracle!'

Something in his expression gave her pause. She looked about her, her eyes troubled. Her senses caught an ominous tenseness. 'But those men? Why are their swords drawn? What... what was happening here?'

Moro was sneering. 'Those swords were drawn to do you service. To deliver you from a peril in which I, poor fool, believed that you stood.' And upon that he leapt at her and seized her by the shoulders, fiercely. 'Traitress! Is this the faith you keep? Is this your steadfastness? Was it to discover this that I left my post in Crete, for which I may yet be broken?'

'Discover?' Sternness surmounted her bewilderment. 'What, pray, do you imagine that you have discovered?'

'Imagine? Have you left room to imagine anything? Have I not seen? Have I not heard?' Still clutching her slim shoulders in his hairy jewelled paws, his white, disordered countenance within a foot of her own, he raved on. 'I landed at Rimini today, so as to ride to deliver you. And here tonight I begin by saving the life of the man I had come to kill. Ironical, isn't it? As ironical as your riding so desperately to save the man from whom I had come to save you, you faithless woman!'

If he paused then, it seemed to be because his rage was choking him.

'Faithless, am I?' There was a sad, twisted smile on her pale lips. 'But where is your faith, Ottavio?'

'Only a fool's faith could survive this evidence. And I am not a fool.'

'No. A madman.'

'Because I will not listen to your lies? Because I will not be deluded by them when the truth stands stark before me? You rode in wild, fearful haste to save this man: this man of all men; this man whom your father was forcing you to wed against your will; this man for whose death you must, therefore, have prayed had you been loyal to your vows to me. Can any lies destroy that, or explain the slobbering fondness in which you ran to him? What has he become to you? That is all that I desire to hear from you. Answer me!' He shook her roughly. 'What has he become to you?'

She threw up her head, and never had Colombino seen those proud eyes of hers so cold and proud as at this moment.

Abruptly she twisted from Moro's grasp. The action loosened the cloak in which she was modestly wrapped. It fell open, disclosing the slim body loosely clad in the borrowed leather hacketon. She was breathing hard in fury.

'God of Heaven! Am I some baggage for your handling and your insults? I am Samaritana da Polenta.'

The reminder only served to inflame his savage, aggressive nature; the barren, domineering mind was hardened in its obstinacy.

'I am well aware of that: of the treacherous house from which you spring and of the wantonness that's in the blood of its women since that Francesca da Polenta who in Rimini made a cuckold of Malatesta.'

Colombino saw her gloved hand tighten upon the riding-whip she carried; he saw her lips part to speak, yet remain silent; he saw the glance of cold disdain with which she withered the Venetian; then abruptly he found himself addressed by her.

'I beg you, sir, to conduct me hence.'

He was very prompt to obey, but as promptly found himself checked by Moro.

'Ah, that, no. I am not to be mocked. You'll take the consequences, my girl, of this rash journey. Before you came I had offered terms to this rascal, this fellow for whose sweet sake you confront alone the perils of the road in man's attire.' Slobbering like a drunkard in his passion, his mouth awry, insult in every line of him, he pointed with a shaking hand to her booted legs. 'In man's attire, with the effrontery of a harlot. So that he renounced you, I would spare his life. But now that I hold you, his renunciation is not needed. You'll come with me to Crete, my girl. Not in honour, as my wife, since you're soiled goods, no longer fit for that. But you'll come with me. Do you understand? That will teach you and your rascally lover what it means to make a mock of Ottavio Moro.'

Her answer was swift and sudden as a lightning-flash. It was delivered with her whip across his evilly derisive face.

'You vile hound! You pitiful tyrant bully!' Thus in a royal anger. Then her voice broke. 'O God! The shame of ever having loved you! The scalding shame of it!'

Moro had fallen back with an inarticulate cry, his hand to his face, livid now save where a red wheal was angrily rising to mark the course of her whiplash. A moment he pondered her with the eyes of a wild beast. Then his hand went to his sword-hilt.

With what murderous intent he drew will never be fully known; for before the point had cleared the scabbard, Colombino acted. Swiftly he caught up the three-legged stool by which he had remained standing, and using it as a battle-axe, he stretched the Venetian insensible upon the earthen floor.

That made an instant stir, both among Moro's followers ranged by the fireplace and Masaccio's knaves who were crowded in the doorway. But promptest of all was Masaccio himself. With immediate perception of what must follow, a perception rendered instinctive by the experience of many a rough-and-tumble, the burly ruffian had whipped out his sword almost before Moro reached the ground.

As Moro's men began the movement of a charge to their leader's rescue, Masaccio's foot was on Moro's breast, his point at the Venetian's throat.

'Back there, all of you, or by the belly of Bacchus I'll pin your master to the floor like a beetle.'

That checked them, and, whilst they stood in huddled apprehension, the bravo laughed at them. He threw out his chest. He became grandiose as he addressed Colombino.

'Thus Masaccio pays his debts. I told you I was your man, my

135

lord. I pray you take madonna hence whilst I keep these foreign hogs at bay.'

'Hark!' Samaritana's hand was on Colombino's arm. Once again from the distance came a sound of hooves, the drumming now of a numerous company. 'This will be Don Pablo. I sent him urgent word to follow.'

Colombino smiled down upon her. 'You seem to have forgotten nothing, madonna.' Then he stepped to Masaccio. 'Give me that sword. I'll take your place, whilst you go outside and hold up this troop for me.'

Thus he was left there, with Samaritana beside him, and Masaccio's five sound knaves just beyond, ready at need to oppose themselves to a rush by those ten Cretans.

But Moro's men, held in check less by this than by the menace to the life of their lord, had no thought to attempt a rush. The perception that this thunder of hooves that was rolling nearer heralded an overwhelming enemy force had made them apprehensive for their lives.

One of them attempted to make terms. Colombino cut him short.

'Throw down your weapons, all of you, if you hope for mercy.'

He was obeyed, and so they waited there in a queer silence for some moments until outside the arriving horsemen clattered to a halt and the night became noisy with their voices.

When presently Moro's senses had returned, and he sat up bewildered, his face smeared in blood from the cut which the stool had dealt his brow, he found the place swarming with men-at-arms in steel and leather, and he saw the Lady Samaritana standing between Colombino and a swarthy, corpulent fellow who broadly grinning at him.

Some of Moro's own men came to raise him up. If as his wits cleared he became conscious of his peril, it robbed him of none of his arrogance. He shook himself out of the supporting arms of his knaves, wiped the blood and sweat from his face, greenishly livid under its tan, and stood squarely before the corpulent Don Pablo, who so obviously commanded these newcomers.

'You'ld best not let your fools interfere with me,' he warned the Spaniard. 'I am Ottavio Moro, son of His Serenity the Doge, and the Most Serene Republic's Procurator in Crete.'

Don Pablo's fat, jovial countenance grinned at him. 'It rests with my Lord Colombo whether you're to become the Most Serene Republic's Procurator in Hell. And I think it's very likely.'

'At your peril, sirs!'

Don Pablo swung to his master. 'Your orders, my lord?'

Colombino stroked his chin. 'I can scarcely claim him. He belongs to Monna Samaritana.'

Samaritana, ever cold and proud and so much mistress of herself now that none might guess the wound she had taken, slowly shook her head.

'He is no man of mine,' she disowned him. 'That is overpast, if, indeed, it ever was. For until tonight I have never known him. I knew only the pretended self with which he deceived me. Do with him as you will, Ser Colombino; yet I would have you spare his life, not for his own sake, but for yours.'

'It's in his face,' said Don Pablo, 'that he'll be hanged sooner or later. There's an opportune tree just outside...'

Colombino broke in. 'Let him go his pitiful ways. Let him go back to Crete and his procuratorship.'

Don Pablo sighed his resignation. 'Yet the Cretans are docile, inoffensive people. It's a little hard on them.'

Moro glared at him, wild-eyed, speechless, then found Samaritana claiming his attention.

She had come to stand squarely before this man to whom she had betrothed herself in defiance of her father, and for whose sake – believing him fine and noble, as women will believe their lovers – she had been ready to endure all things. Steadily she met now his wild, baffled glance, and her words dropped ice-cold upon his overheated brain.

'You asked me several questions tonight, and to all of them, yourself, you supplied the answers, to your own ignoble satisfaction.

But there was one question which would have been the first on the lips of a man of heart or brain, which you forgot to ask: Whence sprang the danger to Messer Colombino from which I rode to save him? Which is to say: By whom and why were men set on to murder him?

'Let me give you the answer now, so that you may ponder it on your way back to Crete, and draw from the story a lesson for your future.'

And she told him of Colombino's chivalrous renunciation, to the hurt of his ambition and reckless of the rancour he must provoke by the pretence under which he made it. It was a tale so simple and obvious, supplying so clear an explanation of Masaccio's attempt upon the Captain, that it compelled immediate belief even in the jaundiced mind of Moro.

'And now, sir,' she ended quietly, 'you possess the answer to your question as to what there is between Messer Colombino and me that I should ride through the night to save him, fronting the perils of the road, alone and thus, in man's attire, with the effrontery of a harlot, as you so delicately observed.'

She ceased, and stood with a little, twisted smile considering the Venetian's stricken countenance. Then, abruptly, she turned her back on him.

'If you will give me leave, Ser Colombino, Masaccio and his knaves will escort me back to Ravenna.'

Only then did Moro shake off the paralysis that held him. He sprang after her, with a pleading, broken cry. 'Samaritana! Samaritana! Forgive! I did not know. How could I guess so much?'

'You guessed other things so easily. Ignoble things. This you could not guess because it asks a nobility, a faith that does not lie within your nature. I thank God for the timely discovery of it.'

Those were her last words to him. She beckoned Masaccio to attend her, and went out.

Colombino followed, to hold her stirrup. When she was mounted, he stood irresolute beside her in the gloom, his hand upon the neck of her horse.

'I have yet to utter some word of thanks,' he murmured.

'Not to me. None are due. You heard what I said to that man. In what I did tonight to serve you I performed the least duty that your nobility imposed upon me.'

He looked up. A shaft of light from the inn door glowed now upon her proud, finely featured face, pallidly wistful.

'No more than that?' he asked her, very softly.

There was a pause in which she seemed to seek words, and when she had found them her voice choked upon them.

'What else could there be? I loved Ottavio Moro. So much. My heart is weeping a little over the shards of a broken idol.'

He sighed. His voice was low, his face invisible to her, in the shadows.

'Of my love for you, madonna, you hold, I think, the proof. It is deep and strong and it will last. I ask for nothing now, nor ever shall, save that I would have you remember that in any need I exist to serve you. To know it may lend you strength. To know that you believe it will bring some radiance to my life. That is all, madonna. Remember.'

'Could I forget?' she choked.

He took his hand from her horse's neck, and stepped back.

'God guard your journey, madonna,' he said steadily.

'And keep you safe and fortunate,' was her answering wish.

He watched her ride away with Masaccio and his band. Then slowly he turned to find Don Pablo standing, a bulky silhouette, in the light of the doorway.

'An unprofitable night for everybody, it seems,' he sighed. 'There's been a general shipwreck of intentions here at the Neptune Inn.'

'Who knows?' wondered the Spaniard. 'Who knows in this world what is shipwreck and what is salvation? All things are causes, Captain: seeds in the womb of time. Out of evil comes good, and out of good comes evil. None ever knows until time gives birth to the effect.'

Chapter 5

THE LADY OF LA BOURDONNAYE

i

Of all that Colombo da Siena had said to Onorato da Polenta, nothing was more truthful than that there was likely to be war in Naples over the succession. They were nearer to it than he supposed, as he discovered when heavy-hearted he came back to Siena, and took his way at vintage-time to his villa on the heights of Montasco.

Scarcely was he returned when he was sought there with news of this unrest by three prominent members of the Signory – the Council of Fifteen – which ruled the State. They were his friend Petrucci, Annibale Piccolomini, a young kinsman of that gracious, scholarly Pope, Aenea Silvio Piccolomini, who ruled as Pius II, and Ettore Malavolti, who disputed with Petrucci the leadership of the Republic of Siena, successfully for the moment since he held the high office of Prior of the Fifteen.

They told Colombino in detail of the war clouds gathering over Naples, where King Ferdinand – the bastard of Alfonso of Aragon, who had wrested the kingdom from the House of Anjou – sat enthroned. They confirmed the rumours that had been abroad in the Italian Peninsula for months to the effect that John of Calabria, the son of old King René, of Anjou, encouraged and supported by the King of France, was arming and secretly making alliances with the aim of reconquering the dominions of his house.

The struggle if it came would be a stern one, and might involve the whole of Italy. For in the North the Duke of Milan allowed it plainly to be seen that war would find him on the side of Aragon, and in the South the Pope was throwing the weight of his influence into the scales on the same side. Siena could scarcely hope to keep out of the garboil. At the same time the Signory was not prepared to yield to urgings of the Piccolomini that the Republic should declare for Aragon. It preferred to wait upon events before approaching a decision. In the meantime lest decision when it came should find the Republic unprepared, these prominent patrician representatives of the State, welcoming Colombo's timely return, hastened to prevent him from disbanding the troops he had brought south.

They found him oddly cold, and, for a man who lived by war, so singularly indifferent that Malavolti's suspicions were instantly aroused.

'If,' said Colombo, 'the Republic chooses to quarter my men at her own charges, and to pay them for doing nothing at say three-quarters of the rates they would receive if they were actively campaigning, that is the Republic's affair. The matter, of course, can be arranged.'

'And yourself?' asked Malavolti, his dark eyes very watchful.

'Myself?' Colombino shrugged, and hesitated. Distaste and lassitude were written plainly upon his face. 'I am a little weary of campaigning. I need rest. Body and soul. I hope to find it here in my vineyards. There is no need to take me into account.'

'There is every need,' said Piccolomini, the oldest and gravest of the three. 'Without you, your army is merely a rabble of men. It is the Company of the Dove the Signory desires to retain, and there is no Company of the Dove without Colombo.'

'There are my captains. Sangiorgio and Caliente. Both leaders of great experience.'

'This, sir, is frivolous,' said Malavolti.

'Regard it as you please. My heart's not in it.'

'Your heart's not in it!' Malavolti stood up, a tall man, with the lithe, graceful vigour of a panther. His handsome, swarthy face grew dark. The full-lipped, sensual mouth was grimly set. 'If offers were to come to you from the Angevins, would your heart be in it then?'

Colombo's expression of weariness deepened. 'I have said that you may have my men. You do me the honour to say that without me to lead them they are of small effect. But of what effect am I without them? Are you answered?'

'Not as directly as I could wish.'

'Oh, as to that, I might have added a reminder that I am a free agent, to be constrained into the service of no party, but to take service as I choose. Your tone seems almost to deny me such a right.'

Camillo Petrucci hastened to the rescue. 'No, no, Colombino. It is just because we recognize it that we are here, so as to forestall any other who might seek to engage you.,

'And, after all,' added Piccolomini, 'you are a child of Siena, and you could not wish to find yourself ranged on the side to which Siena is opposed if Siena should come into the conflict.'

'I thank you for that justice,' said Colombino, and he disregarded Malavolti's open sneer. 'Disabuse your minds. As I have said, my heart is not in it. Not in campaigning, I mean. I have been almost constantly under arms for three years now. I need repose, and my vineyards need me.'

'This we could recognize, my friend,' said Petrucci gently. 'But consider. If war should come, it cannot come now before the spring. The season is too far advanced. This ensures you a rest of close upon six months. By the end of that time you should be weary of resting. And meanwhile over this period of inaction, at a time when there are no hirings, the Republic will pay you a retainer of a thousand ducats a month in addition to providing for your company. That, in fact, is the offer we have been sent to make. It does not seem to me an offer that you can or should refuse.'

Not if he's honest,' said Malavolti.

Colombino let that pass. He stalked the length of that spacious, handsome room, his thumbs in the girdle of his crimson houppelande, his chin on his breast. His thoughts were with Samaritana, and his last sight of her as she rode away into the darkness outside the Neptune Inn. It was a vision of her that was to recur whenever she rose in his thoughts, and that was to be very often. It seemed to him that in going, as he had then seen her go, she had borne away with her all his zest and all his ambition, leaving only lassitude in his soul. There was no salt now in life. All achievement was insipid, all exertion seemed futility. Just as a man bruised in body craves rest and is content to lie inert, so he, bruised in spirit, found himself urged to bucolic inaction. But there was with him, too, the knowledge, however little there might at present be the feeling, that these wounds would heal. He was not too young to realize this. Presently with returning vigour of mind the need of action would return also. If it did, and if war came, where else should he be but on the side that Siena took?

Slowly he paced back, watched by those three pairs of eyes.

'Very well,' he said, at last. 'I will accept the engagement.'

It was only Malavolti who paid heed to the lack of enthusiasm, to the weary indifference of Colombino's tone. And when he commented upon it afterwards to his companions, as they rode back to Siena, he was silenced by their opposition, which in Petrucci was hot with indignation.

There was no publication of that engagement, since this might have appeared as an announcement that Siena had already decided upon her course of action, which was very far from being the case. But there was publication at about that time of the engagement by the Angevin party of Jacopo Piccinino, who ranked just then as the first soldier in Italy, the distinguished son of a father distinguished in the same trade, and the commander of the most formidable company of mercenaries that stood for hire in the Peninsula.

Piccinino's engagement was the work of the Count Gaston de La Bourdonnaye, who for some months had been flitting like a stormy petrel up and down Italy, seeking to enlist on Anjou's behalf the support of her princes and communes. Because of the known attitudes of the Pope in the South and the Duke of Milan in the North, Monsieur de La Bourdonnaye met with less success than he had hoped. But he was not on that account dismayed. The enlisting of great mercenary companies was at least as important as winning the favour of states; and so long as he succeeded in the former, it might ultimately be his to constrain the latter by the display of force which his side could make. The hiring of Piccinino had been an important step. So important that if he could add to it the engagement of Colombo da Siena and his Company of the Dove, John of Calabria, well supported in addition by French troops, would be in such strength as the other side could hardly hope to equal, and Aragon might abandon its pretensions.

At the same time, if he could win the support of the Republic of Siena primarily and ostensibly the only object of his descent upon it, he would be fully compensated for his failure with other lesser states.

As the envoy extraordinary of the King of France, he was received in Siena with all the honours due to his exalted office from a State at peace with his master. There were festivities attended by all who were of any consequence in the Republic, and Camillo Petrucci dragged the reluctant Colombo from his retirement at Montasco so that he might bear his part in them. The palio was held in the Campo with more than ordinary magnificence; there was a joust, over which the Comtesse de La Bourdonnaye presided, and in which Colombo, who in addition to being a great captain was of a singular address in arms, carried the day over all comers; and there were banquets and balls and elaborate masques without end for the entertainment of the Frenchman and his lovely, wistful young Countess.

When, however, it came to politics, Monsieur de La Bourdonnaye found the members of the Council as vague and lethargic as in festive matters they were precise and active. Cursing the elusive Italian subtlety of the Piccolomini, the Petrucci, the Malavolti, and the Squillanti, he took the resolve, after three weeks of wasted endeavour, to make sure of Colombino, let Siena do what it might.

He attempted to broach the matter to the Captain one evening after the performance of a comedy of Giumelli's at Petrucci's palace, where for the time Colombo was housed. He sought him out in a corner of the vast glittering room in which the play had been given.

'You take your ease these days, my Captain. It is most just. No man has better earned it; no man has a better title to rest upon his laurels. And they are brave laurels, as is well known even beyond the confines of Italy.'

From his stately height Colombino looked down upon this stocky man in the middle forties, powerful and ungainly, and caught from his prominent light eyes a suggestion of anxiety. He smiled, and inclined his head a little as if in acknowledgment of the compliments.

'There is peace in Italy at present. A miraculously unusual condition.'

'But ephemeral. The elements of strife are present.'

'As for that, they always are.'

'Oh, but very definite. That is why I am in Italy.' His tone grew confidential. 'To prepare on behalf of the King my master. It is a subject on which I should esteem a word with you.'

'At your good pleasure, my lord.'

'You are gracious. The King of France has a proposal for you that I think you will account worthy of his well-known munificence.'

'I am honoured to deserve his regard. But at present I am in the service of the Republic of Siena.'

'Already!' The Count was manifestly taken aback. 'And the term of your engagement? Is it permissible to ask that question?'

'I am retained on a monthly stipend, my lord.'

'But the term of it?'

'No term is set.'

The Frenchman brightened. 'Why, then, it may be determined in a month at any time.'

Colombino shook his head. 'Not as I understand it, sir. And not as Siena understands it.'

'Understandings, my Captain, do not constitute engagements. The service of the King my master confers not only honour but emoluments such as I venture to think no other service today could offer you.'

The condottiero smiled. 'Then it were best not to tempt me by disclosing them. For I account myself indefinitely bound.'

'No man could be that,' said the Count, and he was about to develop the argument when Ettore Malavolti, swaggering of gait, effusive of manner, came to interrupt them.

'What do you conspire, you two?'

'Conspire?' cried La Bourdonnaye.

Malavolti's smile grew broader. 'What else should keep two gallants in a corner, and one of them a Frenchman, when there are ladies languishing for your attention?' He slipped a hand through La Bourdonnaye's arm. 'The incomparable Caterina Squillanti offers you the opportunity to be avenged upon her husband for the ardent love he is making to your Countess.' And with a nod to Colombino, he drew the Frenchman away, and carried him off to interrupt a very close communion between the insolently beautiful Marchioness Squillanti and that dainty patrician fribble Silvio Pecci.

The twain looked up almost in resentment. Shouldered, as it were, aside by the masterful Malavolti, the exquisite, perfumed, effeminate Pecci departed in reluctant resentment, and reluctant were the dark eyes of the young Marchioness that followed him. The shrewd Frenchman was not slow to draw the obvious inference. He was not desired. Malavolti's announcement had been the merest pretext to separate him from Colombino.

It showed him clearly from which quarter the wind was setting. Not only were the patricians of Siena shy of his attempt to bind them to his master's interest, but they were equally reluctant that there should be any understanding between him and their great condottiero. It became necessary to walk delicately in this matter, and to mask his aims until they should be achieved, until Colombino should be bound by definite engagement. And it was no less necessary to proceed with the greatest care with Colombino himself, so as to disentangle him from the bonds which Monsieur de La Bourdonnaye conceived already to exist between the Captain and the Republic of

Siena. This might demand protracted and intimate intercourse; and if these suspicious patricians became aware of anything of the kind, they would at once assume the purpose for which La Bourdonnaye was cultivating the society of Colombino, and no doubt they would take their measures to frustrate his aims.

This was the problem now plaguing the envoy extraordinary of the King of France. But kings do not choose dullards for this office, and La Bourdonnaye was no dullard. That he looked a dullard was perhaps an advantage. A stocky man, as I have said, short, thick-set, and powerful, he carried aggressively erect on a short neck a face that was brutally handsome, very big in the nose and very square in the chin. But his blue eyes normally were dull, and when they became alert they merely succeeded in giving him a foolish expression. His brow receding to his iron-grey hair was at once narrow and shallow. He lisped a little in his speech, he was ostentatious in his dress, ingratiatory in manner, and he had the loud and ready laughter that proclaims the empty head. But his head was far from empty. He could be subtle as any Italian of them all, he was troubled by no sense of moral values, and did not know what it was to have a scruple where man or woman was concerned.

The problem of providing a cloak for the intimacy he desired with Colombino did not long exercise him. It was solved by the following morning; and since the solution entailed the collaboration of his Countess, he instructed her without either delay or qualms.

'At the banquet to be offered by the Commune tomorrow evening to this Florentine tradesman, de' Medici, you will meet again that handsome upstart, Colombo da Siena. You will recall that it was from your own delicate hands that he received the trophy in last week's tourney. It is impossible that you should not admire him. Tomorrow night you will display that admiration unequivocally. Opportunity will be provided. If you should even go the length of a little wantonness, that will not perturb me. I desire you to arouse in him a more than ordinary interest. You should not find it difficult.'

There was no astonishment in the eyes she raised to look at him. Only loathing. And not merely loathing of the task imposed upon her, but of the man who imposed it.

They were standing in a room of the mezzanine of the palace in the Via Flavia, near the Campo, which the Salimbeni had placed at the disposal of the envoy extraordinary. It was a long, low-ceilinged chamber, handsomely hung with tapestries in blue and gold, and lighted by wide mullioned windows that overlooked the street. A shaft of sunlight filtering through the gules of the armorial bearings on the glass set a rosy glow in the middle of the room and a patch as of blood upon the wood mosaics of the floor. Elsewhere the long chamber was full of shadows, and it was into these that Madame de La Bourdonnaye, had she obeyed her instincts, would have crept. But she dared not move whilst the pale eyes of her lord were compellingly upon her.

Twenty years younger than the Count, a slight, frail, dark-haired woman, seeming little more than a child, her little oval countenance, sharply outlined in its close-fitting coif, was of a winning purity of feature and expression. Gentle and good and innocent were her eyes, and hauntingly wistful, betraying the unhappiness into which she was come, since her spirit had been broken by the brutal, sneering, domineering man to whom she had been given in marriage.

Why he should have married her was a question that she asked of Heaven daily. He had wearied of her so soon. In the unrestrained indulgence of an insatiable sensuality, he had put upon her indignity after indignity by the very flagrancy of his infidelities, until she knew herself for an object of contemptuous pity. Yet, like the dog in the fable, guarding the grass for which it had no appetite, he had ever been swift to display a vain man's jealousy if the dainty charm of her which had staled for him exercised the least allurement over other men.

Therefore, accustomed though she was to being used as a contemptible pawn in his schemes, her surprise at his present commands almost outweighed her indignation. It seemed to her that she could not rightly have understood him, and she said so.

'Must I always explain myself?' He wondered impatiently. 'Can you never perceive anything for yourself? I desire this soldier freely at my house. But I do not want it suspected that it is my company he seeks or keeps. Do you understand now?'

Shame resuscitated in her a spark of the spirit that once had been hers. 'I understand.' She threw up her chin, and stood straight and tense. 'But you shall not put my honour in pawn for any of your schemes.'

The rebellion took him entirely by surprise. His heavy black brows went up. He stroked his shaven, masterful jaw.

'Shall I not? Ha! Shall I not? Are you not my wife?'

'Your wife? Your Countess, if you please. No more than that. In the eyes of the world…'

He interrupted her. 'Just so. It is with the eyes of the world that we are concerned.'

'And in the eyes of the world you will play the part of the complacent husband? You? And for this purpose I am to act the wanton…'

She was allowed to go no further. Experience should have warned her of the futility of opposition to his wishes. His hand took her by the wrist. It was a hand as powerful as it was hideous: a short, round paw of stubby fingers and diminutive nails. Its mangling grip, that seemed to crush bone and sinew, made her writhe in pain. She bit her lip, to stifle an outcry. His light eyes narrowed in a cruel smile, as if he gathered a sadic pleasure from the physical suffering he inflicted.

'Madame, these are matters for my decision; not for yours. You understand what I require of you.' Derisively he ran on: 'You have, I know, a high opinion of your charms. They have been – have they not? – so often extolled by the gallants I have never known you reluctant to encourage. Do not be reluctant now. Exert those charms. Take joy in the freedom I give you to practise your natural feminine arts. You have not only my leave, but my command.'

He released her, and she shrank away from him, nursing her mangled wrist. A dry sob broke from her, whereupon with a laugh he changed abruptly from arrogant cruelty to nauseating cajolery. He came to pat her shoulder.

149

'There, there! What's to cry for? Where was the need to provoke me? To be stupid? You know that in my heart I am fond of you, whatever I may say or do.' His tone became more coaxing. 'After all, it is a little thing that I ask. Do you suppose I relish it? Do you know me so little as that after all these years? It is really worse for me than for you. But great issues hang upon it. We men of state are no better than slaves. Slaves of duty. There, Valérie! I count upon you.'

She made him no answer beyond a shudder. But with that he was content.

ii

Monsieur de La Bourdonnaye counted confidently upon the dread of him in which his Countess went. But if the accident of circumstance had not served him here – and procured not the make-believe he commanded, but reality – he would have counted vainly on this occasion, so nauseating was the task to the dignity and purity of his lady.

As if Fate conspired to serve the Frenchman, it happened that the Countess was seated at that banquet, as became her rank, on the right hand of Camillo Petrucci, who presided, and that she found Ser Colombino on her left. There was, therefore, no need to create the opportunity for an assault upon the Captain's sensibilities. The opportunity was presented to her ready-made. But because of her repugnance to grasp it, her husband's satisfaction was soon dashed. She sat mumchance, a white-faced, piteous little figure, answering in monosyllables when addressed, her wits in a frozen paralysis. And the more insistently her husband scowled command at her from the table's farther end, the more firmly this paralysis enclosed her.

Thus until Fate stepped in again to take a hand, and Colombino, exercising himself to animate this petrification of womanhood beside him, suddenly precipitated a situation actually in excess of Monsieur de La Bourdonnaye's desires.

'Madame, you have bruised your wrist!'

Flung into panic by the discovery and the tone of solicitude in which Colombino announced it, she hurriedly withdrew the hand that had been resting on the board beside her plate. A hoop of brilliants clasped about the empurpled flesh served to stress rather than to disguise the bruise.

As the astonished glance of the tawny-headed young soldier followed the retreating hand, he saw a tear merge with the brilliants to sparkle amongst them a moment before vanishing.

'You are in distress, madame!' He spoke in a fluent French that was softened by a Tuscan intonation.

The hum of voices, the clatter of dishes, the clink of glass, the flitting of black-and-white livened servants, the music of flute and viol from the gallery overhead, all served to cover the sharpness of his exclamation. But the expression on his countenance, as he leaned towards her, was visible. It was one of pitying tenderness, and Monsieur de La Bourdonnaye from the distance, perceiving only the tenderness and missing the pity, was relieved at last. His Countess was behaving with unostentatious obedience.

What she was saying to him, with her wistful little smile was: 'It is nothing, sir. I beg that you will not give heed.'

'Not give heed? Not give heed to the distress of a lady? Of a lady so sweet and gentle?'

He spoke without hint of illicit gallantry. The deference of his tone contradicted any assumption that his words were those of an amorous opportunist.

'Countess, if I can serve you in any need, you have but to command me,' said that servant of chivalry.

She flashed him a sudden, frightened glance. It was not in her experience that men made such proposals without hope of guerdon. The grave sincerity of his regard reassured her in part. Yet her answer was not entirely without mistrust.

'Mine is no need that you can serve.'

But the very words, the very sadness of the voice, beckoned him further along the road from which she sought to wave him. Pondering ever that discoloured wrist, his clear-cut, shaven face grew set and stern. All that was knightly in him surged up now, dispersing the listlessness that had lately hung about his spirit. The thought of Samaritana, though she might be lost to him, came to him in that moment as an encouragement. She must commend his chivalrous interest in this lady's wrongs, his purpose to discover and to right them.

'I ask myself what bracelet you have lately worn, madame, what gyves. A man's hand might have done that. What do I say: a man's? A beast's, perhaps. If you were to tell me, madame, I might so dispose that you would be safe in future.'

Her panic increased. She could not guess what might be her husband's design; but from his odd anxiety to mantle it, she must assume that it boded no good to Messer Colombino. Horror of the vile part of a decoy was deepened as she looked into the face of this young soldier, so stern in all but the dark eyes, which were gentle and tender. Suddenly she perceived the adventitious opening offered, and took her decision.

'You may so dispose, indeed, if you will do as I shall ask you. This bruise, sir, was suffered on your behalf.'

'On my behalf?' He was aghast. By his tone he almost seemed to draw back.

Across the room she met her husband's glance, watchful again and menacing. She swung to confront Colombino more squarely. She set her hand familiarly upon the grey velvet sleeve of his doublet, and startled him by speaking on a note of strident laughter.

'In pity laugh with me. We are watched. Laugh, Monsieur Colombino.'

He was quick to understand. The counterfeit laughter on her lips and the terror in her eyes made it very plain, and he laughed as he was bidden whilst listening to what else she had to say.

'Presently, when we rise, when the dancing comes, could we not slip away? Then I will tell you all.'

'It shall be contrived,' he promised her, whereupon both laughed again, as if at some quip that had passed between them. And they laughed so frequently thereafter that more than one eyebrow was raised and more than one nudge exchanged to see Colombino, who had been so staid and dull of late, grown of a sudden so merry with this Frenchwoman.

At the end of supper came a party of mummers to perform a comedy. After this the musicians in the gallery were reinforced, and the floor was cleared for dancing.

Monsieur de La Bourdonnaye led forth the wife of Camillo Petrucci, whilst Petrucci himself looked round for Madame de La Bourdonnaye. He discovered that Colombino had forestalled him. Because he loved Colombino as a brother, he smiled upon what in another he would have resented as a presumption. If he smiled no longer when presently it was perceived that the Captain and the exalted lady who was the guest of Siena had left the hall, at least he leapt at no such assumptions as Malavolti came to mutter in his ear.

'Our captain and these French grow a thought too fond of one another.'

Petrucci shook his dark young bead. 'There's no ground for scandal. I know enough of Colombino's present mind to acquit him of gallantries.'

'That is the mischief.'

'The mischief?'

'Just God! Is it obscure? We know the real purpose of the Frenchman's presence in Siena.'

Petrucci understood. He laughed the suspicion to scorn. 'Colombino is pledged to us.'

'Reluctantly, you'll remember. His heart is not in it. We have his own word for that. Do you begin to suspect why? There might be more profit in other service.'

Petrucci frowned in displeasure. Their political rivalry apart, he cared little for Malavolti. 'Colombino is pledged to us,' he repeated, his tone significant.

'The Frenchman may bribe him to break the pledge.'

'He may try, you mean.'

'He may succeed. After all, a mercenary is a mercenary.'

'And therefore he need not have bound himself to us, although he is a Sienese. Having done so, that is the end of the matter. To break with us now would be a treason to the State, and Colombino is no traitor.'

'He is the son of one. These things run in the blood.'

But now Petrucci became angry, and showed it. 'Colombino is my friend. Who insults him, insults me. Will you remember that, Malavolti?'

'I'll remember it. Nevertheless, I'll keep a watch on him. The matter is too grave for assumptions. Where is Colombino wandering with the lady? And why does La Bourdonnaye remain so calmly indifferent of a disappearance that is in danger of rendering him ridiculous? Is there no clear inference? Has she not been deputed by her husband to do that which her husband hesitates to do openly himself? May it not even be that she is to ensnare the senses of our captain? Men who are not to be bribed by gold into dangerous paths will tread them, nevertheless, to pursue a yielding woman.'

Petrucci kept his temper by an effort. 'You began by saying that the matter is too grave for assumptions. What else do you offer me? I'll need a mind as foul as yours to heed you.'

He swung on his heel, and left Malavolti staring after him with a smile on his full lips and a frown at the base of his hawk nose.

Outside, on the balustraded terrace above the fair garden behind the Communal Palace, Colombino paced beside the little Countess. There was not even the warmth of a summer night to excuse their conduct, for autumn was now at hand, and the air was chilly. But Madame de La Bourdonnaye heeded this as little as the proprieties that must condemn her. Pacing there at his stalwart side she told him everything. And this without recklessness; for, as she pointed out, she accomplished two objects at one and the same time. She made herself safe with her husband by this apparent compliance with his orders, and she made herself safe with her honour and her conscience by this full revelation.

Colombino's speculations upon the French envoy's motives were at present stifled by concern for the lady. But when he began to express it, he found himself checked by her.

'Monsieur Colombo, I had a little comedy to play with you. Chance has helped me at least to play it honestly. That is all. I do not desire to be an object for your compassion.'

'I am an ambitious man, madame. I aspire to spurs. I am impatient for them. Meanwhile, I do what I can to practise the virtues of chivalry.'

'If I had not perceived that, monsieur, I should never have employed such frankness with you. I thank you from my heart for your courtesy and patience. I shall remember them... and you. Now, let us go back.'

'I will ask you to remember also that if yet you should need me, I am ready. Here is my pledge of it.'

He took her right hand from where it hung beside her, raised it, and pressed his lips to the bruised wrist.

The tears mounted to her eyes, the tenderest of smiles parted her sensitive lips as she looked down upon his bowed head, the thick, tawny hair of it confined in a caul whose little jewels sparkled faintly in the moonlight.

Curious glances met their return to the brilliantly lighted hall, from the searching gaze of La Bourdonnaye to the disdainful smile of Caterina Squillanti. The insolent beauty opened her mind to Silvio Pecci, who hovered as usual about her.

'A timid mouse of a woman, to behold her. Yet from lewdness borrowing courage to hunt a lion. There's no virtue in any Frenchwoman.'

Silvio giggled. 'And no taste, it seems.'

The young marchioness looked him over with raised brows. 'Why, Silvio, what's amiss with Colombino? He's too fine a man to waste himself on such a ninny.'

'You say it but to vex me,' lisped the fribble. 'He has height and thews; he needs them in his trade. But a helot, standing for hire, an upstart, dissembling in arrogance a natural coarseness, and reeking of the stables.' Fastidiously he waved a pomander ball before his nostrils, as if imagination evoked the offending smell. 'Not a man whom my heavenly, fastidious Caterina should describe as fine.'

She curled her insolent lip.

'Are you afraid I'll give you cause for jealousy?'

'Always. It is my haunting dread. But not where that swaggering captain is concerned. He is well enough for Frenchwomen. I wish the Countess joy of him.'

Monsieur de La Bourdonnaye wished not quite so much. Back in the Salimbeni Palace that night he took his lady sharply to task.

'It was illusion I desired of you, madame. Not reality. You and that Sienese springald between you have all but made a mock of me.'

She shrank before the bitterness of his reproach. 'I did no more than you commanded.'

'Than I commanded? Must I forever curse the day I mated with a fool?'

Before his stupid injustice she was swept by a gust of almost ungovernable rage. The emotion because rare was the more violent. It lent her courage to answer him in scorn.

'If you conceive your honour touched, there is a ready way of healing it. I do not doubt that Messer Colombo will be ready and willing to give you satisfaction.'

This turned him livid. 'So! So! You do not doubt it, eh?' He came close, and dominated her by his bulk if not by his height, for she was almost as tall as he: 'What passed between you in the moonlight, ninny?'

Terrified, already in anticipation feeling the blow she feared, yet she gave her tortured soul the luxury of braving it. 'He kissed this bruised wrist of mine and told me to remember if in any need that he aspires to knighthood.'

She held out to him the hand he had maimed. For a moment, taken aback by her audacity, he stood glowering upon her; then suddenly he laughed, swung on his heel and left the room.

iii

Monsieur de La Bourdonnaye was content to leave the room when he did because, from what his Countess told him, he considered that his aim was achieved. The rest was comparatively no matter.

Three days he waited for what, it appeared to him, must be the inevitable sequel: for Colombino to come, like a moth to a candle, in quest of Madame la Comtesse.

Then, time being precious to him, his patience gave out. 'This Sienese cockerel is a half-hearted gallant for all his big talk, or else prudence makes him shy. A Frenchman in his place would have been here upon the morrow. But these Italians... Devil take me if I shall ever understand them. It was for my sins, I suppose, that I was sent to Italy.' He sat gloomily considering, glowering at his wife across the table at which they had just dined. 'Well?' he thundered suddenly. 'Have you nothing to say?'

She jumped. 'What...what can I say?'

'Oh, nothing. Nothing. But there's something you can do.' He had suddenly taken the resolve. 'You will pay our captain a visit today.'

'I?' She stared at him with dilating eyes.

'Do not be alarmed. I do not mean you to go unprotected. My presence shall curb his amorous fury. I have to talk to him. And since in spite of your allurements he will not come to us, why, we must go to him.'

'But if you are going, why do you require me?'

'Because, if I went alone, Siena would surmise what I do not want it to surmise. Your going will make the visit appear to be one of courtesy: a pleasure-trip to his vineyard.'

They set out a half-hour later, the Countess in a mule litter, with the leather curtains drawn back, so that all the world might behold her, the Count following on horseback, and followed in his turn by a couple of grooms.

A ragamuffin stretched at full length and fast asleep in a doorway opposite the Salimbeni Palace awakened suddenly just as the little procession turned the corner, and went padding after it.

By narrow streets sparsely tenanted in that post-prandial hour, the French party came to the Porta Tufi and the Convent of the Olivetani, and so out of the city. In the heat of the afternoon they toiled up the slopes of Montasco, swarming with peasants harvesting the grape, and came by fragrant orange groves and lemon groves at last to the four-square, rosy embattled house upon the heights.

In the courtyard, where men-at-arms kept guard as if the place were royal, grooms bestirred themselves to take charge of the horses.

Within the cool shadows of the marble-paved hail, a young chamberlain in black with a gold chain upon his breast despatched a page to announce these illustrious visitors.

Then to escort them into the august presence of the great condottiero came a corpulent, jovial fellow, splendidly dressed, whose black eyes twinkled merrily, who spoke French like a Gascon, and described himself as a Spanish captain in Messer Colombo's service.

It was all very impressive to the Frenchman; but most impressive of all, when at last they reached him in a setting made princely by all that Italian art could furnish, was Colombino himself. Very stately and handsome in a crimson houppelande that was embroidered with gold, the Captain welcomed them to Montasco with the airs of a prince. Protesting himself profoundly honoured by their visit, he bowed low over the hand of the pallid, rather breathless Countess.

An hour was wasted in compliments and courtesies and nothings, in which Don Pablo, whom Colombino had retained, bore a gay part. La Bourdonnaye began to grow impatient. The Spanish Captain's presence rendered confidential talk impossible. So La Bourdonnaye invented a sudden interest in viticulture, so very natural, after all, in a Frenchman, alluded to the industry he had observed in Messer Colombo's extensive vineyards, and begged his host to afford him the opportunity of surveying them at greater leisure. Madame was a little tired. It would be inconsiderate to drag her with them. Therefore, she had best remain indoors, with perhaps Don Pablo to entertain her.

With perfect understanding, and dissembling the dislike with which Monsieur de La Bourdonnaye inspired him, Colombino led him forth, across the courtyard, over the drawbridge to the terraced height, whence the vineyards were all in their full view.

But it was not of vines or viticulture that they talked. The Count began, in the French manner, with a world of compliments. He spoke of Monsieur Colombo's great feats of arms; of his universally recognized mastery of the art of war; of the magnificent organization and equipment of the Company of the Dove. He alluded almost in awe to Monsieur Colombo's defeat of the Venetian army before Ravenna, and protested eloquently the high esteem with which Monsieur Colombo was regarded by the King of France.

After these hors d'oeuvres he came to more substantial matters.

He would be frank. War was inevitable in Naples as soon as the winter was overpast, and the King of France would naturally support the Anjou claimant. Monsieur de La Bourdonnaye was in Italy to prepare the ground. From the Commune of Siena he could obtain no satisfaction; Petrucci, Piccolomini, Malavolti, and the other patricians all eluded him whenever he approached the subject. The inference was clear, and not surprising. The Pope's Holiness would be on the side of Aragon, and the Piccolomini influence in Siena would either bring the Republic into line with the Pope's wishes, or, at best, cause it to stand neutral.

It was, from his point of view, regrettable; but after all, once it came to war, what mattered was not political support, but troops and the man to lead them. Anjou, as Messer Colombo would have heard, had already enlisted Piccinino and his free company. If to this formidable support Anjou could add that of Colombo da Siena and the Company of the Dove, no anxieties touching the issue need then trouble them.

At this point Colombino interrupted the oration.

'I thank you for that compliment. But if you come to me with a proposal, you come too late, as I have had already the honour of informing you. I am pledged to Siena.'

'I know, I know, and the terms and the extent of it. But as I have already told you, a monthly retainer may be determined at the end of any month. Your patience, Monsieur Colombo. Hear, at least, what the King my master offers.'

He paused, standing squarely before Colombino, hand on hip, his big head thrown back on his short neck, and delivered himself impressively.

'The proposal is a year's engagement at a stipend of two hundred thousand ducats, and at the successful close of the campaign the fief of Benevento with the title of Count. There is an offer, my Lord Count of Benevento, that will set a crown to your career.'

Colombino's startled countenance was evidence of the impression made upon him by this dazzling proposal. Monsieur de La Bourdonnaye accounted all done but the signing. Then, to his infinite amazement and disgust, the soldier, recovering his calm, slowly shook his head.

'You do not overrate your master's munificence, my lord. And it profoundly flatters me. But I can but answer yet again that I am already pledged. Let us talk of it no more.'

La Bourdonnaye went white. His breathing quickened. 'Vertudieu! You cannot mean that upon a mere legal quibble you will refuse a greatness that rarely comes to a condottiero of twice your years?'

'A legal quibble?' Colombino laughed. 'Did you ever hear of Carmagnola, and how he fared at the hands of Venice in like case?'

'There is no parallel. That was treason.'

'It was never proved against him. There was no trial. They lured him away from the protection of his army, and took off his head. A political assassination. And here at home, in this very Siena of ours, we have the case of Gisberto da Correggio, a condottiero like myself, in the pay of the State. Presumed guilty of communication with the enemy, the Council sent him a courteous invitation to attend a conference. He went to it, unsuspecting and almost unattended. He was stabbed to death in the very council chamber by order of my friend Petrucci. That is the way in Italy with captains of fortune who do not observe the spirit as well as the letter of their engagements.'

'But if you fear…'

'No, no,' Colombino interrupted quickly. 'I do not say that, my lord. It would not be true. It is merely to show you what would happen if I were base enough to yield to the temptation of an offer of unparalleled munificence. My duty, Lord Count, as I conceive it, is to Siena, and from that duty I definitely tell you that I will not be turned.'

Monsieur de La Bourdonnaye was in despair. His head was no longer erect. It drooped, and he stood almost hangdog before his host. But one last effort he must make to secure at least something.

'I see that it would be idle to press you further into taking service with Anjou. But if you will not serve with us, will you, at least, not serve against us? Will you stand inactive during this campaign, pleading ill-health or what you will?' He went on quickly before Colombino could interject an answer. 'For this neutrality, if Anjou is victorious, you may still have Benevento and the countship. I am empowered to pledge the King of France to that.'

Colombino, tall and straight, and the very embodiment of young, athletic vigour, looked down upon him, smiling. 'Do I look sick? Do you suppose the Fifteen would be in any doubt upon the nature of my illness?' He took the Frenchman by the arm, and swung him round, so that they might retrace their steps. 'Lord Count, you shall not waste your time to tempt me further.'

By an effort Monsieur de La Bourdonnaye kept the signs of anger from his face and bearing. This failure, coming in the train of so many others that had marked his mission to Italy, was a bitterness he could not swallow.

'At least, sir, give thought to what I have said. My offer is not one to be lightly dismissed. Some way may open. Come to me soon in Siena, and we will talk again.'

But Colombino shook his head. 'It were best there should be no more visits between us, monsieur. Your journey to Montasco is scarcely prudent. Be sure the Fifteen will not be in ignorance of it, and Communes have been suspicious of captains of fortune ever since Gisberto da Correggio's business. They are very prone to act upon suspicion, and I care little for risks that are fruitless.'

So justified were these fears of his that he was not the only one

who at that very moment was alluding to Gisberto da Correggio. In
his house in Siena, Camillo Petrucci was listening to Malavolti, who
had brought Antonio Piccolomini to support him.

'They are all of one breed, these captains of fortune.' the patrician
was inveighing. 'Who seemed more deserving of trust than Gisberto
da Correggio? And in this Colombo I tell you now that we have
another Gisberto.'

'I'll need proof of that before I begin to believe you;' said
Petrucci.

'Isn't it proof enough that the French envoy is with him now at
Montasco? Why should Monsieur da La Bourdonnaye give himself so
much trouble?'

'It is certainly suspicious,' Piccolomini agreed. 'You'll admit so
much, Camillo.'

'I will not admit it. You yourself entertained La Bourdonnaye, and
you, Malavolti. Are you then both to lie under suspicion of conspiring
with France?'

'We are members of the Fifteen. Proper persons to be sought by
an ambassador. And to what end did he seek us? To seduce us into
declaring for Anjou. Isn't that what he has gone to do at Montasco?'

'Assume it so. What then? Did you succumb, Malavolti? Did you,
Antonio? Did any of us? Why, then, should Colombino? By what
right do you suppose it?'

'Because I know the breed, the corruptibility of these soldiers who
stand for hire. But there! You'll never heed a warning until it is too
late.'

'It would at least be prudent to keep his movements under
observation,' ventured Piccolomini, who stood fearing an explosion.

Petrucci shrugged wearily. 'Do so, by all means. But don't come
deafening me with your silly suspicions of a man whom I know to
be the very soul of loyalty.'

'Terrarossa's son!' said Malavolti, raising his eyes to Heaven.

Petrucci looked at him sternly. 'Terrarossa's son, as you say. I
would I could be as sure of your loyalty, Malavolti.'

The blood receded from that swarthy hawk face. Deep in the soul of this man, who accounted himself the first among the patricians of Siena, there had been dark stirrings of ambition. Under Petrucci's stern, challenging eyes he was asking himself now whether he had ever by incautious word or deed betrayed those still inchoate aspirations.

'You dare say that to me!' he blustered, his voice hoarse.

Then Piccolomini got between them. He took Malavolti by the arm.

'Come, come. In God's name! Will you two make a quarrel out of this? What's to do, we know. When we have something more than suspicion we'll seek you again, Camillo.'

'I shall have to wait through eternity,' Petrucci answered them as they departed.

iv

Monsieur da La Bourdonnaye came back to Siena in a vile humour, a deal of which he vented upon his wife.

His failure with Colombino, which seemed so definite and final, coming in the train of all the other failures he had made of his mission, meant that he must return empty-handed to France. The King his master would not be likely to heed explanations. That he had been unlucky would not excuse him. Those who serve kings must know how to control their luck. The Count saw nothing but disgrace ahead of him.

Bitterly he set the blame of this frustration upon his wife. She had been wanting, he told her, in allurement. Whilst by her conduct with Colombino she had made her husband ridiculous in the eyes of the Sienese as a potential cuckold, yet she had not known how to render it effective. A woman of ingenuity, with half the parade of wantonness that she had made, could so have enslaved the senses of this young man that he would have become the creature of her will. He concluded by desiring to be informed what good she was in life and by his usual complaint that he was cursed for having mated with a fool.

She suffered these infamous upbraidings in a stony silence, her soul sick to death within her. One day, she knew, her senses would burst from so much repression and she would go mad. Until then she must bear this rough and heavy cross as best she could.

'It is the end,' he announced. 'I have failed here, just as, thanks to you, I fail everywhere. If I were a coward I should not return to France. For God alone knows what the King will have to say to me. Anyway, in Siena there is no more to be done. We had best pack and quit.'

He was moving towards the door as he spoke. On the threshold he paused to turn and gloom upon her where she sat, awaiting some retort that should justify a further indulgence of his wicked humour. None coming from that white-faced, suffering woman, he stamped out.

But it was not yet the end, as he had protested. Whilst his servants packed, he brooded, cursing Colombino, whom, next to his Countess, he now regarded as the chief author of his ills. If the fellow would not serve Anjou, at least he might have consented not to serve against Anjou. It was his refusal to stand neutral which weighted the scales too heavily in Aragon's favour – for Monsieur de La Bourdonnaye had no longer any doubt that Siena, following the Holy Father's lead, would ultimately resolve to range her forces on the side of Aragon. Neutrality was not much to have solicited, and great was the price he had offered for it. Yet this upstart captain of fortune had flouted him with a refusal, had almost laughed at his offer.

Into his brooding came an inspiration that ripped the blackness of it like a flash of lightning.

If Colombino's service could not be enforced, his neutrality most certainly could be. Quite simply. In one way or another he could be removed.

His company remained, a company which, with its auxiliaries, Monsieur de La Bourdonnaye had carefully informed himself, was now no less than four thousand strong. But, however numerous or powerful, it remained an inert mass without the guiding mind of Colombino. Nor was that all, as the Frenchman saw the matter. It was long odds that once Colombino were removed, he would be succeeded in the command of the Company of the Dove by one of his present lieutenants; and with them it should be easy to make terms. Sangiorgio was a Florentine, Caliente a Spaniard; so that neither would be bound by sentimental ties to Siena, and neither would consider himself under the engagement to the Republic into which Colombino had entered.

His hopes began to rise again from their nadir. He slept upon the notion, nor moved to act upon it until the following afternoon, by when he had considered in detail what was to be done.

More than ever now he needed the collaboration of his Countess. To secure it he sought her, and found her idling listlessly alone in the long room of the mezzanine. He came to stand over her where she sat, and for a long moment silently considered her with his contemptuous, dominating glance. When at last he spoke it was on a sneering note.

'What did you tell me that our captain said to you that night when he slobbered on your wrist? Was it not that in your need you should remember that he aspires to knighthood? Was it not?'

'It was,' she breathed.

'Well, well. Your need is now. You shall send word of it to this mirror of chivalry.'

She raised a white face from which weariness and misery had almost crushed the last vestige of beauty. 'I? Send him word?'

'It is what I said. Do you add deafness now to your other infirmities?'

She strove for calm under his hateful smile.

'What is the purpose of this? What are you intending?'

He laughed. 'Are we alarmed for our ardent knight, our flaming champion?' Then, lest his mockery should provoke obstinacy and so give him trouble, he changed his tone. 'No need for any fears. There is no harm intended him. No abiding harm. Listen, Valérie.' He drew up a chair and sat down before her, his knees almost touching hers.

'Listen carefully.

'We start at daybreak for Leghorn, where a ship is waiting to take us back to France. If I am not to return under a cloud of failure, to face the anger of the King, disgrace, and God knows what else, something must be done. You will realize that. What I can do is little enough when compared with what the King expects of me. But still it is something. It will save me from returning quite empty-handed. If I cannot bring Colombo into the service of Anjou, at least I can prevent his going into the service of Aragon.' He leaned forward, and set a hand impressively upon her knee. 'Let a message from you fetch him here tonight, and he goes with us to France.'

She would have risen then. But the pressure of his hand upon her knee restrained her.

'How does he go? How?'

'How?' He was leering again. 'Have you no arts to draw him? Do you not know how to beckon so that he would follow you to the ends of the earth?'

'You know that he would not. Why do you mock me with this?'

'If he be, indeed, so insensible to your beckoning, as your husband I must naturally resent that insensibility. I must compel by force what you could not induce by sweetness. All that I need of you is a message that will bring him here tonight.'

'You mean to ruin him, then?'

He shrugged. 'In the pass to which things have come, it is his ruin or mine. Naturally I prefer that it be his. Perhaps you don't agree with me. But that's no matter.'

An odd courage of defiance rose in her. 'Why should I agree with you? Messer Colombo has never harmed me.'

From his expression she thought that he was going to strike her. But he curbed himself. 'Ah! I shall remember that. I treasure up these words of yours, madame. One fine day there will be a reckoning.' He pushed back his chair, and rose, peremptory. 'Meanwhile, the letter.'

He strode away to a writing-pulpit set in the light of the window, beside a tall screen of brown leather heavy with golden arabesques.

He pulled open a drawer, and took from it writing-materials: some sheets of parchment, an ink-horn, a pounce-box, wax, silk, quills and a sharp, slender knife for trimming them.

'Come, madame.'

But as, although she had risen, she still stood hesitating, he raised his voice. 'Pâques Dieu! Will you come, or must I fetch you?'

Despising herself for yielding, she crossed the room with dragging feet, and sank into the chair he had set for her.

He patted her shoulder now with that false cajoling tenderness, more detestable to her than his roughness.

'Come, come, Valérie. You must help me in my need; for your own sake as much as for mine.' He thrust a quill into her hand. 'Now write,' and he dictated:

Messer Colombo – In dread peril and necessity I recall your treasured words that in my need I should remember that you aspire to knighthood. My need is now and terrible, else I should never venture upon this boldness. By the chivalry of your nature, by the knighthood of your aspirations, I implore you to come to me at the fourth hour of night. We are leaving Siena. My husband has already departed ahead of me for the coast, otherwise I could not avail myself of the only help I know in all the world. Come alone and in secret, informing none. Unless you do this, then it were best for my honour's sake that you do not come at all. I send you the key of the garden gate. That way you will not be seen. I shall be waiting for you in the garden.

He placed a key upon the pulpit as he ended. 'Fold that into the letter. But first, sign. Sign your full name.'

So far she had mechanically obeyed him, sobbing at intervals in fear and grief; and he had smiled to see the irregular, straggling hand, conceiving what colour this would add to the tale the letter told of a woman writing in terror. But now, under his command to sign, a sudden unconquerable repugnance assailed her. Nothing should make her set her name to this piece of treachery that was to lead to his destruction, perhaps to his death, a man who had used her with an unselfish tenderness. No terror of this monster she had married should bring her to consummate that vileness. Contemptible had she been in writing a word of it. Rather should she have suffered death. Again one of those rare gusts of rebellious rage swept through her soul.

She flung down the quill, and rose, and in the very act of rising put forth her left hand to seize and crumple that treacherous sheet.

But as swift to guess her purpose as to thwart it, he caught her wrist. 'What now?'

She stood face to face with him, and his eyes were terrible. But they had lost the power to terrify. The martyr's spirit had entered into her.

'I will not sign. I will be no party to your infamy.'

He was standing with his shoulder to the leather screen, almost leaning against it. 'You will sign,' he said quietly. 'As there is a God in Heaven, you will sign.' But if his voice was quiet, the rage of him found expression in his hand. Again, as once before of late, it seemed to her that bone and sinew of her delicate wrist were being crushed to pulp. She swayed, half-swooning from the pain of it, and he smiled cruelly in her eyes. 'Now sit again, and sign,' he said with the quiet, mocking assurance of one who knows that resistance is at an end.

Her left wrist in his grip, her eyes, oddly glazed, staring into his, her right hand groped upon the pulpit, as he supposed, for the quill, and his smile grew broader, his grip began to relax.

v

That letter came to Colombino at Montasco just as dusk was falling. It disturbed him profoundly.

Little more than an hour ago Sangiorgio had ridden in from Siena with an account of ugly rumours current there.

'It is being said that you have sold yourself to the French; that, in spite of your engagement by the Fifteen, you will be found if war comes on the side of Anjou. It is not nice. In a tavern by Sant' Ovile I broke the jaw of a man who said that you are another Gisberto da Correggio. He'll utter no more lies for a month or two.'

Colombino stared at him. 'In God's name, why should they say this?'

'You have been too close with the French envoy is their explanation. He is known to have been seeking you here at Montasco. The foul minds of your fellow countrymen cannot suppose the visit innocent.'

Colombino thought of his father, and fetched a sigh. Always because of the sins of his sire must he earn distrust. 'The Devil take rumour,' he laughed at last. 'Let it run until it chokes itself.'

'Ay, ay. But be discreet, child. Now that you know what it feeds on, do not harbour relations with this Frenchman.'

'It's not my intention, as I've already told him.'

And now, so close upon the heels of that, came this appeal from the Frenchman's lady. He pondered it awhile, then ordered his chamberlain to introduce the messenger, a lackey out of livery. He questioned him closely; but all that he elicited was that the fellow had the letter from the hand of the Countess with orders to ride hard, and that the Count had set out already for the coast, to take ship.

Colombino dismissed him, and considered further. He had misgivings. With rumour already accusing him, if it were known that he had gone secretly by night to seek Madame de La Bourdonnaye, not even her husband's absence might prevent his accusers from seeing in this thing done by stealth the proof of their suspicions. They would assume that the Countess was acting as her husband's deputy; that the Count's departure that same day was merely a strategic movement to mask his aims. Upon less evidence than this Gisberto da Correggio had been put to death. After all, knowing how La Bourdonnaye had once sought to use his wife, remembering the mood in which La Bourdonnaye had last left him, could he be sure that those assumptions would be utterly without foundation?

That on the one hand. On the other was his compassion for the Frenchman's ill-used lady. He remembered the bruised wrist. A vision of Samaritana rose before him. The desire to deserve of her an esteem which he might never earn because she would never know of those deserts, the knighthood of his aspirations to which the letter alluded, the chivalry to which he had erstwhile pledged himself, put it upon him not to set a possible danger to himself above the possible danger of the gentle lady who appealed to him for help.

In the end he called for his horse and his arms, and set out alone through the deepening night.

Thrice as he rode, he drew rein sharply to listen; for it seemed to him that there was too persistent an echo to his horse's hoofs, where he had never before observed an echo. Then he told himself that never before had he had occasion to observe it, for never before had he ridden alone this way in the dead of night. And yet the sense that he was being followed persisted.

At the Tufa Gate, which was closed when he reached it, his identity proved a sufficient passport. He left his sweating horse at the gatehouse, and went on afoot through the silent streets, to his destination. It was just upon the fourth hour, which is to say it wanted about an hour to midnight, as he entered the narrow lane that ran behind the Via Flavia.

The key fitted smoothly. The tall door in the garden wall swung noiselessly inwards. He entered, closed and locked the door again, and stood a moment listening among the shrubs. A footfall in the lane outside renewed in him that suspicion of a follower. Was the ever mistrustful Council already watching his movements as a result of those rumours which Sangiorgio had reported?

The question was swept from his mind by a movement near at hand. A shadow loomed beside him, a light hand touched his arm, and he heard in a trembling whisper the voice of Madame de La Bourdonnaye.

'God reward you for answering my prayer, Monsieur Colombo. Come with me.'

The house before them stood in darkness, save for a light from one of the windows of the mezzanine. But tapers were burning in the hall, to light them up the wide staircase. She led the way in silence. He followed closely. The stillness of the house was natural at an hour when all would be abed.

The long room of the mezzanine into which she ushered him was ablaze with light. Coming from the gloom, he was for a moment dazzled by it. Two golden candle-branches, in each of which burned a dozen tapers, stood upon the walnut table in mid-apartment. The illumination seemed to him absurdly excessive.

As she softly closed the door, he turned to face her. Instantly his heart smote him. Her cheeks were of a deathly pallor, her eyes swollen with weeping and set in dark stains which rendered very piteous their appeal. She shook so violently that she seemed scarcely able to stand, and there was a world of meaning in the pressure of her hand upon her heaving breast.

In a stride he was beside her.

'Calm, madame; calm, I beseech you. I am here to serve you, whatever be your need.'

And he was a figure to inspire confidence, his stalwart vigour stressed by his raiment. His hose was of brown leather and of brown leather was the close-fitting tunic buttoned to his very chin over a slender shirt of mail. He removed his dark blue cloak, and tossed it aside with his hat, as if making ready for whatever the emergency might demand.

'Tell me your need of me, madame.'

She attempted to speak. But her voice rattled hoarse and inarticulate. She made a beckoning movement, and dragged herself towards the writing-pulpit, he following, indeed, almost in step with her. Having reached the pulpit, she staggered aside to make room for him, waving him on, and pointing with her shaking hand to the space behind the tall leather screen.

Obediently he advanced, and then recoiled again. He turned his head to question her with startled eyes; then resolutely he stepped forward once more.

Behind the screen lay the Count de La Bourdonnaye, supine, at full length, a grin on his blue lips, whilst his glazed eyes stared up at the frescoed ceiling.

Colombino went down on one knee beside him and verified that he was quite dead. The breast of his doublet was soaked with blood, and from the left side a white, slender, ivory haft protruded. Colombino took it between finger and thumb, and drew it forth. From that haft sprang a blade, slender and sharp for the trimming of quills. It was quite short, yet long enough, as it appeared, to have reached the heart of Monsieur de La Bourdonnaye.

He stood up, and came out again into the open. Gravely he looked into the distraught face and tragic eyes of the Countess. Because she was swaying where she stood, supporting herself upon the back of the writing-chair, he went compassionately to set an arm about her shoulders. For a moment she nestled against him, shuddering and sobbing; then, at once conducting and supporting her, he led her away and set her in a tall armchair that stood by the table. On the table's edge he perched himself, so that he immediately faced her. He addressed her calmly in the hope of inducing calm.

'Compose yourself, madame. How did this happen? Tell me.'

The question that she asked him supplied the answer.

'What do they do in Italy to parricides? To women who kill their husbands? Do they send them to the fire?'

'So. You killed him,' said he, quietly as if the stabbing of husbands were the most ordinary of occurrences. 'Well, well, that need surprise no one who knew him, and his ways with you. There is your wrist, and... But what is this?' He had caught her left hand, and surveyed the evidence of a fresh brutality.

Forth now, in a voice broken at first by sobs, but gradually growing steadier, came the tale of that afternoon's events, to the point where, maddened by pain and by his brutal insistence, her fingers idly groping on the pulpit had closed upon that frail pen-knife. Scarcely knowing what she did, acting upon wild impulse, she had plunged it into his breast. She had not meant to kill. She had not meant anything. She was, she explained piteously, a desperate, agonized creature without intelligence, acting upon blind instinct.

He soothed her. He stroked her arm and then her little dark head, as a brother or a father might have done, and so at last encouraged her to continue.

'He fell there where he lies, behind that screen. I sat in terror at the pulpit, and so I must have sat for a full hour before I realized that he was dead, expecting him at every moment to rise up and kill me. Then a servant came in quest of him. I told him that my lord was from home, that he had gone out alone and might not return for a day or two. I scarcely knew what I was saying.

'After that my wits began to work again. I understood, and I was spurred on by a new dread. The treacherous letter he had made me write lay there before me. I realized that the lying need of which it spoke had suddenly become the truth; that chance had made you my only friend in Siena; and that my only hope lay now in your chivalry.

'And so, at last, I signed the letter, and despatched it: the letter he had dictated. Little he thought in what circumstances his words were to be used to summon you, or that the events would make true the lies he compelled me to set down.' A shiver ran through her. 'Oh, my God! My God!' She clutched his arm with both her hands, and again came that fearful question: 'What do they do to such women? How do they punish such crimes in Italy?'

'Crime?' he echoed. 'Child, this is no crime.'

'Not in your eyes, who know. But who else will believe my tale? Monsieur Colombo, help me. I implore you. In the sweet name of Mary the Mother. I have endured so much. My life has been so sad and ugly. Let me go end my days in a convent. But do not let...'

He was on his feet, at her side again, his arm once more about her shoulders, drawing her against his flank. 'Hush! Hush! There is nothing to fear. Nothing. Give me but time to think. Let me consider well what is to do. But comfort you, meanwhile. I shall find a way. Be sure I shall find a way.'

When, however, he came to give it thought as he paced to and fro, his chin upon his breast, he discovered a weakening of the confidence with which he had sought to inspire faith in her. And meanwhile she sat huddled in her tall chair, following him with eyes of hungry, piteous hope.

Thus until a loud knocking below, reverberating through the silent house, came to startle them both. She came to her feet, only to sink down again, limp and terrified.

The knocking continued, more peremptory and accompanied by shouts of command, until hastily aroused servants went to open.

Thereafter the house grew full of sound: the stamp of feet, the clank of arms, the clamour of voices. It came surging up the staircase like a tide, and broke violently into the long room of the mezzanine.

The invasion was headed by Malavolti, with, at his heels, the lean, austere Petrucci, the grizzled Piccolomini, and the elderly florid Marquis Squillanti. After these came three other members of the Council, and behind these again a half-dozen men-at-arms in steel caps and corselets.

Their eyes swept negligently over the woman, crouching terror-stricken in her chair, and settled upon Colombo, who stood beside her, straight as a lance, his tawny head bare, his glance arrogantly questioning, his hand by instinct on the hilt of his heavy dagger.

The sight of him seemed to give them pause. He had the impression as of a gasping recoil in them, and he was vividly conscious of the dismay and sorrow that overspread the ascetic countenance of Camillo. Then it was to Camillo that Malavolti turned, and what he said was merely the ruthless expression of what was in the minds of all of them.

'Now, my doubting Thomas, let your eyes assure you. There he stands, caught in his treachery; another Correggio, selling his country and his masters; another Judas. Do you need more proof?'

Petrucci stood dumb and stricken, whilst from the others came snarling execration to an ominous accompaniment of the soft, tinkling slither of weapons plucked from their scabbards. A movement towards Colombino was already beginning when he checked it by his question.

'Will you tell me what this means, my masters?'

Petrucci roused himself to answer him, at the same time flinging out an arm like a barrier to restrain the others. There were undertones of anger in the sorrow of his voice, a reflection of scorn in the sadness of his eyes.

'It is rather for you to explain your presence here, Colombino, at dead midnight, having come in secret and alone, slinking in by the garden gate with the key that was sent to you.'

'You set a watch upon me, do you?'

'It had become necessary in the view of some. I was not of those. I was too foolishly trusting, persuaded that your loyalty would be proof against any bribe that might be offered.'

'You see,' said Malavolti. 'It was in our knowledge that bribes were being offered. This very day we intercepted a letter from the King of France to his envoy here, urging him at need to increase the price he was to pay you. It is idle to protest. We but waste words.' And his glance eloquently invited action.

But again Colombino contrived to stay them, and this time by a laugh. 'I see. I see. And so, you poor witlings, you men of little faith and less intelligence, to you proof that a bribe was offered is proof that I accepted it. You reason like statesmen, as God lives.'

Squillanti, heavy and massive, took a hand. 'And your presence here, is that proof of nothing? The manner of your coming? Does that look like honesty? Does a man with nothing to conceal enter a house like a thief in the night?'

And Malavolti added: 'Will you quibble in the face of death, you lying traitor?'

The mutter behind him became an uproar. 'Enough words! Let him go the way of Correggio!'

'A little patience, sirs,' Colombino begged them. 'You've all night in which to murder me. But you had better hear something from me first, rather than discover it for yourselves afterwards, or you may be following me down to Hell rather sooner than you think.

'It is quite true that I came here secretly; like a thief in the night, as you say, Squillanti. Quite true that I came to hear what the King of France might have to propose to me.'

'You give us news,' sneered Malavolti fiercely.

'I think I shall do. News of how I answered.'

'Are we to take your word for that?' demanded Piccolomini.

'Not unsupported. I can supply some evidence. Look for yourselves.'

He stepped quickly back, pulled away the screen, and let it crash forward flat upon the floor.

They stood at gaze, aghast, and their very breathing seemed suspended.

After a moment Colombino spoke again.

'For any man who hurt my honour with assumptions that I could be seduced from my pledged allegiance, what other answer could there be but this?'

They sucked in their breaths again. Their awe of the deed was transmuted into awe of the doer. There was a shuffling stir amongst them, and suddenly Colombino found himself gripped in Petrucci's arms.

'That I should have doubted!' was Camillo's penitent cry. 'That I should have let myself so easily be persuaded! You may forgive me, Colombino; but I never shall forgive myself.'

'On my soul,' Squillanti was growling, 'that is my case, too.'

'And mine,' said Piccolomini.

Malavolti stood shamefaced. 'I am the worst offender of all. I confess it frankly. My wits have led me astray. But there's an amend to make, and it's for all of us to make it: to stand as a bulwark between Colombo and the wrath of France at his noble, this truly Roman answer to a seducer.'

They were loudly swearing it, swarming about him, heaping blessings on his name, when at last he drew their attention to the Countess, still crouching there, white-faced and terrified, scarcely believing yet that the lightning by which she had thought to be blasted had been deflected.

They fell silent then and grew ashamed of their heartless boisterousness in the presence of the widow. Malavolti waved away the men-at-arms. Then with his brother patricians he bowed low to her, very solemnly, and with them departed.

Colombino lingered still when all had gone. He had still a word to say to the Countess. Her very action now showed him how necessary it was. For whilst their steps were still upon the stairs, the murmur of their muted voices in the air, she suddenly rose and came with sobs to cast herself at his feet, to seize his hand and bear it to her lips.

'What do I not owe you? What do I not owe you?' she was wailing.

He took her by the arms, and drew her gently up. 'I see that you have not understood. What I did was to save myself as well as you.'

She shook her distracted head. 'If I had not sent for you, you would have been in no such need. Every night of my life I shall thank God that I did, and for what you did. Every night I shall pray for you. What else have I with which to repay you but my prayers?'

'It is very noble payment, madame; far greater than the deed deserves. But this remains, madame. Listen. You will be departing now to France. I must not see you again before you go. I must not linger even now. For in the eyes of those men it remains that I am the slayer of your husband. And any relations of mine with his widow must hurt either her honour or the belief in which those men have taken their leave. Therefore, I can do no more, and I can stay no longer.'

'I understand,' she said. 'I understand.' But her eyes were full of sorrowful bewilderment.

He released the arms he held, and took her hands. 'God guard you, madame, and bring you yet to happiness.'

Then, as he stooped to bear her hands to his lips, she snatched them away, took his tawny head between them, and kissed him on the mouth.

Afterwards he was wont to say: 'I had my knighthood from Ferdinand of Aragon, and it was the Queen of Naples who buckled on my spurs. But it was the kiss of Madame de La Bourdonnaye that bestowed upon me the knightly accolade.'

Chapter 6

THE LADY OF CANTALUPO

i

The history books will tell you that Monsieur le Comte de La Bourdonnaye died of an apoplexy. That is what Siena was told and France believed, since his widow confirmed the tale on her return.

In Colombino's career that death marks a definite step and is directly responsible for all that followed, so molelike is the burrowing of Destiny to her ends. What an ordinary faith in an ordinary loyalty would not have earned him was earned him by the reaction of the Fifteen from their mistrust. In his loyalty, had they never believed him disloyal, they would have seen no more than the commonest duty which he owed the State. As it was, they came to regard him as steel that has been tested in the furnace, and they so magnified him that when the buds were breaking in the following spring and the rumblings of war at last exploded, nothing would content them but that he should be given the supreme command, appointed Captain-General of the allied forces of the Pope and the Sienese which were ranged on the side of Ferdinand of Aragon.

The Marquis Squillanti, a soldier of experience who had been Gonfalonier of Holy Church, had some claims to that exalted office, and might, through the Holy Father, have swayed the Piccolomini and the Petrucci into admitting those claims now. But even he, under the general spell, waived his rights in favour of Colombino and consented to take service under him.

The appointment is said to have moved the scorn of Jacopo Piccinino, that famous rascally soldier-son of a famous rascally soldier-father, who commanded on the Angevin side. Boastingly he announced that it was clear the gods desired to destroy the House of Aragon. Not only was he in great force, having recruited heavily in the Cantons, but the King of France, it was known, was sending an army by sea to his support, so that presently his preponderance should be overwhelming. At once to facilitate his junction with this French force when it arrived, and to mark his contempt of his opponent, he chose to march south with his Swiss auxiliaries along the western seaboard, ready to deliver battle upon Roman soil whenever it should be offered.

Now whilst this march of Piccinino's across enemy country may have been marked by some violence and depredations, yet it had no quality of conquest or occupation. He would not waste his strength in the Pontifical States by attempting to reduce strongholds which he would have to garrison. Avoiding all minor engagements, and keeping to the plains, he moved steadily south, husbanding his resources for the conquest of Naples and for the battle which he would have to fight when Colombino at last decided, as Piccinino supposed that decide he must, to dispute his passage.

The odd thing was that Colombino showed no such inclination. He, too, was moving south, but parallel with Piccinino, and at a distance which he showed no disposition to diminish. Whilst Piccinino hugged the shore, and went unchallenged by Ostia and Ardea, Colombino kept beyond the hills, coming down by Arsoli and Subiaco, content through the eyes of his far-flung scouts to watch the progress of his adversary.

Soon it began to be said that Piccinino's unchecked advance could be explained only by hesitations on Colombino's part. Of what was he dreaming? If things continued thus, Piccinino would presently be playing havoc within Neapolitan frontiers, intimidating the barons into throwing in their lot with Anjou so as to avoid the destruction of their fiefs.

In Rome the Holy Father was blaming himself for having permitted the Sienese to over-persuade him in the matter of the supreme command. In Siena there was a growing dismay at the supineness of their chosen leader. In Naples, Ferdinand of Aragon grew apprehensive where hitherto his confidence had been buoyant. In general there was a free expression of the opinion that the greatly vaunted and hitherto fortunate Colombo da Siena was revealing the poverty of his mettle now that at last he found himself opposed to a really experienced soldier. Of the many who announced it in laughter, none laughed with greater relish than the lady of the Neapolitan fief of Cantalupo, a lady who once had been Countess of Rovieto.

Tagliavia, in his *History of His Own Times*, says of this Madonna Eufemia de' Santi whom he opines might with greater propriety have been named Eufemia dei Diavoli – that she was perhaps the sweetest morsel ever used by Satan to bait a hook for man's perdition. Considering the delicate, winsome beauty Antonello da Messina painted – in the picture that already has been mentioned – you feel that here was a lady who must have drawn most men to be her slaves, be it by awakening the chivalry of some, or by arousing the less exalted emotions of others.

It may be that such women are the victims of greater temptations than their less favoured sisters. It may be that the evidences time brings them of their power lures them irresistibly to abuses of it. In this may lie all the secret of the frailty which Tagliavia discovers beneath the saintly aspect of Madonna Eufemia.

We have seen of what vindictiveness was capable this lady who without consciousness of duty was overconscious of her rights. We know what was her resentment of Colombino's just indignation and withdrawal from her service. That she had abundantly provoked it weighed for nothing with her. In regarding it as a treachery, she was possibly sincere. And that resentment festered in her. It festered the more as she saw this detested man pass so easily from strength to strength until he stood acknowledged the first captain in Italy. It put a climax to her rage to hear of his appointment as Captain-General of the forces of Ferdinand of Aragon. The greater, therefore, was her exultant relief when already the initial stages of the campaign were revealing that he had accepted a burden to which his shoulders were unequal. And this notwithstanding that the man she had now married held his fief from the House of Aragon and was therefore heart and soul on the side of King Ferdinand.

He was a septuagenarian, no less, this Marquis of Cantalupo, this Lord Amedeo degli Amedei, who had taken to wife a woman not yet thirty. It was in Florence, six months ago, that he had come under the spell of her enchantments, and had cast away the prudence with which through seventy years of life he had been equipping himself. He ignored the slurs unkindly rumour set upon her fair name, was deaf to the implication that she possessed arts of ensuring widowhood when her capricious nature began to find a husband tiresome, and that an old man of seventy was not likely long to be tolerable to her lively, ardent nature.

The truth, if that old gossip Tagliavia, is to be believed, is that she found him scarcely tolerable when she led him to the altar. But whilst she might have commanded all the lovers that her heart could desire, it was not likely, that being a little tarnished, she could easily have commanded another husband who, like Cantalupo, would raise her again to the high estate from which she had fallen when the Scaligeri drove her out of Rovieto.

Less tolerable still did she find him when he disclosed his attitude upon the outbreak of war. Loving his ease and good cheer, and being of the opinion that he had reached an age at which a man is entitled to the peaceful enjoyment of these blessings, he decided, like many another Neapolitan baron, to hold aloof from the coming strife. She did not mince words. She had never learnt to do so. She described his attitude as pusillanimous. She would have him spend himself, his health and his gold, in raising men so as to support the Anjou claimant, and this although his sympathies were avowedly with Aragon.

It was not that it mattered to her whether Anjou or Aragon ruled in Naples; but it mattered very much to her that all the odds should be piled upon the side against which Colombino fought, so that this insolent upstart should at last be overthrown.

The common talk that Colombo da Siena was obviously out-generalled, unable or unwilling to come to grips with the formidable Piccinino, brought her at last the dear assurance that there was no cause for her anxieties and that her fondest wishes were about to be fulfilled.

Even among Colombino's officers some murmurings began to make themselves heard, and at Segni, where the army lay one April night, under the shoulder of Lepini, whilst Piccinino was beyond that line of hills somewhere in the neighbourhood of Nettuno, Squillanti – urged to it, no doubt, by letters from Siena – came to reproach Colombino with his inaction.

Colombino received him in a room of the cottage which he had made his quarters. He heard him in silence. Then he spread a map upon the table.

'You are a soldier of great experience, Lord Marquis. Propound me a plan.'

Squillanti, with the facility and light-heartedness of the critic, propounded three in quick succession, blushing for each in turn when Colombino had demonstrated its unsoundness. After that he was disposed to sulk. He was a stolid man of a full, powerful habit of body, round of face with a small, pursed mouth and the bluest of eyes under dense black eyebrows. His hair was grey and he cropped it short. He was close upon fifty years of age, but very vigorous in spite of a slight lameness from a wound taken in one of his early campaigns.

'It is easy to find fault,' he grumbled.

'It is what I desired you to understand,' said Colombino.

'Yes, yes. But what plans have you?'

'None yet. But I have a hope. If that bears fruit, my plans will take shape of themselves. I have studied Piccinino's methods. He has one only strategy. I am making it easy for him to apply it.'

For the rest, he announced, he would not be urged or bullied. He would act in his own time and in his own way. He was in command, and the responsibility lay with none but himself. He would know how to discharge it.

When, however, on the very next day, a Sunday, his scouts brought word that Piccinino was marching south at speed, Squillanti's excitement was not to be curbed. Without ceremony he burst in upon the Captain-General who sat in council with Santafiora and Caliente. He raved that before night Piccinino would be at Terracina, on Neapolitan soil, that already it was too late to stop him.

'It is,' said Colombino. 'I agree with you in that.'

His calm was a goad to Squillanti's fury. 'The man has outwitted you!' he declared.

'It is what everyone will suppose. Expecially Piccinino.'

'Will they be wrong, sir? Will they be wrong?' The Marquis banged the table. 'Answer me.'

Colombino did not answer. He was listening to something other than the voice of Squillanti. A horse furiously ridden came to a rattling halt outside the cottage.

'That may be Nervo at last,' he said, his eyes on Santaflora.

The Florentine went to open, and an officer sprang in, and breathlessly delivered himself without preambles.

'He left Nettuno at peep of day.'

'Yes, yes. We've known that for some hours. But the galleys?'

'Galleys? What galleys?' interjected Squillanti.

'Four Papal galleys that Piccinino seized in Nettuno yesterday. Four light vessels of fifty oars. Well, Nervo?'

'Two of them have put to sea, one going straight out into the west, the other steering northwest. They were out of sight when I left. A third has gone forth, following the coast at a distance of a couple of leagues. The fourth is at anchor outside the bay, just off Point d' Anzio. One of Piccinino's officers is on each, and Bernardone is in command of the galley that has remained at anchor. Apart from their rowers each is very lightly manned, a score of men at most.'

Colombino nodded, musing. 'You are very well informed, Nervo.'

'I went down into Nettuno after they had left. There was no difficulty in gathering the information.'

'Anything else?'

'Nothing else, Sir Captain.'

'Excellent.' Colombino rose. 'It but remains to follow Piccinino, and as ostentatiously as possible. About it, sirs.'

Sangiorgio and Caliente went briskly out. Nervo, being dismissed, followed them. Squillanti lingered.

'There's no time to lose, my lord,' Colombino admonished him. 'We march within the hour.'

'Better late than never, I suppose,' the Marquis grumbled, since to this he could offer no objections.

But he had some objections to offer that same afternoon. For instead of marching down the valley where the going was direct and easy, Colombino sent his army toiling westward over the hills towards the sea, and rolled it down the slopes of Lepini as if marching on Nettuno, in full view of Bernardone's galley where it rode at anchor a mile or so from the shore.

'Do you do this so that Piccinino's captain may laugh at you?' wondered the irritated Squillanti.

'Will he laugh, do you suppose?'

'I can almost hear him.'

'Why, let him, then. It is the last laugh that counts, my lord.'

As after that they drove south, on the heels of Piccinino, Squillanti had no more to say until the morrow.

They had come by then to Terracina, and Colombino's scouts brought word that Piccinino stood before Gaeta. Sangiorgio, Caliente, and Squillanti were with the Captain-General. They made a mounted group on a green eminence whence they could look out over the sea smooth and sparkling in the April sunshine. Colombino, standing in his stirrups, shading his eyes with his hand, scanned the horizon on which the Pontine Islands were faintly visible. Beyond those and some brown-sailed fishing boats in the middle distance, there was nothing to be seen.

'We will take to the hills again,' he announced, and added in answer to Squillanti's stare, 'so as to afford them some more matter for laughter.'

The army, proceeding without haste, turned its back upon the sea, and moved inland once more, until by dusk they had come to the foot of the valley to the east of Mount Lepini, from which they had earlier emerged.

'Some day,' said Squillanti, 'I shall understand all this. I suppose that we are really making war, and not just strolling about in the hills to amuse ourselves.'

'We are not pausing here,' said Colombino.

'I feared we might be.'

'No, no. Sangiorgio will bivouac here tonight with a thousand men; a mixed force, horse and foot, pikemen and crossbowmen. From here, strictly maintaining the same distance between himself and Piccinino, he will move as Piccinino moves, but always keeping to the hills and woods, so that Piccinino shall not have cause to suspect that less than my entire army is moving with him.'

'And the army itself?' asked Squillanti.

The answer took away his breath, convinced that him Colombino's wits had left him. 'That army goes north again, to encamp at the spot we left yesterday morning, before we marched down to Nettuno.'

'But, by all the devils…'

Colombino interrupted him. 'I have told you that Piccinino has only one trick of strategy.' And to soothe Squillanti he now proceeded to explain it.

ii

In a day in which victories were seldom more than strategic, Piccinino was perhaps justified in crowing victory because having, as

185

he put it, eluded the forces of Colombino, he had crossed the border and had come to stand upon Neapolitan soil. And so that no doubt should remain in the public mind on the score of this victory, and also so that the temporizing Neapolitan barons should be brought to perceive where their interest lay, the little Perugian – Piccinino was a native of Perugia – in a manner worthy of the traditions inherited from his sire, seized several minor townships, and delivered them over to pillage and rapine by his mercenaries.

Secretly jubilant at these excellent beginnings of misfortune for Colombino, the Lady of Cantalupo found in the events an argument with which to whip her lord into declaring for Anjou. Cantalupo was an important fief and the influence of its Marquis was considerable. If he declared for Anjou, many other barons who stood waiting upon events would follow his example, and this defection from Aragon would further diminish Colombino's already very slender chances of recovery.

The difficulty lay in that Cantalupo was staunchly loyal to Aragon.

If the burly, phlegmatic, rather dull-witted Marquis could even listen patiently to his sweet lady's persuasions, it was only because of a fond reluctance to offer opposition to any whim of hers. Like most elderly men in his case, he was of a doting uxoriousness. By submission to her every caprice, he sought to make amends for all that age and increasing infirmities compelled him to deny her ardent temperament. Indulgence of her present caprice was, however, a thought too dangerous even for his uxoriousness. But whilst unswervingly determined to hold by King Ferdinand, he could not, he dared not, give that determination utterance. He took refuge from her displeasure in a display of temporizing. Before declaring himself against the House of Aragon and his vassalage, he preferred, he protested, to wait and see what shape affairs assumed.

'You'll wait too long,' she warned him, and he winced at the tartness of her voice. 'Will you wait until Piccinino is before your walls?'

He was a large, gross, jovial fellow, bald and florid, who, as I have said, loved good cheer and laughter. He advertised these predilections in his guffawed reply.

'If so, I shall not wait an instant longer.'

He pulled her with good-natured roughness to his massive knee, and chuckled as he fondled this slight, lovely object of his worship, who might still have seemed a child to a much younger man than Cantalupo.

'You treat me lightly,' she complained. 'And I deal with serious matters. Let me go.' She struggled with him. But he held her in a hug that was like that of a bear, and kissed her resoundingly, however much she might seek to strain away from him.

'Will you sulk and frown because I'm not such a fool as to make rash engagements? It may not be very noble in me; but believe me, it is very prudent. One of the lessons age teaches is that prudence is better than nobility. The first is a necessity in this world; the second a mere adornment.'

'That is a hateful creed,' she condemned him.

'Maybe, child. Maybe.' He chuckled again. 'But it makes for your security as well as mine. Be thankful then.'

'That I've mated with a coward?'

'Coward! Pshaw! Words break no bones, child. Kiss me, and let us change the subject.'

'I tell you this is serious. When Piccinino stands before your walls, where then will be my security?'

'Piccinino! Pooh! He's a long way off. At Benevento, and not likely to move northward. So long as we don't invite trouble, our peace here isn't likely to be disturbed. The war will be fought out round Naples.'

This was her cue; this, and his earlier cynical assertion that if Piccinino were to appear before his walls he would not wait an instant longer to declare himself. She perceived, she thought, how she might force his hand.

That same night she wrote a letter to the Angevin commander, inviting him to come to Cantalupo. The Marquis, she explained, was utterly devoted to the House of Anjou, but he needed a pretext to declare himself. His so declaring himself must result in materially strengthening the cause by ensuring the adherence to it of many who now hesitated. Therefore, so that Cantalupo might save his face, she urged Messer Piccinino to make the necessary demonstration in force.

Next morning, in the town, she found a messenger secretly and swiftly to bear that letter to the Angevin captain in his camp at Benevento.

No answer could have been more prompt. Four days later Piccinino appeared before Cantalupo with a detachment of a thousand helmets, having left his camp and the main body of his army in the charge of his Lombard Captain Castrocaro.

The news of his approach filled the old Marquis with alarm. He remembered the brutalities perpetrated elsewhere by Piccinino's soldiery. There proved, however, to be no cause for his fears. Piccinino's lances rode in orderly fashion up the main street of the little township to the massive grey castle above, as if assured of welcome there.

With a dull anger in his heart, and taking bitter shame in secret at the extent to which he was practising his philosophy of preferring prudence to nobility, the Marquis left his drawbridge lowered and his gates wide, and waited bareheaded in the courtyard, his winsome lady beside him, to give courteous welcome to the soldiers of Anjou.

Amid all his secret chagrin, he had at least the satisfaction of perceiving that he ensured the immunity of his fief from damage. For when quarters had been found for the troops, a stern injunction to them was issued by their leader to be orderly in their behaviour.

For Piccinino himself and a couple of officers in immediate attendance upon him, the best rooms in the castle were instantly made ready.

The Marquis, pursuing his detested rôle, exerted himself ingratiatingly to entertain his unwelcome guest. In this he was supported by his lady with an affability which at first he assumed to be as entirely counterfeit as his own, but which within a day or two he perceived to be entirely real. This perception went to increase his resentment of Piccinino's presence and his detestation of the condottiero, about whom, when all is said, there was little that was engaging.

Like his father before him, who, as the name implies, had been a little man, Piccinino was short, bow-legged and sturdy, a coarsely featured, hairy fellow, with the speech and manners of a stable-boy. In this uncouth exterior, however, Madonna Eufemia's fastidious daintiness seemed to perceive nothing repellent. She fawned upon the soldier almost from the hour of his arrival.

On his first night at Cantalupo, whilst they sat at table after supper, she fell to praising the astuteness with which he had given Colombino the slip and crossed the Neapolitan border; she even lauded the policy of atrocities by which he had struck terror into the temporizing barons; and generally she expressed an unstinting admiration of his shining soldierly qualities and a firm confidence in the ultimate triumph awaiting the Angevin arms under so able a leadership.

The Marquis listened to all this, writhing in secret torment, a false frozen grin upon his lips, whilst Piccinino, deprecating the praise in a manner which yet accepted it as no less than his due, preened himself under the discernment of this exquisite lady. They spoke of Colombo da Siena. Madonna was of the confident opinion that the knell of his fame was already sounding.

Piccinino was contemptuous in his agreement. 'What is this fame of his? A bubble blown by insolent fortune.'

'Indeed, indeed! In the past he has enjoyed easy successes, only because he has never yet been face to face with a real soldier. Now that in you, Ser Jacopo, he meets a master of the art of war, he falters and stumbles in the very first steps of the campaign. And he will go on faltering and stumbling. For I have cause to know that under his swaggering exterior, this impudent upstart carries a heart as craven as it is treacherous. The triumph that awaits you, Ser Jacopo, is scarcely worthy of your splendid prowess.'

Whilst the Marquis suffered a spasm of nausea at the grossness of the flattery, Ser Jacopo bowed, intoxicated. Then, turning to his host, he cast over his swagger some lingering rags of modesty.

'Your reception of me at Cantalupo, my lord, will have done a deal to smooth my path. In declaring so stoutly against the Aragon bastard, you have set an example which every cravenly hesitating Neopolitan baron will be sure to follow.'

The Marquis grunted agreement with a fact that was a torment to his soul. Then he eased himself of some of his secret spite.

'Yet, sir, I almost wonder whether to ensure this, it could be worth your while to leave your camp and come to Cantalupo. As a consequence, you might easily lose more than you are gaining.'

Piccinino's black brows came together in a frown. 'I take your meaning. But...' He curled his lip and tossed up his stumpy hands in a gesture of contempt. 'I am but two days from Benevento. And I have time to spare until the landing of the French.' And now, as he proceeded, he disclosed his aims, disclosed that stroke of strategy – the only stroke in his repertory, according to Colombino – by which he counted upon annihilating the enemy. Vainglory, and the desire dazzlingly to display himself under the stimulating eyes of Madonna Eufemia, were responsible for the disclosure. 'When I set out to march south along the seaboard, I had no other object than to be at hand to receive the French reinforcements. To await them, I would have halted at Nettuno or Terracina, or between the two, if that timid fool Colombo da Siena had not supplied me with the opportunity so to dispose that at a blow I can bring this campaign to an end. I took the chance to slip past him, and cross the border. But from Nettuno I have flung my scouts in galleys out to sea, to meet and inform the French of this, and to bring their army to land at Nettuno, or thereabouts. When that happens, I will turn, and it will then be found that Messer Colombo's army lies between those troops and mine like a nut ready to be cracked between two stones. Unless his compatriot Saint Catherine works a miracle for him, Ser Colombo will then realize the mistake he made when he suffered me unchecked to cross the border.' He laughed, and Madonna Eufemia laughed

with him, and clapped her slim white hands like an excited child.
'Battles, sir,' the condottiero ended, stabbing the table with his
knotty forefinger, 'are won by positions. And so well placed am I that
this battle yet to be fought is won already. Meanwhile, I can wait at
my ease. And my ease could nowhere be better served than here. So
here, by Bacchus, I'll wait for word of the French landing, in grateful
enjoyment of your bounteous hospitality.'

He raised his cup to pledge them; but it was to Madonna Eufemia,
rather than to her lord, that he had addressed his closing words. And
whilst Cantalupo's jaws were set in unobserved disgust, his lady
answered for him.

'And here, sir, you have loyal, cordial friends, who will be at pains
to beguile the tedium of your waiting.'

This was his cue for an impudent gallantry which the presence of
her old husband was powerless to repress in him.

'In your presence, madonna, tedium beguiles itself; or rather,
tedium can have no place.'

He had, you see, pretensions to gallantry, this Piccinino,
notwithstanding his bow-legged clumsiness, and he had not been
slow to perceive in the Lady Eufemia an object worthy of its exertion.
So sweet and frail she appeared to him, and so virginal, despite the
fact that she was now in her third nuptials, and so subtly did she
seem to beckon him that quite early in his sojourn at Cantalupo that
rascally little mercenary found himself in an infatuation.

To the Marquis he gave little thought, and this little was
contemptuous. He took the view that when a senile dotard marries
a young wife, he must be prepared for the consequences of his
presumption; and this view he was at no pains to dissemble. He
would loiter in the evening with the lady upon the ramparts, taking
the air which to any but lovers would have seemed chill, for the
weather had turned cool again in those mid-April days.

Cantalupo, observing this flagrant courtship of his wife by this
ruffian, and his wife's wanton acceptance of that courtship, accounted
himself bitterly punished for a defection to Anjou which it had not
been in his unfortunate power to avoid, and which he could no

191

longer mend. But, at least, he departed from his fond uxoriousness. In remonstrating with her, he no longer humoured her. He was uncompromisingly stern. Yet not on that account did he prevail. He merely aroused impatience in her and a cruel insolence.

'Are you in case to defend me from him? He has a thousand men at his back, and here in Cantalupo he is master. You are stupidly tiresome in your reproaches. Will you accept the consequences if I openly rebuff him?'

'Gladly. As Heaven is my witness!' With that oath, he fell to pleading again. He implored her to remember at once his honour and her own dignity, and not to suffer the insult of this coarse clown's advances.

At this she tossed her golden head. 'I do not perceive the insult. He uses me with all respect. You should remember that he would be a very dangerous man to thwart. And since for all your big words, I cannot depend upon you for protection, I must use such arts as I possess to keep him within reasonable limits. In short, sir,' she concluded, her nose in the air, 'like you, where your loyalty was concerned, I temporize, remembering your creed that prudence is better than nobility.'

At this the unfortunate Marquis raved in exasperation; and the lady with a tinkling laugh and a shrug for his tantrums, went off to render herself once more accessible to the condottiero. Nor in her temporizings, as she called them, was she even as circumspect as she would have her husband believe. When at the end of a week of skirmishing, Piccinino attempted to carry the lady by assault, she stayed him by an implied promise.

'First prove your worth, Ser Jacopo.'

'What proof will satisfy you, my beautiful?'

'The defeat and capture of this Colombo da Siena. When you shall have broken him, I shall refuse you nothing.'

Any man less smugly fatuous than Piccinino must have perceived here the secret of her wantonness: that it lay not in any love of himself, as he so fondly imagined, but in hate of Colombino. He was to be no more than the instrument of its gratification. In the wound which Piccinino's self-love had taken and the jealousy aroused in him by the swift rise to fame of the Sienese captain, she had espied her opportunity to square to the full her accounts with Colombino. In the stimulus which she thus applied to Piccinino, she became the stoutest alloy of Anjou.

'By the Eyes of God,' Piccinino swore, 'I'll lay him in bonds at your feet, so that you may do your pleasure with him.' And on the strength of that promise he advanced upon her and caught her in his hungry arms.

She was still struggling in his embrace when the Marquis came upon them. The spectacle turned him white. He rolled forward on his massive legs, dropped a heavy hand on the condottiero's shoulder, and faced him, his feet planted wide, his bald head shaking with passion. His voice was hoarse.

'You push your demands upon my hospitality somewhat far, Ser Jacopo.'

Piccinino's laugh blended sheepishness with insolence. 'What the devil! If you will lay such tempting viands before a guest, can you blame him for his appetite?' And on that he sauntered, swaggering, away.

Cantalupo, affronted to the very depths of his soul, burning to take that coarse mocker by the throat, and agonized by the shame of the common prudence that restrained him, fell to upbraiding his Marchioness. But here, too, insolence and scorn were all he gathered.

'Are we to have all this again? Is it my fault that he manhandled me? You saw that I was struggling with him.'

'And I saw that you laughed whilst you struggled, which is a wanton's way to ask that her struggles shall be overcome.'

She withered him with her sarcasm. 'Your years should not give you licence to insult a woman because they leave you unable to protect her.' And on that she, too, departed.

iii

The April days that followed, if they sped pleasantly, although tantalizingly, for the condottiero in his inconclusive dalliance, were days of an almost intolerable agony to the Marquis. Dishonoured by Piccinino whose advent had constrained him to disloyalty to his suzerain, he lived on the edge of further dishonour in his private life, and he was as helpless to avert the one as to avenge the other. Yet out of prudence, he must dissemble his hatred of this ravisher of his peace, give him courtesy and entertainment. In this burning purgatory it remained for him only to pray for the speedy landing of the French, so that he might be delivered of his detestable guest.

Fervently was he at this continuous prayer, when in the dusk of a rainy April evening, some two weeks after the coming of Piccinino to Cantalupo, a courier rode a spent horse into the courtyard of the castle, reeled exhausted from the saddle, plastered from head to foot with mud, and hoarsely demanded the Angevin commander.

It happened that the Marquis was in the guardhouse at the time, and heard the call. It also happened that there were none but men of his own present in the courtyard. He kept at Cantalupo a garrison some fifty strong, serving little purpose but that of a guard of honour.

The Marquis stepped out into the rain, thrust aside those of his men who were surrounding the courier, and, with a solicitude so extraordinary that he would delegate the care of the fellow to none of his people, took him by the arm, and conducted him within doors.

Within the cavernous hall, where in the lamplight trophies of arms glittered on the grey walls, the Marquis halted.

'You bear letters?'

'For Messer Jacopo Piccinino.'

'Give them to me.'

'I am to deliver them into the Captain's own hands.'

'I am the Marquis of Cantalupo. I will take them to him, whilst my people care for you.' He held out his hand, his voice peremptory. 'Give me the letters.'

The courier still hesitated for a moment, then overawed by the rank of this big old man, he produced and surrendered a sealed package.

The Marquis summoned Bosio, his castellan, delivered the courier into his care with orders to see to his needs. Bosio led the man away. But other orders must have followed, for the courier was never heard of again.

Cantalupo went to shut himself in his closet. What he did was dangerous. But there was no risk he would not run if it gave him the means of squaring accounts with that villain Piccinino. With a thin-bladed knife he contrived to raise the seal intact, and made himself master of the contents of the letter. His old eyes glittered as he read, a smile shaped itself round the corners of his shaven mouth. Then he burnt the parchment in the flame of the taper by which he had read it, and went to supper with a more pleasant air than he had worn for several days, and a manner towards his guest that was almost cordial. Thereafter he grew still more tolerant, and the smile was not effaced from his lips even when in his very presence the increasingly impudent Piccinino hovered with wooing ardour over Madonna Eufemia.

Thus for four days, and then the end came. It arrived in the shape of news brought one evening when they were snugly at supper. The bearer was no ordinary courier, but one Fidelio, an officer of Castrocaro's, the Lombard captain who had been left in command of the camp at Benevento.

His peremptoriness of manner imposing upon the officer at the gate, he was conducted at once by Bosio to the supper-room, a small chamber that communicated directly with the main hall of the castle, the bleakness of its grey walls relieved by the glow from the heaped logs on the cowled hearth.

The tall, soldierly Fidelio, who bore upon his leather-clad person the evidences of having ridden hard, found a Piccinino in whom he hardly recognized the hard-bitten little captain of the Angevin forces. Rendered foppish for once in his amorous ardour, the condottiero was tricked out in a flaming surcoat of crimson velvet, with the glitter of a jewel or two to enhance his finery, and so much at his ease that it was evident he had no thought for the activities of war.

If the sight of him thus wrought an odd change in the messenger, the sight of the messenger wrought no less of a change in Piccinino. He was on his feet at once, brisk and eager in his instant assumption.

'You bring me word that the French have come at last.' Fidelio, standing within the doorway with Bosio at his side, opened his eyes to gape amazement.

'Bring you word, sir?' His tone was that of a man who does not believe his ears. And again: 'Bring you word? That word you should have had four days ago. It is because there is no answer from you that Castrocaro has sent me.'

'Plague take you, man! Of what are you talking? I have had word of nothing.' Then, sweeping that aside for what he considered the weightier matter, 'but the French, sir?' he demanded impatiently. 'The French? Have they come?'

The answer was a thunderbolt. 'The French, sir, have come...and gone.'

'Come, and gone? What sense is there to that? Damn your soul, man, can't you deliver a plain tale?'

Piccinino stood, a truculent, scarlet figure, leaning upon the massive back of the chair from which he had risen. Beyond the table the Lady Eufemia, her fair, pallid loveliness stressed by the gown of black velvet that sheathed her slim body, with a glow of rubies at her breast, leaned her elbows on the board, to listen. The Marquis sat hunched in his chair, his chin upon his breast, his eyes watchful under his bushy grey eyebrows, his countenance expressionless.

As the messenger began to speak, a look of intelligence passed between Cantalupo and his castellan. Covertly the Marquis made a sign with his left hand, whereupon Bosio slipped unobtrusively from the room.

Fidelio advanced, and brought forth his dreadful tale.

Yves de Bressan, the French commander, guided by the galleys that had been sent out to scout for him, safely brought his little fleet into Nettuno, and had landed there his army some eight thousand strong, between horse and foot, and all splendidly equipped.

'But Colombo da Siena,' he proceeded, 'whom we all supposed to be leagues away in the territory of Naples...'

'Supposed it?' Piccinino interrupted furiously. 'Supposed it? Castrocaro's scouts reported Colombo's army in the hills by Mignano at the time of which you speak.'

'They were deceived, as Colombo meant they should be, by a detachment which he sent forward for no other purpose than to hoodwink us. The main body of his forces, which Bernardone reported to have seen marching south, must have doubled back; for when Bressan landed at Nettuno, Colombo was in strength behind Lepini, watching and waiting for him. That incarnate devil must have guessed the purpose of the galleys you sent out from Nettuno.'

'Do you tell me that Bressan was surprised?' Piccinino had turned pale. 'Had the fool no scouts?'

'He was given no chance to employ them, no chance to do anything. No sooner were his forces ashore than Colombo came down the hills like an avalanche. It seems that he...'

'Never mind what seems! The facts! Give me the facts!'

The facts were that the French were not even given time to form order of battle before the impact. With their back to the sea, unable to retreat, they stood panic-stricken to receive a blow that shattered them completely.

'And this Sienese devil,' Fidelio ran on, 'violating all laws of civilized warfare wrought fearful havoc with his crossbowmen, slaughtering recklessly. The battle lasted not above four hours. Then Bressan surrendered with the five thousand men that remained him. Stripped of arms and armour, their horses and equipment appropriated – an enormous booty – they are now on their way to

Rome. For this Sienese dog has actually refused to observe even the common practice of setting prisoners free after disarming them.'

It was the end of the tale, and a silence followed. Piccinino was speechless. His bearded countenance had turned a nasty yellow; his limbs trembled as if an ague possessed him. He sat down heavily, and took his head in his hands.

Fidelio, having paused for a long moment, now roused his captain and further maddened him by the announcement that this was not by any means the worst of his news.

'Captain Castrocaro bids me report, sir, that since he sent you word five days ago of these events, Papal galleys have come to cruise off Gaeta, completely cutting off our communications with France, whilst Colombo da Siena, with strong reinforcements from Rome, is advancing from Capua, following the course of the river Volturno. Captain Castrocaro has formed the opinion that Colombo's aim is to place our camp at Benevento between himself and King Ferdinand's Spanish forces at Naples. He urges you, sir, to return at once to Benevento so that you may yourself take order against this peril.'

Piccinino, who had listened in a seethe of rage, his hands clenched upon the arms of his chair, his jaw set, found at last a vent for his passion.

'Gesú! Is he an addle-head, this Castrocaro, that he waits there in this jeopardy? Any but a numskull would not have sent this message, but would have come himself, with the army at his heels. To fall back to the north is the obvious countermove, so as to avoid being surrounded. As there is a God in Heaven, it seems that I am served by idiots!'

Pale and limp sat the Lady Eufemia, almost as distracted as Piccinino himself by this blow to all her vindictive hopes.

The Marquis, who throughout had remained immovable and inscrutable, stirred at last. He spoke in a tone of elaborate commiseration.

'Almost, Ser Piccinino, it looks as if the tables had been turned: as if suddenly it is yourself who, in your own image, are become the nut between two stones: a nut ready to be cracked.'

The condottiero's tortured, blood-injected eyes stabbed his host with a glance that was all malevolence. Smiling a little, the Marquis continued.

'Almost does it seem, too, as if the strategic victory of your invasion of Neapolitan territory had been Colombo's and not yours. I mean, as if he had deliberately permitted it, so as to draw you into this trap.'

This was too much for Piccinino. He rose violently, his face a livid, snarling mask.

'By the living God, have you the courage to mock me?'

'Mock!' The Marquis affected dismay, spreading big red hands as if to repel the notion. 'Why, I am all commiseration. I but remark what all Italy will be saying tomorrow, if it is not saying it already.'

This was to turn the sword in the wound. The smart of it, whilst maddening Piccinino, yet made him look more closely to the hand that wielded the poisonous weapon. A suspicion of Cantalupo's secret, malevolent exultation begot in him yet another suspicion, which instantly became a conviction.

'So, you false, treacherous jackal of Aragon, it was for this that you lured me here! So that my leaderless army, left in charge of a fool, might the more readily be taken in the snare preparing for it!'

The Marquis heaved himself to his feet. He plucked off the mask, no longer concerned to dissemble his hostility. 'You rave, sir. In your anxiety to find a cover for your emptiness, a cloak for your error, a salve for your vanity, you rant. And, by my soul, you could scarcely rant more wildly than when you say that I lured you here.'

Piccinino leaned across the table, one of his stumpy hands resting upon it to support him; the other gesticulated wildly, and his face was the face of a devil.

'Will you play the innocent to me? It will need more than that to save your neck. Do you think I have forgotten your sneer that in coming to Cantalupo I might find that I had lost more than I had gained? I understand your meaning now, you false Judas. I should have understood it sooner had not your woman, your bawdy tool, beguiled me with her deceitful languishing. I should have suspected the harlotry she used to delay me here, now beckoning, now repelling me. That and your false friendliness and treacherous letter have made a fool of me. But as God's my light, I'll call a reckoning before I go.'

The Lady Eufemia was crouching in her chair, a vivid fear in her blue eyes. Her lord, however, that man of timid prudences, remained stolidly indifferent before the soldier's furious threat.

'Letter?' he said. 'What letter?'

'What letter?' Piccinino smote the table with his hand. 'The letter bidding me to Cantalupo.'

'Are you a liar, too?' wondered Cantalupo. 'I wrote you no letter.'

'But your woman did. Will you pretend that it was not with your connivance, at your orders?'

The Lord of Cantalupo lost some of his stolidity. Slowly he turned his eyes upon the little lady who sat so tense and still. 'What is this that he says of a letter that you wrote? He lies, does he not?'

She roused herself. She was almost scornful. Perhaps she hoped at his expense to set herself right in the eyes of the condottiero, and thus at least avert whatever now might threaten.

'I did it for the best. You said that if Ser Piccinino appeared before Cantalupo, you would not temporize a moment longer. Therefore I fetched him. So as to put an end to your hesitations. So as to compel you for your own good to declare for Anjou.'

He thrust away the chair by which he had been standing, and strode to her side.

'You fetched him? You bade him come? You traitress!' The colour darkened in his face. He stood menacingly over her, a big ponderous man, still powerful despite his weight of years. Then sudden, and very oddly, he laughed. 'Your neck is slender as a lily's stem; and it would snap as easily between my hands. Do you know why I do not snap it? Because I owe you thanks for something for which I have been thanking Fate.'

Piccinino stormed in. 'Leave comedy. My eyes are open. Wide open. I am not to be fooled twice in the same business.' He swung to Fidelio. 'Before we ride we'll clean out this foul nest. Summon the

guard. Place me this old carrion under arrest. As for the woman…'
He looked at her, and the grin on his mouth was merciless. 'She shall
be my care. My men shall feast on the charms she flaunts so
impudently in her treacherous aims. God's light! But they shall learn
who is the master here.'

Cantalupo startled him by laughing. 'And so shall you, Ser
Piccinino. Is it the guard you desire?' He clapped his hands together
loudly, and raised his voice to call. Almost at once Bosio came in
answer, and at his heels a half-dozen of Cantalupo's men-at-arms.
The Marquis gave his castellan an order.

'You will require the captain of the gate to take up the drawbridge
at once, and to suffer no man to enter or leave Cantalupo until I give
the word. You others, stand to your arms here.'

Piccinino swung this way and that in bewildered anger. 'What's
this? What's this?' He raised his voice to arrest the departing castellan.
'Not so fast, you! It is my orders that count here! You'll wait for them,
if you please.'

But Bosio departed as if the captain had not spoken, a contempt
that turned the raging Piccinino again upon the Marquis.

'Are you all mad in Cantalupo? Am I to put your paltry garrison
to the sword before it is understood that I am to be obeyed?'

The Marquis shrugged his broad shoulders, and sat down. His
ponderous calm moved Piccinino to a yet wilder frenzy, and the Lady
Eufemia to a round-eyed, palpitating wonder.

Into the soldier's blasphemous ordures of speech, the Lord of
Cantalupo's voice cut coldly, peremptorily.

'Attend to me, you foulness! Instead of crowing so loudly about
being master here and about hanging me from my own battlements,
you had better realize that the gin has snapped upon you. I am not
your prisoner. You are mine. And preserve your calm, I beg. For at
the first sign of violence these men of mine will cut you down.'

Piccinino's rage was engulfed in amazement. This thing was too
fantastically incredulous. The news that Colombo da Siena was
marching on Benevento had gone to the old dotard's brain, and had
intoxicated him.

201

'You fool, have you forgotten that I have a thousand men at hand?'

'They are outside the castle walls, and the drawbridge is being taken up.'

'How long do you suppose it will take them to give an account of your mouldy walls and their futile defenders?'

'Not long, perhaps. But certainly longer – much longer – than it will now take Colombo da Siena to reach Cantalupo.'

'Cantalupo?'

'Of course, you would not think of that. This Messer Fidelio's information about Colombo's movements is incomplete. It is no doubt true that he is marching along the river Volturno. It is certainly true that he is marching northward. For what really is happening is that he is on his way to Cantalupo, informed that, wherever your army may be, you yourself, Ser Piccinino, are being held here for him.'

From bloodless lips came Piccinino's voice, now hoarse with passion.

'You sent him that assurance! You dared!' Then, at last, he showed a further, belated, understanding. 'The courier sent by Castrocaro five days ago? The letter he carried announcing de Bressan's defeat? You intercepted it! You withheld it from me!'

The Marquis leered at him. 'You were so happily engaged that it would have been a cruelty to have disturbed you. You were in such exalted enjoyment of the hospitality my lady offered you in Cantalupo that I had not the heart to distress you sooner than necessary with this news.' He slewed round to face his pallid marchioness. 'You will have understood by now, madonna, that your letter to Messer Piccinino was not the only invitation that went out from Cantalupo. Indeed, it was your invitation to Messer Piccinino that provided the occasion for mine to Colombo da Siena.'

It is doubtful whether the Lady Eufemia or the Captain-General of Anjou was his bitterest enemy at that moment. There was no candour now in the eyes of the lady as they glared their mute hatred of her lord; and Piccinino might have read in her white, distorted face that he had too rashly judged her in league with her husband to betray him.

But Piccinino, in the fierce anguish of contemplating the terrible position in which he found himself, no longer can have troubled to give thought to the manner in which it had been brought about.

Hands were laid upon him and upon Fidelio by Cantalupo's men-at-arms. The Marquis offered sardonic apologies.

'It is necessary that I should place you in safety, sir. But do not let it vex you unduly. It will be for no more than a day or two, until Ser Colombo arrives.'

iv

The Marquis of Cantalupo had acted when he did because his hand had been forced by the arrival of Fidelio. When he said that Colombino would arrive in a day or two, he expressed a hope rather than an assurance. As a matter of fact it was a full week before Colombino arrived.

Eager though he might be to lay hands upon the Angevin commander, the Captain-General of Aragon in his forward sweep had found himself, as a result of his calculations, so excellently placed to end the campaign at a blow that Piccinino and Cantalupo must wait a while.

The forces of King Ferdinand acting in concert with his own and in accordance with his directions, he held the camp of Benevento in a ring of steel, and this ring he began to close. Castrocaro, finding himself beset on every side at once and by forces materially in excess of his own, broke down under the responsibility thrust upon him by the absence of his chief. He acknowledged himself out-generalled, surrendered at discretion, since he could obtain no other terms, and suffered himself to be disarmed. The war was finished, the Anjou hopes were dead, and Ferdinand was firm upon the throne of Naples; and all this accomplished in the turn of a hand, as it were, by a man at whose fancied ineptitude Italy had been laughing little more than a week ago.

'I hand you the palm,' Squillanti told Colombino on the night of that victory. 'Never again in my life will I doubt your purposes. I have seen something of war, and I have some notion of myself as a soldier. But here you baffled me. And yet…' He hesitated. 'There is something I shall never understand. When you marched south parallel with Piccinino, with forces fully equal to his own, was surely the moment to have fallen upon him, before the arrival of the French. You risked his being reinforced before you delivered battle. Still, since luck served you so well, as it happens…'

'Luck?' Colombino interrupted him. 'Oh, well, yes. Fortune in these matters must never be denied. But I was not served by luck as you suppose. There was always the chance that just this might happen. Piccinino, as I kept telling you, has one only trick of strategy, and if the opportunity served, I thought he would not fail to try it. If the French sails had shown on the horizon, I must instantly have fallen upon Piccinino, to deliver battle before he could be reinforced. But as long as no sails showed, I waited. And in the end he did as I supposed. He slipped past me, counting that I would follow, and ready to turn again the moment he had word that the French were in my rear. Between his own army and Bressan's he would crush me. But I only made pretence to follow. The galleys he sent out assured me of what was afoot. I doubled back to wait for Bressan. Then, when I had smashed him, I had Piccinino in the position in which he so fondly imagined that he would catch me. He was between my army and King Ferdinand's, and his doom was sealed. Patience, my dear Marquis, is the highest virtue a commander can possess. And I possess it. We'll go and explain all this to Piccinino. It will amuse the little devil.'

And so, with a force some four thousand strong – the main body of the army, with its long convoy of prisoners, being sent on to Naples – Colombino rode to Cantalupo. He rode into it without striking a blow, for Piccinino's thousand, demoralized by the events and in no case to stand before this overwhelming force, dissolved and vanished at his approach.

In the main hall of the castle, the old Marquis awaited him, and at his side stood his reluctant lady, whose presence he had constrained. For in these days the last dregs of his uxoriousness had been cast out, and he commanded now where formerly he had coaxed and begged.

Colombino entered. He was in light armour, trailing a wine-coloured cloak, a youthful, vigorous figure with the bearing of a prince and a princely train of attendant officers.

Stepping briskly ahead of his following, he advanced towards the Marquis. Only for a heartbeat did his firm step falter, his smile grow rigid; and that was when his glance alighted upon the slim little figure in black that stood with heaving breast and downcast eyes at her lord's side. Only then did he recall the fact, heard months ago and forgotten in the press of his active life, that Eufemia, once of Rovieto, had married the Marquis of Cantalupo. Recalling it, he wondered for an instant whether in coming here, it was he who had walked into a trap. Then, remembering the troops at his heels, flowing through township and castle, he perceived the idleness of the thought, and went boldly on.

He was embraced by the Marquis and greeted with cordial words of welcome and of loyalty to Aragon. Then he turned perforce to take the hand extended to him by the Marchioness. He bowed over it stiffly, and bore it to his lips as the forms demanded. It was ice-cold, and all of ice seemed the lady who stood before him without raising her eyes.

He stepped back, and was beginning to express his thanks and the thanks of his master for the great service the Marquis had rendered, when Cantalupo interrupted him.

'Not to me these thanks. Not to me, sir. *Palmam qui meruit ferat.*' He was smiling as he spoke; but it was an odd smile, thought Colombino, for it seemed to hold more bitterness than mirth. Smiling so, he half-turned to his lady. 'It is to Madonna Eufemia here that you should address your thanks for this fresh laurel added to the crown you so nobly wear. There was, I believe, some old debt between you two which she was anxious to discharge. For this she brought Jacopo Piccinino here, so that he might be taken and held for you. And she employed arts of which she is mistress to drug his senses until the time should be ripe to secure him.

'It is thus that she pays her debt to you. It is for this that she deserves your thanks, for this service to you and to the cause of Aragon, which is her last act in this world.'

Colombino recoiled. He had perceived by now at least in part the source of Cantalupo's bitterness. 'My lord!' The cry was startled from him.

But now the smile of the Marquis was reassuring. 'Do not misunderstand me, sir. I have prevailed upon Madonna Eufemia to remain here until today, so that she should do you honour and receive your thanks. It is only to this end that she delayed her departure. She goes to Rome, sir; to the convent of the Poor Clares. There in prayer and humility and poverty she proposes to purge herself of the contamination of a world which no longer interests her, in preparation for a better world to come.'

Chapter 7

THE LADY OF SQUILLANTI

i

Once again Colombo da Siena was to profit by a revulsion of feeling.

Whilst in any case his defeat of Piccinino must have been hailed as a great victory, it was magnified by the shock to the popular mind which had been persuading itself of his incompetence. He who deceives an enemy is acknowledged a skilful general, but he whose deception involves at the same time a people is acclaimed a genius by those whom he has hoodwinked. To do less would be to depreciate their own perspicacity.

Just as the reaction from suspicions of his loyalty in the matter of Monsieur de La Bourdonnaye had resulted in placing his loyalty solidly beyond doubt, so now the reaction from assumptions of his ineptitude made his military talents shine the more dazzlingly.

The considerable fame hitherto enjoyed was as nothing to the fame into which he now entered. Naples prepared a triumph for him. King Ferdinand rewarded him with the fief of Ostiamare and the title of Count, and bestowed the accolade upon him, whilst the Queen, with her own hands, buckled on his spurs. The Pope had sent him the Golden Rose and offered him the gonfalon of Holy Church, which Colombino, aiming higher still, had gracefully declined.

To one so honoured abroad, his native Siena was moved to offer signal homage, and like Naples prepared a triumph for his home-coming.

Under archways of blossoming ramage, swathed in bunting and flanked by banners, through streets that had been carpeted with boughs and strewn with flowers, past houses gay with tapestries and cloth of gold and silver, through a press of acclaiming townsfolk, noble and simple, young and old, to the blare of trumpets and the shouts of the multitude, the young soldier of fortune, looking like an incarnation of the Christian Mars, Saint Michael, rode into the city of his birth, and saluted the she-wolf on her pillar in the Campo. The May sunshine flashed from his silver armour as from a mirror, and in the eyes of some fervent ones seemed to set an aureole of light about his tawny head. For he rode bareheaded, on a great white charger with rich trailing housings of damask, its head adorned by a golden artichoke. A sleek esquire in crimson rode a horse's length behind him, bearing his dove-crowned helmet, his lance and his mace. Colombino's face, cast in such squarely austere lines that it seemed hewn of granite, was flushed though grave, and he bowed to the acclamations as a prince might bow to his subjects.

The incense of worship and wonder in which he moved in the days that followed, under the homage of great men and the allurement of inviting glances from more than one great lady, must have turned a head less level. Or perhaps it was that his yearnings, set ever upon that distant lady in Ravenna, left him no appetite for the present feast. Had she been at his side to share his glory, how different it would have been and how treasured for her sake! But in her absence he was constrained to draw upon his fortitude so that he might ably bear his part in the festivities that succeeded each other in his honour, impatient to be done with it all and to be free to depart to the peace of his villa at Montasco.

Squillanti was his host during those days in Siena, and an assiduous host who spared no pains to make the occasion glorious, by a succession of banquets, balls, and jousts, and lesser entertainments.

And in all that he contrived for the delight and magnification of his guest, he was seconded by his Marchioness with an assiduity that exceeded even his own. A woman as famed for beauty as for gallantry, Squillanti's lady had left an ache in many a stout heart since she had wed the Marquis. That she meant to leave none in Colombino's was plain enough from the utter frankness with which in those days she offered herself to his attention. But Colombino, with his thoughts elsewhere, remained unconscious of her wooing, however flagrant it became. He was blinded perhaps by weariness; a weariness, ever increasing, of the role of hero of the hour which he found thrust upon him.

At last it was coming to an end. A ball in the Squillanti Palace was marking the close of these festivities.

The ambassador of the Most Serene Republic of Venice was among the foreign envoys present, and this ambassador was Colombino's old acquaintance Francesco Gritti. The influence in Venice of the Gritti family had been too great for Messer Francesco's permanent disgrace. He had never ceased to be a member of the Ten, and having borne, himself, the expense of his mistake, the Most Serene Republic had speedily and graciously forgotten it. Indeed, Messer Francesco seemed to have forgotten it himself. At least, he showed no sign of rancour towards Colombino for the past, but was amongst the loudest now in his adulation.

To the delight and flattery of this ambassador of the Serenissima, they were dancing the stately Veneziana in the great hall of Squillanti's palace, and all that was noble in Siena and able to move with reasonable nimbleness upon two legs was taking part in this new dance.

The Marquis himself had led forth Madonna Silvia Piccolomini, who, as the Pope's cousin, was just then the Lady Paramount in Siena; Camillo Petrucci had followed with Messer Gritti's lady, who, though already well advanced in years, yet took the eye by her semi-Oriental Venetian splendour; the exquisite Silvio Pecci moved gracefully with Squillanti's demurely radiant young Marchioness; the most noble Ettore Malavoiti, very tall and scornful, and conspicuous as a magpie in black-and-white silk – as if the colours of Siena were peculiarly his right – was partnered with a golden-headed lady of the Roman House of Orsini.

Colombino, having excused himself on the score that the figures of this new dance were strange to him, had gone to watch the gay scene from the stone gallery above.

Weary though he might be of all this, and glad to think that tomorrow at last he would be free to return to the peace of Montasco, yet in the honours of which he had been the recipient there was much in which he might take satisfaction. Of all the flattery bestowed upon him, one that perhaps really touched him was the offer made him by Venice, through her envoy Francesco Gritti, that now that his engagement with Siena was at an end he should enter the service of the Serenissima and assume the command of her army. Exhausted though Venice might be by her long-drawn war with Milan for the prepotency of the North, yet such faith, said Messer Gritti, did Colombo da Siena inspire, that if he could be persuaded to become her condottiero, she would rouse herself to renew the struggle.

Colombino had temporized, neither accepting nor refusing. He confessed himself a little weary of war; his vineyard required attention – his usual excuse on such occasions – and for a few weeks at least he would make no decision. Messer Gritti, professing to respect the soldier's inclinations, had written to the Council of Ten, urging them to increase the stipend they had offered.

Pondering now this amended proposal and watching the surprising nimbleness of a man of Messer Gritti's years and gaunt frame, Colombino found amusement in contrasting the Venetian's present attitude towards him with what it had been at Ravenna, when Francesco Gritti had stood a prisoner before him with a halter round his neck. The thought of Ravenna brought with it the thought of Samaritana and the ache that ever accompanied it. It so absorbed him that he was scarcely aware of footsteps approaching from beyond the pillar against which he was leaning.

Presently a man and a woman came to lean upon the rail of the gallery. Like himself they had ceased to be actors so as to become spectators. Without perceiving him they had entered his line of vision, and he saw that they were his hostess, the slim, dark young Marchioness, and the exquisite Silvio Pecci, who, it now occurred to him, was too frequently at her side.

Silvio's high-pitched voice came clearly to his ears; his tone was one of mincing mockery.

'Of the many things for which your Squillanti was not fashioned, the service of Terpsichore is one. His dancing is that of a festive bull. I never behold him but I think of that Cretan horror, the Minotaur.'

If it shocked Colombino that any man should address Squillanti's lady in such terms, her laughing answer, clear above the strains of flute and viol, shocked him more.

'You will add, Silvio, that in me you see another Ariadne and in yourself the heroic Theseus.'

'I confess it was in my mind.'

'An ingenious mind, my Silvio.'

'Does it not describe us?'

'A trifle flattering to you, I think. You may be skilled in finding your way through labyrinths. But you would faint in the presence of the Minotaur.'

Colombino thought that this was rather better. There followed a pause. Then said Pecci, in a voice that had turned sour: 'I lose your esteem, I think, Caterina.'

'No, no. My esteem never went the lengths of considering you a Theseus. Your fibre is too delicate, Silvio, for that part.'

'Are you defying me?'

'On the contrary. I am restraining you. The lute is your proper weapon, sir; the lists of Cupid are your proper battleground.'

'I thank you, madonna. I am diminished in your eyes since this captain of fortune has brought swaggering bluster into fashion.'

'Cease, or you will put me out of humour. You grow tiresome, Silvio.'

'Tiresome?' Anger was kindling in his voice. 'Tiresome! Oh, I grow tiresome, madonna mine. Shall I tell you since when? Since the return of this fine captain from the wars. By the Host! It nauseates a man to see the fawning adulation lavished on this mountebank, this upstart, this adventurer.'

'You mean that it nauseates you, Silvio. But not a man. No, nor a woman either.'

Messer Silvio caught his breath. 'You are so shameless, then, as to confess it?' Thus, out of light words had the storm gathered. But as he now raved on, he disclosed that it had been brewing earlier. And he disclosed to Colombino matters that served to heal the Captain of his blindness. 'My faith, there was not the need to tell me. I have seen your eyes when you looked at him; and I have read their message; for once it was so that you looked at me.'

'May God forgive me for it. For you were never worth looking at, Silvio.'

'Ah! And this Colombino, then...'

He got no further. The soldier, shaking off his embarrassment with the hesitation that had held him there, an unwilling listener, stepped forth into their view.

'Did I hear my name?'

They started round in swift confusion. Squillanti's lady flashed him a glance from nun-like eyes, all innocence and chastity, then looked away, the colour stirring in her lovely, pallid face. Messer Silvio struck a pose of dauntlessness, hand on hip, his head thrown back.

'Whence do you spring, sir?'

'Spring? Sir, I do not spring. I walk. I pass. I overhear my name. Or was I mistaken? If so, let me pass on.'

'We were speaking of you, yes,' the lady admitted. 'All the world is doing that, and not only in Siena. Messer Silvio was saying...' She turned to find her gallant melting into the shadows of the staircase. 'Oh, but does it matter what he said?'

'Rarely, I should imagine.'

'And at such a moment? For your sojourn here draws too swiftly to its end. Tomorrow you depart.' She looked away again, down into the throng below, which danced no longer, and added softly: 'Alas!'

His voice was coldly formal.

'I am as fortunate in my going as in my staying. To continue here might be to lose the little modesty Siena has left me.'

'Does your welcome surprise you? Are you not worthy of all, and more?'

'Certainly not worthy that you should think so.'

The long, demure eyes, so startlingly blue against her smooth black hair, came slowly round to look into his own. The nun-like face had an expression that was certainly not nun-like.

'Worthy of all that I could think of you.' Her tone had dropped to a caressing murmur that no coxcomb could have misunderstood. Nor did Colombino now, who was certainly no coxcomb and found here no coxcomb's satisfaction.

That she was the wife of a brother-in-arms and a host who had nobly entertained him rendered doubly odious a situation which he could no longer misunderstand; and for days thereafter he would shudder as he wondered if he could have extricated himself without brutality had not Squillanti himself at that moment come limping towards them on his massive but unequal legs.

'Silvio told me that I should find you here. Our guests begin to leave. I need you to help me speed them, Caterina; and you, too, Colombino. For yours is the leading part tonight.'

ii

Late that night, as Colombino was climbing into the great canopied bed in the chamber of honour which he occupied, the door was softly opened to admit the Marquis, who came, in bedgown and slippers, with the announcement that there was a grave matter upon which they should have an understanding.

For a moment the soldier was caught by a suspicion that his host was concerned with Madonna Caterina's undisguised preoccupations, and in his soul he damned the lightness of all women that must forever be setting men at grips.

He frowned as he watched Squillanti re-lighting the candles which Colombino had just extinguished in the massive golden branch that stood on an ebony table in mid-chamber. After that the Marquis limped to the bed, and sat down upon the edge of it, his florid countenance portentous.

As he opened his mind, the soldier's wonder grew with his relief to hear himself harangued upon the politics of Siena. Being relieved, his wonder presently turned to weariness, and he sought to stem the flood.

'My dear Lord Marquis, you waste your rhetoric. What have I to do with theories of government? I am but the tool of governments. My functions are brutally practical.'

Squillanti raised a massive hand, pursing the lips of his curiously small mouth. 'A little patience! Consider me the distracted state of this unfortunate republic, in prey to parties, each seeking, under the pretence of patriotism, to serve its own advantages. We have the Fifteen, the Nine, the Popolani, the Riformatori, the Signory, and the Balia. Was ever government so complicated? So many factions, each striving with the others for supremacy? They make the world hideous with their turbulence. Siena in prey to this internecine strife lies languishing; her trades and her arts are paralyzed. Let this continue for a little longer, and we shall be the meanest state in Italy. Could a better example be found of the evils of communal rule? Could a stouter argument be urged in favour of government by a prince; such a government as Florence has already adopted?'

'Probably not,' said Colombino, stifling a yawn. He agreed so that they might be the sooner done.

But Squillanti seemed merely at the exordium.

'What Florence has done for her honour and salvation, Siena can do.'

'I see.' Colombino was indifferent. 'You would replace the republic by a prince. Why not?'

'Just so. Why not?' But Squillanti was so tight-lipped and so direct of glance that the soldier realized that further disclosures were impending. A heavy hand was laid on Colombino's wrist. 'What has been done in Florence by a family of apothecaries turned usurers, by these Medici, who blazon upon their shield the pills with which they laid the foundations of their fortune and house, may surely be done here in Siena by a soldier of distinction, a man well-born, enjoying the universal esteem of his fellow citizens, a man who in the eyes of the people must appear as a natural leader by right of something better than purges.'

There was an end to Colombino's indifference. He was shaken into sudden attention. He was even not untouched by fear. 'God save me!' was his ejaculation, and wide-eyed he remained staring at his host.

Smiling darkly, Squillanti stroked his double chin. 'I have startled you.'

Colombino essayed a short laugh. It expressed merely nervousness.

'Faith, you point the way either to the throne or to the headsman. I can't determine which.'

'Bah! We can forget the headsman. Nothing worth achieving was ever achieved without risk. But here the risk need not deter us. I have weighed it. I have taken soundings. And I can tell you that, with the exception of a few self-seekers, none of the patricians of Siena will oppose the project.'

'But will they support it?'

'I am assured they will. Besides, it is not for a man of spirit to count the obstacles when duty so clearly points the way. No man who loves Siena can remain indifferent whilst these jackals fight and snarl over her for their own profit. It is out of love for Siena that I am impatient to strike this blow for the restoration of order and the encouragement of the arts and crafts by which states grow rich and powerful. The man who accomplishes this, Colombino, will be hailed – and rightly hailed – as the saviour of his country.'

Colombino sat propped on his pillows, the eyes of his body dreamy, the eyes of his soul dazzled. If the ambition which has ever lain deep in the heart of every soldier of fortune had languished in him of late under the discouragements procured him first by the Lady of Rovieto and then by the Lady Samaritana, it was nevertheless still alive, and it was being reinvigorated now by the breath of the Marquis Squillanti. His earliest inspiration had been the career of that great condottiero Francesco Sforza, who had risen to be Duke of Milan and the most powerful prince in Northern Italy. And now, abruptly, possibilities almost as great were opening before himself.

That he was the man for this, he never doubted. Nor did he doubt that the revolution Squillanti suggested would be for the good of Siena; so that patriotism came to quicken the lively stirrings of his ambition. That the patricians of Siena should be prepared to accept him for their duke, as he understood Squillanti to be saying, did not seem odd, considering his recent achievements and the love that Siena was displaying for him. But it might be less easy, he thought, to persuade the people that they would prosper better under the government of a prince. That was a belief to which they must gradually be educated.

This thought he expressed, and thereby provoked Squillanti's scorn.

'If by the people you mean the plebs, the populace, that is never to be educated. In all ages it is ready to listen to the first seducer base enough to flatter it and to lead it by its foolish nose with lying promises of the effortless acquisition of the treasures of the earth. We are not without such rogues in Siena. But if a state is to prosper, its populace must be dominated, not educated. Education is for men whose minds are equipped to receive it, for patricians, for natural leaders. In this I have already made more than a beginning. I know that we can count upon the Primerani, the Alamanni, upon Ventura d' Allegretto, upon Silvio Pecci, and perhaps even upon the

Piccolomini and the Salimbeni. Petrucci I do not trust, because I believe him to be too ambitious. I mean that he would support the scheme if it aimed at giving him the throne. But he would never suffer another Sienese to achieve that ascendancy over him. Malavolti is in the same case. Already he disputes with Petrucci the title of first citizen to Siena. And there are a few others whom it would be just as dangerous to enlist. But we have enough without them. And if your duty to your country moves you as it should, we have in your free company the strength to impose our will.'

He paused there, and looked searchingly into the soldier's face that was set in stony gravity.

'I have been frank with you, Colombino. Now, the fate of Siena is in your hands.'

At last Colombino raised his dark, glowing eyes, and looked straight into the eyes of his host. He had taken his resolve.

'Since in my soul I believe with you that a prince will be for Siena's good, I am your man. God helping me, I will do my duty by the State.'

Squillanti flung himself forward and hugged him in an embrace that left him momentarily breathless.

'I knew that I could depend upon you!'

Colombino, now all eagerness, asked him for instructions.

'Leave all to me,' he was answered. 'Away with you to Montasco and your vineyards until I give the word to strike. I will keep in touch with you. Meanwhile, disband none of your men.'

'I'll need some pretext for that. I do not maintain an army in my pay when there is no prospect of a hire.'

'I've thought of it. Venice supplies the pretext. It is known that Gritti is wooing you with offers from the Serenissima.'

'I have no notion of accepting them.'

'You need not say so yet. Temporize with Gritti, and let it be known that you are temporizing. That will sufficiently account for keeping your army standing.'

On that they parted for the night, and Colombino lay down, not now to sleep, but to stare into the dark and irradiate it with visions

217

of empire. And into these visions of his stole the slender, graceful wraith of Samaritana. Old Onorato da Polenta had died some months ago, and in Ravenna Samaritana ruled with the help of her priestly cousin. It was two years since that night at Bellaria when her own romance had been shattered and he had looked upon her for the last time. By now perhaps the wound that Moro had dealt her would have healed, and the memories she must hold of Colombino could not be of a kind to render him mistrusted or unwelcome. If he were Duke of Siena there would be about him a glamour which might serve to captivate her. He could bear her the offer of a nobler crown than that of Ravenna. It should be worth while, then, to make the attempt. If it succeeded and she consented to share his throne, how the inspiration of her would widen his horizon! To Siena he would link Lucca and Pisa, first by force of arms and then by a wise government that should make for their prosperity and give their people peace. Then he might even bring Florence under his sway, wresting its government from the hands of those murderous pill-makers, and so build up in Middle Italy a hegemony as great and powerful as either Venice or Milan in the North.

The skies were suffused with the flush of dawn before Colombino sank at last from these exalting dreams into quiet slumber.

iii

On the morrow Colombino rode away to his noble villa on Montasco, there to pursue his fond dreams of dukedom; to plot the laws he would enact for the sound government of his people, the militia he would raise for the State's defence, so that predatory mercenary companies might no longer drain its resources, and the other measures he would take to render Siena prosperous, happy, and formidable among the states of Italy.

His gloom was at last completely dispelled. Sangiorgio and Caliente found him joyous and gay once more as he had been in the old careless days before the Rovietan adventure. And this was because daily the hope of Samaritana now grew stronger, and when he dreamed of her, it was no longer to sigh over something lost to him. The conviction grew daily that the road he trod was leading him straight to her, as indeed it was, if not quite in the way that he imagined.

Messer Gritti rode out to visit him; a Gritti who choked down the gall in his heart, so that he might laugh with Colombino over that old business at Ravenna as at something which if bitter in the experience was in retrospect a jest. Colombino entertained him nobly, and was entirely inconclusive. He would say neither yes nor no at the moment to the proposals the Venetian made him. But he promised, at least, that he would not keep Messer Gritti waiting a moment longer than was necessary, and constrained to be content with this Messer Gritti went his ways once more, promising to come soon again.

Silvio Pecci was his next visitor; a Pecci swelling with importance in those languid, summer days, to find himself neck-deep in a conspiracy that was to revolutionize the State. He brought letters from Squillanti, reporting favourable progress. And after Pecci came other messengers from the Marquis with further letters, all very ambiguously couched, so that their real meaning should be clear to Colombino alone. These letters Colombino punctually answered.

And then, when he had been some ten days at Montasco, Caterina Squillanti came riding one noontide into his courtyard, hawk on wrist, attended by a falconer and two grooms.

She protested to him, when he stood bareheaded to receive her, that the pursuit of game had lured her farther afield than she suspected, until, finding herself in the neighbourhood of Montasco, she had resolved to cast herself for an hour or two upon his hospitality.

So hollow was the pretence and so arch her tone that Colombino must suppose she did not desire him to be deceived. It was in his thoughts, and certainly in his too sanguine hopes, that she might have been sent to him by Squillanti with news.

She was very fine in green and gold, the close-fitting, high-waisted corsage opening low, her sleeves tight to the elbow and thence spreading like wings on either side of her to mingle with the voluminous folds of her gown. Of green and gold, too, was her turban, made fast by a silken band that came tightly under her chin. Thus framed, her delicate, pallid face looked more than ever nun-like.

Colombino was severely courteous. It was most opportune, he announced, that he was about to dine. His poor table would be honoured, little though his celibate house might be designed for a lady's entertainment.

She rallied him on this when they came to table, and its noble equipment and lordly service were displayed for her; for Colombino was in all things fastidious. He bore her raillery with grace, and with still better grace her intelligent praise of last year's vintage of Montasco, served in finely blown Murano glass. It was a deep amber wine resulting from Colombino's marriage of Orvietan vines to the rich Montasco soil. He was proud of it, and accounted it worthy of the vessel from which it was poured, a tall golden jug, designed by Della Quercia, studded with bosses of amethyst and turquoise.

When at last the cloth was raised and the servants having departed they could be more at ease, he asked her for the news of which he supposed she might be the bearer.

'News?' Her brows, so fine that they might have been drawn with a pencil, were raised. Her blue eyes opened wider at once in wonder and reproach. 'Do you make me welcome, Ser Colombino, only for the news that I may bring?'

Courtesy prescribed a denial.

'You need but to look in your mirror, madonna, to find the answer to that question. Still, since you will have news...'

'But I have not,' she interrupted him, and so disabused his mind. 'I have no purpose here that is not solely my own. Is it not flattering? Will you not say that you are flattered?'

'It needs no protesting. Since it was built, my house has never been more honoured.' Even as the mechanical words escaped him, he accounted them treason, remembering that Samaritana had sat there once, on the occasion when her father had sought him. It drew a sigh from him, brought a shadow across his face, and caused him to remind his visitor of the distance between Montasco and Siena.

Frowning, she glanced up at him. Then shyly laughed.

'What haste to be rid of me, Lord Count of Ostiamare!'

'No, no,' he protested. 'It is just that I would not have your fair name suffer for an imprudence, however dear to me the imprudence might be.'

The kindling of her glance, the faint colour creeping into her cheeks as she looked at him, warned him that he had been betrayed by courtesy into saying too much.

'Is that the truth?' There was a melting eagerness in her tone. 'Is my imprudence dear to you?'

'Who visits me, honours me. Who takes a risk in visiting me honours me doubly.'

She set her elbows on the board, and cupped her chin in her long, slim hands. Thus she gazed upon him with solemn and intent allurement.

'Why so timid, Colombino? Why tread so cautiously when there are no rebuffs to fear? Don't you yet guess that there is no hurt I would not take for you?'

He inclined his head, his lips tight. 'I am honoured, madonna. Honoured beyond my deserts.'

She frowned, her tone was plaintively impatient. 'You talk too much of honour and honouring. You have no other words for me. Colombino, why so formal, and so cold? You speak as if from the lips alone. Your heart remains silent. Colombino.'

He smiled with a certain whimsical sadness. 'Perhaps I lack the adventurous spirit, save in soldiering. And then… Squillanti is my friend.'

She seized this explanation avidly. She was of those who have a gift for understanding as they wish. Audibly she caught her breath. She leaned farther over towards him. 'And if that were not the case…?'

'Does it profit us to speculate? Is it even wise?'

'Oh, a fig for wisdom! Wisdom is the thief of all the joys of life. Can it be that you fear the Minotaur: this bull of a man to whom they married me?' Her hands came from her chin, and were stretched palm upwards across the table to him. 'If I bid you to be brave, Colombino?'

'I have no valour of that kind, madonna.'

This gave her pause. She was chilled. The little colour that had crept into her cheeks faded out again. Slowly she sat back in her tall chair, keeping her eyes upon him, and they were now questioningly grave. She sought an explanation of this restraint in him, of this aloofness. That there should live a man who simply did not want her could not occur to this Caterina Squillanti whose days had been spent in defending herself from the ardours of too many wooers. Her speech faltered a little.

'You mean…you mean…because you are Squillanti's friend?'

'That were reason enough.'

Her lovely mouth, so red in that white face, was twisted into a queer, deprecatory smile, and then at last, to Colombino's infinite relief, came interruption. A sudden sound of steps and voices broke forth beyond the closed door. The voices were raised in altercation; they were his chamberlain's and another's, one who too insistently demanded admission to his presence. And he prevailed; for abruptly the door was flung wide.

Across the threshold surged a vision of white and crimson, of slender legs, of long waving crimson sleeves and golden hair. All this beauty belonged to Messer Silvio Pecci. Behind him the agitated chamberlain still protested.

Colombino, who faced the entrance, stood up, and raised his hand to wave the chamberlain away. Monna Caterina, looking over her shoulder, gasped upon beholding that elegant, angry presence.

Messer Silvio advanced yet a pace or two, then struck an attitude as the door closed behind him. He glared in horror upon the lady, then shifted his furious glance to her host.

'So this is why you sit behind closed doors!'

To another it must have been matter for indignation. But not to Colombino. He laughed outright at the impudence of this fribble. He was suddenly at ease; for he knew how to deal with men.

'My good Silvio, it is not my habit to dine in public, whether alone or with a guest. But it flatters me that you should make so free with my poor house. This is to treat me like a brother.'

Silvio gave no heed to the irony. The lady was absorbing his attention, supplying the focus for his wrath. He came a little closer. He breathed the furious mockery that springs from a wounded soul.

'I saw Gino, your falconer, in the courtyard. You should not leave your servants at the gate when you are secret and private within. It betrays you, madonna. Nor when you come to Montasco should you mask intention under such paltry make-believe as hawking. The wooded valleys of the Asso and the Ombrone are scarcely hawking country. Such poor invention, madonna, serves only to reveal the very thing you would be hiding.'

She was on her feet, and in her white face her eyes burned with a fierceness to match his own. Indeed, for all the jealous rage that choked him, hers was the deeper, deadlier fury.

'You dared to follow me? You dared, you insolent, yelping lapdog!'

He acted scorn of the notion. He laughed unpleasantly. 'Follow you? I? Disabuse your mind. I came here seeking the Count of Ostiamare. It is by accident that I stumble upon your shamelessness.'

Colombino had moved slowly round the table. He conceived that it was time to intervene, that Messer Silvio's impertinence had been sufficiently indulged. Standing a half-head taller than the tall young patrician, he took him now by the shoulder in an ungentle grip, and span him round, so that they faced each other.

'Jackanapes, this is my house. This lady is my guest. You'll show a proper respect for both, or my grooms shall fling you on the dunghill, which by your manners I take to have been your birthplace.'

Silvio sucked in his breath and recoiled. By instinct his hand sought the jewelled hilt of the heavy dagger hanging before him from his golden girdle.

'God's Passion! Do you talk of birth, you knave begotten by a traitor?' He swung again to the lady. 'For that is the thing you've taken for a lover, madonna. I give you joy of him, and him of you.'

Colombino, oddly calm, clapped his hands.

Instantly the door opened again to disclose the chamberlain, who had not moved from its other side. Colombino looked at the exquisite.

'Will you depart unaided, sir?'

Wickedness unspeakable glared back at him from that weak, handsome face. Pecci drew himself up with a sudden assumption of lofty dignity.

'I was the bearer of a message for you,' he said. 'A message from this lady's husband on a matter of grave importance, as you may surmise. It concerned a dukedom. A matter that might set a noose about some necks I could name. Since I am dismissed, you may seek the news for yourself in Siena.'

On that, abruptly, he swung on his heel and stalked out, and Colombino, for all the misgivings the fellow's words had sown, disdained to hinder him.

Not so, and for quite other reasons, Monna Caterina.

As the door was closing upon the brilliant white-and-crimson figure, she rustled up to Colombino, and clutched his arm, her face intent and fierce.

'There was mischief in his tone. Menace. Do not let him go. Kill him! Kill him!'

He masked in a smile the repugnance her ruthlessness aroused. He shrugged.

'Shall I do murder for so little?'

'So little?' She looked up at him in an amazement that quickly changed to scorn. 'So little? After what he said to you? After what he said to me? To me! You heard him, didn't you? His insults? Can you forgive them?'

'I have already forgotten them.'

'My God! Is it only in battle that you are brave?'

'Perhaps it is.'

Thus at a blow he shattered the infatuation with which she had plagued him.

'But what are you?' she asked, her lip curling in scorn of him. 'Lord God! And I thought you were a man.'

It was the last word she ever spoke to him. Having uttered it, she turned and swept out, her chin in the air, leaving Colombino wistful, yet relieved. All that he perceived was that she had gone. Of the mischief that she had sown he took no heed. Yet already it was germinating fiercely, soon to yield a crop of horror.

iv

It was twenty miles from Montasco to Siena, and in the course of that long ride Messer Silvio Pecci had leisure to reflect. Cooling with reflection from the hot rage in which he had flung away from Colombino, it amazed him as much as it had amazed the Marchioness that he should have been permitted to depart. To explain it he could but suppose that surprise had momentarily numbed the condottiero's wits. From this it was but a step to the conclusion that presently, rousing himself, Colombino would be after him, seeking his very life. For his own safety now, Colombino must desire the destruction of Messer Silvio. Apprehension swelled in his pusillanimous soul. Self-preservation became his only thought, and however he might ply his wits, he could see one only way to ensure it.

It was an ugly, treacherous way, and it would set some heads aloft on pikes to decorate the city walls. But fear and jealousy of the condottiero, acting in alliance, whipped him recklessly forward along the only path to safety that he could perceive. Among the heads to fall would certainly be that of this braggart captain; and another would be Squillanti's. He almost sniggered to think that thus at one blow he would deprive the wanton Caterina of both husband and lover. She should learn what it meant to break faith with Silvio Pecci. The sense of his power for vengeance gave him consequence in his own eyes. That others would share the fate of Colombino and Squillanti gave him no pause. So that he made himself safe he cared not how many heads might fall or whose.

He took a night for reflection. He pondered well whom he could trust to be the recipient of the betrayal he intended. First to his mind came Piccolomini, the Pope's cousin and one of the foremost gentlemen of Siena, who had not, after all, been brought by Squillanti into the conspiracy because he was accounted honestly devoted to the State as it existed. But Piccolomini was Colombino's friend, and he might destroy the plot without destroying Colombino. Next he considered Petrucci. But Petrucci, too, was Colombino's friend, and even more close with him than Piccolomini. Besides, he regarded Petrucci as a self-seeker whom it would be dangerous to trust.

His choice fell at last upon that prominent and resolute member of the Signory, Ettore Malavolti, and he rode out to seek him at his country house on the Arbia.

The disdainful tolerance with which that arrogant patrician welcomed Messer Silvio was turned to horror when he learnt from him of the plot to overthrow the Republic, and to still deeper horror when he heard the names of the persons implicated.

'Miserable wretch! Why do you bring this tale to me?'

'Because I have not the courage to go before the Signory. I…I am too conscious of my fault in having even listened to these seducers. You are an understanding man, Malavolti. The Signory might not account my disclosure the amend that it is. But you see that. You see that, and you will make the Signory see it. The glory of unmasking this infamy will be yours. You will…'

'Leave that,' he was harshly bidden. 'Who cares to count such glory? It is barest duty. They would set up a duke, would they? The fools! The knaves!' He turned on the dainty gentleman with flashing eyes. 'You may thank God that He inspired you with this timely penitence of your treacherous practices. Thus at least you save your neck.'

'I am more concerned,' said Pecci, relieved by this assurance, 'to save the Republic.'

But Malavolti sniffed and sneered at him. 'Heroic, are you not? You rise from this dunghill with its filth upon you, and cry: Behold how clean and pure I am. You earthworm!'

'I suppose,' lisped Pecci with a sigh, 'that I deserve your scorn.'

'Suppose it? Be sure of it, and be damned!' He swung on his heel and paced the long room in fury, waving his long arms. 'They would set up a duke!' he cried again. 'Lord God! They would ape the Florentines! I marvel that they, too, did not choose a pill-maker for their prince.' He came to a halt, his arms akimbo, towering dominant over the pallid Silvio. 'Go to bed. It is too late to ride again tonight. In the morning we will talk of this again. The Signory must be warned at once, so that these scoundrels may be dealt with as they deserve. There'll be a crop of beads in the Campo before the week is out. Give thanks to God before you sleep that you have had the sense to save your own. Go, man. My servants will light you.'

Pecci went, thankful to escape from that scornful presence. But when they met again to break their fast upon the morrow, the storm appeared to have passed from Malavolti's soul. He must in the course of the night have found reason for relenting from his angry contempt of his guest, for now Pecci found him almost affable.

'Before we announce this matter to the Signory, there is a problem to be solved. It has kept me wakeful. The matter is not quite so simple as it seemed.'

'I perceive no complication,' ventured Silvio.

'But you will when I expound it; and you shall help me to resolve it.' He rose and went to the window, thence surveying his lordly park which stood gold-tinted in the sunlight. 'It's a fine day. Suppose we take a walk. I find it assists thought. Besides, we can talk at ease as we go, without fear of eavesdroppers.'

It was not for Pecci in his delicate situation to thwart any of Malavolti's wishes or to pester him with questions. They set out.

227

But as they wandered farther and farther through cool, leafy glades beside the sparkling waters of the Arbia, it was not of plots, but of nature and its glories that Malavolti discoursed with all the fervour of one who is something of a poet in his keen sensuous perceptions.

Particularly, when they came to it, he desired Pecci's attention to a wide circular pool, a great basin hollowed in granite by the torrent. Its sides were green with moss that was like velvet until within a foot or so of the water, where they became smooth as polished steel. Trout were poised in its clear greenish depths.

'Lovely is it not?' said Malavolti in ecstasy. 'To me it is as some vast jewel; a tourmaline upon the noble breast of Italy. We call it Leda's Bathing Pool.'

'Why Leda's?' quoth the foolish Silvio, so as to be amiable.

'Because it would be in some such crystalline bath that Jupiter surprised her.'

His fancy captured, laughing at the conceit, Messer Silvio leaned forward to obtain a better view, and in that moment Malavolti thrust him vigorously in.

Spread-eagled he took the water, scattering the trout.

He rose gasping and spluttering.

High above him on the basin's rim stood Malavolti, and since Malavolti's laughter pealed through the glade, Messer Silvio supposed himself the victim of a brutal jest. All the world knew that there was a vile streak of brutality in Malavolti. Silvio cursed him now with what breath he had.

'Will you laugh while I drown, brute beast?'

'You would laugh yourself if you could see yourself: so like a fly in a bowl of milk.' And at the conceit Malavolti laughed still more heartily.

Silvio's rage began to turn to panic. 'Lend a hand, in God's name! Don't you see that it is impossible to climb out without assistance? Lend a hand! This jest has gone far enough.'

But Malavolti never moved. He stood there, hands on hips, surveying the swimmer in his drenched finery of white and crimson.

'You are very well where you are,' he answered him. 'I am sorry that I have no Leda for you. But unless you emulate Messer Jove, and like a swan grow wings on which to raise yourself, the Ledas of this world will trouble you no more.'

With that for farewell this merry gentleman turned about, and went off through the woods, to make his way back to his villa and turn his mind to the more serious business that awaited him.

That evening he rode armed into Siena with an escort of a dozen helmets. His destination was the Squillanti Palace. Invading it, he took the Marquis by surprise, seized his person, and proceeded to a systematic hunt through his papers. The risk he took in this high-handed action was negligible, since the information Silvio had brought him assured him of the existence of incriminating letters. He found them, and in them abundant confirmation of Silvio's tale, evidence that would take off a dozen of the noblest heads in Siena.

Content, sardonically soothing Squillanti's distraught lady, who raged and threatened to make him pay with his life for this brigand outrage, he carried off the Marquis to the Public Palace, and sent messengers in haste to summon the Signory, the Captain of the People, and the Podestà.

To these, when they were assembled, Malavolti vauntingly proclaimed himself the Saviour of the State. Sternly he denounced the plot to overthrow the Republic, and named the plotters, putting forth his documents in proof.

Within the hour Squillanti's associates were under arrest, and the city was in an uproar. The tocsin was sounding from the Mangia Tower, the militia was called out, and whilst the streets rang with the cries of 'Treason!' and 'Popolo!' men flew to take up arms. All night Siena was in ferment. By morning a motley citizen army, some ten thousand strong, was afoot and surging in the great space of the Campo about the pillar of the she-wolf. Acclaiming Malavolti as the preserver of Siena, this army stood at the orders of the Captain of the People, to defend the State from a treachery the full extent of which no man as yet could gauge.

V

Colombino, twenty miles away at Montasco, remained in ignorance of these events until word of them was brought to appal him that afternoon by his friend Camillo Petrucci.

That tall, spare, elegant, and in the main gentle ascetic showed himself for once as a flame of wrath. Colombino, listening, stricken and dismayed, to the tale he unfolded, yet perceived quite clearly the source of the merciless scorn with which he invested his words. The conspiracy had offended Petrucci in his ambitions. Accounting himself, and not without reason, the first man in the State, the Lord of Siena without the title – just as Cosimo de' Medici had been before he was made Duke of Florence – it wounded him not only that there should have been a plot to set up a prince, but that the plotters could have thought of bestowing the dignity upon any but himself. In the same way it offended him to witness the high-handed manner in which Malavolti had taken charge of the situation, achieving thereby a prominence which for the moment at least completely eclipsed the prepotency of Petrucci.

All this, however, was in Camillo's tone and manner, rather than in his actual words. These were concerned with a relation of the events, with the known details of the discovery made, and with the names of the men denounced and convicted. Squillanti, Alamanni, and Allegretti were already with their Maker. Swift justice had been done upon them, and their traitor heads were grinning down from the Ovile Gate upon the city they would have betrayed. A like justice awaited all the others when they should be taken.

Colombino sat at his writing-table in the noble chamber he made peculiarly his own. His chin in his hands, his elbows on the board, he listened to Petrucci, who was restlessly pacing as he talked.

To shut out the scorching August sunlight and preserve a coolness in the room, the shutters had been almost entirely closed, and Colombino was grateful for a gloom that partly spared him the effort of setting a mask upon his emotions.

His first and natural suspicion was that Silvio Pecci was the brewer of this mischief, and that it was he who had placed Malavolti in possession of the facts upon which that gentleman had so promptly acted. But finding no mention of his own name amongst those denounced, and gathering from Petrucci's manner that no suspicion of participation yet attached to him, it began to seem to him that the betrayer could not, after all, be Silvio. If Silvio had disclosed the plot, he could have done so only with the object of destroying Colombino, who was to be regarded as the principal member of it, since it was on his behalf that the whole wretched business had been set on foot.

He broke the silence he had hitherto maintained – for he had scorned to simulate surprise – to ask a question.

'You named Silvio Pecci among the conspirators. Has he been taken?'

'He has disappeared,' said Camillo shortly. 'We suspect he was forewarned of what was coming. But we shall find him, and he'll go the way of his fellows.'

When they found him, thought Colombino, the present singular oversight where he was himself concerned would no doubt be repaired.

He sat crushed by deepest dejection, in which, however, fear for himself played little part. The dissipation of his great dream of dukedom and more, to be shared with the adored Samaritana, was of little affliction at the moment compared with his remorseful grief at the thought of all those noble lives cut off by the justice of the State for the attempt to make a prince of him. And he could spare pity, too, for the lady of the Marquis Squillanti, widowed and bereft of support by these grim events which her own levity had precipitated. Bitterly now did his conscience reproach him with his ill-starred ambition, but not quite so bitterly that he could agree with the fierce denunciations Camillo was uttering.

'There is one for whom death was too light a punishment. Something worse than death should have been designed for the man who in his reckless presumption aimed at being duke; the man responsible for all this havoc; the man who recklessly sacrificed these poor fools to his own cursed ambition.'

'Is it not possible,' said Colombino, 'that it was they who tempted him?'

'Tempted Squillanti?' Camillo was scornful.

'Squillanti?'

'Yes. Squillanti. Didn't I mention it? It was Squillanti who aimed at being duke.'

'Squillanti!' Colombino echoed again. 'There surely you are at fault.'

'At fault? Not I. You may suppose it. But there is no error possible. The papers found by Malavolti make it clear. Besides, we have Squillanti's own word for it. He was racked before he died. And he confessed.'

'Confessed?'

Colombino was bewildered. He took his elbows from the table, and sank back into his chair. In thought he went back to the night on which Squillanti had tempted him. He strove to recall the precise words used by the ill-starred Marquis, and recalling them realized how readily he had applied to himself terms which were intended to describe the other. The soldier of distinction, the man enjoying the universal esteem of his fellow citizens, the man who must appear to the people as a natural leader. He remembered now, and understood. Thus in his conceit had Squillanti, the Gonfalonier of Holy Church, described himself; and Colombino in his conceit had misapplied the description.

Quite suddenly, and without any mirth, he laughed outright; a hollow sound that set Camillo staring at him in that twilight.

It was for this, to make Squillanti Duke of Siena, that he had thrust his neck into a noose, a noose which might presently be drawn tight if any of his letters to Squillanti should come to be discovered. Truly it was matter for laughter, and for dull rage, too, that the dead Marquis in his presumption should have supposed that Colombino would lend himself to the gratification of that ambition.

Scorn of himself, and of the witlessness of his too-ready assumptions, consumed him after Petrucci had departed, and abode with him, keeping him inert until late in the afternoon when another visitor reached Montasco.

vi

The young chamberlain who announced this newcomer announced at the same time that he was cloaked, hooded, and masked, and that he would give no name.

Colombino's consideration was brief. If conjecture could not take him far, it could, at least, take him far enough to conclude that this would be someone from Siena with news.

A muffled figure, tall, erect, and treading strongly, was introduced, and disclosed, when the door had closed again, the person of Ettore Malavolti.

If Colombino was uneasy, he did not display it. He rose to greet the man who had unmasked and was casting aside his hooded cloak, the only man who, according to the exasperated expressions of Petrucci, had derived any profit from the Squillanti affair.

'The Saviour of the State!'

The sarcasm of the greeting brought a frown and then a laugh to the tall patrician's swarthy, aquiline countenance, clearly revealed, for by now the shutters had been thrown back, and the room was suffused with light.

'I do not surprise you, it seems, on this day of surprises. For it must have been that to you.'

'As to many.'

'But scarcely of the same kind. For you the chief surprise must surely have been that, whilst so many foolish heads were being shorn

233

off, no breath of suspicion should yet have uttered the name of one whom you know to be as deeply implicated in this treason as any of those impeached.'

So! It had come. But the odd thing was that it brought him no dismay. Afterward he confessed that this must have been because he sensed that here a contest awaited him. Malavolti's opening words and ironical tone were as the preliminaries of a swordsman about to engage.

Stern and cold, looking straight between the eyes of that dark, mocking face, 'What name have you in mind, sir?' Colombino asked.

'You cannot guess?'

'Why trouble, since you are here to tell me?'

'You guess that, at least. And you could easily guess the rest, since the name is your own. No need for dissimulation. It would merely waste our time.' From the breast of his tunic, Malavolti plucked a sheet, and proffered it. 'I found this letter among Squillanti's papers.'

Colombino leaned across the table to take it. It was his letter to Squillanti, with the news that Messer Gritti had been to see him, but that he temporized and thus maintained the pretext under which he kept his army standing. He frowned as he weighed the expressions he had employed. Still frowning, with something haughty in his stare, he looked at Malavolti.

'Does this incriminate me?'

'Less, much less, than two other letters which I found with it. But still, enough. It would not be easy for you to explain why Squillanti should be interested in your keeping the Company of the Dove at its full strength. Nor yet what you mean when you speak of a pretext. And you might be asked to explain these matters on the rack.' Malavolti smiled. 'At such times the fertility of a man's invention will commonly desert him. And the rack has been very busy in Siena these last four and twenty hours.'

'I gather that you are threatening me. It's a rashness I don't understand.'

'Threatening you?' Malavolti laughed outright, and now the ring of his laughter surprised Colombino by its sincerity. 'You may well not understand a rashness that would proclaim me a fool. Should I come to you in secret? Should I thrust myself into the lion's den if I came to threaten? My dear Colombo, use your wits. If I were not your friend, you would not now be alive. Ask yourself why I, who have spared no other man concerned in this conspiracy, should have refrained from denouncing you with the others. Ask yourself.'

'I have done so. But I can't find the answer. They tell me that your credit stands high in Siena for the shambles you have made there. If it was in your power to increase that credit by yet another victim, I don't know why, being what you are, you should not have done so.'

'This is to play comedy,' said that grim comedian, with a careless smile. 'Leave heroics. Let us be practical. I am, above all, a practical man, without false sentiment of any kind. Sentiment is an expression of weakness, either of the head or of the heart. It is not for you and me, who are strong men.'

'The association flatters me.'

'I hope so. For I look to see it carried further. Much further. I take my opportunities when I perceive them. Had I yielded to mawkish sentiment I should not now be hailed in Siena, as you hailed me, as the Saviour of the State. Petrucci is in a foam of rage to see his star obscured. Piccolomini has shut himself up with his spleen at my ascendancy.' He laughed his rich, deep-throated laugh, and, entirely at his ease, found himself a chair and sat down.

'So let us be frank with each other. You will perceive the futility of dissembling when I tell you that my information of your share in the business does not rest upon these letters. I had it all from Silvio Pecci. It was he who betrayed the plot to me, chiefly so that he might pull you down. That woman of Squillanti's… But that's no matter. The irony is amusing. The lovely Silvio betrayed a dozen men, so that he might destroy just you; and of that dozen, you are the only one who has escaped so far.' He paused. 'You do not even smile, Colombo.'

235

'It is not amusing.' And then for an instant he yielded to his passion. 'God's blight on that fribble! I should have strangled him with my hands when he was here.'

Malavolti sat back, and threw one shapely, vigorous leg over the other. He toyed with a gold tassel at the breast of his purple tunic. He sighed as he smiled. 'So often we are wise too late. Take warning, my friend. Do not commit that error twice.'

'Shall we be coming to the matter that brings you here? Will you tell me why you spared me whilst sending so many worthy men to their doom? For this, I take it, is what you have come to tell me.'

'Of course. And you are wrong to sneer, as you shall come to agree, I hope.

'When that poor pimp Silvio chose me rather than another for his disclosure, it was because he knew my love for Siena. What he did not suspect' –and now Malavolti became slowly emphatic– 'was that I should perceive merit in the plot. When I came to take thought, I was persuaded that a duke would be to the advantage of the State. The only thing I could not approve was the person chosen by the plotters for the office. Squillanti was certainly not the man. A good-natured, clumsy blunderer who suffered from a delusion, amongst others, that he was a great soldier. The gonfalon of the Church was his ruin. If he had not been a fool to the marrow, he would never have brought such a creature as Silvio Pecci into the business.' He affected gloom, and heaved a sigh. 'I was sorry to take off Squillanti's head. I had an affection for the man. But there was no help for it. All had to be removed; that is to say, all but you, Ser Colombo. Do you wonder why? Yet surely it is clear. Because you and your army will be as necessary to impose the duke of my choice upon Siena as to impose Squillanti. Do you begin to understand?'

'At last. And the duke of your choice?'

'Can you not guess? Do you know a better man than myself?'

'Yourself! The Saviour of the State!' Colombino laughed in anger, and smote the table violently with his hand. 'God's light! And to further your treacherous ambition, you play the patriot, and bring a dozen of the noblest heads in Siena to the block!'

'And thereby so establish myself in the people's trust and love that my transition to the dukedom is already half-accomplished. Don't overlook that.'

'I am in danger of overlooking nothing. If this is what you came for, you might have spared yourself the journey. You may be the duke of your own choice; but, as God's my witness, you are not the duke of mine.'

Malavolti betrayed no resentment. His smile grew tolerant even.

'I think I understand. After all, it seems that you are not immune from the weakness of sentimentality. That is what is stirring in you, masquerading as righteous indignation. If you were ready to set up a duke in Siena, it must be – for I assume you honest – that you thought Siena would fare better under a duke. Can you truly suppose that my merit is less than Squillanti's?' He stood up suddenly, majestic in his carriage, in his height and vigour. 'Surely you behold in me a man of firmer purpose, a man of the fibre necessary for government. If you were ready to support Squillanti, why should you not be ready to support me?'

'Support him!' Colombino ejaculated. And there he checked, smothering the ironic laughter that was struggling to his lips. He turned aside and strode to one of the windows. He leaned upon the sill, and stood looking out upon the courtyard where the shadows were lengthening. Of what avail to tell the truth to this mocker? He spoke without turning.

'I lend myself to no more attempts to set up a duke in Siena.'

He heard Malavolti's sigh, and turned at last as his visitor began to speak. 'You drive me to odious extremes by your obstinacy. I may not be the duke of your choice, as you have told me; but you are certainly the soldier of mine. Since together we cannot fail, I cannot do without you. Therefore, either you support me as I invite you, or I must do my duty by the State. I must discover those letters that you wrote to Squillanti. You perceive that I have no other choice, especially as I have been so frank with you.'

It was never more fortunate for Colombino than at this moment that he was a man of deliberate thought. He perceived quite clearly the deadly peril in which he stood. No indulgence of the hot rage that surged in him against this laughing scoundrel would avail him here.

'There is something that has escaped your calculations,' he said slowly. 'The man who denounced me to you, this Silvio Pecci, will never suffer that I, the one man whose ruin he desired, should escape. Indeed, he may impeach you with me, for not having used your knowledge of my guilt.'

Malavolti uttered a chuckle of relief. 'Is that where the shoe pinches? Faith, if you suppose that I overlooked that, then you are right to suppose me unfit to rule. My friend, that danger was the first thing I perceived. And I removed it. Messer Silvio will trouble us no more.'

He went on to relate quite frankly and with relish, as if taking pride in his subtlety, the story of yesterday's morning walk with Silvio, and its abrupt ending in a pool of the Arbia.

'In Leda's Bathing Pool. "I am sorry that I have no Leda for you," I said to him, and left him swimming there, like a fly in a bowl of milk.' He laughed at the memory of it and at the amusing image he had used yesterday, and now used again. And he repeated it: 'Like a fly in a bowl of milk.'

Colombino pondered him with amazed disgust, less perhaps because of that cold-blooded murder for purposes of calculating greed than because he could find amusement in remembering and relating it. Malavolti perceiving only the amazement in the soldier's glance, and accepting it as a tribute to his lively wit, crossed the room, to set a friendly hand upon his shoulder.

'So let no thought of Silvio prove the obstacle. He's been safe in Hell these six and thirty hours. Come, now.' His tone became one of friendly cajolery. 'Consider where your interest lies. You'll find me a better master than ever Squillanti would have been. When I am duke, your place will be assured.'

Colombino's soul was shuddering under the touch of that jovial murderer's hand; his pride was in revolt against the promise of patronage from such a man; his impulse was to strike the self-assured smile from that mocking, masterful face. Instead, however, he came out of a momentary absorption to answer Malavolti as the man required.

'So be it,' he said. 'Since you have disposed of Silvio, you have disposed of my objections.' He smiled. 'For the rest, I really have no choice.'

'In that you are perhaps more fortunate than you yet perceive.' Malavolti, gay now that he had prevailed, slapped his shoulder with amicable vigour. 'We understand each other, then?'

'Oh, yes. Be sure of that. You'll stay to sup?'

But Malavolti shook his head. He had come in secret, and he would not have his unmasked face beheld by Colombino's servants. He would drink, however, a cup of Montasco, to pledge their association.

So when he had resumed his mask and cloak, the wine was brought. It was the same that Caterina Squillanti had drunk there two days ago. How all the world had changed since then!

Malavolti savoured it, and spoke of it in terms of praise.

'You must see my vineyards as you go,' said Colombino. 'I will walk down the hill with you to set you on your way. I am proud of my vines. So proud that I begrudge the time my soldiering steals from them.'

And so, Malavolti leading his horse and the condottiero stepping beside him, they went down that southern slope of Montasco, which fell away to the densely wooded valley of the turbulent Ombrone.

The soldier now was lost in the husbandman. With pride and knowledge Colombino pointed out the features of the place he had fashioned: his method of training the vines, so as to ensure for the fruit the maximum of sunlight, and in particular his laborious provision for irrigation. On the lowest terrace of all he brought his guest to the vast estang, and explained to him the sluices opening to the river, so that flooding might be avoided in time of water-plenty.

Malavolti admired the pleasant lingering-place that Colombino had here created. The rocks over which the water had been led to cascade into the estang were guarded by a colossal stone figure of

Hercules leaning upon his club. About three sides of the great tank pillars of rough-hewn granite carried a framework of beams, over which lemon and orange trees had been trained to make a cool and fragrant roof. Seats of white marble invited repose in that green shade beside the placid sheet of water which reflected now the ensaffroned evening sky. But Colombino was still the husbandman and engineer.

'This,' he explained, 'ensures water for our fields beyond in times of drought. A deal has been drawn off today. As you see, the level has sunk considerably. But it will be full to the rim again by morning, and meanwhile there is no lack. The depth is fully twenty feet.'

Malavolti stood beside the low parapet and looked down. Near the smooth sides of the tank the water, some six feet below, was green with vegetation, patches of which bore now a snowy bloom. He commended the fine storage so easily procured. He must do something of the kind on his property of the Arbia.

'Now what in Heaven's name can that be?' wondered Colombino, and pointed.

To follow the indication of his hand, Malavolti craned farther out over the water.

'I can see nothing,' he complained.

'You need to get a little nearer,' said Colombino, with a queer, sudden laugh.

A moment Malavolti strove desperately against the hands that had seized and were impelling him. Then he plunged headlong down to plumb the water's depth, even as yesterday on the Arbia he had sent another.

With a foot on the parapet and an elbow on his knee, Colombino leaned over to survey the floundering, discomfited patrician.

'I follow your advice, Malavolti. This time I do not make, as I did with Silvio, the mistake of being wise too late.'

Malavolti, scarcely able to swim, kept himself precariously afloat by frantic struggles. His eyes bulged in his upturned, livid face.

'Scoundrel! Inhuman beast! Will you see me drown?'

'Only sentiment could persuade me to rescue you. And sentiment, Malavolti, as you so truly said, is not for strong men such as you and I.'

He took his foot from the parapet, and turned away. Malavolti began a screech that ended in a gurgle. Colombino stepped back, on a sudden thought.

'And I am sorry that I have no Leda for you in your watery adventure.'

But it is to be doubted if the wildly splashing Malavolti heard him.

Colombino went to untether the patrician's horse. He loosed the girths, and removed saddle and bridle, lest these should lead to easy identification. Then, with a stinging cut across the hams, he drove the animal into the woods by the river.

It was almost dark when, with a tranquil conscience and the sense of justice poetically done, he regained his villa. In the hall he summoned his factor.

'Orlando, I observe that the estang is in danger of becoming foul. You will open the sluices tonight, and let all the filth that has gathered in it go down the river.'

Chapter 8

THE LADY PARAMOUNT

i

Pandolfini, the Sienese chronicler from whose records so much of my history of Colombino is derived, makes philosophy at this stage. He draws attention at length to the furtive manner in which Destiny spins her threads and the tortuous ways by which she leads man to fulfilment.

If you mark the sequel you will agree that he is justified. It will reveal that events which in themselves seemed almost disconnected were in effect the solid links of a chain that Destiny was forging. If the chance affair of Monsieur de La Bourdonnaye had not come to cast into relief, though spuriously, the solid Roman quality of Colombino's loyalty, he would never have been appointed Captain-General of Aragon in the Neapolitan campaign. Had he not been vouchsafed that opportunity to cover himself with glory, he would not have been accorded his triumph in Siena on. his return, and consequently could not have been under the delusion which made him involve himself in the Squillanti conspiracy. Had he not so involved himself, he would not, as he did upon realizing the peril in which he stood when that matter was discovered, have consented to avail himself of the Venetian proposals. And had he not done this, Venetian aims would never have sought fulfilment, and that which follows for Colombino would never have come to pass.

The decision to enter Venetian service was taken on the same night that saw the end of the ambitious Malavolti, and was the direct result of that unsavoury business.

The letters Colombino had written to Squillanti still existed, and they might at any moment be brought to light. Their terms had been guarded, and in themselves they might not be enough to compromise him. But when taken in conjunction with the fact that he had kept his army standing at full strength, he could not hope to give them an innocent explanation. He might, of course, at once disband this army. But that would afterwards appear as a measure taken in panic upon the discovery of the conspiracy, and supply merely a further measure of incrimination. To say that he had held his force together whilst considering the Venetian proposals would hardly suffice. Unless he ended by accepting these proposals, that would probably be regarded, and rightly, as a pretext. Whilst nothing might quite definitely be proved against him, yet the suspicion would be so strong as to represent a risk in believing him innocent. And it was not the way of Italian states in the quattrocento to shoulder these risks out of any humanitarian considerations. The fate of Carmagnola at the hands of Venice and of Gisberto da Correggio at those of Siena were proof enough of this.

If Colombino had temporized so long with Venice, it was, we know, for his own ends. At heart he had no intention of entering the service of the Serenissima. Of what his experiences were when he had served her under Colleoni in his early days, we have no details. But it does seem clearly to transpire that he had no love for the great Republic of the North, and I suspect that had his hand not now been forced, had he not been under the necessity of finding a definite cloak for his part in recent events, he would not on that same night have despatched a messenger to Siena, inviting the Venetian orator, Messer Grimani – by whom Messer Gritti had lately been replaced – to do him the honour of a visit on the morrow.

Messer Grimani came with alacrity and betimes, borne in a mule litter, for his obesity had bred in him a reluctance for the saddle.

The interview was brief and definite. Colombino's captains, Sangiorgio and Caliente, were with him when he received the envoy, and both were jubilant at the decision which their leader was about to announce.

Grimani was of the utmost affability, and produced his parchments, setting forth the terms and the princely stipend upon which the Count of Ostiamare was to assume supreme command of the Venetian forces in succession to the great Colleoni, for a term of three years.

Colombino gave the parchment little more than a cursory glance. Now that his resolve was taken, he was in haste to have done. He signed and sealed the bond, and received in exchange the signature of His Serenity the Doge.

Grimani rubbed his hands. 'And now that this is happily concluded, Lord Count, I already have for you the orders of the Serenissima.'

'You gentlemen of Venice waste no time.'

'We take it by the forelock. My courier will leave today with the welcome news. On receipt of it, the Venetian captains will be ordered to assemble on the Brenta there to encamp and wait for you to come and take command. Their strength will amount to some fourteen thousand men. With the six thousand of your own – the Company of the Dove and your auxiliaries – you will be at the head of a magnificently equipped army of twenty thousand. With such a force you should easily excel the great achievements that already honour your name. The question now is, How soon can you set out?'

If Venice was in haste, so was Colombino. The sooner he were gone the better, lest anything should yet happen to prevent his going.

'Within a week,' he promised.

Grimani nodded. 'Excellent. Ten days at most to move your company to the Brenta. You will be there before the middle of

September. The year wears on, so that, as you see, there is need for haste.'

'I perceive it. And from the Brenta whither?'

'Orders will reach you when you are in camp there. It is probable that I may be the bearer of them. So that we shall meet again. I set out for Venice myself today.'

When he was gone, Colombino sat glooming, chin in hand. 'He will bear me orders from the Ten,' he grumbled, his lip curling as he looked at his captains. 'That is ever the thorn for him who serves Venice. Always a commissioner of the Republic at his elbow to spy, to report, to order, to direct, to thwart. A malediction on that service! There is no trust in it. Always is the Serenissima as suspicious as a jealous woman. But we are pledged, and that's the end of it.'

'You'll find it prove a glorious beginning,' Sangiorgio soothed him. 'To stand where Colleoni stood, and at your age, child?'

'The only great soldier whose heart they did not break.'

'Because like yours it was too big and stout for their breaking.'

'What I have I derive from him. Colleoni! It is not ten years since I commanded ten helmets in his company. And now! I would he could have lived to see it.'

But whatever his reluctance to serve the Most Serene Republic and whatever his forebodings, he did not lose sight of the need to be gone from the Sienese with all despatch, and true to his promise, within a week of signing, the Company of the Dove was marching north, a long line of horse and foot, or men-at-arms and pikemen, of crossbowmen, of engineers with a siege-train drawn by oxen, and a rear-guard of sutlers with their carts and pack-mules. Within the time prescribed this host had come to the vast encampment in the flat low-lying lands by the mouth of the Brenta, just south of the lagoons, where breezes from the Adriatic tempered the September heat which was still torrid in that year.

There, whilst awaiting marching orders from the Most Serene, he was actively employed in drilling and in consolidating into a homogeneous force the various mercenary companies that went to make up this great army under his command.

What leisure these duties left him, Colombino fell into the habit of spending in the little neighbouring town of Chioggia on the lagoon.

Returning thence one afternoon, when he had been a week or so in the camp, he came within a half-mile of the town upon a grey friar and a mule. The mule, tethered to a sapling, was cropping such green blades as it could find among the parched grass by the dusty roadside. The friar, who had been sitting near it, rose at Colombino's approach, and stood forth, a tall, grey figure, whose face was lost within the shadows of his cowl.

Colombino, conceiving that he understood why the fellow should thus put himself in his way, groped in his scrip for a coin, without, however, slackening the pace of his big white charger. This constrained the friar to fall aside. But he hailed the rider, employing the conventual phrase:

'God give you peace, noble Captain.'

Colombino laughed as he answered him: 'God take away your alms, little brother.' Nevertheless, he tossed a piece of silver down into the dusty road as he sped past.

He heard the friar's voice behind him raised to shout. He supposed it to be a scandalized rejoinder to his jest, and laughed again as he rode on.

ii

A little later that day when, having returned to camp, Colombino sat at his ease in the splendid pavilion that had been set up for him, seeking profit and finding entertainment in an indifferent copy of the *De Re Militari* of Vegetius, a shadow fell across his papers. Looking up to see who so unceremoniously came to block the light, he beheld in the entrance a tall, closely cowled grey friar.

From the depths of the cowl came greeting. '*Pax tibi.*'

'*Et tibi pax,*' said Colombino carelessly, to add more sharply: 'Who are you? And how come you past the guard?'

246

'What guard would hinder a poor little mendicant brother?'

'Is it alms you seek?'

'No. An explanation.' The voice, rich and full, held none of the humility the man's kind professed. Unbidden, and without ceremony, he advanced to the camp-table, his hands folded before him within the capacious sleeves of his coarse habit. 'I come to ask why you should return me evil words for good.'

Then Colombino remembered him, and understood the question. A mild resentment of this presumption was blended with amusement.

'You mistook me. I answered you in kind. The peace you augured me would take away my livelihood, which lies in war. Each to his trade, little brother.'

'Each to his trade, as you say. But what trade is yours? Is it such a trade as Judas Iscariot drove?'

Colombino frowned. But supposing that he had to deal with some insane fanatic, he kept his temper. 'I do not remember to have heard how Judas earned his livelihood; nor at this time of day can I suppose it matters. You are interrupting me, little brother. I beg you to go with God.'

The friar, however, was not to be dismissed. 'I had in mind a transaction by which Judas earned some thirty pieces.'

'Sir Friar, you push my patience somewhat far. To what evil invention have you been giving heed?'

'Invention? You have the short memory that supports an evil conscience. You will have forgotten Ravenna and Onorato da Polenta? That you were once in his hire? That he esteemed you so highly, was so deceived in you, that he betrothed to you his daughter Samaritana, his only child? That you, counting your pledge as naught when it otherwise suited your greedy ambition, betrayed his trust and went your ways, leaving him at the mercy of his enemies? Have you forgotten all this?'

Colombino came to his feet, his countenance set and grey, so that the lines of it seemed sharpened. His eyes were terrible.

'When truth is seasoned with the spice of falsehood, then all the tale's a lie, Sir Friar.' Lightly and swiftly he stepped round the table. 'If so be that you are indeed a friar.'

Without other warning he swept back the man's cowl, and so uncovered the narrow, pallid countenance of Cosimo da Polenta.

They stood a moment eye to eye, a sneer on Cosimo's face, surprise on Colombino's.

'What do you want of me?' the soldier challenged him.

'To say what I have said,' replied the priest.

'You deal, then, in futilities. As for what lay between me and Samaritana, that concerns none but her and me.'

'It concerns every man of the house and blood whose honour you slighted.'

'Vain words. As vain as the paltry lie that I left the Lord Onorato at the mercy of his enemies. I so broke up his enemies that they never again raised a hand against him in his lifetime. God rest his soul.'

'You pray for him, do you? It's in your part. Order masses for his soul whilst treacherously advancing the evil that is brewing for his house.'

'Is your mind unhinged, Sir Priest?'

'Are you not paid by Venice to subdue Ravenna, and so undo what you were paid to do by the Lord Onorato? Is there in all the world a trade more treacherous and base than yours?'

'I see. I see,' said Colombino, and grew yet more contemptuous. 'Why, you lunatic, it is war with Milan that is afoot, as all the world knows by now. That is the sole purpose of my hire.'

Cosimo's dark glance gave him plainly the lie. 'Does it say so in your parchments? Is there any express condition in them that you shall serve only against Milan? Is not your hire for the occasions of the Most Serene?'

Colombino hesitated on a sudden doubt, which he as suddenly dismissed. 'Ravenna is not one of those occasions.'

'It happens that I am better informed. This coveted southern outpost is to be swept up by you in passing, and annexed at last to the Most Serene Republic.'

The doubt returned, and grew in Colombino's mind, thrusting out resentment. But he resisted it. 'I do not believe you.'

'It comes as news to you, does it? The poor pretence!'

'So far is it from a pretence that if I did believe you, I must resign my command.'

Bitter mockery was in the other's laugh. 'Comedian! Will you even pretend that you would dare to play with Venice as you played with Ravenna? Will you?'

The colour was creeping back into Colombino's face on a rising tide of anger. His mouth was hard.

'You have doled out insolence enough. You had better go. And quickly.'

Instead, Messer Cosimo came yet a step nearer. His face was yellow.

'First hear what else I have to say. I come from Florence. I have been there to warn the Signory of these Venetian intentions, and I have made some stir. The Signory will not tolerate a Northern prepotence such as Venice aims at establishing. Florence is already arming to intervene and to join hands with Milan. With Florence in the field and yourself removed, Ravenna should be safe. The first is assured. I am here to ensure the second. I bring you this!'

On the word his right hand flashed forth from the concealing sleeve to deal a lightning stroke. But the soldier caught the gleam of steel in that swift hand, and instincts as swift moved him to ward the blow. Before attack and defence had even penetrated his consciousness, he found himself grasping Cosimo's wrist between both his hands. After that, at grips, they swayed and staggered across the pavilion. Then, interlocked, like a pair of wrestlers, they went down and rolled over together.

But from the moment that the surprise had failed, the issue was in no doubt. When Colombino had at last wrenched away the dagger, he rose and stood over his assailant. Cosimo struggled to his knees, and in that posture remained on the defensive, panting.

'Madman!' the soldier growled at him. 'What shall I do with you? Shall I summon my provost-marshal to take you out and hang you, or shall I give you back your dagger in your throat?'

Cosimo, livid and breathless, glared baffled hate at him for only answer.

Thus for a long moment they remained. Then the rigidity of Colombino's expression softened. He spoke quietly. 'If I do neither, it is because I perceive a better use for you. Get up! You shall bear a message for me to your cousin Samaritana. Tell her that in no circumstances shall my hand be ever raised against her. Tell her that if your assumptions were correct and her patrimony imperilled, rather than be the instrument of those who imperil it, I and my company would hasten to preserve it for her. Bear her that message with my duty and homage, Messer Cosimo. Here, man, take your dagger.'

Cosimo picked up the weapon so contemptuously flung to him. He came to his feet and took a step forward, his body bent, his face blank in incredulity.

'You mean...' He checked, and drew himself erect. 'I can't believe you. I...'

'I know. I know. You are like all the rest. Not even your priesthood makes it easier for you to believe good than evil. But whether you believe me or not, convey my message. And you had better go, sir. I do not want to be under the necessity of explaining you if you are found here.' He turned his back upon Cosimo, and flung himself as if weary into a chair.

Cosimo stood yet a moment hesitating. Then, he drew the cowl over his head, folded once more his hands into his sleeves, and crossed slowly to the entrance. There he paused, and turned.

'I will convey your message,' be said. 'God will not forgive you if you have lied.'

Colombino answered nothing. He sat as if he had not heard.

Cosimo stepped out into the sunlight. The main body of the camp lay ahead of him, a city of canvas, green and brown and white, with bannerols fluttering here and there from the summits of the tents, and a glimpse of soldiers moving in the lanes between them, sauntering, hurrying, or lounging. Somewhere in the distance a drum was beating. Cosimo turned to the right, and with his face to the sea moved at a calm, leisurely pace over the parched grass. He had come level with a group of huts, a score of paces from Colombino's pavilion, when suddenly the daylight was blotted from his sight.

A cloak that was being tightly twisted enveloped his head. Strong hands gripped him on either side, and held him powerless. Then in silence and in darkness, helpless to resist the pressure exerted, he felt himself being hurried swiftly away.

iii

Messer Paolo Grimani, the commissioner of the Most Serene Republic, sat on the edge of a day-bed in his pavilion. It was a tent equipped with a splendour almost barbaric, enriched by a luxury of hangings, of carpets, of gilded furniture and other appointments for which heavy toll had been levied on the East.

His worthiness was making a simple collation of figs and rye bread which he washed down with a heavy golden Greek wine. He was waited upon by a graceful, fair-haired stripling in scarlet with the winged lion wrought in gold upon his breast.

Into this scene of peaceful luxury came a young man in a steel cap in which the little tuft of scarlet feathers proclaimed the officer. He was mildly excited.

'We have him here, Excellency.'

'Ah!' The commissioner dusted some crumbs from his plump fingers, passed a damask napkin across his lips, and looked up with dull, slow-moving, benign eyes. In general the appearance of this sluggish, obese, middle-aged man suggested the amiable imperturability of an Eastern idol. 'There was no fuss? No alarm?'

'None, Excellency.'

'Very good. Bring him in.'

251

The officer stepped to the entrance to issue a command, then stood aside. Into the pavilion two men-at-arms hustled a man with a cloak about his head. They loosed the cloak, and pulled it away together with the cowl, leaving Messer Cosimo da Polenta to blink at the portly commissioner of the Serenissima.

Messer Grimani gravely considered that proud, dark face, and still more gravely the black hair above it, falling in a fringe across the brow.

'For a little brother of Saint Francis,' he said, 'your tonsure needs enlarging. We have ways of doing it; ways involving the use of whipcord. They are detestable, but I see no alternative, unless you tell me that you are not really a little brother of Saint Francis, and at the same time tell me who you are and what was your business with the Captain-General of the Venetian forces.'

Cosimo glared at him. 'You do not frighten me.'

'My friend!' Grimani protested.

'And you cannot torture me without sacrilege. I am a priest.'

'Just so. Just so,' the benign Grimani agreed. 'But unless you tell me who you are, how am I to believe you? You will be reasonable, I hope. You come here in disguise. So much is obvious.' He shrugged his fat shoulders. 'It would be a dreadful thing to put you to the question, and then discover that you are a priest. It might be even more dreadful for you than for me. I do not know.'

'If I answer you, it is because I have nothing to conceal. Neither my name, nor my business here. I am Cosimo da Polenta, cousin of the sovereign Countess of Ravenna.'

Grimani betrayed no emotion of any kind. 'Then I need not ask you what your business was. At least not yet. Take him away, Ser Montone, and keep him close.'

But Cosimo had yet a word to say. 'I'll make no secret of my business. I came to kill your Captain-General.'

This stirred Grimani at last. He sat upright, and his dull eyes quickened.

The officer interposed: 'He had a bare knife in his hand when we took him. It is here.'

Grimani waved it away. 'Messer Colombo?' he asked the officer.

'Oh, I did not succeed,' said Cosimo. 'He wrenched the knife from me. That he restored it to me was a sign of his Satanic pride. I...'

Grimani seemed to have lost interest from the moment that he learnt that the attempt had failed.

'Take him away, Montone. Do as I said. See that he communicates with nobody. I shall want him again.'

When they had taken him out, Grimani returned to his figs and his rye bread. Then he put up his legs.

'Set a cushion behind me, boy. So.' He lay back at his ease with a gusty sigh. 'Now send someone to the Count of Ostiamare's pavilion...'

He was interrupted. One of the guards appeared in the entrance, the flap of which was kept raised.

'The Lord Count of Ostiamare to see your worthiness.' Colombino came in as light of step as he was heavy of countenance.

The commissioner lifted a jewelled hand in greeting, pointed to the golden jug on the table at his elbow, and ordered the page to pour a cup for his potency.

But the soldier waved away the lovely Murano goblet and ignored the chair that was set for him. His tone was as blunt and peremptory as the words he uttered.

'I am come to ask your worthiness for precise information upon Venetian intentions in the approaching campaign. Precise, if you please.'

Those dull eyes which betrayed nothing and missed nothing looked at him mildly. 'You inquire most seasonably. I was about to send for you. Orders from the Serenissima have just reached me.' He swung his feet to the ground. 'Help me up, boy.'

Leaning on the arm of his page, he heaved himself from his low couch, and crossed ponderously to the table in the middle of the tent, there to unfold and spread a map. He beckoned Colombino to his side.

'This red line marks the Venetian frontiers on the mainland which this war is to teach Milan to respect.'

Colombino studied the map, frowning, then tapped it with an impatient forefinger. 'Here is something I learn for the first time. Ravenna, I see, is placed within the intended frontier.'

'Ah, yes,' Grimani lisped. 'That is the only change in the old line, the only increase of territory desired. But very important. Ravenna is a strong place, necessary as a southern outpost to the security of Venice. The letters I have just received from the Ten order that you open the campaign by proceeding to reduce and occupy it as soon as may be. No resistance is to be expected.'

Colombino straightened himself, and looked down from his fine height upon the portly Venetian. 'In our compact, Messer Grimani, there was no mention of this.'

His worthiness seemed unconscious of the asperity in the Captain's tone. Reflectively he pursed his lips and stroked his smooth round chin. 'Not specifically. No. Ravenna was not mentioned. But what then? Your hire is for three years. It would be not only idle, but impossible to specify all that may be required of you within that time; for it is something that no one could foretell. Your engagement is for all undertakings that the Ten in their wisdom may desire.'

'Sir, shall we leave quibbles?'

'Quibbles?' Mildly reproachful was the lift of Messer Grimani's brows. 'If you dispute what I have said, the quibbling will be yours, Lord Count.'

Colombino made a gesture of impatience. 'Your worthiness has been less than frank with me.'

'I? Less than frank? Sir, I am incapable of a lack of frankness with you. Read your parchment, sir. Refresh your memory.'

'If my parchment confirms what you have just said, then, sir, we are in a misunderstanding.'

'But how is that possible? How else could your engagement run?'

Colombino felt himself entangled. He was in despair. 'We are in a misunderstanding, nevertheless,' he insisted. 'Fortunately, it is not yet too late to correct it. If I am required to march against Ravenna, you may have back your parchments. I cannot continue in Venetian service.'

Grimani looked up at him in positive distress. 'Lord Count, this is not reasonable. Since when has a captain of fortune dictated to the State he serves in what undertakings he will serve it?'

'I am not dictating, sir. I am resigning my command.'

'And your grounds?'

'Once I took the pay of Ravenna to deliver her from Venetian dominion. I cannot now take the pay of Venice to execute a renewal of that condition.'

The distress in Grimani's face gave place to a benignly tolerant surprise. But Colombino observed for the first time how shrewd and hard could be those eyes which appeared so dull and sleepy. 'You set me a riddle, sir,' said the Venetian, smiling up at him. 'You hint at reasons which elude my simple wits.'

'I hint at nothing. I state quite plainly what honour forbids.'

'Honour!' Messer Grimani blew out his cheeks in mock gravity. 'Oh, the big, round, fat, senseless word! Honour! And on the lips not of a moonstruck knight-errant, but of a mercenary soldier who makes a trade of arms! A portent!' He laughed, and swung aside. 'Zannino! Here, boy, give me that cup.'

Colombino became impatient. 'However your worthiness regards it, I hope you understand me.'

His worthiness paused with the wine-cup almost at his lips. But his manner lost none of its jocularity. 'Then you hope for the impossible. I know of no reason why a condottiero who was on one side yesterday should not be on the opposite side tomorrow. It commonly happens. It supplies one of the reasons why we are never done with wars in Italy. No, Sir Captain.' Still smiling, he shook his head. 'I am still very far from understanding.'

'That you should not understand the motive is no matter, so long as you understand the fact. And the fact, sir – I state it clearly – is that sooner than march upon Ravenna, I will resign my command.'

The Venetian stood looking into his cup. He took a draught before replying, and he took his time in drinking. When, at last, having returned the cup to the page, he spoke, his tone and manner were as smoothly urbane as ever.

'This, Lord Count, if you will suffer me to be frank, is rankest folly. When I said that I did not understand, I was wanting perhaps a little in candour. After all, I have heard – as who has not? – that once you were to have married the Lady Samaritana da Polenta, who is now Countess of Ravenna. I must suppose that some of the tenderness which such a relationship will sometimes leave behind is responsible for your reluctance. Very romantic. Oh, very. But a captain of fortune, sir, is a practical man concerned with life's realities.'

'I have the weakness to account honour one of life's realities: honour, sir, which to you is just a fat, round, senseless word.'

'But – Mother Most Holy – we are not in the age of chivalry!'

'For your worthiness, perhaps not. For me… In short, since honour forbids me to undertake anything against Ravenna, it is idle to talk further.'

Even now Messer Grimani displayed neither heat nor dismay. He fingered his double chin a moment thoughtfully, then shrugged his fat shoulders, and wandered back to his day-bed.

'If you will commit a folly, why, then, you will.' He sat down. 'But it is not for me to release you from your engagement. I have no such power, as you should know. All that I can do is to send word of your wishes to His Serenity and the Council of Ten. Decision rests with them.'

'At your pleasure.' Colombino bowed. 'But your worthiness will understand that my own decision is irrevocable. If we are to march upon Ravenna, there is an end to my command.'

'I will so inform His Serenity. You will, of course, do nothing until I have his answer?'

'I shall hope that his answer will permit me to continue in his service.'

'That, too, I shall have the honour to communicate to him.'

They parted on this note of courtesy, and Colombino, back in his pavilion, summoned his marshals, Sangiorgio and Caliente.

When they had heard what was afoot and what were his intentions, Sangiorgio did not dissemble his dismay. A practical man, he deplored the almost certain sacrifice of a three years' engagement on excellent pay to a mere matter of sentiment, and being a man who bluntly spoke his mind, he said so.

But Don Pablo was of a mellower nature. He had a notion of what Madonna Samaritana meant to Colombino. He had been present that night at the inn at Bellaria, and he remembered. He turned upon his brother captain.

'Mother of God, Giorgio, sentiment is of the soul! Will you weigh ducats against it? Are you just a huckster-at-arms?'

'You may call me that; and yourself the same at the same time. It's well to call things by their proper names. It helps the understanding. That's why I say that sentiment should be left out of these affairs.'

Colombino looked at the gaunt old soldier. 'You may be right, Giorgio. It just is not my view in this. It might be best if I resigned my leadership of the Company of the Dove.'

This dismayed Sangiorgio as much as Caliente, and the voices of both were raised in protest.

'What are you saying, child?' cried the Florentine. 'Without you there is no Company of the Dove. And perdition take the Doge, the Ten, and all the rest of them! The Company of the Dove marches where you will and when you will. Naught else was ever in my mind. I only bewail the necessity to give up this well-paid service.'

'The necessity is not yet. His Serenity may think it worth while to sacrifice Ravenna rather than the Company of the Dove.'

But the Doge's answer when four days later it came did not support this hope. His Serenity expressed distress that a difference should have arisen at a moment rendered critical by the news that Florence was arming to ally herself with Milan. This circumstance alone made it impossible to release the Count of Ostiamare from his engagement, and His Serenity was confident that the existing difficulties could be removed. To this end he invited the Count of Ostiamare to come to Venice and confer with the Council of Ten.

257

Messer Grimani, having read the letter to him, awaited his reply. It was promptly given. With a confident smile Colombino announced that he would set out at once. For the letter had revealed to him the strength of his own position and given him the assurance that in the conference to which he was summoned, it was his will that must prevail.

But his captains, when presently he told them of it, met his smiling confidence with furious dismay.

'Are you stark mad, child?' cried Sangiorgio. 'Will you go into the lions' den?'

'I have been in lions' dens before.'

'Brave Daniel! But this is the Lion of Saint Mark! It has wings! It stoops like a falcon! Gesú!'

And Don Pablo, with a vivid morphological oath, asked him had he forgotten the fate of Carmagnola.

Colombino seated cross-legged in his pavilion laughed at their agitation as they stamped to and fro before him.

'What have I to do with Carmagnola?'

'Could cases be more parallel?' Sangiorgio demanded. 'Like you, Carmagnola was in command of the army of Venice, and his conduct did not meet the approval of the Most Serene. With fair words, such as they send you, he was invited to attend before the Ten, whom the Devil confound. When they had him there, away from his troops, they did not even weary him with a trial. They just told him that they no longer trusted him, and they decapitated him between the pillars in the Piazzetta.'

Colombino remained scornful. 'I am not like Carmagnola.'

'You'll be uncommonly like him by the time they've taken off your head.'

This Colombino disregarded. 'Carmagnola,' he said, 'was trafficking in betrayal.'

'So it was supposed,' answered Sangiorgio. 'But it was never proved. The same will be supposed of you: your proposal to resign your command and withdraw your company will be described as treason.'

'That is the pure truth,' added Don Pablo. 'Pura verdad! Heed it, Don Colombo. Heed it, by God! Don't make a widow of your company.'

'Listen to me,' Colombino bade them, very earnest now. 'There are facts and factors here which render your fears phantasmal. Florence is arming to join Milan. This makes things serious for the Serenissima. The preponderance of force upon which she counted has vanished, gone over to the other side. Suppose now that the Ten were to treat me as they treated Carmagnola, you, Sangiorgio, would be my natural successor in the command of the Company of the Dove. What would be your immediate decision?'

'March to join the Duke of Milan. Join him at need without pay, and let the Company of the Dove pay itself out of the pillage of the Venetian cities we should sack.'

'In what case, then, would Venice find herself? To the forces of Milan and Florence would be added six thousand of the best and most experienced troops in Italy today by which the Venetian army would be diminished. That would be enough for the Serenissima, I think. Rather than embark upon a foredoomed campaign, she must sue at once for peace. And do you suppose that the Ten will not perceive this just as clearly as we perceive it? They are not fools, these Venetians. You begin to see, I hope, the difference between my case and Carmagnola's? And that's not all. It is the Venetian desire to annex Ravenna that has brought in Florence. This makes it doubly important that Venice should retain my services. It is to persuade me, perhaps to try to bribe me, that the Ten require my presence. When they perceive me to stand firm, they will realize themselves checkmated, and Ravenna will be saved to Samaritana da Polenta.' He rose. 'It is on this that I go to break a lance with them in the name of chivalry.'

They were convinced. Colombino had set the thing in a light that left no shadows, and he started that same day for Venice to do the same by the Council of Ten.

He was accompanied on that short journey by Messer Grimani, with a page and two esquires for only escort. A sumptuous barge of ten oars, sent by the Serenissima, awaited them at Chioggia, and bore them swiftly to that wonder-city of the lagoons.

Colombino was landed on the steps of the Morosini Palace, a tall, yellow mansion whose Gothic windows overlooked the Grand Canal. It was placed, Grimani informed him, at his disposal for as long as it should be his pleasure to remain in Venice. Within that sybaritic interior of marble walls, tessellated pavements, carpets that were like jewels, and richly frescoed ceilings, he found all prepared for his lavish entertainment, a regiment of lackeys and a kilted, Dalmatian guard of honour. All this, he thought, was to treat him as a prince, and very proper.

iv

He was summoned next morning to wait upon the Doge. Landing at the Piazzetta, and greeted by a blare of trumpets from the Slavonian guards drawn up to honour him, he strode between the ominous granite columns of Syrian origin, and under the spell of the fantastic, voluptuous beauty of the place in the mellow golden light of that September morning, he entered the ducal courtyard, passed up the great staircase, and so into the palace.

In the Council Chamber, to which he was instantly conducted, he found the Ten assembled, and beheld amongst them the lean frame and cadaverous countenance of his old acquaintance, Messer Francesco Gritti.

At the middle of the semi-circle which the councillors formed, and a little above them, sat enthroned the Doge, Cristoforo Moro, a grey-faced, elderly man with a hard, tight mouth and cold, deep-set eyes, who for all his patrician blood was coarsely featured as a peasant. He glowed in the official chlamys of cloth of gold and his head was crowned by the golden horn that was the emblem of his princely rank.

The officer who had introduced Colombino conducted him to a gilded chair, each arm of which was carved into the shape of a lion with a forepaw resting on an open book. There he found himself at the focus of the semi-circle formed by the councillors in their shimmering robes of crimson silk.

Messer Grimani, who was also present, was invited to a stool set immediately below the ducal dais.

His Serenity, in a voice that was naturally harsh and deep, at once opened the proceedings. They were informed, he announced, by Messer Grimani of the Count of Ostiamare's reluctance to march against Ravenna, and they had, therefore, invited him to come before them and frankly state his reasons for this reluctance.

Listening to him, Colombino found himself dividing his attention between what the Doge was saying and the reflection that this was the father of a man who once had crossed the seas from Crete to seek his life. Repressing the vivid memories the thought evoked, Colombino made shift to answer.

Speaking quietly, he confined himself to a repetition of what already he had told the commissioner. It did not agree with his notions of honesty that he should take the pay of the Serenissima to destroy that which he had taken the pay of Onorato da Polenta to establish.

The deep-set eyes of the Doge considered him coldly. Otherwise there was no expression on that repellent face.

'If that is all your difficulty, Lord Count, you are too late. For already you have taken the pay of Venice.'

'The moneys shall be returned, Highness.'

Someone laughed, shortly, unpleasantly. Colombino, looking sharply towards the sound, perceived it to have been emitted by Messer Gritti. He understood at once that he could be assured of at least one active enemy in this assembly, and that Gritti's friendliness in Siena had been purely official, in itself a sham, a mask upon a vindictiveness that nothing could extinguish.

'You do not understand,' said His Serenity. 'The money was an earnest, a symbol of the binding nature of your engagement with the Most Serene Republic. And if you know anything, sir, of the history of the Most Serene, you will know that just as she never breaks an engagement, so she never tolerates the breach in others.'

'She will have to tolerate this, unless Your Serenity agrees to my terms.'

From Gritti came the snarling interjection: 'Terms!'

It provoked a rustle of silken robes and a subdued murmur of resentment. The Doge, however, remained coldly inscrutable.

'So you offer terms? We had best hear them.'

'That Ravenna be left in the enjoyment of her independence.'

This time, but for the Doge's imperiously uplifted hand, the interruption would have been general. His Serenity's voice became acid.

'So that you, sir, our hired servant, permit yourself to dictate to us upon matters of policy! It is as amusing as it is audacious. And yet it is, I suppose, what we should expect, from a man whom we find practising with the enemy.'

Colombino was moved inwardly to indignation at this early hint that his captains had been right. Since such words were used to him, it must be in the minds of the Ten to deal with him as they had dealt with Carmagnola. They had invited him here, so that they might trap him. Presently they should perceive their miscalculation. He was coldly haughty in his answer.

'Practising with the enemy? I? What fable, sir, is that?' Instead of answering him, the Doge's glance sought the attendant officer. 'Ser Barnabò,' he said, and made a sign.

It was evidently something preconcerted, for the officer stepped at once to the door, and opened it. Beyond the threshold two Slavonians waited with a prisoner. This prisoner, the officer beckoned forward, and when he had entered, closed the door upon his guards.

'Look at that man,' the Doge commanded. 'And tell me if you know him.'

Colombino turned, and, to his surprise, beheld Cosimo da Polenta in his black priestly gown.

'I know him, yes,' and Colombino named him.

'His presence will supply the answer to your question. You will not trouble to deny that disguised as a friar he penetrated the lines on the Brenta, and visited you secretly in your tent. In leaving you, he was arrested by the orders of Messer Paolo Grimani.'

The Doge may have thought to dismay him by this display of the secrecy and thoroughness of Venetian methods. He awakened only the scorn which accusation based on rash assumption must ever deserve.

'Since it is true, why should I trouble to deny it? But that Messer Cosimo should have visited me unbidden is very far, it seems to me, from proving that I practise with the enemy.'

'Does he not represent the enemy? One of the enemies? And was it not just after his visit that you announced your scruples to Messer Grimani? Does that prove nothing?'

'It proves the truth. That his visit made me aware of Venetian intentions concerning Ravenna.' Then, with an abrupt change of manner, he took a bold, impatient tone. 'And, anyway, I am not here upon my examination, but to state to you the terms upon which I will continue in your service.'

The smile that broke on the grey face of the Doge was almost sinister.

'It happens that the possession of Ravenna is a necessity to Venice for the security of her mainland provinces; and you should understand, sir, that the necessities of the Republic cannot yield to the personal scruples of one of her servants.'

'That I readily admit. Therefore, it only remains for me to take my leave, and depart from Venetian service.'

Again there was that impatient, resentful stir among the Ten. But Cristoforo Moro remained stolid.

'There are grave obstacles to our permitting it. You are aware that Florence has entered into alliance with Milan, thus increasing the odds we have to encounter.'

'Just as I am aware that it is your intention concerning Ravenna that has brought Florence into that alliance. Ravenna, sirs, is a wall against which you'll break your obstinate heads.'

263

'The feelings you betray show plainly how little guaranty we should have, if we consented to release you, that you would not pass with your company into the service of the other side. Indeed, we have every reason to assume that you will have that course in view.'

'I am prepared solemnly to engage myself to enter no service making war on Venice.'

'We have already seen, sir, how you treat an engagement.'

'What you have seen is that I treat it with fidelity even when it is overpast.'

'God give me patience with you, sir! We cannot argue forever. My brethren here agree with me that, since we can now place no trust in you, we cannot suffer you to depart again.'

The agreement of the Ten was instant, unanimous and loud.

It brought Colombino to his feet in a bound.

'Will you bray at me?' he thundered, and by his voice and attitude cowed them into silence. Every line of his face had hardened. It had assumed again that aspect of being carved of granite, and his deep-set eyes were terrible. He swept that crimson semi-circle with his glance, and brought it at last to rest upon the Doge. He spoke as if he were upon the drill-ground. 'Let us be plain. Am I a prisoner?' He paused for an answer, stern, haughty, formidable. After a moment, interpreting that silence, he relaxed again, and subdued his voice to a tone of cold rebuke. 'I came here in response to Your Serenity's invitation and trusting to your good faith.'

Gritti broke in, to mock him with the very thought that was in his mind.

'So did Carmagnola, in like case. Like you he swaggered here before us with a soldier's hectoring ways. Like him you may....' He spread his bony hands, his yellow face cracked across in an evil grin, expressing the hatred that at long last was to be gratified.

Not in all his life had Colombino been moved to such anger as that which now boiled within him. But he repressed it. He allowed only his contempt of them to show upon the surface, and in that contempt he laughed now in Messer Gritti's face.

'If you think to constrain me by threats, my masters, you waste your breath. And you, Messer Gritti, lie clumsily and loutishly out of your spite when you compare me with Carmagnola. There is no man knows better than yourself the quality of my integrity. I made you sweat once for doubting it, and that stirs your malice, I suppose. The only similarity between Carmagnola's case and mine lies in the treacherous manner in which by fair words he was lured to Venice by the Council of his day.'

There was such an explosion of wrath as only an ugly truth provokes. Every member of the Ten was on his feet, fury in voice and gesture, calling upon His Serenity to make an immediate end of this insolence.

But Colombino was not yet done. 'Hear yet a word, sirs!' He plucked a folded parchment from the breast of his purple tunic. 'When I came, I offered you a choice. You might retain my service if you abandoned the undertaking against Ravenna. Now that I know you better, that offer is withdrawn. I am not Carmagnola. I am Colombo da Siena; and I do not serve such masters.' He ripped the folded sheet across and yet across, and flung the rags of it at the feet of the Doge. 'There, sirs, is your parchment.'

Eleven pairs of eyes considered him balefully in the hush that followed. Grimani's was the only countenance that remained gloomily wistful. His Serenity, with no vestige of serenity left in his livid countenance, harshly cawed two words.

'The guard!'

The officer flung the door wide, and rapped out a command. Four Slavonians in red, with steel caps and corselets, clattered in, and ordered their halberts.

But Colombino had yet a word to say. So far he had merely displayed the husk. The kernel was still to offer these gentlemen. One backward glance he swept as the guards came in, and almost smiled to see how white and startled was the face of Cosimo da Polenta. Then he was confronting the Doge once more.

'Before Your Serenity pushes rashness too far, you would do well to weigh the consequences, and realize that you are in danger of precipitating the very thing you have good cause to fear. My marshals, Giorgio di Sangiorgio and Don Pablo Caliente, have my clear orders that, in the event of any harm befalling me, they are to march the Company of the Dove into the service of the Duke of Milan. From what Your Serenity has already said, I know that you perceive what this would mean for Venice. There will be an end to your hopes in this campaign. Indeed, there will be no campaign, unless you insist upon wooing destruction.'

That he had left clear commands was an inaccuracy, perhaps. But negligible since he no more than stated the avowed intentions of his captains. A silence of utter dismay was presently followed by angry, excited gibberings, which Moro finally quelled. Very grave, he addressed the officer.

'You will remove both your prisoners. But you will keep them both at hand until I call for them again.'

Colombino and Cosimo were led out, to leave the Council to deliberate in secret upon the fate they would measure out to the audacious condottiero.

In the antechamber, where they waited, the prisoners were under no restraint, and here to Colombino pacing restlessly came a very subdued and humbled Cosimo.

'Lord Count, you have made me sick with shame. In all humility I ask your forgiveness for the words I used to you, the attempt I made upon you. I would that the Lord Onorato could have lived to know how deceived he was.'

Colombino was touched by this proud man's contrition.

'You had but the appearances upon which to found your judgment. That is how men must ever judge.'

'If I live to leave Venice, Samaritana, at least, shall know of this. All of it. She shall learn how nobly you have borne yourself so as to champion her helplessness.'

'Yes. You owe me that.' The soldier's face grew wistful. He sighed. 'I could wish her to see in this a proof of the devotion that has never faltered since the day when for her own sake I renounced her. Tell her that, too, Ser Cosimo. And give her this.' He detached from his breast a great emerald set in brilliants that had been the gift of the Queen of Naples. 'Beg her to keep this in memory of one who is ready to give all in her dear service.'

Cosimo stared at him with round eyes. The hand in which he took the emerald was shaking.

'She is that to you? I do not understand. She is that to you, and you...'

Ser Barnabò, bethinking himself that this muttered conversation, scraps of which had reached him, might be against the wishes of the Ten, broke in to part them, so that Messer Cosimo was left with his perplexing problem.

A moment later a summons came from His Serenity, but now only for the Count of Ostiamare.

Conversation among the Ten was fading to a hum when Colombino advanced once more to the gilded chair, and took his stand by it.

The Doge cleared his throat. There was anxiety in his sunken eyes, and in the kneading movement of his gnarled hands upon the arms of his throne.

'Lord Count, your presumptuous bearing before us, the insubordination you have shown, and the threats you have been so bold as to utter, are responsible for any harshness in our decision concerning you.

'You hold us in check by the threat that your army will go over to the enemy if we take against you any of the measures which your conduct justifies.

'In the duty which we have to the Republic, we must meet this threat by a counter-threat, and your check by a counter-check.

'Messer Grimani will return to the army on the Brenta today. He will inform your marshals that they are required to place themselves and the troops of the Company of the Dove at the disposal of Messer Orlando Gonzaga, who goes to replace you in the supreme command of the army. Messer Grimani will warn your captains that any attempt on their part to evade this order, or otherwise depart from the engagement to serve the Most Serene Republic into which you entered for them, will be attended by your instant decapitation here in Venice.

'You remain, meanwhile, a prisoner in our hands; but merely as a hostage. So long as your captains are submissive, you shall be courteously entreated. For the sake of all concerned, and particularly for your own, we hope that your captains and your men love you well enough to refrain from conduct which you will pay for with your life.

'That is all, Lord Count.'

The droning voice ceased. Colombino stood a moment stiffly upright. Then he swept a bow that took in the whole assembly, turned on his heel, and went out, his head erect, his heart of lead. For not even the reflection that at least he had saved his head from being taken off immediately could console him for his failure to save Samaritana from becoming the victim of Venetian acquisitiveness.

Without accomplishing this, he had temporarily sacrificed his liberty and placed his life in a jeopardy from which he might never extricate it.

His marshals had been right. He should not have come.

v

The Council of Ten sat long in secret session after Colombino's removal.

And outside in the antechamber with his guards sat Messer Cosimo, listlessly waiting, in ignorance of the Council's decision touching Colombino, whom he had seen depart under escort, and wondering, but almost without hope, what might be the decision touching himself.

For two long hours he waited, staring at those tall closed doors, and when at long last they opened, it was merely to give egress to Messer Grimani.

The portly envoy approached him, his manner smooth and friendly.

'You are to come with me, Ser Cosimo.'

It surprised him that their destination should be the camp on the Brenta. But on the morrow, having been housed for the night in one of Messer Grimani's tents, he discovered that this was merely a stage on the journey, made because of the business with which Messer Grimani was charged.

The envoy's interview with Colombino's captains, of which Messer Cosimo knew nothing, had been a violent one. That is to say, his communication had been violently received. He himself had preserved, if with some difficulty, his mild benignity, even when Don Pablo had threatened to cut him into collops. His unanswerable arguments, however, had prevailed, and assured that Orlando Gonzaga, the new commander, was not likely to have trouble with the Company of the Dove, Messer Grimani set forth again on the morrow with now a strong escort to attend him.

To Cosimo's ever-increasing wonder, they rode to Ravenna. They reached it in a deluge of rain on the afternoon of the following day.

Cosimo, informed by then that Messer Grimani came as the envoy of the Serenissima to the Countess, and conceiving no reason against it, was sponsor for him and his fifty lances not only at the city gate, but also in the rocca, where in his cousin's name he ordered quarters to be placed at their disposal.

But when he would at once have conducted Grimani to the Countess, who nowadays had her apartments in the fortress, the portly ambassador excused himself. He pleaded fatigue. He would rest awhile before seeking audience. Meanwhile, let Cosimo announce him. Also, Cosimo, no doubt, would have much to tell his cousin after his absence. The amiable Messer Grimani was too considerate to deny the cousins the satisfaction of a preliminary private interview.

Gratefully the priest went in quest of Samaritana. He found her in the principal chamber of the apartments she had made her own on an upper story of the rocca, the doors of which opened onto an embattled parapet, commanding a view of the sea to the east and of the wide plains that swept away to the distant hazy line of the

Apennines on the west. It was a prospect all blurred that afternoon by mist and rain.

She rose as he entered and rustled forward to greet him, a Samaritana upon whom the two years that were sped since her disillusion had made no visible impression. She was not more than twenty-two, and the resilience of youth had absorbed the shocks of the blows that Fate had dealt her.

'What does it mean, Cosimo? They tell me you come with an escort of Venetians.'

'The escort is for Messer Paolo Grimani, envoy of the Serenissima. I merely accompany him, more or less as his prisoner. I come from Venice.'

'From Venice? You have been to Venice? On my behalf?' Her eyes grew tender.

Although little in this narrative may hitherto have led you to suppose it, yet Cosimo da Polenta was of an orderly mind. He knew that if time is to be saved and understanding ensured, a tale should be told from the beginning. And so he told his tale now from the moment of his seeking Colombino on the Brenta.

The only interruption he suffered was when he came to relate his attempt on Colombino's life and the reasons that had spurred him to it.

'You believed that!' she cried out.

He smiled. 'I believed it then. But I know better now. I have learnt a good deal since, although there is still a good deal I do not understand at all. Yet you...' He broke off. 'But we will come to that at the end. First let me render a full account.'

When he had rendered it, he proffered the jewel and faithfully delivered the message with which Colombino had charged him. To his amazement there were tears in her dark eyes, and her sensitive lips quivered as she spoke.

'Yes. That is Colombo da Siena, as perhaps none knows him but I. To the world he is just a soldier of great skill, the first captain of mercenaries in Italy. To me he is a very perfect knight, a survival from another age.'

'He is this to you?' Cosimo's amazement vibrated in his voice. 'I go from bewilderment to bewilderment. There was an affront he put upon…'

'There was no affront. All that is false.' She looked up, sitting straight and slim in her tall chair of gilded leather, her hands in her lap, and in one of these the glowing emerald. 'There was sacrifice, as there is now. Yes, you may well stare at me. In my cowardice I have allowed these things to be believed. My father would never have forgiven me had he known the truth. Since his death it has never occurred to me to speak of it to you. But if you had told me of your intentions, you would have heard the tale.'

He heard it from her now, and so, at last, all that still puzzled him was made clear. He was profoundly moved, scornful even.

'I do not wonder that you feared to tell your father. But this pledge you gave Moro…'

'Don't you understand? All that ended that night at Bellaria. I saw him then for what he was. A devil. He used threats to me. Vile threats that disclosed his loathsome nature. But why talk of it?'

'And Colombo, then? This man of whom you can speak so tenderly?'

She understood, and shook her head, a sad little smile on her lips.

'Could he return, after such a departure? Besides, he was not the man to return unless he thought I wanted him. I remember so well his words. "When I marry, I shall hope to be a husband, not a penance; a lover, not a hair shirt to a woman's tender flesh." How was he to know…' She checked, and lowered her eyes.

'That you would make him welcome? Is that what you would say, Samaritana?'

'Why should I not? You are not only my cousin, but a priest. Regard it as a confession. It will ease me to speak of it. Afterward, when I had leisure here to think after my return from that ride to Bellaria, when the wounds of my disillusion had healed, and I could contrast him with the worthless man whose arts had infatuated me, then yes. I wanted him back. I ached for him, Cosimo, and every night I have prayed that he might one day return. This' – she looked at the jewel in her palm – 'this and his dear message give me hope.' And then from wistfully contemplative, her manner changed abruptly to apprehension. 'But where is he now?'

Cosimo had yet to tell her that he supposed him to remain in Venetian hands.

She sprang up, suddenly white, her eyes wide. 'He lives?' she cried. 'At least he still lives?'

'Oh, yes. He lives. Messer Grimani assured me of that. They and he are in a stalemate. They dare not put him to death, because if they did, the Company of the Dove would join their enemies, and these are already overwhelming.'

She moved a moment aimlessly about the room in agitation.

'This Venetian who comes with you? This Grimani. Bring him to me. Bring him at once.'

Cosimo made haste to obey, such haste that when presently Grimani was ushered into her presence, his portliness was a little out of breath.

She stood to receive him, straight and tall, her slenderness stressed by the mourning gown of black velvet that sheathed her from foot to neck. The only ornament that relieved it was an emerald set in brilliants worn upon her breast.

Grimani took a sensualist's pleasure in the contemplation of her stateliness, her graceful lines, and the nobility of that young face, showing white as ivory between the collar of the funereal black gown and the lustrous black hair above. He bestowed a courtier's approval upon the dignity with which she gave him welcome, as sinking to the chair by which she stood, she invited him also to be seated, and to state his errand. Cosimo went to take his stand behind her. Thus Messer Grimani was confronted by two pairs of eyes.

His opening startled both of them.

'Madonna, the gravest issues bring me here. At this moment it is not too much to say that the fate of Italy is in your hands.'

She stared at him, then her lip was raised in a little smile of deprecation. 'You are pleased to flatter me,' she said.

'You think so? You shall judge.' He leaned forward, an elbow on his massive knee. 'Venice, as you know, is preparing to renew the struggle with Milan, so as to ensure her rights on the mainland. To render them permanent and so as to reduce the danger of further wars by which the people are harassed, the Serenissima aims at enlarging her frontiers at certain necessary points. The discovery that Ravenna is included in these aims, and the advocacy with the Medici employed by your cousin Messer Cosimo da Polenta, has resulted in a declaration by Florence that if we go further with these intentions the Signory will cast her lot with Milan. The alliance, I understand, has not yet been signed. But the resolve is formed. This may be merely the beginning of a conflagration that may involve the whole of Italy. So long as the issue was left between us and Milan, the danger would have been circumscribed. But once Florence takes the field, who shall say what other states may not feel themselves compelled to bear a hand? You perceive, madonna, the gravity of the moment: the ruin, the desolation of which this may be the eve?'

'That I perceive. But not for what I count in it.'

'I shall hope to make it plain. Milan desires strife no more than we do, who have been driven to it by the sense of injustice under which we lie. A compromise is possible. Some of the guarantees we ask for in the shape of strongholds on the mainland, Milan if left alone will yield. In the fate of Ravenna, Milan is not interested. But if Florence joins her, then Milan will go forward, and all compromise will be impossible. Now Florence is being brought in upon your representations. Therefore, it is possible that upon your representations she might consent to hold her hand, and all the threatened misery and carnage of war will have been averted. Is not that worth while, madonna?'

He pursed his lips, the incarnation of benevolence, folded his hands, sat back, and awaited her reply.

'An argument of humanity!' was the scornful comment of Cosimo, who saw clearly whither they were going.

But Samaritana was in perplexity. 'Do I understand, sir, that Venice will relinquish her claim upon Ravenna?'

The envoy's sigh seemed to rise from the very depths of his corpulent being. 'I would it were possible. But Ravenna is the crux. That is why I say, madonna, that the fate of Italy lies at this moment in your hands. This southern outpost is imperatively necessary to the security of Venice.'

'What you are asking, then,' she said slowly, 'is a voluntary abdication on my part in favour of Venice; a surrender to Venice of my heritage.'

'The Serenissima will make the amplest compensation, madonna. I am empowered to offer...'

'Compensation!' she interrupted him, and there was a glow of anger in her dark eyes. 'Does the Serenissima perceive in life nothing but trade and barter? What of my duty to the people whom I was born to rule?'

'Yes. Answer that,' said Cosimo.

Grimani pursed his heavy lips. 'Duty,' he said slowly, reflectively. 'Duty. Yes. Duty to a people implies love; the desire best to serve their interests; to assure them, as far as may be humanly possible, peace, so that they may be prosperous, secure, and happy. That, I take to be a sovereign's duty.'

'We agree so far.'

'Then let me make bold to ask, are you, is the House of Polenta, in case to do this by the people of Ravenna?'

It was a simple question, yet a startling one. Samaritana looked up at her cousin. Cosimo answered the look.

'A sophistry to serve Venetian greed.'

Grimani, impervious to insult, gravely shook his head. 'Oh, not a sophistry. A fact. Venetian greed, if you choose so to describe Venetian sentiments, may be anxious to urge this fact. But it does not distort it. What has been the history of Ravenna independence in the past? How many sieges has this city sustained? How many times have its hapless citizens been given over to pillage and rapine? How many times has the countryside been ravaged by enemy troops?'

'Are you reminding me of Venetian atrocities?'

'These things have been suffered not only at the hands of Venice, and they have been suffered because the rulers of Ravenna have not had the necessary strength to intimidate attack. In what case are you now to withstand it, madonna? Florence may come to your aid. It is not impossible even that Florence may be able to retain for you this patrimony. But whilst your pride of sovereignty may thus be gratified, what will have happened to your people? To this people to whom you say that you have a duty? Will Florentine intervention save this smiling countryside from becoming a cockpit, from being ravaged and desolated?'

She was very white, tortured by the undeniable force of what he said. Her long, slim hands were twisting one within the other.

'Am I, therefore, to subject my people to a foreign yoke? Is that the inference I am to draw from this?'

'A foreign yoke! A yoke! The well-worn, specious word. The inevitable pretence that people are galled by a foreign yoke and not by a native one. To govern it is necessary to impose a yoke. But has the yoke imposed by the Serenissima upon her subjects been very hard to bear? Under it the people are secure and happy. For it is a yoke that gives them protection. Let the banner of Saint Mark be hoisted over this citadel, and I dare to say that not in generations will the people of Ravenna be disturbed again by war. Are they happier under a Polenta rule, with the constant menace of powerful neighbours hanging over them? If you love your people of Ravenna, madonna, if the duty towards them which inspires you is a duty to procure their good, you can find one only answer to my question.'

She sank together where she sat. Her head was bowed in thought. Grimani employed terrible arguments to which, let her wits search as they would, she could find no answer such as she desired. It was Cosimo who answered for her.

'Sir, you but give voice to the fears of Venice. If the Serenissima had not suddenly become afraid of the task to which she has set her hand, she would not send you with these specious arguments. She would send her troops, recking little of this desolation which you so much deplore.'

275

Grimani looked at him in sorrow. 'You are a priest, sir. An argument of humanity should not move your scorn. Nor should it be rashly regarded as a sign of fear. Venice fears nothing but the things I have stated. Ravenna is necessary to her, and be sure that Ravenna she will possess. But she desires to possess it without carnage, the memory of which might dispose the people so ill towards her that she would be constrained to rule them harshly. That, too, is something for your consideration, madonna. Your abdication in favour of Venice would be accepted by your people, thus doubly ensuring on the part of the Serenissima a benevolent rule. As for our being afraid – to revert to that – it is probable that, as Florence comes in on one side, others will come in on the other. But if that does not happen, we can confront the armies of Milan and Florence without fear. Already in the Cantons we are raising fresh troops, to strengthen the powerful army on the Brenta, which includes, in the Company of the Dove, the best and most experienced soldiers in Italy today.'

Thus craftily, keeping what he supposed to be the master-argument to the end, he brought the question round to Colombino. She stiffened where she sat.

'The commander of that company is a prisoner in Venice,' she said, and now her voice was strained.

'A hostage, merely. A hostage for the good conduct of his troops. We could not otherwise depend upon it. His captains might commit a rashness. If it comes to war, that may yet happen, even so, though I pray that it may not. For I have a great regard – as who has not? – for the Count of Ostiamare; and it would be a grievous loss to Italy if he were cut off. But war is war, and as matters stand, his survival is one of the risks of it.'

'And now you play upon my cousin's fears with that!' cried the intransigent Cosimo. 'It is brave.'

'It is kind,' Grimani corrected. 'It is no more than fair to her that she should perceive all the risks that will attend the failure of my mission here.'

There was a spell of silence. She sat, her head bowed once more, her soul in travail, her wits confused by the dreadful choice that she was offered. The arguments with which Grimani had answered her urgings of duty seemed to her overwhelming. If duty meant love, then she would best serve a people, whom she saw herself without the strength to protect, by abdicating to a power whose might would safely shield them. But was she truthful with herself? Was this readiness to believe the envoy's assertions being urged upon her by her fears for the man who had placed himself in jeopardy on her account? She made a little moaning, despairing sound, almost without realizing it, and again appealed for assistance to her cousin.

'How do we answer him, Cosimo? Perhaps you can see more clearly than I. Tell me.'

'Since you can ask me...' he began, and checked there. 'It is all specious, yes. It may even be true. But...' On a sudden thought he looked at Grimani whose sleepy eyes were watching them with veiled anxiety. 'Can you even be sure that at this time of day, the Lady Samaritana's abdication will cause Florence to draw back?'

'Ah, yes,' she cried, leaning forward in a fresh anxiety. 'What if it should not?'

Grimani rose, as if by standing he could increase impressiveness.

'Whether it does or not, I can pledge the Serenissima that in none of her interests shall the Lady Samaritana suffer. Compensation shall be paid her as may be agreed, and she need not doubt the Serenissima's munificence.'

'It is not of the compensations that I am thinking, sir. This gentleman who out of loyalty to me has placed himself in jeopardy?'

'Will be in jeopardy no longer, rest assured.'

'You pledge yourself to that? You swear it?' She, too, had risen.

He bowed. 'I swear it. But not even so much is necessary. For by your own voluntary abdication of the thing to defend which he sets his engagement at defiance, you will have made an end of his need to maintain that attitude.'

'That is not enough for me. I desire this clearly. Will the Serenissima, if I agree, set the Count of Ostiamare at liberty? Let me have it clearly, sir.'

'Clearly, then, you may depend upon it.' Having said this, he waited with parted lips for her reply in an anxiety he no longer troubled to dissemble.

She turned to Cosimo, who stood chin on breast, his brow dark.

'Help me,' she begged him.

'I cannot,' he said. 'I am a priest, and I thank God for it. May He pardon me if at moments I have tried to be a man of state. This decision is for you alone. The only advice that I may perhaps offer is that you take time for thought.'

'What thought can alter the situation?'

Cosimo shrugged, inclined his head and spread his hands. 'Though your father might turn in his grave to hear me say it, your only present choice is between love and pride.'

'I thank you, Cosimo.' The colour was creeping into her pallid cheeks as she faced again the envoy.

'Here is my answer: On the day that you deliver the Count of Ostiamare safely into my hands, you shall have the abdication of all my rights in favour of the Most Serene Republic.'

Grimani bowed. 'That decision, madonna, does you more honour than you may yet perceive.' His voice grew resonant with sincerity. 'It is a decision for which your people of Ravenna will hereafter come to bless your name. Yet before I can fully pledge the Serenissima, before the Serenissima can release the Count, there must be an end to the state of war.'

'How?' He had stricken the breath from her again.

'Do not be alarmed. It will follow. But I ask your suffrages. I began by saying that it was upon your representations that Florence was brought to take up arms, and that, therefore, upon your representations she might be persuaded to lay them down. I ask that you make, be it in person accompanied by me, be it through Messer Cosimo, those representations.'

'Will Florence yield to them?'

'I do not make that a condition. I merely ask that you present them. When you have done so, the Count of Ostiamare shall be delivered to you safely in exchange for the parchments you have promised me.'

'Whatever happens in Florence?'

'Whatever happens.'

vi

There was no rashness in Messer Grimani's promise, for there was no flaw in that shrewd statesman's calculations. He knew that at heart Florence no more desired a Milanese than a Venetian hegemony in the North; that her considered poiicy would be to side with neither, so that the balance of power should not be disturbed. Her present intervention was the result of yielding to sentiment by the Medici on behalf of the House of Polenta, and if upon sentimental grounds again the Lady of Ravenna were to beg the Florentines to withdraw a support which she no longer desired, Messer Grimani was persuaded that the Magnificent Lorenzo would be not only willing but relieved.

And as he reckoned, so it came to pass. More. When Grimani urged on her behalf that the good of the people was the prime consideration which had moved her to place Ravenna under the banner of the winged lion, the great Lorenzo who, sincerely or otherwise, was known to avow that the good of a people should be the supreme law of a prince, placed upon her decision the benediction of his approval.

The rest lay between Messer Grimani and the Medici and between the Medici and the Signory of Florence; and the question of Florentine alliance with Milan perished under the breath of the shrewd Venetian.

When this had happened, the lady, who for two years had prayed rather than hoped that one day Colombo da Siena would seek her in Ravenna, could wait no longer for his coming. She would return to

279

Venice with Messer Grimani, and there, upon receiving the price she had exacted, execute the deed that gave Ravenna to the Republic of Saint Mark.

With no suspicion of the pattern being woven by other hands than his own into the destiny of which he conceived himself the only master, Messer Colombino languished in the Morosini Palace, a close prisoner. He was courteously treated, it is true; but deprived of weapons, constantly under the immediate guard of Messer Barnabò, who never stirred from his side and even slept in his chamber, with a dozen Slavonian soldiers within hail. Escape was out of the question. To a man in Colombino's position not merely the palace he inhabited, but all Venice was a prison.

He sought to preserve his calm of spirit, whilst waiting and wondering whether he would ever again be free to practise the art by which he had climbed so high, merely perhaps to end like Carmagnola, ignobly cropped in mid-career by a Venetian headsman.

The black shadow of death lay constantly across his path in those three weeks during which he was left without news of events in the world beyond the lagoons.

The end was as abrupt as it was remote from anything that he could have imagined.

One October morning a barge drew up at the steps of the Morosini Palace, and from under its red canopy landed first Messer Grimani and then Messer Cosimo da Polenta. Turning, these gentlemen handed forth a tall, slim lady, richly cloaked. It was Messer Barnabò who ushered her into the room where the prisoner sat brooding.

Colombino, turning his head to see who came, sat staring a moment before he could believe his eyes. Then, with a gasp, his face white, he rose, and stood as if petrified.

It was the officer who spoke. 'I am happy to announce to you, my lord, that your liberty is restored. His Serenity sends you word by Messer Paolo Grimani that, whilst the hospitality of the Most Serene Republic is yours for as long as you choose to honour it, you are free to depart when you will. This lady is the bearer of the order from the Council of Ten.'

He bowed, and discreetly left them.

Colombino continued to stare. Then he seemed to shake himself.

' 'Faith, liberty were miracle enough for one morning. But you… You are the Lady Samaritana, are you not? God knows I have so often evoked your wraith, called forth your image to the eyes of my soul, that I may well doubt if that does not explain this portent.'

She rustled forward, moving with that grace he so well remembered. She was trembling, weeping, and her lips quivered so that he could not determine whether she laughed or cried. In one of her long, slim hands she carried a parchment bearing a great red seal. A medallion formed by an emerald set in brilliants glowed against the black velvet on her breast.

He moved at last to meet her. She put out her hands. He took them, almost timidly.

'You had need of me,' she said. 'That is why I am here. For two years I have hoped that one day you might come to need me. It was much to hope. But God has been good to me. I bring you deliverance.' She held up the parchment.

He passed a hand across his brow, thrusting back the thick, tawny hair.

'But how is it possible? How?'

'There is no longer to be war. Florence has withdrawn. And Venice in strength has been able to reach an accord with Milan.' But when in a few words she had told him how this had been accomplished, he cried out in indignation.

'Mercy of Heaven! Now I understand. The cunning of these Venetian foxes misses nothing. I was a hostage in their hands for more than the submissiveness of my captains. I was to serve them so that they might bend you to their will, even to the sacrifice of your sovereignty of Ravenna. The infamy of that! And you? For me…?'

'For you and for Ravenna,' she insisted. 'Though perhaps more for you than for Ravenna. But we Polentas never could wield sovereignty so as to protect our people. Under the shield of Saint Mark they will be secure and at peace.'

'These, too, will be the arguments of Venice.'

'They are. But true none the less.'

'The real truth is that their sly, treacherous speciousness has tricked you into signing away your patrimony.'

'Oh, no.' She looked into his face, and smiled tremulously through tears. 'It was not their arts that prevailed with me. It was my duty. My duty to you, Messer Colombo.'

'Madonna, you owed me no duty.'

'Did I not? Have I forgotten, do you suppose, the renunciation that you made, and how you made it, reckless of the execration you provoked? Could I suffer you now to sacrifice to me, as you were doing, your liberty, perhaps your life?'

'There is no parallel...' he was beginning.

Her interruption was almost fierce. 'That is true. There is none. Still, I have done the little that I could. I lay it at your feet.'

'Samaritana! Oh, Samaritana!'

He looked at her so gravely, as if he asked a question with his eyes. And her eyes answered him, it seems. For upon that he took her in his arms, drew the black head against his shoulder, and after a silent moment softly laughed. 'That this should come to pass! And by the agency of these Venetian gentlemen. That this lovely, lovely dream in which I am should be reality! When first I sought you to wife, Samaritana, it was so that I might possess Ravenna. For love of you I renounced it, and you have renounced it now for love of me. It is very well.'

Rafael Sabatini

Captain Blood

Captain Blood is the much-loved story of a physician and gentleman turned pirate.

Peter Blood, wrongfully accused and sentenced to death, narrowly escapes his fate and finds himself in the company of buccaneers. Embarking on his new life with remarkable skill and bravery, Blood becomes the 'Robin Hood' of the Spanish seas. This is swashbuckling adventure at its best.

The Gates of Doom

'Depend above all on Pauncefort', announced King James; 'his loyalty is dependable as steel. He is with us body and soul and to the last penny of his fortune.' So when Pauncefort does indeed face bankruptcy after the collapse of the South Sea Company, the king's supreme confidence now seems rather foolish. And as Pauncefort's thoughts turn to gambling, moneylenders and even marriage to recover his debts, will he be able to remain true to the end? And what part will his friend and confidante, Captain Gaynor, play in his destiny?

'A clever story, well and amusingly told' – *The Times*

Rafael Sabatini

The Lost King

The Lost King tells the story of Louis XVII – the French royal who officially died at the age of ten but, as legend has it, escaped to foreign lands where he lived to an old age. Sabatini breathes life into these age-old myths, creating a story of passion, revenge and betrayal. He tells of how the young child escaped to Switzerland from where he plotted his triumphant return to claim the throne of France.

'…the hypnotic spell of a novel which for sheer suspense, deserves to be ranked with Sabatini's best' – *New York Times*

Scaramouche

When a young cleric is wrongfully killed, his friend, André-Louis, vows to avenge his death. André's mission takes him to the very heart of the French Revolution where he finds the only way to survive is to assume a new identity. And so is born Scaramouche – a brave and remarkable hero of the finest order and a classic and much-loved tale in the greatest swashbuckling tradition.

'Mr Sabatini's novel of the French Revolution has all the colour and lively incident which we expect in his work' – *Observer*

Rafael Sabatini

The Sea Hawk

Sir Oliver, a typical English gentleman, is accused of murder, kidnapped off the Cornish coast, and dragged into life as a Barbary corsair. However Sir Oliver rises to the challenge and proves a worthy hero for this much-admired novel. Religious conflict, melodrama, romance and intrigue combine to create a masterly and highly successful story, perhaps best-known for its many film adaptations.

The Shame of Motley

The Court of Pesaro has a certain fool – one Lazzaro Biancomonte of Biancomonte. *The Shame of Motley* is Lazzaro's story, presented with all the vivid colour and dramatic characterisation that has become Sabatini's hallmark.

'Mr Sabatini could not be conventional or commonplace if he tried'
 – *Standard*

Printed in Great Britain
by Amazon.co.uk, Ltd.,
Marston Gate.